Her
UNTAMED
Warrior

Her
UNTAMED
Warrior

**MICHELLE
WILLINGHAM**

**HARPER
ST. GEORGE**

MILLS & BOON

HER UNTAMED WARRIOR © 2023 by Harlequin Books S.A.

The publisher acknowledges the copyright holders of the individual works as follows:
STOLEN BY THE VIKING
© 2020 by Michelle Willingham First Published 2020
Philippine Copyright 2020 First Australian Paperback Edition 2023
Australian Copyright 2020 ISBN 978 1 867 29829 8
New Zealand Copyright 2020

MARRYING HER VIKING ENEMY
© 2019 by Harper St. George First Published 2019
Philippine Copyright 2019 First Australian Paperback Edition 2023
Australian Copyright 2019 ISBN 978 1 867 29829 8
New Zealand Copyright 2019

MIX
Paper | Supporting
responsible forestry
FSC® C001695

Published by
Harlequin Mills & Boon
An imprint of Harlequin Enterprises (Australia) Pty Limited
(ABN 47 001 180 918), a subsidiary of HarperCollins
Publishers Australia Pty Limited
(ABN 36 009 913 517)
Level 19, 201 Elizabeth Street
SYDNEY NSW 2000 AUSTRALIA

Printed and bound in Australia by McPherson's Printing Group

CONTENTS

Stolen By The Viking
Michelle Willingham

RITA® Award finalist and Kindle bestselling author **Michelle Willingham** has written over forty historical romances, novellas and short stories. Currently she lives in southeastern Virginia with her family and her beloved pets. When she's not writing, Michelle enjoys reading, baking and avoiding exercise at all costs. Visit her website at michellewillingham.com.

Books by Michelle Willingham

Harlequin Historical

Sons of Sigurd

Stolen by the Viking

Untamed Highlander

The Highlander and the Governess

Warriors of the Night

Forbidden Night with the Warrior
Forbidden Night with the Highlander
Forbidden Night with the Prince

Warriors of Ireland

Warrior of Ice
Warrior of Fire

Forbidden Vikings

To Sin with a Viking
To Tempt a Viking

Visit the Author Profile page
at millsandboon.com.au for more titles.

Author Note

Stolen by the Viking is the first book in the
Sons of Sigurd series. Alarr Sigurdsson is about to
enter an arranged marriage when he and his tribe
are attacked on the day of the wedding. He is badly
wounded, and he doubts that his fighting abilities
will ever be the same. He intends to kill his enemy,
but a brave Irishwoman, Breanne Ó Callahan,
won't allow him to threaten her foster father. He is
torn between vengeance and his own desire for a
woman who sees past his scars to the man within.

This series is a five-book continuity, and I thoroughly
enjoyed working with four other authors whose
books will follow mine. You can look forward to
Rurik's story by Harper St. George; followed by
Sandulf's story by Michelle Styles; then Danr's book
is by Jenni Fletcher; and the final book in the series
is Brandt's story by Terri Brisbin. We had a wonderful
time brainstorming plot and character ideas, and I
hope you'll try all five books!

If you'd like me to email you when I have a
new book out, please visit my website at
www.michellewillingham.com to sign up for my
newsletter. As a bonus, you'll receive a free story,
just for subscribing!

DEDICATION

To Kat Schniepp, for your daily encouragement, words of wisdom and for being my friend all these years. You have walked a difficult road and come out stronger. And with your help, so have I.

Prologue

The kingdom of Maerr, Norway—ad 874

It was the morning of his wedding. Although most men would have welcomed the day, Alarr Sigurdsson had the sense that something was not right. The shadowed harvest moon last night had promised an ill omen, and the wise woman had cautioned him to delay the marriage.

Alarr had ignored the *volva*, for he was not a man who believed in curses or evil omens. The union would bring a strong alliance for his tribe. He had known Gilla Vigmarrsdottir since they were children, and she always had a smile and was even-tempered. She was not beautiful in the traditional way, but that didn't matter. Her kindness made him amenable to the match. His father, Sigurd, had negotiated for her bride price, and the *mundr* was high, demonstrating their family's wealth.

'Are you ready to be chained into the bonds of marriage?' his half-brother Danr teased. 'Or do you think Gilla has fled?'

He didn't rise to Danr's bait. 'She will be there.'

Alarr had worn his best tunic, adorned with silver-braided trim along the hem, and dark hose. His black cloak hung over his shoulders, but it was the absence of his weapons that bothered him most. His mother had asked him to leave them behind, claiming that they would only offend the gods. It was an unusual request, and one that made him uneasy, given all the foreign guests.

Her beliefs did not mean he intended to remain defenceless, however. During the wedding, he would receive a ceremonial sword from Gilla as a gift, and at least he would have that. Weapons were a part of him, and he took comfort in a balanced blade. He felt more comfortable fighting than joining in a conversation.

It was strange being the centre of attention, for he had two brothers and two half-brothers. As the second-born, Alarr was accustomed to being overlooked and ignored, a fact that usually allowed him to retreat into solitude and train for warfare. The intense physical exertion brought a strange sense of peace within him. While he practised with a blade, he didn't have to compete with anyone, save himself. And now that he had earned his status as a fighter, the men respected him. No one challenged him, and he had confidence that he could win any battle he fought.

Not that Sigurd had ever noticed.

Although his father tried to behave as if they had no enemies, Alarr was no fool. There was an air of restlessness brewing among the tribes. He had visited several neighbouring *jarls* and had overheard the whispers of rebellion. Yet, his father did not want to believe it.

Danr shot him a sidelong grin. 'Are you afraid of losing your innocence this night?' With that, Alarr swung his fist, and Danr ducked, laughing. 'I hope she is gentle with you, Brother.'

'Be silent, unless you want me to cut out your tongue,' he threatened. But both knew it was an idle threat. His half-brother was never serious, and he often made jests. Fair-haired and blue-eyed, all the women were fascinated by the man, and Danr was only too willing to accept their offerings. Alarr knew that his half-brother would find his way into a woman's bed this night.

The scent of roasting meat lingered in the air, and both cattle and sheep had been slaughtered for the wedding feast. Sigurd had invited the leaders of neighbouring tribes, as well as their daughters. Undoubtedly, he would be trying to arrange future weddings to advance his own position. Although Sigurd was a petty king, it was never enough for him. He hungered for more status and greater power.

Alarr walked towards his father's longhouse and found Sigurd waiting there. The older man had a satisfied expression on his face, though he was wearing only a simple woollen tunic and hose. His hair was greying, with threads of white mingled in his beard and hair. Even so, there was not a trace of weakness upon the man. His body was a warrior's, lean and strong. Sigurd had bested many men in combat, even at his advanced age. 'Are you ready?'

Alarr nodded, and they walked alongside one another in silence. Outside their settlement, his ancestors were buried within the Barrow. The graves of former warriors—his grandsire and those who had died before him—were waiting. There, Alarr would dig up a sword from one of the burial mounds. The weapon would become his, forged with the knowledge of his forebears, to be given to his firstborn son.

After a quarter-hour of walking in silence, Sigurd paused at the base of the Barrow and gestured for Alarr to choose. He was glad of it, for he already knew whose sword he wanted.

He climbed to the top of the Barrow and stopped in front of the grave that belonged to his uncle, who had died only a year ago, in battle. Hafr had trained him in sword fighting from the moment Alarr was strong enough to lift a weapon. There was no one else whose sword he wanted more.

He and his father dug alongside one another until they reached the possessions belonging to Hafr. Alarr tried to dispel the sense of foreboding that lingered while he respected the ashes of his uncle. The sword had been carefully wrapped in leather, and Alarr took it, uncovering the weapon. The iron glinted in the morning light, but it would need to be cleaned and sharpened.

'Do you wish to take the sword?' Sigurd asked quietly.

'I do.'

His father then reached out to seize the weapon. Once he had given it over, Sigurd regarded him. 'Much is expected of you with this marriage. Our kingdom of Maerr has risen to great power, and we need to strengthen our ties with the other *jarls*. You must conceive a son with Gilla immediately and ensure that our alliance is strong.' He wrapped the sword in the leather once more and set it aside. 'Perhaps my brother's wisdom and strength will be yours, now that you have his sword.'

Alarr gave a nod, though he didn't believe it. He wanted the sword because it gave him a tangible memory of his uncle. Hafr had been more of a father to him than Sigurd, whether he'd known it or not. Alarr had spent most of his life trying to gain Sigurd's approval, to little avail.

They reburied the ashes of his uncle, along with Hafr's worldly possessions, before returning to the settlement. Alarr walked towards the bathhouse, for it was time for the purification ritual. He had not seen Gilla since her arrival, but he had seen several of her kinsmen and a few others he didn't recognise.

When he entered the bathhouse, the heat struck him instantly. Steam rose up within the air from heated stones set inside basins of water. Wooden benches were placed at intervals, along with several drying cloths.

Alarr stripped off his clothing and saw that three of his brothers were waiting. His youngest brother Sandulf was there, along with his older brother, Brandt, and their half-brother Rurik, Danr's twin. Unlike Danr, Rurik was dark-haired and quiet. In many ways, Alarr found it easier to talk with Rurik. They trained together often, and he considered the man a close friend, as well as a brother. Their youngest brother, Sandulf, had a thirst to prove himself. He had dark-blond hair and blue eyes and had nearly put adolescence behind him. Even so, Alarr didn't like the thought of his brother fighting in battle. Sandulf lacked the reflexes, though he'd trained hard. He feared that only experience would help the young man gain the knowledge he needed now.

'Whose sword did you choose?' Sandulf asked.

'Hafr's,' Alarr answered. At his answer, Rurik met his gaze and gave a silent nod of approval. His brother had also been close to Hafr, since Sigurd had distanced himself from his bastard sons.

Alarr strode towards the wooden trough containing heated water. He began the purification ritual, pouring the warmed water over his body with a wooden bowl and scrubbing off the dirt with soap. As he did, Brandt remarked in a low voice, 'There are many strangers among the guests. Did you notice?'

'I did,' Alarr answered. 'But then, our tribe is well known across the North. It's not uncommon. And we know that Sigurd wants to make other marriage alliances.' He sent a pointed look towards Rurik, which his half-brother ignored.

Even so, Brandt looked uneasy. 'He's endangering our tribe by bringing in warriors we don't know. Some were from Éireann.'

The island was several days' journey across the sea. Sigurd had travelled there, years ago, and had brought back a concubine. She had given birth to Rurik and Danr a few months after her arrival and had never returned home, even after Sigurd set her aside. Although Saorla had died years ago, this was the first time any visitors had come from Éireann. Alarr wondered if there was some connection between the visitors and his half-brothers.

Regardless, he saw little choice but to let the foreigners witness the marriage. 'They are already here now. We cannot deny them our hospitality.' With a shrug, he added, 'Sigurd likely invited them in the hopes of wedding one of their daughters to Rurik or Danr.'

'Possibly.' Brandt thought a moment. 'We cannot deny them a place to stay, but we can deny them the right to bring in weapons. We will say it is to abide by our mother's wishes.'

It was a reasonable request, and Alarr answered, 'I will see to it.' He reached for his clothing and got dressed.

'Wait a moment.' Brandt approached and held out a leather pouch. 'A gift for your wedding.' Alarr opened it and found a bronze necklace threaded with small pendants shaped like hammers. It was a visible reminder of Thor, a blessing from his older brother.

He stood so Brandt could help him put it on. Then Alarr looked back at his brothers, unable to cast off the sense that something was not right at all. Perhaps it was the unknown warriors, or perhaps it was the knowledge that he would be married this day.

A sudden premonition pricked at him, that he would not marry Gilla, as they had planned. Alarr knew not why, but the hair on the back of his arms stood up, and he could not set aside his uncertainty. He tried to dispel the restlessness in anticipation of the wedding. Like as not, every bridegroom had those feelings.

Sandulf trailed behind him. 'May I join you, Alarr?'

He shrugged. 'If you wish. But we are only exchanging the *mundr* and Gilla's dowry. You may want to wait.' The wedding activities would last most of the day, and there were enough witnesses without needing Sandulf there. 'You could return when we make the sacrifices to the gods. That part is more interesting.'

His brother nodded. 'All right. And in the meantime, I can watch over our guests and learn if any of them are a threat.'

'Good.' He understood his youngest brother's desire

to be useful, and it might be a wise idea to keep a close watch over the visitors.

Alarr departed the bathhouse and watched as his brothers went on their way. Brandt joined him as he approached the centre of the settlement. His older brother said little, but his face transformed when he spied his heavily pregnant wife, Ingrid. There was a moment of understanding that passed between them, along with joy. Alarr wondered if he would ever look upon Gilla's face in that way when she was about to bear a child.

'It won't be long now,' he said to Brandt. 'You'll be a father.'

Brandt nodded, and there was no denying his happiness. 'Ingrid thinks it's a boy from what the *volva* told her. I hope they are right.'

Alarr walked alongside his brother until he reached Sigurd and Gilla's father. It was time to discuss the bride price and dowry. But before they could begin, they were interrupted by his mother. She hurried forward and whispered quietly to Brandt, whose face tightened. Then he gave a nod.

'I must go,' he said to Alarr. 'There is a disturbance with tribes gathering to the north. I should be back later tonight for the wedding feast, but I've been asked to intervene and prevent bloodshed, if possible. I am sorry, but it cannot wait.'

Alarr inclined his head, wondering if this was the ill omen the *volva* had spoken of. It also struck him that his mother had spoken to Brandt and not to him or to her husband. She did not like Sigurd, but then again, it was possible that the king already knew and had ordered Brandt to go in his stead. Sigurd's presence at the wedding was necessary.

'Do not go alone,' Alarr warned his brother.

'Rurik will accompany me, along with a few other men,' Brandt promised. His gaze fixed upon his wife, who was walking towards the other women, and his features softened. 'I will return as soon as I can.'

'Go then,' Alarr said. 'And return this night for the feasting.' He clapped Brandt on the back before turning his attention back to the negotiations.

Sigurd was already bargaining with Vigmarr as the two exchanged the dowry and *mundr*. Since they had already agreed upon the bride price, it was hardly more than a symbol of the union to come.

Alarr saw Gilla standing behind her father. She wore a green woollen gown with golden brooches at her shoulders. Her dark hair hung below her shoulders, and upon her head, she wore a bridal crown made of woven straw, intertwined with flowers. Her smile was warm and welcoming, though she appeared slightly nervous.

Beside her, the *volva* was preparing the ritual sacrifice to the gods. The wise woman began chanting in the old language, supplications for blessings. Several of the guests began to draw closer to bear witness, and the scent of smoke mingled with the fresh tang of blood. The slain boar was offered up to Freyr, and the *volva* took a fir branch and dipped it into the boar's blood. She then made the sign of the hammer, blessing them with the sacrificial blood, as well as the other wedding guests.

Although Gilla appeared amused by the ritual, the sight of sprinkled blood upon her face and hair made Alarr uneasy. He watched as the wise woman then sprinkled the boar's blood on each of the guests. But instead of the guests revering the offering, there seemed to be an unspoken message passing among several of the warriors. Alarr could not shake the feeling that this was an omen of bloodshed to come.

Let my brothers be safe, he prayed to the gods. *Let them come back alive.*

Alarr watched the men, his attention caught by the tall Irish king. He didn't know if Feann MacPherson had come as an invited guest, or whether he had arrived of his own choice. It might be that he wanted an alliance or a wedding for his daughter, if he had one. The king wore a woollen cloak, and there were no visible weapons. Yet the man had a thin scar along his cheek, evidence of an earlier battle. His dark hair was threaded with grey, but there was a lean strength to him.

When he saw Alarr staring, his expression tightened before it fixed upon Sigurd. The hard look was not of a man who wanted an alliance—it was of a man itching for a fight.

Someone needed to alert the guards, but Alarr could not leave in the midst of the ceremony. He searched for a glimpse of Danr or Sandulf, but they were nowhere to be found. He only saw his aunt nearby, and she could do nothing.

You're overreacting, he tried to tell himself. But no matter how he tried to dismiss his suspicions, his instincts remained on alert. He could not interrupt the ceremony, for it would only humiliate his bride. This was meant to be a day of celebration, and Gilla's smile was bright as she looked at him.

She was a kind woman, and as he returned her smile, he forced his thoughts back to the wedding. Friendship was a solid foundation for their union, and he inwardly vowed that he would try to make this marriage a good one.

He stood before her, and Sigurd brought the sword of Hafr that they had dug from his uncle's grave. Alarr presented it to Gilla, saying, 'Take this sword as a gift from my ancestors. It shall become the sword of our firstborn son.'

She accepted the weapon and then turned to her father to present their own gift of another sword. 'Take this sword for your own.'

The blade had good balance, and he tested the edge, noting its sharpness. Gilla knew of his love for sword-fighting, and she had chosen a weapon of quality. It was a good exchange, and he approved of her choice.

Alarr placed the ring for Gilla upon the hilt of the sword, and was about to offer it, when he caught a sudden movement among the guests. Feann cast off his dark cloak and unsheathed a sword from where it had been strapped between his shoulder blades. His men joined him, their own weapons revealed. The visible threat made their intentions clear.

Sigurd's face turned thunderous at the insult, and he started to reach for Alarr's sword.

He handed the weapon to his father and commanded, 'Take Gilla to the longhouse and guard her.' The last thing they needed was his father's hot-headed fighting. 'Vigmarr and I will settle this.'

He took back his uncle's sword from Gilla, and her face turned stricken when she murmured, 'Be safe.'

His father heeded his instructions and took Gilla with him, along with a few other men. His aunt joined them, running with her skirts clenched in her hands. He heard his mother scream as she fled towards another longhouse in the opposite direction. Only when the women were gone did Alarr breathe easier.

It was a mistake. Chaos erupted among the guests as his men hurried towards the longhouse where they had stored their weapons. King Feann uttered a command in Irish, and his men surged forward, cutting down anyone in their path.

Alarr ran hard, and iron struck iron as his weapon met an enemy's blade. He let the familiar battle rage flow through him, and his uncle's sword bit through flesh, striking down his attacker. The weapon was strong, imbued with the spirt of his ancestor. Alarr swung at another man, and he glimpsed another warrior behind him. He sidestepped and caught the man in the throat before he slashed the stomach of his other assailant.

The volva *was right*, he thought. *It was an ill omen.*

Already, he could see the slain bodies of his kinsmen as more men charged forward in the fight. Alarr searched for his brothers, but there was no sign of Sandulf or Danr. By the gods, he hoped they were safe. If only Brandt and Rurik had been here, they could have driven off their enemies. He caught one of his kinsmen and ordered, 'Take a horse and ride north as hard as you can. Find Brandt and Rurik and bring them back.' The man obeyed, running hard towards the stables.

A strange calm passed over him with the knowledge that he would likely die this day. The shouts of kinsmen echoed amid the clang of weapons, only to be cut short when they died. The Irish king started to run towards the longhouse, but Alarr cut him off, swinging his sword hard. The older man caught his balance and held his weapon against the iron.

Feann paused a moment. 'Stay out of this, boy. The fight isn't yours. Sigurd has gone too far, and he will pay for his crimes.'

'This is my wedding, so the fight *is* mine,' Alarr countered. He swung his weapon, and the king blocked his blow. 'And I am not a boy.' He was beginning to re-alise that Feann had travelled seeking vengeance, and his intent was to slaughter Sigurd. But what crimes was he talking about?

They sparred against one another, the king toying with him. Alarr struck hard, intending to stop the man. But with every blow, he grew aware that Feann was stalling, drawing out the fight. It was then that he saw men surrounding the longhouse where his father was protecting his bride. Gilla's father, Vigmarr, was fight-ing back, trying to defend them.

And then Alarr caught the unmistakable scent of smoke and fire.

He renewed his attack, slashing with his sword as he fought to find a weakness. Feann parried each blow, and when the screams of the women broke through, Alarr jerked his attention back to the longhouse.

A slashing pain struck him in the calves, and he saw the king withdraw a bloody blade, just before his legs collapsed beneath him. Alarr met the man's gaze, waiting for the killing blow. Instead, Feann's expres-sion remained grim as he wiped his blade. 'If you're wise, boy, you'll stay on the ground.' Then he strode towards the longhouse.

Alarr tried to rise, but the agonizing pain kept his legs from supporting him. He called out to his men to attack and defend the longhouse. But a moment later, he watched in horror as the fire raged hotter. Someone threw open the doors, and Sandulf staggered out. Four other men emerged from a different door, and Alarr struggled to his knees. He spied the slain bodies of his father… Gilla… Vigmarr and his wife…

His stomach lurched, and Alarr turned his gaze back to the sky, hating the gods for what they had done. A lone raven circled the clouds, and he could only lie in his own blood while his enemies cut down the remaining wedding guests and returned to their ships.

In the dirt beside him, he saw the familiar glint of a golden brooch.

Chapter One

Ireland—ad 876

The heavy slave collar hung around Breanne Ó Callahan's throat. Her mouth was dry from thirst, and she could hardly remember how long it had been since she was taken captive. The days blurred into one another, for she had been stolen from her foster home and sold into slavery. The trader had locked her in chains, and she had travelled for days in a wagon with the other women. She knew that he intended to sell her in the marketplace at Áth Cliath, for he could get a higher price for her there.

Exhaustion weighed upon her, and her body ached from bruises where she'd been beaten. It had been especially humiliating when they had taken her to the healer. Although it had been a woman who had touched her, her cheeks still burned at the memory. The healer had verified her virginity, and Breanne knew it was the only reason she had not yet been raped. The slaver knew that he could command a higher price for her innocence. She tried to clear her mind of the terrors rising and the fear of being held down and claimed by a stranger this night.

Breanne clenched her hands together in a vain attempt to keep them from shaking. Thus far, no one had come for her. She had searched in vain for any sign that her foster father had sent men to save her. They might not know where she was being held captive. With each day that had passed, her hope had begun to fade.

Do not surrender, she warned herself. *Not yet.*

There might be a chance at escape with so many people in the marketplace. She held fast to the frail hope, even as they dragged the first woman to the auction block. Breanne did not know her name, but the girl began to sob at her fate.

The trader called out the woman's value and stripped her naked in the marketplace. The girl whimpered when he extolled the virtue of her slender body and soft breasts. He turned her around, and there was no denying the lustful gazes of the men.

Breanne turned her attention to the crowd of people, searching for a way out. There were a dozen wooden carts rolling through the streets, and if she could only get to one of them without being noticed, she might hide herself among the barrels or beneath the straw. She would have only precious seconds to act, and only then if she could break free. Her wrists and ankles were chained together, but if she shortened her stride, she could still run. All she had to do was wait until the woman before her was sold. She was last among the women, a lucky place, for soon there would be no one chained to her and she might be able to flee.

Her brain warned that it would be nearly impossible to escape notice. Not if she was running with an armful of chains. But even so, she tried to keep hope. If she imagined the alternative, the panic would rise up and overpower what little courage she had left.

The first woman was sold to a fat merchant, and he seized her hair as he pulled her forward. He groped her bare breast, laughing before he covered her body with a rough shift. Breanne suppressed a shudder. During the auction, her gaze fixed upon a row of three carts. One of them might serve as a place to hide—but first, she needed to create a distraction.

An outdoor peat fire burned nearby, and she spied another cart filled with straw. A fire, she decided. It would allow her to flee unnoticed while the others attempted to put out the blaze.

The second woman was sold, then the third. But before the fourth climbed up to the block, Breanne saw a taller man drawing near. His dark hair hung to his shoulders, and his piercing blue eyes stared at her. He appeared to be one of the *Lochlannach*, a fierce warrior from across the sea. His skin held a darker tone, and an iron chain containing three hammers encircled his throat. He looked like a man who had spent the entire summer upon the waters.

Breanne lifted her chin and stared back, refusing to let him intimidate her. A hint of a smile lifted his mouth, as if he had accepted her challenge. *Danu,* what if he attempted to buy her? It was clear that she had caught his interest. He appeared to be a man accustomed to getting his own way.

She noticed his strong hands and the way his shoulders filled his tunic. Unlike the fat merchant, there was no trace of weakness in his body. A vision flared in her mind, of being stripped naked before this man. Her body flushed at the thought. His blue eyes never left hers, and she felt a strange pull within her, as if he had somehow caressed her flesh without a single touch.

The warrior took another step closer, and this time, she noticed his slight limp. He wore armour, and a sword hung from his side. Who was he?

Her heartbeat pounded, and she had no more time to wonder, when the slaver dragged her up the stairs towards the block. He held the length of chain in his arms, and Breanne locked her gaze with the *Lochlannach*, wondering about his intentions. It would not matter. She would be no man's possession.

She feigned weakness, reluctantly drawing close to the block. Though she continued to walk forward, she waited until she could feel her captor's grip on the chain going slack as he prepared to strip her naked.

Now.

Breanne dived forward, leaping from the block towards the crowd. As she'd predicted, the unexpected motion jerked the chain from the slaver's hands. She lunged through the crowd of onlookers, making her way towards the wooden carts ahead.

Many tried to stop her, but she shoved her way past them. The weight of the manacles on her wrists and ankles impeded her movement, but she would do anything to escape.

But a moment later, a hand caught her chains and dragged her backwards. Breanne fought to free herself, but the chains held fast.

'Let me go,' she gritted out, but she could not move. When she turned around, she saw the face of the *Lochlannach*. His expression was unyielding, like iron.

He wrapped the chain around his arm, making it impossible for her to escape him. His blue eyes were chips of ice, with no pity in them. Her heartbeat quickened, for she knew he would never release her.

'Please,' she begged.

He ignored her, holding the chains with one hand as she struggled to free herself. The slaver approached and raised his hand to strike her. Before his fist could make contact, the *Lochlannach* caught the man's wrist and held it. He spoke in a foreign tongue she did not understand, but his tone brooked no argument. The slaver started to argue, but the man ignored him. Instead, he reached into a pouch at his waist and withdrew a handful of coins. He placed them in the slaver's palm, and the man's protests were silenced.

And so, it was done. She had been bought by this *Lochlannach*. Hatred rose up within her at the thought of being this man's slave or worse, his concubine. She struggled again to free herself, but it was no use. He kept the chain tight, securing her firmly at his side until he reached his horse. In one motion, he lifted her up, before he swung up behind her.

He spurred the animal and rode towards the outer edges of Áth Cliath. Throughout the short journey, he said nothing at all. She almost wondered if he was even capable of speaking her language. Her only consolation was that he had not attempted to touch her...yet.

The uneasiness inside her intensified, doubling her fears. He was a raider and a Norseman, one who would take whatever he wanted. Why had he bought her? She wanted to believe that it was only a moment of chance, a sudden whim.

But he had been watching her and waiting. He had

stopped her from fleeing the slave market, and now, he had claimed her. Gods be merciful.

They reached the river, and he dismounted from his horse, lifting her down. Breanne wondered if she could dive into the water, but he dispelled any thoughts of escape by keeping her chains tight. Inwardly, she cursed the man for taking her. She wanted to return home to Killcobar, and now she might never see Feann again. He and her foster brothers were the only family she remembered, since her parents had died years ago. Was Feann even looking for her? Or worse, had he given her up for dead?

Her heart ached at the loss of her home and family. The pain welled up inside her, mingled with loneliness and fear. She knew not what would happen to her any more. It seemed as if her life had crumbled into pieces, scattering to the wind.

The *Lochlannach* led her towards the docks until they reached a small boat where another man waited for them. The vessel was not large, and the sail was tied up against the mast. Her captor lifted her inside, and she glanced down at the dark water, wondering if she had the courage to jump. The other man seemed to guess her thoughts, for he shook his head in warning.

The Norseman spoke to the other man in the language she did not know. Another flare of anxiety caught her, for she feared they might take her to their country. She might never see Éireann again, and the thought terrified her.

'Who are you?' she asked, even knowing that they might not understand her. The men lifted the anchor and began to row out to the open water. As she'd predicted, they did not answer her question. Once again, she eyed the water, wondering if she dared to jump. But then, the chains would only drag her down to the bottom of the river and cause her to drown.

Though it was still morning, the sky was dark and heavy with moisture. Clouds obscured the sun, and soon, fat raindrops splattered upon her. Breanne welcomed the water, trying to quench her thirst by opening her mouth. The Norseman seemed to notice, and he held out a drinking skin, tipping it against her lips. She took a sip, and the water was stale but welcome. When she had finished, he took it back. Then he reached inside a wooden container and pulled out a heavy fur of seal skin. He lifted it over her, and she realised that it would shield her from the rain.

She was taken aback by the gesture. Why should he care if she were drenched from the rain? It poured over him and his shipmate, soaking through his dark hair. Though he rowed steadily, he kept his gaze fixed upon her.

His attention unnerved her, reaching deep within. Though he had bought her as his slave, she could not deny that he had shown kindness. And it was difficult to reconcile the two parts of this man. What did he want from her?

She remained still while the rain fell steadily. Both men were soaked now, but they appeared indifferent to the elements. When she eyed the other man, she saw that he was watching her with interest. There was no sense of surprise, as if he had expected to have a female slave aboard the ship. It made her question what else he knew.

Breanne huddled beneath the seal skin, and they continued to row until the river met the edge of the sea.

Áth Cliath was now behind her, and she could see only a light fog and the water surrounding them everywhere. Once they were further out to sea, the Norseman gestured for her to put out her chained wrists. He withdrew an awl and a small hammer, and she understood his intention. Within moments, he had hammered out the pin and her chains fell to the bottom of the boat. Next, he removed her neck collar, and she rubbed at the chafed skin, feeling relief from the weight. Last, she extended her ankles, and he removed the chains there, as well.

Her wrists were raw, and she tried to ease the soreness. She didn't quite know what to think of this man. True, there was nowhere she could run, now that they were nearing the open sea. Perhaps he'd meant to offer her comfort, and for that, she was grateful.

Even so, she could not dispel her suspicions. She was his captive, and he had no intention of freeing her. Was he trying to soften her distrust? Or perhaps he did not want her to fight him when he forced her to share his bed. Breanne swallowed hard, trying not to think of it.

During the journey to *Áth Cliath*, countless hands had groped her, and she had fought to protect herself. They had laughed at her, and she'd received a few bruises when she had struck back.

Breanne gripped the edges of the seal cloak, shutting her eyes to try to blot out what was to come. Though this journey would grant her somewhat of a reprieve from his attentions tonight, she did not doubt that the *Lochlannach* meant to use her for his own pleasure. His blue eyes stared upon her with interest, and her body prickled at the thought of his hands upon her bare flesh. She tried to dispel the thought, but the more he stared at her, the more she sensed that he would not be a brutal lover. Instead, she imagined those rough palms caressing her skin, arousing her. Without warning, her breasts tightened against the thin fabric of her shift and she caught her breath. He was handsome and stoic, a fierce warrior with undeniable strength. At the thought of him pressing her back against the sleeping furs, she could not suppress the unexpected response from her body.

And by the gods, she knew not what he would do to her.

Alarr sailed with Rurik, grateful that his brother had maintained the silence. He didn't know if his captive knew any of their language, and he didn't want to take the risk. For that reason, he had spoken little on the journey, until it was in the early hours of the next morning.

He'd been tracking King Feann's foster daughter for the past sennight, fully intending to use her as a hostage. He had paid a soldier to take Breanne and bring her to him, with the understanding that she would remain unharmed. Instead, the man had betrayed him, selling her to a slaver who had taken a shipment of women along the coast. It had taken several days to track her to Áth Cliath, and Alarr was irritated by the delay. But now, he realised that there was an unexpected advantage, for she would know nothing of his connection to Feann. He could learn more about her foster father's weaknesses if he could coax her to talk.

Although Feann had not been the one to plunge the blade into his father's heart, Alarr knew the Irish king had been involved in the plot. There was no question that the man had travelled across the sea, seeking the death of his enemy…but why? What had Sigurd ever done to Feann that would cause such a response? He needed to uncover the secrets that veiled his father's death.

After the wedding massacre, his brothers had taken him into hiding to recover from his wounds. They had burned the bodies of Gilla and her family before burying their ashes. Alarr had kept Hafr's sword as a reminder of the tragedy. King Harald Finehair had stripped his brother Brandt of his claim to Maerr, giving it to his aunt's husband, Thorfinn. Thorfinn had declared them outlaws, and Alarr and his brothers had no choice but to leave Maerr. But not before they had all sworn a blood vow of vengeance. Every man who had played a part in the wedding slaughter would face justice for what he had done.

Alarr had asked Rurik to accompany him to Éireann, while there were rumours that others had gone to Alba and even to Constantinople. Within a year, Alarr hoped to scatter the ashes of their enemies so that they would find no place in Valhalla.

And Breanne, foster daughter of King Feann, would be used to gain the information he needed. Although his knowledge of the Irish language was not strong, Alarr had learned enough to understand it during the past year. Rurik's grasp was better, since his mother had been Irish.

He'd understood every question Breanne had voiced, along with her frustration when he'd refused to answer. But he had given her a crust of bread and some dried meat, which she had devoured. He and Rurik took turns keeping guard until at long last, she had succumbed to sleep, curled up against the seal fur he had given her.

Breanne Ó Callahan was a beautiful woman with hair the colour of a sunset—gleaming red and gold in the light. Her green eyes reminded him of the hills in Maerr, and there was no doubting her courage. She had a strong will, and he admired her refusal to weep or yield. There were bruises on her face, neck, and arms, as well as the raw flesh at her wrists and ankles, but she had not complained of pain even once.

They had sailed through the afternoon and night, using the stars to mark their path. Rurik slept for a time, and Alarr caught an hour of rest before dawn broke across the sky, revealing the southern coast of Éireann. They would reach the Hook Peninsula soon, and Alarr intended to shelter there and rest for a few days. His father had spoken of Styr Hardrata and his wife Caragh, who had formed their own settlement near the coast. The thought of a true bed with furs and a fire were a welcome respite from the miserable rain that had not once relented. Even in morning, the clouded sky offered very little light.

'What will you do with her?' Rurik asked quietly.

'She will give us the information we seek about Feann, and we will use her to get inside the gates of Killcobar. After that, I care not.'

Rurik adjusted one of the sails, and in the distance, they could see the flare of torches from the harbour. 'Do not get too close to her, Alarr. Question Breanne if you must, but do not soften.'

He understood his brother's warning. When it came to women, he found it difficult to remain harsh. His mother had taught him to be kind to maidens, and he could not cast off his upbringing so easily. And there was no doubting that Breanne was a temptation.

A darker voice within him whispered that he could claim her as his concubine. It would be another act of retribution against King Feann to dishonour his foster daughter in such a way. He imagined this beautiful woman curled up against him, her bare skin warming his. Her reddish-gold hair was tangled against her face as she slept, and he wondered what it would be like to have that silken length against him.

'She will tell us everything,' he said. 'But only if we let her believe that we mean her no harm. We will say that we are taking her home in the hopes of a ransom.'

'You're going to betray her,' Rurik said quietly.

It was unavoidable, and Alarr refused to feel any guilt. He had journeyed across the sea for many days, keeping his rage at the forefront of his mind. 'I will do what I must. The woman should believe that we are helping her. Afterwards, I will kill Feann for what he did to our father and me.'

Alarr adjusted the sails as they neared land, and he centred his mind upon the settlement ahead. Absently, he rubbed at the scars on his calves. It was nothing short of a miracle that he'd managed to walk again. The healer had treated his wounds, wrapping them tightly so the muscles could heal. For the next year, he had struggled with every step, and even now, he had a limp. No one spoke of his fighting skills any more. They knew, as he did, that his days of being a warrior were over. He could barely keep his balance, much less defeat an enemy. It ground at his pride, a festering resentment that would never fade.

The dark memory of his wedding day lingered within

him, an ever-constant reminder of what he'd lost. Alarr wanted to avenge his family's honour, and the surest way to reach Feann was through his foster daughter. He would revel in the moment when he could avenge his family, watching the life fade from Feann's eyes. And after he'd killed his enemy, the ghosts of his past would be silenced at last. If he lost his own life, he cared not. He was no longer the warrior he had once been, and he would rather die than be less of a man. All that mattered now was vengeance.

When they drew closer to the pier, Alarr took a length of rope. Breanne stirred from sleep the moment he touched her. 'Where are we?' she asked.

He didn't answer but bound her hands tightly in front of her. Annoyance flared in her eyes, but he would not risk losing such a valuable prisoner.

'Of course, you're not going to answer,' she responded. 'You probably don't understand a word I'm saying.'

Alarr helped Rurik tie off the longboat, and when Breanne tried to climb into the water, he jerked the rope binding her hands and pulled her back. She cursed at him, but he ignored her.

Once the longboat was secure, he stepped into the hip-deep water and reached for his captive. She fought him, but he held her tightly and strode through the waves until they reached the shore. The settlement lay a short distance from the water's edge, closer to the river. Alarr lowered her to the sand but kept her rope in his hands, forcing her to walk alongside him.

'If you think I am going to remain your slave, you are mistaken,' Breanne muttered. 'The moment you try to sleep, I will disappear. And may the gods curse you if you dare to lay a hand on me. I will cut it off first.'

She continued to voice her frustration, cursing them with every step. They walked from the water's edge, up the sandy hillside, to the open meadows. A few sheep grazed nearby, and they continued their path towards the fortress in the distance. Only when they had reached the gates did she stop her endless words. The settlement was newly built, and even beyond the walls, Alarr could see that construction of several longhouses had recently begun.

Four warriors guarded the gates with long spears, and there was no sense of welcome in their demeanour. Alarr approached with Rurik and greeted them. 'Tell Styr Hardrata that Alarr and Rurik, sons of King Sigurd of Maerr, have come to seek shelter.'

One of the men inclined his head and departed, but they were forced to wait until he returned with Styr's permission to enter. Only then did the guards allow them inside the settlement.

By now, the inhabitants had begun to stir. The guard led them towards one of the longhouses near the centre, and they passed by men carrying peat for the outdoor fires. An old woman stirred a pot, adding raw meat to the stew as she stared at them.

Weariness made his vision blur, but Alarr continued walking with Breanne's ropes in one hand and Rurik at his side. Although he had never met the Norse leader, he hoped to learn if the man had any connections to King Feann or if he had any knowledge to share.

They followed the guard inside and passed by several tables as they approached the dais. Styr Hardrata rose from his chair and came to greet them. The leader was tall, with dark-blond hair and a light beard. His brown eyes held a welcome, but there was also a sense of caution, as if he would not hesitate to strike them down if they were a threat.

'We bid you welcome, Alarr and Rurik, sons of King Sigurd.' His gaze narrowed upon Breanne, and he exchanged a glance with his wife. 'Who is your hostage?'

Alarr jerked the ropes forward. 'She is a concubine I bought from Áth Cliath. I intend to ransom her to her foster father, King Feann of Killcobar.'

Styr's wife appeared unsettled by their captive. Her long brown hair was braided and bound at the nape of her neck, and she wore a cap. Her violet eyes softened with sympathy. 'Let me take her, Alarr. She is hurt. I will see to her needs and talk with her.'

The leader introduced her, saying, 'This is my wife, Caragh. Will you allow her to tend your hostage?'

Alarr considered it a moment. 'As long as she is not permitted to leave the settlement.'

Styr gave the orders to his men and nodded. 'If she tries, they will bring her back again.'

'Untie her,' Caragh ordered. 'She will come with me. You may speak with Styr a while, and I will make a place for all of you in one of our longhouses. I know you will be wanting to rest after your journey.'

Alarr could hardly suppress his yawn, and the young woman smiled. 'Perhaps on the morrow, you can help our men with the harvest. We would welcome your assistance.' There was no doubting that this was how she intended them to repay their debt, by offering labour in exchange.

Even so, Alarr was uneasy about letting Caragh take Breanne with her. He didn't trust his slave not to flee, but neither could he insult his hosts by implying that they could not keep her hostage.

'Bring her to me as soon as you can,' he agreed. It was the only thing he could say without offending Styr's wife. He could only hope that allowing Breanne some small measure of comfort would be the first step towards earning her trust.

'You must be weary,' the woman said. Breanne was startled to hear the Irish language flowing so easily from her. Her expression must have revealed her shock, for the woman introduced herself. 'I am Caragh, formerly of the Ó Brannon tribe. My husband is Styr Hardrata.'

'I am Breanne Ó Callahan.'

'And your foster father is King Feann, is he not?'

She nodded, wondering if Caragh could help her. 'He is. I am trying to get home again. I was taken captive and sold into slavery.'

'These men are taking you home,' Caragh said. 'Did you not realise?'

No, she hadn't. But then, the men had told her nothing at all—not even their names. 'I cannot speak their language. They have said nothing to me.'

The young woman's eyes turned sympathetic. 'Well, I would not say that they are bringing you home out of kindness. More that they intend to ransom you.'

That sounded more realistic. But even so, Breanne could hardly believe what she was hearing. She had tried to escape, and the *Lochlannach* had bought her. 'Why would they do this? They don't even know me.'

'They are mercenaries. And you're wrong—they know exactly who you are.'

Now, it made more sense why the *Lochlannach* had taken her captive, if he had known that she was the foster daughter of a king. But how? She had never journeyed to Áth Cliath, nor had she seen this man before.

Perhaps they had overheard something in the marketplace. Someone else might have recognised her, or he might have heard a rumour. There was no way to truly know. But the realisation that they were bringing her home—even for a ransom—caused such a wave of gratitude, she could barely suppress her smile of relief.

'Who are they?' she questioned. 'They have not even told me their names.'

'The older man is Alarr and the younger is Rurik. Both are from the kingdom of Maerr.'

She had never heard of it, but then, she had never left her homeland or travelled anywhere outside of Éireann.

'Would you care to bathe and change into a clean gown?' Caragh offered.

'I would be so grateful.' Breanne had only the rough shift that the slavers had forced her to wear and the seal fur that the men had given her to keep warm.

'I will take you to one of the longhouses. I fear we have only begun building our settlement, and there are many shelters that are still unfinished. We hope to have them completed before winter, but we need the help of every man.' She offered a slight smile. 'I had thought, for a time, that Styr and I might travel across the seas. But now we decided to stay here for the winter...' She rested her hand upon her stomach, and Breanne understood her unspoken blessing of a child to come.

Caragh led her back towards a small partitioned room that contained a wooden trunk. She opened it and sorted through garments until she chose a green gown. 'Here. This might fit you.' She held it out, but Breanne was reluctant to take it.

'It's too fine,' she argued. 'I cannot accept something so beautiful.'

'You may wear it until you are home again,' Caragh said. 'And then send it back to me.' There was no other choice, so Breanne accepted the woollen gown. The stitching was delicate, and she had no doubt it would be warm and comfortable.

Caragh led her back outside towards a different longhouse that was partially finished. On the way, she caught the attention of a young man and gave him orders in the Norse language. Then she took the gown from Breanne. 'I will send you a maidservant to tend your bath. I will give her the gown, and she can help you dress afterwards.'

Breanne thanked her, and Caragh brought her towards the far end of the longhouse. Another partition hid the wooden tub from public view. It was not large, but the idea of warmed water was a luxury that she welcomed.

While they waited for the servants to fill the tub with the hot water, she told Caragh of her foster father's ringfort where she had grown up. A hollow feeling seized her inside. Had anyone searched for her? Or had they given up, believing she was dead or ruined? It hurt to imagine that Feann had turned his back on her and discarded her as a foster daughter. But it was a real possibility, one she had to accept. She was not of his bloodline. An ache settled within her heart at the thought of being forgotten and alone.

After the tub was filled with hot water, Caragh added scented oil to the bath. A young maidservant joined them, and Breanne allowed them to strip off her garments before she settled into the steaming tub.

The warm water consoled her, and she kept her knees drawn up, sinking down as low as she could to immerse herself. She leaned back, dipping her hair into the water, and the maid gave her soap for washing. She scrubbed away the dirt, wishing she could scrub away the memories of captivity so easily. Her wrists and ankles burned from the sores made by the manacles and the ropes. The maidservant brought a linen drying cloth, but before she could help her out of the tub, the *Lochlannach* returned.

She covered herself and glared at him. If he had come here intending to glimpse her naked body, it would not happen. 'Get out,' she ordered.

His blue eyes stared at her, but instead of leaving, he turned around. 'If you want to return home, you must learn to obey.'

It was the first time she had heard him speak her language. The sound of his words had a foreign cast to them, and she suddenly realised that he had kept silent on purpose. She motioned for the drying cloth and the maid brought it to her. In a swift motion, Breanne shielded her body and wrapped the drying cloth around herself, before she stepped out of the tub.

'I have no reason to obey,' she countered. 'And I am not afraid of you.' It was a lie, but she spoke the words with mock confidence, hoping he would believe them. It unnerved her to realise that he had understood every word she had spoken.

'What is your name?' she demanded, wanting to hear it for herself.

'Alarr Sigurdsson,' he answered. 'Of the kingdom of Maerr.'

'I am Breanne Ó Callahan,' she answered. 'My foster father is King Feann MacPherson of Killcobar.'

'I know who he is.' He turned at that moment, and his gaze fixed upon her. 'I recognised you the moment I saw you. And you are worth more than a slave.'

'How could you possibly know me?' she demanded. 'I would have remembered you.' Heat flared in her cheeks when she realised what she'd said. But it was too late to take back the words. Breanne tightened her grip upon the drying cloth, and in that heated moment, she grew aware of his interest. He studied her face, his gaze drifting downward to linger upon her body. There was no denying that he wanted her.

But worse was her own response. She was caught up in his blue eyes and the dark hair that framed a strong, lean face. There was a slight scar on his chin, but it did nothing to diminish his looks. The *Lochlannach* warrior was tall and imposing, his physical strength evident. Only the slight limp revealed any weakness.

'What do you want from me? A ransom?'

He reached out and cupped the back of her neck. It was an act of possession, but instead of feeling furious, his sudden dominance made her flesh warm to the touch. His blue eyes stared into hers as if he desired her, and she was startled by the unbidden response. Though she tried to meet his gaze with resentment, her imagination conjured up the vision of his mouth descending upon hers in a kiss. This warrior would not be gentle... no, he would claim what he wanted from her. Heat roared through her, and she thought of his hands moving down to pull her hips against his.

That might be what he wanted from her, after all. She was well aware of how female slaves were used as concubines. The thought shamed her, but another part of her was intrigued by this man. She could not deny the forbidden attraction, and she had the strange sensation that his touch would not be unwelcome.

As if to make his point, Alarr stroked the nape of her neck before releasing her. 'You will remain with me at all times, obeying everything I ask. If you do this, then I will remove your bindings.'

'When?' she demanded.

'When you have earned my trust. Not before.'

His arrogance irritated her. Was he expecting her to become a slave in truth, subservient to every demand? Never. She could not pretend to be someone she was not. The instinct arose, to tell him that he would be waiting an eternity. Then again, if there was any truth to his words, she would be hurting her own chances of getting home.

'You ask a great deal of me,' Breanne said at last. 'I do not know you, and I do not trust you at all.' He was no better than a mercenary, and she had no doubt that there was a great deal he had not revealed. But then, what choice did she have? She needed an escort to bring her home.

'I have not forced myself upon you,' he pointed out. 'This, I could have done many times. I could also have given you to my brother.'

She reddened at his words, for they were true. He *had* treated her with honour, though he had kept her bound. She would not have trusted him either, were their situations reversed.

'I am grateful,' she said honestly.

'If you do not run away, we will take you home to your father. But if you defy me, you will face consequences.'

She stiffened at the overt threat. 'If you beat me, he will know of it. And you will not be rewarded.'

'I never said I would harm you.' His voice had gone deep, almost seductive. She took a step back, fully aware of her nakedness beneath the drying cloth. Never had a man looked at her in this way, and she could hardly breathe. His hand moved to her face, drawing an invisible line down her jaw. Beneath the drying cloth, her breasts rose up, almost aching to be touched.

And suddenly, she realised that this man was dangerous in ways she'd never even imagined.

Chapter Two

It took an effort not to react to Breanne after her bath. Her skin was rosy from the heat, and damp tendrils of hair framed her face. He had watched as a droplet of water had spilled down her throat to the shadowed hollow between her breasts. He'd wanted nothing more than to push the drying cloth away, revealing her body. *She is the foster daughter of your enemy*, he'd reminded himself. He needed to gain her trust, and leaving her untouched was necessary.

Alarr had turned his back to allow her a measure of privacy while the maid dressed her in Caragh's gown. While they were occupied, he ordered another servant to bring him a length of silk. After Breanne was dressed, Alarr bound her wrist to his with the silk, ensuring that she could go nowhere.

'Is that truly necessary?' she asked. 'I cannot leave the fortress.'

'It is. You have not yet earned my trust.' He did not want her to even imagine thoughts of escape. Her hair was wet and combed back, dampening the edges of the green gown. It fit her waist perfectly and clung to her

curves. There was no denying the beauty of Breanne
Ó Callahan. Her gown brought out the green in her
eyes, and the soft rose of her mouth. He wanted to taste
her lips, to make her understand how badly he wanted
her. Having her hand bound to his only tempted him
more.

As they passed among the others to walk outside, he
saw the men glancing at her with interest. He glared in
response, warning them not to look, and most turned
away. She was not theirs to admire.

Alarr led Breanne to the longhouse where Caragh
had offered them a place to stay. Inside, there was a
sleeping pallet and a long curtain that could be drawn
across the space. Breanne appeared uneasy about the
private space and tried to step back from it. He took
her hand and drew it closer to his. With her wrist bound
in silk, she could pull back a short distance, but nothing more.

'We have journeyed for over a day without stopping,'
he said to her. 'I intend to rest with you at my side.'

'I am not tired,' she started to protest, but he pulled
her closer.

'You will lie beside me.' He didn't trust her not to
run, and he was weary from lack of sleep.

The fear on her face revealed her suspicions, but he
added, 'Have I not said it is not my intention to claim
your innocence? If I give you back to your foster father
untouched, it is worth more to me.'

She still appeared uneasy, but he pulled her near
and forced her to lie down on the pallet. He curled
his body against hers, and her hair was wet and cold
against his face.

'Sleep,' he ordered. He only intended to rest for an hour or so—long enough to get through the day.

But with her body nestled close, he grew aware of her light scent. She tried to keep her distance, but he saw that her skin was prickled with gooseflesh. Despite her words, she was not immune to his presence. But perhaps that was only her fear, not an answering desire.

Beside him, he could feel her tension. She was not about to fall asleep, no matter how much he might want her to.

'What is it?' he demanded. 'I have said I will not harm you.'

She hesitated for a time. The silence stretched out until at last she whispered, 'You knew who I was in the slave market. How is that possible? I've never seen you before.'

He wasn't about to give her the truth. 'It does not matter.'

She refused to relent and continued her questions. 'Aye, it does. I want to know your purpose.'

He gave her no answer, for he owed her nothing. And still, she remained persistent. 'What of my foster father? Do you know him?'

Never would he forget the man who had cut him down, causing his limp. Nor the man who had plotted to murder his father. The taste of vengeance was bitter upon his tongue, but Alarr held no pity towards the man. Even after over a year, his leg often ached from the phantom pain of the blade. There were days when he felt like an old man with ancient bones, especially after a hard rain.

But at last, he answered, 'I have seen King Feann before.'

'How?'

This time, he reached over and touched her lips. 'Sleep. Unless you want me to bind your mouth closed.'

She grew quiet at that, but he realised that Breanne Ó Callahan was not a woman who would obey meekly. Nor would she submit to his commands. Were she not the daughter of his enemy, he might have admired her spirit.

As it was, he intended to heed his brother Rurik's advice to not grow attached to this woman. Breanne was beautiful, and there was no doubt that his body craved hers. But she was a means to an end, and he had to somehow force her to lower her barriers and give him the information he sought. He needed to know everything about the fortress—the number of guards, the weapons, every door and every threat. And the only way he could gain such information was by winning her trust.

Yet Alarr had to maintain his distance, as well. He could not let temptation interfere with his plans. He was prepared to risk his life for revenge, and he did not expect to survive the battle, given his physical weakness. But at least he could claim Feann's life even as he surrendered his own.

Beside him, he could feel her attempting to loosen the length of silk, to free herself. In silent answer, he drew the silk tighter around his arm and gripped her body close. She would never escape him—not while she held the answers he sought.

'I don't like you,' she informed him.

'I don't like you either,' he lied. 'But you are worth a great deal of silver. And in the end, both of us will get what we want.'

'My foster father will have you killed,' she said. 'If you believe he will pay a ransom for me, you are mistaken.'

'Because he does not want you back?'

'Because he has a strong army, and they will cut you down and take me back.'

Alarr tightened his grip around her and began fishing for information. 'Feann is a petty king. He has no more than a dozen men.'

'You are wrong,' she countered. 'He has at least fifty men. Perhaps more.'

It was likely an exaggeration, but he didn't doubt that the Irish king had fifty men who were loyal to him, even if they weren't soldiers. Yet, Breanne had revealed possible numbers, which was useful. He knew if he simply rode into Killcobar, they would slaughter him where he stood. He needed his own warriors to cause a distraction, men who would fight while he avenged Sigurd's death. His brother Rurik would join him, but it would be more difficult to get others to endanger their lives. He could ask Styr for men, but the *jarl* would not grant fighters unless Alarr gave something in return. He would have to think upon it.

After some time, Breanne stopped fighting him. She softened as she slipped into sleep, and her body relaxed against his. It was strange to hold a sleeping woman in his arms, but the sensation was not unwelcome. The scent of her hair and skin sent a bolt of arousal through him. He could imagine leaning down to kiss her throat, cupping her breasts and stroking them until she gasped from her own desire. The image made him grow hard, and he gritted his teeth.

Breanne snuggled against him in her sleep, and the

motion deepened his discomfort. He wanted her badly, and now, he was starting to understand that returning her untouched might be more difficult than he'd imagined. It was not only her beauty that attracted him—it was her fiery spirit of rebellion.

Now was not the time to seduce this woman, for he had to remain fixed upon his goal. Breanne was a distraction, and there was no honour in pursuing her when it could come to naught. It took every ounce of control he had, but he refused to touch her. Instead, he closed his eyes, knowing that sleep would be an impossible feat.

It was early evening when Breanne awakened, after Alarr touched her shoulder. She rose from the pallet, her wrist still tied to his.

'We will eat now,' he said and led her from the sleeping space. She was starving, so she made no protest when he led her to another longhouse where men and women were gathering. Already she could smell the roasted meat and fish, and the yeasty scent of bread nearly brought tears to her eyes. Although Alarr had given her travelling food, it had been nearly a fortnight since she'd had a proper meal.

Alarr opened the door and guided her inside. Long trestle tables were set up with benches, and the people gathered together as one tribe to eat. Children sat upon their mother's laps, while others teased one another as they fought over better seats. She was overwhelmed by the number of people, but Styr and his wife Caragh welcomed them and guided them to their places near the dais.

It made her self-conscious being bound to Alarr.

Though she understood that she was his prisoner, it made her uneasy for everyone to see it. He led her to sit down and then regarded her. 'If I remove your bindings, will you vow to stay and eat?'

Her heart pounded at the thought of precious freedom. A part of her longed to seize the moment, to flee and hope that she could escape. But the logical part of her brain warned that this was a chance to earn his trust. She could not simply run; she had to make her plans carefully.

'I swear it.' She looked him in the eyes as she made the promise.

He stared as if he didn't quite believe her, yet there were so many people inside, it would be nearly impossible to go. Finally, he gave a nod and untied the silk binding, unwrapping it. 'You will remain at my side at all times. Do not go anywhere without my permission.'

She inclined her head to agree and rubbed at her wrist. Alarr gave her a trencher, and upon the bread was roasted mutton with carrots and a thick sauce. She was so hungry it took an effort to eat with good manners when she wanted to stuff it into her mouth as quickly as possible. The meat was warm and savoury, and she had never tasted anything so good. Alarr ate beside her, but she noticed that he never took his eyes off his companions. He was alert to his surroundings, fully aware of everything.

Though she'd believed he was friends with Styr and Caragh, it appeared that he could not ever be at ease. Like a man on guard, his gaze focused upon the doorway when each man entered. His body remained tense, his hand near his weapon.

The other man he'd travelled with, his brother Rurik,

was dining with some of the younger warriors. Although he listened to the tales of the other men, he said nothing. Once or twice, she caught him looking at his brother, but he appeared ill at ease, even among other *Lochlannach*.

As she sated her hunger, Breanne followed Alarr's example and studied each of the men and women. They were very similar to her own people, telling stories, laughing, and sharing in food. Caragh, doted upon her husband, and she reached over to touch him in small ways. There was nothing but love in every gesture, and Breanne found herself feeling envious.

No man had ever looked upon her in the same way Styr looked at Caragh. Or even with desire, as Alarr had looked at her when she'd emerged from bathing. Her skin tightened at the memory. But she could not stop the worry that no one would come for her. It had been weeks, and the isolation caused an ache deep inside her.

She had grown up among the MacPherson tribe and had believed that she was like a daughter to Feann. He had allowed her to sit beside him on the dais after his wife had died. She had cared for his sons as if they were her brothers, and now all were being fostered with other family members to strengthen tribal bonds. But now she wondered if her presence had been a burden after the death of her parents. It might be that Feann had only intended to marry her off to further his own alliances.

They don't want you, a voice inside murmured.

She tried to push back the doubts, but it was hard to believe that anyone cared about her now. A coldness gripped her inside, the loneliness and fear taking root.

'What is it?' Alarr asked from beside her.

'It's nothing.' She didn't want to tell him anything, though he did appear concerned.

'You look pale.' He eyed her, and she met his expression without offering any answers. There was no reason for her to reveal the truth to this man. They were strangers, and she owed him nothing at all.

'I am fine,' she repeated.

'No, you're not.' He tore off a piece of bread, still waiting.

He could wait a very long time, as far as she was concerned. Breanne glared at him. 'If I'm not, it's only because I am your captive. And even if you do intend to bring me home, I despise being a prisoner.'

'I removed your bindings, did I not?'

She flushed, not really knowing how to reply. It was easier to shrug than to say anything.

'You have nothing to fear from me, so long as you obey,' he said.

She bristled at his command and sighed. 'Obedience is all men ever want.'

'For your protection,' he said softly. But then a moment later, his gaze narrowed as if he'd just thought of something else. 'Or is there another reason you are afraid? Was there someone you left behind who is searching for you? A husband, perhaps?'

She sobered, feeling embarrassed by his questioning. Though she hadn't planned on saying anything, she blurted out, 'Feann *was* planning to choose a husband for me. Until I was taken.' At the time, she had been eager to wed, wanting a family and a home of her own. A true home—not a foster home where she felt like an outsider. But now, that dream had burned into ashes.

'Was he planning to wed you to another king?' Alarr

demanded. He appeared almost displeased by the news, and beneath his tone there was a hint of jealousy. She didn't want to imagine why. Though she had tried to remain shielded from his interest, there was no denying the heat that had sparked between them.

'I don't know which suitors Feann was considering.' She took a sip of the mead and found it sweet. 'Possibly someone favoured by King Cerball. It matters not now. No man will have me to wife anymore.' There was no self-pity in her words—they were fact. What man would wed her after she had been held captive by a *Lochlannach* warrior? No one would believe her if she claimed she was untouched.

'Was there a man you had hoped to marry?' He tore off a piece of bread, not making eye contact with her. Instead, his gaze was fixed upon Rurik.

She could hardly believe they were conversing about her future, as if he were a friend. And yet, it was almost too easy to confess her thoughts to a stranger. What did it matter if he knew her innermost feelings? After he returned her to Feann, they would never see each other again.

And so, she admitted, 'I was hoping for a kind man, one who has all his teeth.' She suppressed a grimace at the thought, for it was not uncommon for young noblewomen to be married to older kings.

'What of your parents? Wouldn't they arrange the match instead of Feann?'

She shook her head. 'My parents have been dead for years. Feann has been my foster father since I was two years of age. He allowed me to stay, since I have no living family.' At least, none that she had ever met. Given a choice, she preferred to remain with the man who had cared for her all these years, rather than strangers. Once or twice, she had asked him about who was governing her homeland, but Feann had been vague about the answers, saying only that her lands at Clonagh had been claimed by King Cerball and were under his protection. Whenever she had asked about them, Feann had warned her to put those thoughts far from her mind. Her father had been executed as a traitor and his lands were forfeit. She didn't know how her mother had died, but Feann had refused to speak of it.

The truth was, she felt no connection to Clonagh, since she had never visited the lands. It wasn't difficult to set aside her legacy and look towards a different future. She had always believed she would live with her husband.

Alarr poured more mead for her. 'Do you remember your family at all?'

Breanne shook her head. 'Feann was more of a father to me than anyone else.' She said nothing of her father's betrayal, for she had been warned never to speak of it, and Feann believed it was dangerous.

'Do you think he claimed your parents' lands upon their death?'

Breanne shook her head. Her suspicions rose up at so many questions, but she finished by saying, 'Feann is not a conqueror. He's a good man.'

A sudden darkness came over Alarr's face, as if he did not care for the king. Breanne ventured, 'You don't agree with me, do you?'

He masked his emotions immediately. 'I hardly know him.'

But somehow, she didn't fully believe him. Alarr stood, and the sudden motion made him catch the edge of the table for balance. He reached for her hand and led her towards the dais. As they walked, she noticed his limp was more pronounced than usual. Perhaps his scowl was from pain instead of something her foster father had done.

When they reached the table where Styr and Caragh were dining, the young woman smiled at her in friendship. Alarr spoke with Styr in their native language, which Breanne could not understand. Instead, she drew closer to Caragh and asked in a low voice, 'What are they saying?'

Caragh answered, 'Alarr has asked us for men to accompany you to Killcobar. In return, he is offering his services to us.'

'What services?'

'It is time to harvest the grain, and we need many hands to accomplish the work. We are also trying to build the remaining longhouses before the winter sets in. Our people need shelter, and we cannot fit everyone here.'

'So he intends to bargain our labour in exchange for escorts?'

Caragh nodded. 'It is reasonable enough. But while Styr may send men to protect you, I do not think they will fight.'

Breanne nodded and lowered her voice so no one else could overhear her. 'It would be better if Alarr brought me home without asking for a ransom.' It was possible that Feann would grant him a reward if he asked for nothing. 'If he makes a demand for silver, I cannot say what my foster father will do.'

Caragh's face turned grave and she spoke quietly to her husband in the Norse language before she turned back to Breanne. 'We have come to an agreement. You will stay with us for the next fortnight, and afterwards, Styr will send a dozen men to guard you on your journey to Killcobar. But they will remain outside the gates.' It was clear that they would not allow their own men to face any threats.

A fortnight was far too long. Breanne shook her head. 'I cannot remain here for longer than a few days.'

'It will take more time than that to harvest the grain,' Caragh argued. 'My men cannot leave until it has been stored for the winter.'

Breanne understood the woman's dilemma and tried to find a compromise. Alarr and Styr were engaged in their own conversation, but she still kept her voice low. 'Will you allow me to send word to my foster father? It might put his mind at rest if I tell him I am staying here by choice.'

'Feann would send only men to fetch you,' Caragh predicted. 'And I don't believe Alarr would let you leave with them.'

Breanne sobered, knowing that she was right, 'No. He wouldn't.' Although he had unbound her wrist to allow her to eat, she had no doubt that he would bind her again this night. His behaviour was possessive, almost overprotective.

Alarr stood with Styr, and he sent her a warning look to stay with Caragh. The two men walked down from the dais to speak with Rurik, giving them a measure of privacy.

Caragh eyed her with sincerity. 'You must understand why we will not risk a fight within our gates between Feann and Alarr. We will not allow the king's men inside our settlement. Else it would bring harm to our own people.'

Frustration blossomed within Breanne when she realised there was no choice but to back down. 'I can stay for a sennight, but no longer. Afterwards, if you have finished harvesting your grain for the winter, will you send your men to accompany us?'

Caragh nodded. 'We will. Or you can leave beforehand, if you believe Alarr and Rurik would provide adequate protection.'

She hesitated. Although both men were *Lochlannach* fighters, there was no denying that there were dangers in travelling with such a small group. Two arrows could bring them down, leaving her unprotected.

'You are right,' she admitted. 'It would be safer to travel with more men.'

Caragh brightened. 'Good. We will be going out to work in the fields in the morning, and we would welcome your help.'

Breanne was embarrassed to admit the truth. 'I have never harvested grain before. I know very little about it.'

'The men will cut the stalks, and we will collect the grain and shake the kernels free.' Caragh said. 'The women will show you how.' She stood from her chair and offered, 'On the morrow, I will show you how to bind back your hair and use the folds of your gown as an apron.'

Breanne followed her, and as they neared the men, she cast a look at Alarr, waiting for permission. He inclined his head and said, 'You may go with her.' Then he added, 'But do not run away.'

His warning irritated her, for she did possess honour. Caragh and Styr had offered their hospitality, food, and shelter. She would not try to run—not when she now knew Alarr's intent was to ransom her. If she bided her time, she would reach home once again. The thought brought an aching within her, the fervent desire to be back at Killcobar.

And yet, she somehow sensed that it would not be the same again.

Alarr rose at dawn to work alongside the men. Although the morning air was cool, they had stripped off their tunics, wearing only hose. Each man had a scythe for cutting the wheat, and Styr divided the fields so that the men were spread out over different sections. The sun had just risen, and the scent of ripened grain filled the air.

Alarr welcomed the physical activity, for it gave him time to think. The motion of swinging the scythe caught him in a rhythm, and he allowed his mind to drift. It was backbreaking work, but he found satisfaction in watching the stalks fall to the ground.

Behind the men, the women gathered the fallen stalks. He kept a close eye on Breanne to ensure that she had no intention of escaping. She had bound her hair beneath a length of cloth like the other women, and she wore a gown with a wide apron. The women followed behind the men, gathering the stalks of wheat in their aprons, before they returned to place the grain in large baskets. Some of the older women and children were seated with large baskets, running the stalks through their fingers to harvest the wheat berries.

Alarr turned back to the field, slicing through the grain in a steady motion. He kept his steps slow, to disguise his limp. As he worked, he tried to piece together the faces of the men who had come to his wedding. But the only face that remained constant in his memory was Feann. The king's men had surrounded the longhouse and set it on fire, slaughtering those inside. The wedding celebration had transformed into a horrifying vision of blood and death. The images were burned into his memory, and he would never forget. Nor could he ever imagine another marriage, if he happened to survive the fight with Feann. The ceremony was tainted with bloodshed for ever.

He glanced back at Breanne. Her steady look held curiosity, but now that she knew he was taking her home, she seemed content to wait. At least, for a time.

They worked from morning until early afternoon, when Styr called a halt to their harvesting. Caragh arranged for the women to bring meat, cheese, and bread to the labourers, along with pitchers of cold water from the stream. Alarr's arms were aching, and although it was not warm, he was sweating from the hard work.

He saw Breanne joining the other women near a large stretch of cloth. They had gathered baskets of wheat berries atop it, and the women each held on to an edge of the cloth, lifting it into the air. They shook the wheat to separate the chaff, and one of the women began singing. Though she did not know their language, he saw Breanne learning the song, and she joined in. The sunlight shone against her face, and she smiled at the other women as she worked and sang.

For a time, Alarr watched her. Strands of reddish-gold hair framed her cheeks, and she was flushed from the warmth of the sun. Rurik came up beside him and saw the direction of his gaze. 'Don't,' he warned.

'Don't what?' Alarr feigned ignorance, though he knew full well what his brother meant. Against his better judgement, he glanced back at Breanne and saw her watching him. Her expression was not one of disinterest, and she flushed before looking away. Alarr turned back, feeling a sense of satisfaction.

'You have to take her back to Killcobar. She's not yours to keep as a concubine,' Rurik warned. 'No matter how fair she is.'

'I know that.' Even so, it didn't mean he couldn't admire what he saw. Alarr walked alongside his brother to a different part of the field and picked up his scythe again. He cut a pathway through the grain, slicing the wheat. Rurik joined him in silence. The exertion felt good, and he was able to hide his limp as he moved slowly. Behind him, the women began gathering sheaves again, and several children helped them. He spied a young girl with dark hair, laughing as she picked up the grain. The sight of the child filled him with a sense of remorse. Had Gilla lived, he might have sired a child by now. But it was more likely that he would never have children.

He sobered at the thought and glanced at the horizon ahead. One fortnight from now, he would face Feann and gain the answers he sought.

The desire for revenge had kept him from falling into despair. During the nights of agony while his flesh had knit itself together last year, he had envisioned Feann falling beneath his blade. It had given him a reason to live, for the gods knew he was now worthless as a fighter. The image of Feann's death was branded in his mind, an inevitable task that he intended to fulfil.

'Alarr,' his brother interrupted his thoughts, nodding towards the other men. 'What are your plans to get us inside Killcobar?'

'We will use Breanne's knowledge of the structure and its defences.' He needed to know all about the interior of Killcobar, and she would give him the information without even knowing what she'd done.

'She will not tell us anything,' Rurik predicted. 'She won't risk her family for our sake.'

'She won't know our intentions,' he answered. 'I will converse with her about her home and she will not suspect my purpose.' By the time she learned the truth, it would be too late. She would despise him, but that hardly mattered.

'And once we get inside the fortress?' Rurik prompted. 'What then?'

'We will give Breanne back to her father and pretend to leave. I will avenge our father's death, as we planned.'

'And how will we escape Killcobar? What is your plan to get out?'

'You will already be gone,' he answered. 'Feann will want us to leave, and I will ensure that he believes we obeyed.'

His brother stopped cold and stared at him. 'Are you *trying* to die? You'll be killed the moment you get close to him.'

He faced his brother. 'Do not doubt that I can kill him. I am not that weak.'

'You've gone weak in the head!' Rurik exploded. 'I

know you are capable of murdering our enemy, but what I doubt is your ability to survive the fight.'

Alarr only stared at his brother, saying nothing at all. He had never expected to live through the battle. He would do whatever was necessary to gain his vengeance—even if it meant sacrificing his life in return.

His brother let out a low curse. 'Why would you do this, Alarr? I won't allow it.'

He picked up his scythe and began walking back towards the others. 'Because you have no choice.' He was weary of living his life as less than a man, a broken warrior. Why would it matter if he lost his life? Every man wanted his place in Valhalla, through an honourable death in battle. This was the way, and in surrendering himself, he would avenge those he'd loved.

And Rurik could do nothing to stop him.

Breanne was finding it difficult to concentrate. Although the women had showed her how to strip away the wheat berries and separate the chaff, she was distracted by the sight of Alarr cutting the grain. With each slice of his blade, his shoulders flexed, revealing his strength. His muscles were thick and hardened from years of training. A few scars revealed tests of battle, and she found herself spellbound by his sun-warmed skin. She could almost imagine him drawing near, a walking temptation. There was no denying her fascination with his body, and it annoyed her. He was her captor. He had bound her in ropes and taken her away as his slave.

But he never treated you as a slave, her conscience reminded her. *He is bringing you home.*

For ransom. It was about silver, she knew. And the

sooner her traitorous body accepted it, the better. But she could hardly tear her gaze away from him.

When the afternoon waned, the men put away their scythes and went to the stream to bathe. Caragh helped her gather up a basket of wheat berries, and they walked alongside one another. 'Thank you for your help,' the young woman said. 'Many hands make the task easier.'

Breanne nodded, noticing that Caragh was walking closer to the stream. It fed into a small lake, and the men had stripped naked and were swimming. She forced herself to look away, but Caragh paused a moment.

'I have spoken to Styr, and we have decided to offer you another choice.'

She didn't understand what the woman meant. 'A choice in what?' When there came no answer, Breanne glanced up.

Caragh studied the men, fixing her attention upon her husband before she looked back at her. 'You could leave on the morrow with a small escort of my husband's men,' she offered. 'They would take you within a mile of the gates, and you could return home without Alarr.'

The offer was tempting, but she pointed out, 'We both know he would never allow me to go.'

'We believe he has another reason for escorting you home,' Caragh ventured. 'One that has little to do with a ransom.'

She frowned, waiting for the woman to continue. 'What do you mean?'

'The kingdom of Maerr is very powerful. Alarr's family has no need of silver. Their wealth far surpasses ours.'

A coldness caught Breanne's spine, and she stared back at Caragh. 'What are you suggesting?'

The woman shook her head. 'I don't know. But there is another reason why Alarr wants to bring you to Killcobar. And ransom is not a part of it—of that I am certain.'

Breanne didn't know what to believe. 'I know that he wants your men to accompany him,' she said slowly, 'but I thought it was for our protection. It's not safe for only three of us to approach Feann's stronghold.'

'That might be true,' Caragh said. 'But were it me, I would try to find out more.'

She didn't understand what the woman was implying. What else was there? He had purchased her and intended to sell her back to her foster father. 'Alarr will not tell me anything,' Breanne argued. 'I am his slave, not his friend. Or, his hostage, I suppose.'

Caragh only smiled. 'I have seen the way he looks at you. He desires you, Breanne. And a man's desire is a good way to get the answers you seek, when his guard is lowered.'

Breanne faltered at the words. Even now, she was aware of Alarr's constant attention. He never took his gaze from her for a single moment. When she turned back towards the lake, she saw him watching her. His body gleamed with water droplets, and his hair was wet. He pushed back the water from his face, and his gaze fixed upon hers. She felt a sudden tautness in her body, a yearning she did not expect. 'I don't know.'

'Come with me,' Caragh told her. 'We will store the grain below ground.' She led Breanne to a smaller shelter. Inside, a ladder was set inside the earth, revealing an underground storage cairn. Caragh climbed

down the ladder and Breanne passed her the basket of
wheat berries. Then she joined the young woman below
ground. The walls were lined with stone, and the air
was cool below. There were dozens of baskets of grain,
and on the far wall, she spied barrels and other wooden
storage containers. The *Lochlannach* tribe had begun
collecting food for the winter, but it would not yet be
enough to feed everyone.

When they returned to the ladder, Caragh paused.
'If you want to go home without Alarr, Breanne, we
can find another way.'

Breanne hesitated, knowing that Alarr would fight
back against anyone who tried to take her. But despite
his possessive demeanour, he had never mistreated her.
With each passing day, he granted her a little more
freedom. She had revealed more about her life than
she had intended, but it was strange to realise that it
had lifted the burden. Nearly a fortnight had passed,
and no one had come for her, save Alarr. To a certain
extent, the ground between them was shifting. It was
not yet friendship…but she did not consider him an
enemy, either. If her father's men tried to harm Alarr,
it would bother her.

And she didn't know what to think of that.

Caragh paused a moment, resting her hand upon the
ladder. 'What do you want to do, Breanne?'

'I'm not certain,' she confessed. 'Alarr did save me
from the slave market when no one else did.' The bitterness returned, even though she realised it was difficult for anyone to track her by sea. 'I feel as if I owe
him the chance to take me home,' she admitted.

And yet, she knew so little about the man. It was far

too soon to trust him. In the end, she said, 'I will think upon it and let you know.'

'As you will. But be careful.' Caragh met her gaze for a long moment before she led the way up the ladder.

The air was warmer above ground, and once they returned to the centre of the settlement, the scent of stew and fish kindled her hunger. The older women had remained behind with the younger babies, and the waiting food was a welcome sight. Breanne searched for Alarr, and when at last he caught her gaze, there was no denying the heat within it. His tunic was damp with sweat, and his eyes drank in the sight of her. He looked as if he wanted to take her hand and drag her into a darkened corner. Her heartbeat quickened at the thought. She felt a sense of guilt about her attraction, but then Caragh's words came back to her. *He desires you.*

Her flush went all the way to her toes. She wasn't accustomed to attention, for she preferred to remain apart from others. Men usually ignored her, except when King Feann had forced her to stand before them. Or when he had seated her beside him on the dais at the queen's place. It made her feel uncomfortable to have so many people watching her. She had only agreed because she knew there was no one else.

She wondered if Caragh's words were true, that Alarr's family had great wealth. Why then, would he go to such a pretence? Or why would he journey so far?

Breanne couldn't imagine any reason at all. If she asked him, he would never admit the truth. She would have to gain his trust, possibly even his interest. He might be more willing to speak if she behaved in a softer manner towards him. She was unaccustomed to using feminine wiles upon a man, but she needed to know if Alarr posed a threat to her foster father.

He joined the other men, lining up for food. She held back, waiting her own turn, but to her surprise, he crossed the space and stood before her. 'You need to eat,' he said, offering her the wooden plate of food.

'But that's yours,' she protested.

She saw that he was about to argue, and instead suggested, 'Why don't we share? If we are still hungry, we can get more.'

At that, he relented. Breanne led him towards one of the outdoor hearth fires and sat upon a log nearby. He joined her and offered her the first choice of the fish. She broke off a piece of trout, but instead of holding it out, she brought it to his mouth. Her fingertips grazed his lips, and Alarr caught her hand. 'What are you doing, Breanne?' His gaze narrowed upon her clumsy attempt to gain his notice.

'Offering you food.' She feigned innocence, but he would have none of it. She realised then, that she had been too obvious. Instantly, she dropped the fish back on the plate. 'If you don't want it, fine.' She picked up the bread and tore it in half, eating her portion without looking at him.

Only then did he take his own bread. She felt her cheeks burning, for he was already mistrustful of her. She should have known that he would suspect any kindness she showed to him.

He offered her the plate again, but this time she took her fish and left him half of it. He ate part of it, but then asked, 'Do you want any more?'

'I've had my fill.' She remained seated beside him, while he finished the remainder.

An awkward silence descended between them, and he said at last, 'If we bring in the harvest sooner, Styr will grant us the escorts. It may not take long.'

She nodded but said nothing. Eventually, Alarr rose from the log and brought the wooden plate to one of the older women, who took it from him. He brought back a cup of ale and handed it to Breanne.

She took a sip and then gave the cup to him. Alarr drained the ale and stood watching her for a moment. She felt the intensity of his gaze warming her skin, and at last, she lifted her chin to stare back. She was caught up in his handsome face, and then his mouth tilted in a slight smile. Breanne felt unnerved by the attention and finally asked, 'What is it you want?'

He studied her and shrugged. 'I need nothing.'

And yet, he continued to stare. His demeanour utterly disarmed her, though she tried to remind herself that it was only an unwanted flare of interest, one that would go away soon. She knew better than to let her wayward thoughts become something more. If his interest was real, then it was only a physical attraction. Alarr would bring her home to her foster father and then leave her behind. She would never see him again.

She was interrupted by Caragh who said, 'Breanne, we have need of your help, if you can join us.'

'Go with her,' Alarr commanded. Without waiting for her answer, he went back to join his brother and the other men.

Caragh took her by the hand and led her towards an outdoor table laden with apples. 'Some of the apples have ripened, and we are drying them for the winter.' On another table, there was a heavy length of wool set out with apple slices to be dried in the sun. She offered Breanne a small knife and bade her join the others at the table.

She began slicing the fruit, grateful for the distraction. Her failed attempts at attracting Alarr's interest embarrassed her, and she inwardly chided herself. She'd never been very good at flirting with a man. Why should today have been any different?

An old woman nudged her and spoke in the Norse language, laughing as she nodded towards Alarr. Breanne had no idea what she'd said, but she flushed at the teasing.

'She offered to make you a love charm,' Caragh said. 'That is, if you're wanting one.'

'No,' she blurted out. 'That's the last thing I need.' She was Alarr's captive, and she did not want to be too close to him. His focused attention already made her ill at ease.

'Oh, I don't know,' Caragh said. 'There are advantages to love.' A soft smile stole over her face, and she lowered her hands to her abdomen. Breanne answered her smile.

'When will your baby come?' she asked.

'In the spring.' The young woman's expression brightened at the thought. Caragh glanced towards the men where she spied her husband. A soft smile came over her face. Then she rose from the pile of apples and left Breanne among the other women.

The old woman nudged her again as she glanced over at Alarr. Then she cackled and passed her another apple. Breanne saw the other women suppressing their laughter, but she stiffened and turned her attention to cutting the fruit. In time, they stopped their teasing.

* * *

After a few hours, it was growing dark. Her neck and shoulders ached, but all the apples had been peeled, sliced, and laid out to dry. She stood from the table, rubbing her sore neck. The women went back to the longhouse where they had dined the previous night, and Breanne joined them. She did not see Alarr or Rurik, and she took a bit of meat and cheese for a light meal. It was already dark outside, and she was weary from the work.

She decided to return to the sleeping space, and when she arrived, she saw Alarr seated on the pallet. Her first instinct was to back away, but then, that would accomplish nothing.

'Come here,' he ordered. 'I have need of your help.'

She obeyed, not understanding what he wanted. When she drew closer, she saw that he was holding a small wooden box that contained an herbal salve. She couldn't quite make out all the scents, but one of them was strong, like mint.

'What is it?' she asked.

He handed her the box. 'I want you to rub this into my scars.' Alarr lifted the edge of his hose and showed her an angry red scar just below his knees. It appeared that someone had tried to cut off his legs, and she was shocked at the evidence of such a violent injury.

'What happened to you?'

'I was badly wounded in battle,' he answered. 'The healer thought I might never walk again.'

'You proved her wrong,' Breanne said. She didn't pry, realising that this was what had caused his limp. He disguised it well, and now that she had seen the scars, it made her sympathise with him.

He added, 'The pain plagues me when I stand for too long. This medicine helps.'

She opened the box and the scent of mint grew stronger. 'You are very fortunate to have survived.' Then she knelt down beside the pallet. 'Turn over.'

He obeyed, and she dipped her hands in the salve. She put a generous amount on his right calf, rubbing it into his skin. The red scar left an indentation in his flesh, and she moved her hands over his legs. His calves and thighs were large, revealing the muscled strength of a warrior. She had never touched a man like this before, and she moved her palms over him in a circular motion. He flinched at her touch, but she gentled it, feeling the knotted muscles beneath her fingertips. 'Are you in pain?'

'Yes,' he gritted out.

She used her fingers to massage his calf muscle, being more careful when she reached the deep scars. Slowly, she rubbed the salve into his skin, pressing gently against the muscles. It was strangely intimate, caring for him in this way. And yet, she recognised the pain he was in. With every touch of her hands, she saw his knuckles clench against the fur coverlet.

For the next few minutes, she tried to soothe the aches, sliding her hands over his skin. Though she supposed she should feel uncomfortable touching him in such a way, the truth was, she found satisfaction in working out the knots. She could tell when she had eased his pain from the way he relaxed beneath her hands. And when he no longer flinched at her touch, she drew back.

'Is that better?'

He rolled over, and the flare of heat in his eyes

caught her by surprise. Without warning, Alarr pulled her atop him. Her legs straddled him, and she could feel the hard length of his arousal. 'No,' he murmured softly. 'It's not better.'

Breanne gasped when he sat up, drawing her to him. Her heart thundered, for she had never been so close to a man before. Her softness embraced his rigid body, and she went utterly still.

Alarr hesitated a moment, his gaze burning into hers with a silent question. When she did not struggle, he cupped the back of her head and dragged her into a fierce kiss. She could hardly catch her breath as he devoured her with his hot mouth and tongue. Shock and desire poured through her, and she clung to his shoulders, hardly knowing what was happening. Never in her life had she been kissed like this. He plundered her mouth, claiming her in a way that provoked a strong desire. Between her legs, she felt her own arousal deepening, and her breasts tightened. God help her, she could not push him away. And she didn't want to.

Instead, she found herself kissing him back, giving in to her own needs. A rough growl came from his throat, and Alarr rolled her on to her back, still lying atop her. He continued to kiss her until her mouth was swollen, her lips bruised. But she hardly cared at all. She was lost in this forbidden moment, unable to think clearly.

The voice of reason tried to intrude, but she silenced it, revelling in the dark feelings. Her body delighted in his touch, and thoughts of surrender spun through her mind. She could give in to his seduction, allowing him to claim her. Everyone would believe that was what had already happened, since he had bought her as his slave. No one would believe that she was still a virgin.

Yet, she hardly knew this man. How could she succumb to these feelings when she knew not his true purpose? She could not trust him, nor could she surrender her innocence.

With reluctance, she broke the kiss and turned her face to the side. Alarr did not release her, but instead, he rolled to his side, pulling her back against his chest. She was cradled against him, and he kept both arms around her.

'Sleep,' he commanded.

Sleep? How could she possibly close her eyes now? Her body was alive with hunger, craving something she did not understand. He was still heavily aroused, and she doubted he could sleep either. But perhaps he recognised the danger and was putting an end to it before it went too far.

Breanne stared at the partition, feeling as if she could hardly bear to be in Alarr's arms. This was not what she had intended at all, not when she had planned to win his trust. Instead, she felt confused and uncertain, almost afraid to move.

She was playing a dangerous game, and he had won the first round. Her heart pounded, and it took a while for her breathing to calm down. It embarrassed her to remember how she had behaved. She had mistakenly believed that she could soften Alarr, gaining the answers to her questions. Instead, he had aroused her so deeply, she was embarrassed at her own reaction. She was allowing herself to weaken, to fall prey to his touch.

Worst of all, she had enjoyed it.

He doesn't truly want you, Breanne warned herself. *He is using you for ransom. You mean nothing to him, and he will leave you.*

She knew this, beyond all doubt. It was foolish to let down her guard for the sake of physical touch. Until now, she hadn't realised how truly lonely she was. Feann had been kind to her, but he was not her true father. Nor had his wife ever been a mother to her. She had always felt isolated and awkward at Killcobar, never knowing why. She was not a MacPherson, but rather, an Ó Callahan. Perhaps that was why she'd never felt at home among them.

She could not let herself fall prey to Alarr's advances, nor could she risk her own desires. For he would only abandon her, just like everyone else.

Chapter Three

Over the next few days, Alarr was torn between keeping his distance and sleeping with Breanne in his arms at night. Something about her presence brought him into a deeper slumber. She made the nights more bearable, and despite the physical frustration, he would not allow her to sleep elsewhere. Sometimes in the morning when he awakened, he watched her sleeping. Her mouth was softened, her fair lashes resting against her cheeks. Though she often braided her hair before she went to sleep, sometimes the reddish-gold strands slipped free, resting against the curve of her face. There was no denying her beauty, and Alarr suspected that any man would be furious at the loss of her.

If Gilla had been taken before their wedding, he would have raised an army of men to find her. Why, then, had no one done the same for Breanne?

It made him wonder if there was another danger he had not considered. He had travelled with the intention of avenging his father's death…but what if Feann was gone from Killcobar? If they attempted an attack, the king's men would slaughter him where he stood.

No, it was better to learn where his enemy was before he made a decision.

This morn, he intended to speak with Styr and begin making his plans. They had harvested nearly all the grain now, and the men had turned their attention towards building more longhouses.

He found Styr upon a ladder, hammering nails into one of the unfinished dwellings. The air was cooler this morn, and Alarr picked up his own hammer and a pouch of iron nails. In truth, he welcomed the constant activity to take his mind off Breanne. Being unable to touch her was its own torment.

He worked alongside Styr for a time, waiting for the right moment to speak. 'Has Breanne's foster father gone in search of her? Or is he still at Killcobar?'

'I've not heard,' Styr answered. He pounded another nail into the wood.

'Did anyone send word that Breanne was taken?'

The leader shook his head slowly. 'There was no news until you arrived.'

Then that meant Feann was trying to keep Breanne's fate quiet. Perhaps to protect her status, Alarr decided. He met Styr's gaze and informed the man, 'I will be taking her back to Killcobar in a few days, if your men can be ready.'

Styr struck another nail into the wood with a mallet. 'They can, so long as the grain is stored. But they will not fight, unless I command it of them.'

'It is not my intent to provoke a fight,' Alarr answered, 'but neither will I be Feann's target.'

'Why do you not send Breanne back to him without a ransom?' Styr asked. 'We both know you have no need of the silver.'

Alarr eyed the *jarl* and hesitated, wondering if he should admit the truth. He decided against it, for Styr would not want to endanger his men. Thus far, he intended to use Breanne as a distraction. After he brought her back, he would pretend to leave with the others. And that night, he would confront Feann alone and gain his vengeance.

The thought of facing the man brought about the dark memory of his battle injury. His calves had a phantom ache, even now, from Feann's sword.

'I believe Breanne was betrayed by some of her foster father's men,' he said at last. 'If they were the ones to sell her into slavery, then it is not safe for her to go alone.'

That seemed to satisfy Styr, and he thought a moment. 'I understand. I will ask our men this night who would like to accompany you.'

'My thanks.'

A sense of guilt slid through him at the half-truth. One of Feann's men *had* taken Breanne and accepted payment for her—but after Alarr had hired him. He had fully intended to steal her away, only to be betrayed when she was sold into slavery. That same man might be there still, and if he were, Alarr intended to seek his own justice.

Yet, it still bothered him that no one had come to search for her. Dozens of men should have tried to find her, and he couldn't understand why they hadn't. It felt as if he were missing information that could later become a threat.

Alarr returned to his work and saw Breanne joining the women. They had gathering baskets and were talking to one another as they walked. Caragh was beside her, and the woman smiled at him when they passed. Breanne's cheeks flushed when she risked a glance.

As Alarr continued to work on the longhouse with the other men, he let himself fall into the steady rhythm of the work. It felt good to labour while his mind drifted to his plans. Yet even as he worked, he couldn't stop looking back at Breanne. Her red-gold hair was bound back into a long braid, and while she spoke with Caragh, she was smiling.

Alarr thought of last night when Breanne had massaged the medicine into his aching limbs. Her touch had aroused him deeply, and he had wanted nothing more than to spend the night pleasuring her. She allured him like no other, and when he'd kissed her, she had kissed him back. He didn't know what was happening between them, but he knew it was wrong. She was an innocent, and he had taken advantage of her. Breanne had succumbed to temptation, but there could never be anything permanent between them. After he took her to Killcobar, she would never see him again. He was prepared to face his own death—but he didn't want her involved. His honour was weary and worn, but in this, he would stand firm. She deserved a man who would be there for her, who would care for her.

As for himself, he was a broken shell of a man. Because of Feann's sword, he'd lost his ability to fight. Even now, running was difficult without a hard limp. He felt like a cripple at times, and the truth was, he'd avoided any raids or skirmishes since he'd been wounded.

It was like a splinter in his soul, degrading him as a warrior. His need for vengeance wasn't only about his father's death…it was for himself. He despised Feann

for what he had done, and he would never stand back
and abandon the matter—even if that meant using Breanne and betraying her trust. He could not let himself soften towards her. There could be no emotion to
threaten his resolve. He would kill her foster father, and
he cared not what happened afterwards. He tightened
the invisible bonds around his conscience, refusing to
even consider mercy. Mercy was not shown to his father
or to him. And Feann would pay the price for murder.

Morning shifted into afternoon, and eventually, Styr
called a halt to their work. They climbed down from
the ladders and began to walk towards the centre of the
settlement, when suddenly, Alarr saw the women returning near the gates. Several were carrying baskets
of apples, but Breanne was not among them.

Caragh came running towards her husband, and
there was a stricken expression on her pale face. Styr
caught her in his arms, and they spoke together in private. The leader glanced at several of his fighters, and
his expression was grim. Then he fixed his gaze upon
Alarr, motioning him to come closer.

'We need men to help us search,' he said. 'Breanne
has gone missing.'

The words took him aback, and for a moment, Alarr
was torn between fear and wondering if she had taken
the opportunity to escape. He had let down his guard
too soon and had allowed her too much freedom. He
had trusted that she would not leave, believing she
would wait until he brought her home.

Yet, after he'd kissed her, he might have frightened
her into thinking he intended to claim her body. He had
wanted to, but he'd kept his restraint. Did she somehow

believe he would force himself upon her? Never would he claim a woman without her consent.

But she might not know that.

He had become too complacent. In the end, she was his slave—and she had likely seized the chance for her freedom. He could not allow her to destroy his plans for vengeance. Not after he'd come this far. He turned to Styr. 'I need a horse.'

Styr barked a command to one of his men, and soon, one returned with a gelding. 'Alarr.'

He turned back and met the leader's gaze. 'What is it?'

'Caragh doesn't think she ran away. She believes Breanne was taken.'

He stilled at that, and his anger hardened into resolve. If another man had dared to take her away, Alarr would bury his blade into the man's heart. Instinct roared within him that she belonged to him.

And yet, she didn't. She had never been his, though he had bought her. Breanne had remained fiercely independent, and he had been attracted to her proud spirit. But if someone had dared to take her, Alarr would not ignore the threat. He would track down her assailant and punish him for what he'd done.

Styr added, 'It happened so fast, Caragh didn't see them. One moment Breanne was helping them with the apples, and then the next, she wasn't there.'

Who could have taken her? Was it one of Feann's men? Or had his earlier instincts been correct, that she had run away? It hardly mattered now—the only thing of importance was getting her back again.

Alarr mounted the animal and rode hard towards the gates. Within seconds, four other men joined him,

Styr among them. He realised, too late, that he should have questioned Caragh further about what she had seen. Instead, they would have to track Breanne, hoping that there was some trace left behind. Though she was his hostage, he could not stop the flare of worry. An unprotected woman could easily become another man's prey.

Alarr rode hard towards the small grove of apple trees further inland. The trees grew in a clearing surrounded by a deeper forest that stretched across the western side of the peninsula. His emotions knotted, but he shut them down, focusing all his efforts on finding Breanne. When he reached the trees, he dismounted and searched for signs that she had separated from the group of women. He examined the grasses, even the slightest bent twig for a clue to discover where she'd gone.

There. He saw a footprint on the edge of the clearing, close to the stream. It disappeared, and he guessed that she had crossed the water and gone into the wood. Though he would have preferred to go on horseback, the woods were so thick, it was not possible. He turned back to the other men. 'Will you take the opposite side and search for her? I will look among the trees.'

Styr gave the orders to split up, and it was then that Alarr realised his brother Rurik was not among the men. He frowned, trying to think when he had seen Rurik last. Yestereve, possibly. Had Rurik gone in search of Breanne?

He tried to hasten his step, but his right leg was unsteady as he tried to run. His left leg was more stable, since the blade had not cut as deeply. But as he continued to limp through the woods, it soon became clear that no one had come this way. He returned to his horse, frustrated that there was no sign of either Breanne or his brother.

Alarr continued to search all afternoon but came up with nothing. He expelled a curse, wondering how he would ever find them.

Breanne glared at her captor, seething at this turn of events. 'Let me go,' she demanded.

'No.' Rurik led her deep into the woods, and branches scratched at her arms as it grew darker. 'Let him believe you ran away.'

'You were supposed to take me home,' she insisted. 'It's why I *didn't* run away.' She jerked back from him and spat. 'At least I showed honour. You have none.' It infuriated her that Rurik would do something like this. She wasn't afraid of him, and yet, she knew not what his intentions were.

'My brother is going to get himself killed. And you're not worth the cost of his life,' Rurik said. He seized the ropes and pulled hard. 'I am taking you back before he begins a war.'

What did he mean by that? 'Alarr isn't starting any kind of war,' she muttered. 'He wants a ransom, that's all.'

Rurik's face twisted. 'Is that what you think?' He let out a sound of exasperation and forced her to continue walking.

Breanne recalled Caragh's warning that Alarr had no need of silver. It sounded as if it were true, now. 'Well, what else am I to think? It's all he's ever told me.'

'And why would he tell you the truth?' Rurik continued his dogged path, and his words cut her down.

She had the sense that he was hiding a great deal, and she pressed the point.

'Then what *is* the truth, Rurik?'

He would not say but forced her to duck beneath a thick oak branch. 'Keep walking, Breanne.'

Did he truly believe she would stay silent and obey? Her own frustration mounted higher. 'And what if I don't want to? I know you even less than I know Alarr. What if you are lying and your intention is to sell me back into slavery?'

At that, he shoved her back against a tree. His blue eyes gleamed with fury. 'My intention is to save his miserable life. And yours.'

'I don't trust you,' she shot back. 'You've dragged me out into the middle of nowhere, and everyone is searching for us. And you can only claim that you're trying to save him.' She raised her chin. 'Why would you need to save him? Why would you think Alarr is going to do something foolish?'

He stared hard at her, as if trying to decide what to say. She saw the indecision in his eyes, and finally he came to his own conclusion. 'Because Feann is the reason why Alarr has those scars. He cut him down, and now my brother cannot fight any more.'

'What do you mean?' An invisible frost seemed to slide within her veins. There was no doubting the seriousness of his words. She had touched the scars, and she knew how much Alarr suffered when he overexerted himself.

But Rurik refused to answer. Instead, he seized her ropes and demanded, 'Walk.'

Numbly, she obeyed. Though she ought to be somewhat grateful that he was taking her home, it was a day's journey from here, perhaps longer. They had no horse, no shelter, and no food. It was clear that Rurik had acted on impulse, and she wondered if he even knew where he was going.

Strange that she should now be wondering how to return to the *Lochlannach* settlement, instead of being eager to go home. Alarr had made her feel safe, whereas she didn't trust Rurik to protect her. He was only one man.

She thought about his claim, that Feann had caused Alarr's wounds. How could that be true? Her foster father had never gone to Maerr, to her knowledge. He had only ever travelled to Britain two summers ago. Surely Rurik was mistaken.

Or had Feann lied?

She decided to try another tactic. 'I need a moment to catch my breath.'

'We have no time. Else they will find us.' The determination on Rurik's face revealed that he was not going to let her ruin his plans. She weighed her options, wondering who she trusted more. Rurik claimed that he was trying to avoid a war…but she was more concerned about Alarr. She believed in her heart that he was a man of honour, for he had never forced her or claimed her as his concubine. Even when he had kissed her, tempting her into surrender, he had not demanded her body. He had treated her as a woman of worth, and that meant something.

She preferred to travel with Alarr, and though he would be angry at his brother, she wanted no part in this escape. Seeing no other choice, Breanne let her body fall slack to the ground, making herself into dead weight.

'I am not going,' she said. 'If you intend to take me, you'll have to carry me.'

The black rage on Rurik's face frightened her, but she forced herself to stare back. Once, Alarr had told her that his brother was known as Rurik the Dark at home. Though it had been a name describing his dark hair, she saw that it also implied a darkness to his mood.

'Get up,' he demanded. There was no mercy in his voice, only a quiet rage.

Breanne drew her knees up, shielding herself in case he decided to hit her. But she did not rise from the ground.

With a grunt of annoyance, Rurik lifted her up and slung her over his shoulder. 'Stubborn woman.'

'I could say the same of you. This isn't safe, and you know it. Alarr will be furious with you.'

'It was my only chance to stop him.'

He strode through the trees as if she weighed nothing, but after a time, he shifted her to the opposite shoulder. She didn't know how to talk her way out of this, but the trees were thinner in this part of the forest. Ahead, she spied a clearing. At least she could gain a sense of where she was.

Rurik slowed his pace and set her down as soon as they reached the edge of the trees. He took her bound hands and pulled her forward. 'I do not want my brother to die. And if Alarr brings you back, Feann will not hesitate to slit his throat.'

'My foster father has never seen him before.'

Rurik shook his head. 'Ask Feann yourself. He will tell you of the raid in Maerr and what happened on Alarr's wedding day.'

She stared back at him. Alarr had never once spoken

of a wife. If anything, she had believed he was a lonely man from the way he'd held her at night. 'His wedding?'

'Ask him what happened to Alarr's bride.' His voice was like stone, hard and unyielding.

'Tell me,' she whispered, though she suspected the truth already. From the harsh look on Rurik's face, the woman must be dead. And if he was somehow right about Feann's misdeeds, then Alarr had a very different reason for wanting to see her foster father.

She started to take a step forward, outside the trees. But a moment later, Rurik jerked her back. 'Wait.'

She didn't understand why he held her, until a few moments later when she heard the sound of a horse approaching. If it was Styr's men searching, she wanted to be found. Before he could stop her, she screamed for help.

Rurik clamped his hand over her mouth and let out a foul curse. 'Be silent.'

She could feel his anger from the way his thumbs dug into her jaw, but what choice did she have? The rider was her only hope.

When she caught sight of them, she saw four men, with only one on horseback. Rurik picked her up, running through the trees. Breanne nearly struck her head against a low branch, but within moments, the rider caught up to them. He reached for the rope binding her hands and pulled it hard. Breanne lost her balance and fell to the ground, and Rurik stumbled backwards since he had tied one end to his arm.

'What do we have here?' the man asked. Breanne kept her head down but recognised him as Oisin Mac-Logan. Her foster father had welcomed him once, and Oisin had wanted to court her as his bride. Something about the man had made her skin crawl. His words were kind, but she had sensed the insincerity beneath them. She had refused him as a husband, and after she'd turned him down, Oisin had been furious.

Breanne prayed he would not recognise her and kept her face hidden beneath her hair. She was angry with herself for alerting Oisin to their presence before she'd known who it was. Rurik had been right about wanting to remain hidden. It was her fault that they'd been found.

'Such fiery gold hair,' Oisin said, dismounting from his horse. 'I know who *you* are.' The other three men joined him, and they formed a circle around Breanne and Rurik, making it impossible to escape.

Her pulse quickened, but she could do nothing when he jerked her to her feet.

'Hello, Breanne. Such a pleasure to see you again.' A thin smile spread over his face. 'Now why would the foster daughter of King Feann be a captive? Did you try to refuse this man as your husband?'

She sensed his unspoken words: *The way you refused me.*

Breanne didn't answer, keeping her gaze fixed upon the ground. She didn't dare look at him, for Oisin was a dangerous man. *Danu*, why had she screamed before she'd seen who it was? She'd been so foolish, and now they would both pay the price. Oisin believed he was above everyone else, and he still resented her for not choosing him as her husband.

He reached out and smoothed her tangled hair. 'Not so highborn now, are you, Breanne?' With a nod to his kinsman, he said, 'Kill her captor.'

Horror washed over her, and Breanne screamed

again as loudly as she could, hoping someone else would hear. When one of the men approached Rurik with a blade, he answered the threat by unsheathing a pair of daggers from his waist. The blades were short, and he would have to move in close to strike a deadly blow.

Breanne picked up the slack in the ropes binding them together. She needed to free herself before the restraints were used against him. She moved in closer, holding the rope so Oisin could not seize it. When his companion lunged towards her, she dodged behind Rurik. He shielded her, but they were easily outnumbered. She needed a weapon of her own. Behind her, she spied a broken branch lying on the ground. It would have to do.

Breanne dropped the rope for a moment and reached for the branch. Though she didn't truly know how to fight with it, she was only trying to keep the men away. She called out once again for help, even knowing that it was futile. A rush of fear filled her as she held on to the length of oak.

The last time she had tried to show courage in the slave market, her escape attempt had ended within moments. She had tried to fight back, only to fail. How could she dare to try again?

Her mind was racing with thoughts of death or being defiled by these men. Oisin would be delighted by the idea of claiming her innocence. He would punish her for daring to refuse him. Nausea roiled within her, and she hated the feeling of being so powerless to fight back.

The other man reached for her, and Breanne reacted on instinct, striking his head hard with the branch. He stumbled backwards, but it did not diminish her fears.

Her hands were shaking as she gripped the branch, trying to defend herself. Although she knew she was no match for these men physically, she had to push them back or die trying.

Over and over, she called out for help, hoping someone would hear them. Their greatest weakness was being tied together. It limited Rurik's movements, and she could not run. 'Give me one of the daggers,' she muttered underneath her breath. 'I'll give you this branch. I need to cut us free.'

He gave no sign that he'd heard her, but when he drove back one of the other assailants, he handed her the blade and she exchanged it for the branch. While he kept the men back, she sawed at the ropes binding them. Within moments, she was free. Rurik fought with renewed vigour, now that they were separated. She tried to give him back the blade, but he would not take it.

'Keep the dagger and run,' Rurik ordered. 'I'll hold them off.'

'If I do that, we're both dead,' she insisted. Their only hope of survival was to fight together. If they separated, it would be too easy for the men to overpower him.

Inwardly, she gave up a fervent hope, *Alarr, we need you.*

If he and the other *Lochlannach* could only find them, there was a grain of hope. Her stomach twisted with fear as she stood at his side. She prayed that the gods would have mercy upon them.

Oisin smirked and eyed his companions. 'When I've finished with her, you can have her next.' He reached for her fallen rope, but Breanne jerked back, keeping away from him. He only laughed, and she realised they were toying with her.

'You need to get help,' Rurik uttered. 'We don't have a choice.'

'I can't leave.'

In answer, he gave her a hard shove. 'We will die if you don't. Take my blade and go!'

Breanne seized her skirts and ran towards the thickest part of the woods, back in the direction of the settlement. Both Oisin and another man pursued her, which was likely why Rurik had demanded it. He had a better chance of surviving against two enemies than four. But she couldn't get caught.

Breanne ran as fast as she could, towards the densest part of the forest. She dodged in between saplings, knowing it would slow Oisin down when he could no longer ride his horse. The men were closing the distance, and she gripped the dagger Rurik had given her.

Over her shoulder, she saw Oisin riding hard towards her while the first man pursued her on foot. Without warning, her foot caught at a hidden root and she went sprawling to the ground. Her wrists ached from landing on them, and she forced herself to grab the dagger and flee. Another tree branch scratched her face, but she barely felt the cut.

Within moments, Oisin caught up to her. He grabbed her arm, twisting her wrist until she cried out and the dagger fell from her grasp. Pain radiated through her as he pulled her atop his horse. He gripped her hair and used it to push her down, so that her head hung over one side of the horse in front of him on the saddle. She could not tell where the other man had gone.

'Did you think I would let you go?' He drew the

horse into a walk, guiding the animal back towards the place where they had left Rurik. 'You belong to me, Breanne. You always have.' His voice was silken, and it made her skin crawl.

She tried to remain calm, but inwardly, she was trembling. Was Rurik still alive? Would anyone come for her? The blood rushed to her face, and she felt a wave of dizziness.

You need to think clearly, her brain warned. *Find a way to escape.*

But a sudden noise caught Breanne's attention. Oisin would not let her raise her head, but she heard him grunt as a man dropped down from the trees and pulled Oisin from the saddle. She lost her balance and landed hard on the ground, the wind knocked out of her.

Though she could hardly breathe, her heart filled up with gratitude when she saw Alarr. His dark hair was pulled back with a cord, and his blue eyes burned with fury. He jerked Oisin to his feet and punched the man across the face, splitting his lip. He cursed at him in the *Lochlannach* tongue, and although Breanne could not understand a word of it, there was no denying Alarr's fury.

She tried to stay out of the way, and her lungs burned as she tried to calm herself and catch her breath. But then she caught the gleam of iron and saw Rurik's fallen blade at Oisin's feet. Her enemy feigned surrender and took another blow to the jaw before he dropped face-down to the ground.

Alarr reached towards the man, and Breanne warned, 'He has a blade.'

Just as she'd predicted, Oisin swung with the dagger in his grip. He barely missed Alarr, who stumbled backwards.

This time, she caught the sudden wariness from Alarr as he struggled with his balance. Although he had caught Oisin by surprise, their enemy took command of the fight. He charged forward and as Alarr tried to sidestep, his leg slipped, and he lost his footing again.

Oh, no.

Her courage faltered, replaced by sudden fear. She knew that Alarr had once been a powerful warrior. The heavy ridged muscles gave evidence to that. But for the first time, she saw him falter in battle. He had hidden his weaknesses so well, she'd never guessed how badly he'd been wounded until she'd seen the scars for herself.

'My brother cannot fight any more,' Rurik had said. And now she witnessed his struggle as he tried to defend himself. Oisin used the advantage and pinned him down. Fury blazed in Alarr's eyes, and he used brute strength to shove the man away. He rolled over to avoid the dagger and then stood—only to have his knee give out again.

We're going to die, Breanne thought. *Unless I do something.* She couldn't just stand back and watch this—not when she could help Alarr.

Oisin started to charge again, but this time, Breanne had no intention of letting this fight continue. She picked up a large stone and threw it at him as a distraction. He spun, and that gave Alarr the chance to take him down. He dragged his enemy against a fallen log and struck the man's face, beating him in a violent rage, as if to lash out at his own weakness. Breanne could hardly bring herself to watch, but before she could move, a second attacker came out of hiding. She called out a warning, and Alarr dodged the death blow, using the man's momentum to push him into Oisin. The man could not stop his motion, and his dagger sank into Oisin's shoulder. The Irishman roared with fury, and he tore the weapon free, slashing his own kinsman's throat.

By the gods, she'd never seen such savagery. If Oisin would kill his own kinsman, what would he have done to Alarr or to her? Breanne scrambled backwards, and Alarr helped her on to the horse. He was about to go after Oisin, but the man dropped to his knees, his face grey from blood loss.

'Leave him,' Breanne said. 'Rurik needs you now.' She didn't know what had happened, but they needed to find him.

Alarr claimed Oisin's mount and swung up behind her. She guided the horse back to where she had left his brother. Along the way, she tried to calm the tremor that held her emotions captive.

'Did you run away?' he demanded. 'Or did my brother take you?' In his voice, she caught the tone of accusation.

'I didn't run,' she insisted. 'This was Rurik's plan, not mine.' She wanted to tell him more, but they were nearing the place where she had left his brother.

Rurik sat on the ground, holding his bleeding arm. Two men were dead beside him, and Breanne breathed a sigh of relief that he'd survived. Thank the gods.

Alarr dismounted and she followed his example, tearing off a length of her skirt to use as a bandage. She went to Rurik and bound his arm for him, asking, 'Are you all right?'

He nodded. 'It's not deep.' For a moment, he spoke to his brother in their native language, and she caught the concern in Alarr's voice. He helped Rurik rise to his feet, and they argued for a moment.

'What's wrong?' she asked.

'I've told Rurik to take the horse, and he's being stubborn. He thinks I need to ride.' The dark look of frustration revealed Alarr's annoyance. His limp was more exaggerated than usual, and she knew that he was angry at himself for it. Rurik claimed that Feann had caused his limp…but it was more than that. The wounds had healed, but Alarr would never again be the same fighter. He had proven himself to be fierce and strong—but one misstep in battle could end his life.

'Were you hurt during the fight with Oisin?' she asked him quietly.

'It's always this way after I run,' he gritted out. 'Riding won't change it. It's not from exertion.' He pointed towards the trees and added, 'My horse isn't far from here.'

Breanne understood that he did not want to show any sign of weakness while his brother was wounded. To Rurik, she said, 'You should ride until we reach Alarr's horse. If you don't lose any more blood, your wounds will heal faster.' Then she turned back to Alarr. 'I will walk beside you until we reach your horse. Then we'll ride together.' She intended to keep her pace slow, for both their sakes.

Rurik didn't seem pleased, but his complexion had gone pale from blood loss. He had killed both men, but he appeared dizzy from the wounds. 'Fine,' he gritted out.

Alarr gave a single nod, but she could tell his pride was wounded. He tried to disguise his limp, but it was nearly impossible.

'How far is it to your horse?' she asked.

'I'm not going to fall over, if that's what you were wondering.' He pointed towards the clearing. 'My horse is just outside those trees.'

Again, she could hear the rigid pride in his voice. She wondered if he would want her to rub the medicine into his scars again, from the pain he was trying to mask. The thought of touching his bare skin made her breathless. After this day, she wanted to feel his body against hers, to fall into his kiss and forget about the danger they'd narrowly avoided. But she pushed away the idle daydreams. She knew it was foolish to imagine there would be anything between them.

'How did you find us?' she asked. 'I had hoped someone would hear my screams, but the settlement is so far away.'

'I tracked you both and rode outside the forest for what I thought would be the right distance. Then I heard your scream.' As they walked alongside one another, his hand brushed against hers. 'I stayed hidden because of the other men.'

'I am so glad you came,' she murmured. 'If you hadn't been there…' She didn't want to imagine the outcome. Oisin would have taken her as his slave and concubine, punishing her for refusing his suit.

Rurik leaned against the horse, closing his eyes from the pain. Breanne watched him for a moment, but it seemed that he was managing to keep his balance on horseback.

'Why did my brother take you?' Alarr asked. 'It's not like him to do something like that. Did you try to coax him into bringing you home?'

'He didn't want you to confront Feann.' She knew

there was far more to his accusation, but now was not the time to discuss it. 'We will speak more of it later.'

As they trudged towards the edge of the trees, Alarr struggled with his limp even more. She let him lean against her for balance, but she could tell from his expression that it embarrassed him.

His horse was hobbled and was grazing. Alarr untied the animal and helped her up before swinging up behind her. A light rain began to fall, and she shivered against the chill. He drew her against him, offering his own body heat.

They rode in silence with Rurik on the journey back to the settlement. Her emotions and thoughts were tangled up, for she was so grateful to him for the rescue, despite his struggle. Alarr was a complicated man, she realised. Although his fighting skills had suffered, there was no denying that he had managed to win the battle.

Yet, she believed Rurik's claim, that Alarr intended to confront her foster father. If the king had attacked during Alarr's wedding, then there was no doubt that he would demand vengeance. He had the demeanour of a man who had lost everything. Such a man was dangerous, for he cared naught for his own life. She didn't know what to think, but she needed to understand his intentions.

And somehow, she had to stop him from harming Feann.

When they arrived back at the settlement, rain had soaked them through to the skin. Alarr called for the healer to tend Rurik's wounds, and he was surprised that Breanne remained with them. She appeared worried for his brother, and only when the healer reassured

them that Rurik would be fine, did her tension seem
to dissipate.

Alarr limped back to their sleeping space, and she
did not speak as they returned to the longhouse. Once
they were alone, she reached into a bundle for a dry
gown. He stripped off his wet tunic, and when he turned
to fetch another, he saw her staring at him. Her green
eyes held interest, and he saw that she was clutching
the gown to her breast. The linen of her underdress was
nearly transparent, revealing the soft skin and curves of
her body. Slowly, she dropped the sodden gown, exposing the curve of her breast and the rosy nipples through
the sheer fabric of her shift.

He hardened at the sight of her and the arousal was
a familiar frustration. He ached to touch her, and the
memory of her kiss made it far worse. But now was
not the time. There was fear in her eyes and the innocence of a maiden. She knew nothing of what she was
offering. Not truly. It was only the instinctive desire to
feel alive after such a close brush with death. His own
body was coursing with the same needs, and his honour was slipping.

'Are you in pain?' she murmured. 'Do you need me
to rub the medicine into your scars again?'

He should refuse, for it was unwise to have her
hands upon him. The thought of her palms caressing
his skin was a temptation he could not deny. His body
was strung tight, desiring her with every breath that
was in him.

But Breanne took his silence as assent. She went to
fetch the box of salve, and he lay upon his stomach,
trying to gather the remnants of his control. He focused on the pain in his muscles, of the never-ending

ache in the scars. When she smoothed her hands over old wounds, he groaned. But it was not from pain—it was from desire.

As she touched him, he dug his hands into the furs. Breanne knew the right amount of pressure to ease the tightness in his flesh, followed by a gentle smoothing touch. He revelled in her hands upon him, until she revealed, 'Your brother said that your wounds were caused by Feann.'

Her statement was like a bucket of ice poured over his body. He rolled over and sat up. Her expression was guarded, a warning in her eyes. 'What else did Rurik tell you?'

'He told me that the attack happened on the day you were supposed to be married. And your brother wanted to stop you from causing a war.'

Alarr wanted to curse, but he held back his anger. He didn't want to tell her any of it. The memories were too raw, and locking them away was the only way to bear the pain. Instead, he held a stoic silence, keeping his emotions in a block of invisible stone.

'Was Rurik telling the truth?' she ventured.

He gave a single nod. 'I couldn't walk for over a year. My brothers took me into hiding and I lived with the healers until I recovered.' The memory of that agony washed over him, along with the feeling of helplessness. He'd been unable to save his father or his wife. Alarr met her gaze and added, 'Feann killed my father, my bride…and my ability to fight. I won't forgive him for it.'

Her face appeared horrified by his confession. Regret and guilt transformed her expression, and she reached out to take his hand. 'I'm so sorry for what he did to you. I cannot change the past, but you saved my life today. And I am grateful for that.'

He sensed that she was nervous about something, but he could not guess what. Slowly, she unbraided her hair, letting it fall across her thin shift.

'I thought I was going to die.' She reached to touch his heart and murmured, 'But you found me when I was in danger. Not my foster father. Only you.'

The slight weight of her palm pressed down upon his guilt. Alarr seized her wrist and held it there. 'Don't pity me, Breanne.'

'It's not pity. You won that fight.' Her green eyes held sympathy, but he didn't believe her. He had barely managed to keep his balance. One wrong motion, and they both might have died.

'I'm not the man you think I am.' He leaned in close, meaning to intimidate her. 'I will have my vengeance against Feann for what he did. And I don't care who stands in my way.'

'And if I stand in your way?' she ventured.

He refused to let her make him into a hero, when he wasn't. 'Stay away from me, Breanne,' he warned. He could smell the aroma of her skin, and he gripped her hand, trying to maintain his control. 'I'm not safe right now.'

'I don't want you to be.' She wrapped her arms around his neck to embrace him, and the fragile hold he had upon his control shattered. He crushed her mouth to his, savouring the taste of her warm lips. She kissed him back, and he could not get enough. His hands moved over her shift, wishing he could tear it into pieces. Instinct claimed him now, and he pressed her back towards the furs, needing her body beneath his.

Alarr wanted to caress her bare skin, making her crave him as much as he desired her. He knew Breanne's virginity should belong to her husband. But when her hands slid beneath his tunic to his bare skin, he no longer cared about anything except touching her. He laid her back upon the pallet, kissing the soft skin of her throat. She gasped, digging her fingertips into his hair and arching her back.

'Alarr,' she whispered, moaning as he tasted her skin. Her eyes were closed, and she bit her lower lip as if she were trying to gather command of her feelings.

His brain warned him again to stop, but he was past the brink of control. He wanted her to fully understand what she was offering, to taste the danger. And if he could touch her intimately, it might frighten her enough to keep her distance.

He peeled back her damp shift, revealing her round breasts. Her nipples were pink, the tips erect and tempting. He gave in to his own desires and bent to taste one. Her shuddering gasp made him grow rock hard.

Never in his life had he needed anyone as much as he needed her.

Chapter Four

⁓⁓⁓⁓⁓

Breanne could hardly gather her thoughts as he suckled at her breast. Sensations flooded through her, and between her legs, she grew wet. No man had ever touched her like this, and she didn't know how to stop him.

Nor did she want him to stop.

Her emotions were tangled up in a knot, and she knew it was a mistake to start this. And yet, right now, she wanted to push away the fear of death and embrace life. She wanted to seize a moment of pleasure, knowing that it would fade away, come the dawn.

A part of her wanted to draw Alarr closer, to convince him to leave her father alone. If he cared for her, he might one day abandon his vengeance.

But for now, she surrendered to his touch, not knowing where it would lead. He feasted upon her, his hands moving lower as he laved one nipple and then the other. He caressed the tip, and she nearly sobbed with delight. It was an aching torment to have his hands upon her, and her brain fought for clarity.

The boundaries between them had lowered. She had

to somehow gain Alarr's affection, if not his trust. He would use her to get close to Feann. She believed that, after what she'd learned of her father's misdeeds. But she couldn't grasp that her foster father would murder innocent women and men. She needed answers, but right now, every thought in her brain disappeared at the sensation of Alarr touching her.

He stripped her shift away until Breanne was naked beneath him. If she didn't speak, if she didn't stop him, he would claim her. And by the gods, she desired this man.

His hand moved between her legs, parting them. When he touched her intimately, fear shot through her, even as her body craved him. Panic rose within her, for she was losing control of herself. Now that she was facing the loss of her virginity, she wasn't certain it was the right choice.

She wanted to tell him to wait, but before she could speak, he slid a finger inside her. She was so wet, so deeply aroused, it made it hard to breathe. Intense pleasure flooded through her, and a moan broke forth from her lips as he used his touch to caress her. Her mind and heart warred with one another, and her fears transformed.

'Alarr,' she breathed. But it wasn't a plea to stop—it was a plea for more.

He misunderstood her and spoke against her lips. 'I warned you that this wasn't safe. When you offer yourself to me, I will take everything you give.' His mouth returned to her other breast, and as his tongue swirled over her nipple, he penetrated her with his finger. Slowly, he entered and withdrew, adding a second finger as he stroked.

The pleasure was blinding. He was taking her higher, and she felt her body straining for release. Before she could plead again, a shuddering wave broke over her, and she arched hard, trembling with a violent eruption. She was shaking so badly she could not gather a clear thought.

'You don't want a man like me inside you, Breanne.'

His claim held a darkness, and she was too weak to make a reply. Instead, she closed her eyes and looked away. She was not ready to offer herself—not even in exchange for her father's life.

A moment later, Alarr stood and straightened his clothing. And then he left without another word.

Alarr slept in another longhouse that night. He had given in to his desires, fully expecting Breanne to push him away. And yet, she had only welcomed him. She was on the brink of surrender, and the intimacy had only drawn them closer. Her body was made for his, and he had revelled in the delight of touching her, of bringing her to fulfilment.

But it was not at all what he'd intended. He had planned to take her to the brink of lovemaking, just far enough to frighten her into keeping her distance. But instead of refusing him, she had responded openly to his touch. By the gods, he'd had no choice but to leave. If he had dared to sleep beside Breanne, he would not have been able to stop himself from claiming her. She would have enjoyed it—of that he was certain. And so would he.

She is your hostage, his brain reminded him. *Yours to do with as you wish*.

And would it not be an even greater vengeance

against Feann, if Alarr claimed the virginity of his foster daughter? What if he became her lover, spending each night in her arms? The idea took root and grew. He was torn between the primal needs and his own sense of honour.

The morning sky was tinted rose and grey as he walked towards the healer's hut. Alarr went to visit with Rurik but found that his brother was still sleeping. The healer sat beside him, and she murmured, 'I gave him medicine last night and again this morn. The cut upon his arm was not the only wound.'

He saw that his brother's ribs were bound up and said to the old woman, 'My thanks for tending him.'

She smiled and stepped back from the herbs she had been crushing with a mortar and pestle. 'I will leave you alone with him for a moment. Though it is unlikely he will awaken after he drank the sleeping potion.'

Alarr was grateful for the privacy. In the dim light of the fire, he saw the profile of his sleeping brother. Regret filled up within him that Rurik had tried to stop him from his vengeance against Feann. Worse, he knew it was because his brother believed he would die. Rurik had no faith in his ability to fight—and was that any wonder? Even when he had tried to rescue Breanne, he had stumbled several times. Had she not intervened, he might not have won the fight.

That knowledge grated upon him still. It didn't matter that he had trained and struggled to improve his fighting abilities over the last year. His body was permanently maimed, and he would never again be the same.

When Breanne had thanked him for saving her, he

had sensed her sympathy—but that wasn't what he'd wanted at all. He had welcomed her kiss, and nothing had pleased him more than to watch her come apart. In that moment, he had become a conqueror, wanting her to desire him as much as he craved her.

Not only was she a beautiful woman, but she had courage. When she had been attacked by Oisin, he'd been overcome by fury. He didn't want any man touching her. He had grown accustomed to waking beside her, and if their circumstances had been different, he might have considered keeping her with him as more than a hostage.

He could not stop thinking of her. What if he *did* seduce her into sharing his bed? She could remain with him for the next few days while he satiated his craving for her. The hunger for her body, the need to quench his desire, was a burning need. She had responded to his touch, her body rising to his call. Every sigh, every moan had only ensnared him more tightly.

But it was dangerous to form any attachment. He knew the risks of confronting Feann. It would likely mean his own death, but Alarr hardly cared. The only ones who mattered were his brothers—and they understood his need for vengeance. He couldn't allow anything to threaten his plans—especially Breanne.

Even more, he knew that once he had taken Feann's life, those green eyes would transform with hatred. And if he claimed her body or worse, filled her with a child, it would hurt her even more. Though he despised Feann, Breanne deserved better.

As he took his brother's hand, he realised that Rurik likely owed his life to Breanne. It unsettled him that she had woven herself into their lives. He had planned to use her for information, but guilt weighed upon him. Breanne would not tell him anything now—not after Rurik had revealed his hatred of Feann. Alarr was torn between the ruthless need for information…and his own regard for her. She was a woman of honour, and it bothered him that he had to betray her. He needed to push her away, to ensure that she despised him. Only then, he could he distance himself.

Alarr was glad his brother was sleeping, for it gave him time alone with his thoughts.

He closed his eyes, bringing back the darker memories of his wedding day. Never would he forget the faces of those who had fallen, of the blood that stained the earth. And of Gilla's sightless eyes staring back at him. The wrenching regret pulled within him, reminding him of his purpose. He could not be distracted by a beautiful slave.

When he strode outside, he tried to mask the limp, but it was impossible. His leg was aching from the exertion, and he made his way towards one of the unfinished longhouses. There, he picked up a saw, wanting to occupy his hands. He measured the correct length and sawed the wood, welcoming the familiar ache of physical effort. A few other men joined him, but as he worked, his mind turned over the problem of Feann. He still knew very little about the fortress, nor did he have a solid plan of how to infiltrate their defences long enough to kill the king.

Styr joined him and said quietly, 'I am glad of your help, my friend. But I would like to have words with you and your brother about your journey to visit Feann.'

'Later,' he agreed. 'Rurik is recovering from his wounds. The healer gave him a sleeping potion.'

Styr paused, resting against the longhouse. 'As you will. But we must come to an agreement about your journey and my men as your escorts.'

He understood the man's unspoken words—that he would not endanger his kinsmen under any circumstances.

'I only want them as escorts to Killcobar,' he said. 'They may remain outside the gates when I speak with the king.'

Styr inclined his head. But then he narrowed his gaze. 'Rurik told me of Feann's role in your father's death.'

'His men slaughtered my father and my bride.' He made no effort to hide the cold fury.

Styr regarded him. 'While I understand your reasons, I cannot let my men be involved in this. If your intent is vengeance, you must go alone.'

'I am asking for your men to protect my brother and Breanne on the journey. I will act alone.'

'But if Feann survives, it will bring war between my tribe and his people.' Styr shook his head. 'This I cannot do.'

'He won't survive.' In this, he had complete faith. Though he knew not how, he was confident that Feann would die.

'And what of Breanne? You would kill her foster father?'

'She knows what Feann did to my family. And to me.' He climbed down from the ladder. 'When Rurik awakens, we will speak again.' He nodded to Styr before he turned back towards the longhouse where he'd been staying with Breanne. She was not there, and he saw her walking towards the healer's hut where he had left Rurik. A hard ache caught him in the gut that she was concerned about his brother's welfare.

He hurried towards her and stopped her before she could go inside. 'I must speak with you.'

He expression remained guarded, but she asked, 'How is your brother?'

'The healer gave him a sleeping potion,' he answered. 'And he had a few other minor injuries that she treated.'

'But he will recover?'

He nodded. 'In a few days, I think.' He reached out to rest his palm against her spine, guiding her away. 'We need to talk about the fate of your foster father.'

Nerves gathered within her, but Breanne knew she had to choose her words carefully. Alarr had strong reasons for wanting vengeance against Feann, and she didn't delude herself into thinking she could change his mind. He led her towards the horses and asked, 'Do you want to ride?'

She glanced up at the sky which was turning amber, the sun rising higher. 'For a short time,' she agreed. There was no doubting that he intended to speak with her about his plans. And somehow, she had to talk him out of them.

He chose horses for them and helped her mount. Breanne followed him outside the gates and noticed that he was leading her south, towards the coast.

After half an hour of riding, she saw the gleam of the water and the reflection of the sun. The sky was a blend of fire and gold, beautiful in its wildness as it embraced the coming afternoon.

He paused when they were near the edge and guided her towards an outcropping of limestone. He helped her dismount, and she went to sit on the pile of limestone while he hobbled their horses, allowing them to graze.

The air was still cool outside, but she hardly felt the chill. Her heart was aching at the thought of what Feann had done and Alarr's need for vengeance. She knew not how to stop him. There was no trace of mercy upon his face, no sense of understanding.

But she knew that he desired her. It was the only weapon she had, and she wondered if she dared to use it. Could she convince him to let go of his anger and need for revenge? Was there any way to change his mind?

A voice inside warned that there was no means of stopping a warrior like Alarr. He would never forgive her foster father for killing his family.

She had so many questions rising up inside. Why would Feann do such a thing, if it were true? There had to be a strong reason. And if Alarr confronted him, he risked his own life. As she studied his profile, she wondered how she would feel if he were to die.

Alarr had rescued her, saving her life when she had needed him most. And beneath his fierce exterior, she sensed that he was a man of honour. He could have forced himself upon her at any moment; yet, he had not. He had awakened her own hunger with his touch, and she had only found pleasure in his arms. But would he listen to her pleas? Or would her feelings mean nothing at all to him? She needed to know more.

'Will you tell me what happened?' she asked quietly. 'On the day of your wedding.'

He came to sit beside her. Without answer, he countered, 'Will you tell me of Feann's defences or how to get close to him?'

'No.' Breanne drew her knees up, staring at the water. 'I cannot betray him. He is the only father I've ever known.'

'He is not the man you think he is,' Alarr said. 'He travelled across the sea with his men and attacked for no reason.'

'He would not have sailed such a distance, if it were not important. That is not his way. Perhaps he was seeking his own vengeance.'

'Sigurd did nothing to him. Their kingdoms are a great distance apart.'

She didn't know the reasons either, but she felt the need to voice another truth. 'Feann was not the man to murder your father. You know this.'

'I blame him, even so. It was his men who surrounded the longhouse and killed everyone inside, including my father and my bride.'

Her heart ached for him, and she fought back the tears that threatened. She couldn't understand how any of this could have happened.

His voice was heavy, laced with bitterness. 'Then they scattered and went to their ships. Any man who pursued them was cut down and left to die. I lost many kinsmen that day.'

She tightened her grasp around her knees, trying to sort out her foster father's actions. 'That doesn't sound like something Feann would do.'

'He did. And he will pay for the deaths he and his men caused. Whether he wielded the blade or not.'

Her heart was pounding, and she knew not what to say or how to stop him. Right now, he was only thinking of vengeance and not what would happen afterwards. She wanted to protect her foster father, but she knew that Alarr would never set aside his plans.

To stall him, she decided to ask more questions. 'How did they attack you?'

'They stood among the wedding guests. Our men were unarmed during the wedding. It was not a fair fight.'

'Why were they unarmed?' Breanne asked, frowning. 'They are *Lochlannach* warriors, are they not?'

Alarr stiffened at her question. 'My mother demanded it.'

'Now why would she do that?' It made no sense for warriors to be unable to protect themselves.

'She claimed it would anger the gods.' But as soon as he spoke the words, she could see the realisation dawning upon him. He knew, without her saying a word, what she was implying.

But Breanne questioned it, none the less. 'Did your mother have a reason to want your father dead?'

'I don't know.' There was so much anger rising within him, it seemed that his temper would burst forth at any moment. She didn't press further, but instead, touched his shoulder gently. His muscles were rigid beneath her hands. Without asking, she massaged the tension from him.

She didn't know why she was touching him. He was her enemy, a man who wanted her foster father dead. But the question now was whether she could turn him away from his desire for vengeance.

She slid her hands to his neck, gently stroking the knots. Instead of granting him relief from his pain, he caught her hands and held them.

'This wasn't why I brought you here,' he said. 'Much as I do want your hands upon me.'

She could hear the edge of pent-up desire in his voice, and the heat of his palms against hers only evoked her own interest. She could not stop thinking of last night, and her cheeks burned at the memory.

'Why did you bring me here?' she asked.

He released her hands and faced her. 'To give you a choice. You helped save my brother's life. If it is your wish not to be there when I face Feann, I could leave you behind.'

She frowned, not understanding his intention. 'Then how would they allow you inside the gates?'

'Rurik and I would break in, and I would challenge the king.'

She shook her head. 'There is no means of getting inside without me. There are no weaknesses in the fortress. The walls are guarded day and night to make sure of it.'

But his offer made her pause. If he intended to breach the walls alone, he would die. She had no doubt of it. 'Will you not hear what my foster father has to say?' she asked. 'It may be that there were other reasons for the attack.'

'Innocent men and women died that day. I will not forget their deaths or my vengeance.'

For a long moment, Breanne stared out at the sea, turning over the problem in her mind. Her foster father had caused Alarr's injuries and the loss of his loved ones. But the man who had cut Alarr down was the same man who had comforted her after the deaths of her parents. Feann had taken her into his home, raising her among his sons, and she loved him. He was the only father she had ever known.

And yet, he had abandoned her when she'd needed him most. It had been weeks since she'd been sold into slavery, and he had never tried to find her. Yet, Alarr had been there for her from the beginning. Even now, he was trying to find a compromise between them, despite his intentions of vengeance. She wanted to believe that she could change his mind.

Her feelings were a storm of confusion. To whom should she be loyal? To the man who had abandoned her or to the man who had saved her? She didn't know what the answer was, not when she was caught in the middle between them.

Alarr had offered her freedom, as if he no longer intended to use her. Did that mean he had come to care for her? He had touched her like a lover, awakening feelings she didn't understand. But if she allowed him to go alone, she sensed that her father would harm him. If Feann *had* gone to the wedding and was involved in the death of Alarr's father, he would recognise him and possibly kill Alarr. She couldn't allow that to happen.

'I will go with you to Killcobar,' Breanne said at last. Not only because she hoped to protect her father, but also because she didn't want Alarr to die. She couldn't put a name to her feelings, but she owed him her life. It wasn't right to turn away from him.

Breanne walked alongside Alarr towards the water's edge. The sun dusted the waves in a glittering haze of light. She removed her shoes and walked along the frigid sand. The icy water matched her mood, and she tried to think of what she could do. The truth was, she didn't want either of them to be hurt.

Alarr trailed behind, and she paused a moment, letting the waves pool around her ankles. But the cold brought a new clarity to her thoughts. There *was* something she could do to protect him and still grant him compensation for his loss, if he were to agree. Alarr might desire vengeance, but bloodshed could be avoided in a different way.

It was a means of putting herself between the two men, shielding them both through her actions. Her nerves gathered up inside her, for she didn't know if she dared to voice her suggestion. It was an unlikely choice, one he might reject.

She didn't even know if it was what she wanted. But if it meant protecting two men she cared about, perhaps it was the best solution.

Breanne turned back to him as she walked through the wet sand. 'This is not finished between us. I will not allow you to harm Feann. But I know of another way you can be compensated for your losses.'

Alarr met her gaze but was already shaking his head. 'There is nothing that would atone for what he has done.'

'Hear me out,' she continued. 'My foster father owes you for your injuries, and if he played any part in your father's death, he must pay the *corp-dire*. The *brehons* will see to it that justice is served.'

'He will never pay a single coin for my sake,' Alarr said.

Breanne steeled herself. 'He would if you become my husband.'

Alarr hadn't known how to answer her, but Breanne pressed her finger to his lips. 'Do not give me an answer yet. Only think about it. It may be a means of avoiding war.'

For her sake, he had held his silence.

After they returned to the fortress, Alarr spent the rest of the afternoon and evening working on one of the longhouses, turning over her suggestion in his mind. Why would Breanne suggest marriage between them? She knew his intentions towards her father. Did she believe that a union would bring peace? Never. He could not abandon his plans, even for her.

She had kept her distance from him for the remainder of the day until they returned to the shelter that night. Breanne turned away from him in their shared pallet, but he could tell from her uneven breathing that she was not asleep. Slowly, he drew her close until she was facing him. 'Why would you believe we should wed, Breanne? Is there not another man you would rather marry?'

In the faint light of the oil lamp, he could see the uncertainty in her expression. Her body was curled towards him, and her cheeks flushed. 'No one would have me to wife. Not after this.'

'You are still a maiden,' he felt compelled to remind her. Although he had touched her intimately, she was innocent in body.

'They never searched for me,' she said. 'Not in all these weeks. Believe me when I say that no man of Feann's kingdom wanted to wed me.' Sadness and humiliation weighted her words. 'I never understood why. Was I not good enough? Was there something I should have done differently?'

Alarr knew not what to say, for he didn't understand

her people's reasons for abandoning her. Had Breanne been his betrothed bride, he would have torn the countryside apart to find her. 'You would never want to marry a man who blamed you for your own captivity,' Alarr said. 'It would not have been a good union.' He paused a moment and added, 'Just as we are not suited to one another.'

'My offer of marriage was about keeping the peace for the time being,' she argued. 'Not necessarily an alliance for the rest of our lives. Only until you are compensated for your losses.'

A temporary marriage, then. But he still believed that was unwise. For if he wedded Breanne, he suspected he could not let her remain a virgin.

He brought his hand to her waist, not really understanding why he had the need to touch her. 'I am prepared to face my own death for his, Breanne. It's why I travelled this far.'

He saw the uncertainty in her eyes and the fear. But he didn't want her to build him up as a hero. Feann deserved to die for what he'd done. There would be no mercy, no turning back now.

She studied him with a sombre gaze. 'If we are wedded, Feann will not harm you.'

Alarr didn't believe that for a moment. 'If Feann already slaughtered my family and my bride, he would not hesitate to have me killed.'

'He would protect you for my sake,' she said quietly. There was an edge of desperation in her tone. 'If we visit Killcobar together, I could talk to Feann. We could reach an agreement.'

He wanted to argue that Feann cared only for himself. Such a man would not listen to reason or agree to

a *corp-dire* payment. The king hadn't even bothered
to search for his foster daughter. But if Alarr revealed
that, it would only hurt her feelings. Breanne held loyalty to a man who deserved none of it.

His mood hardened at the thought. Every time he
thought of that day, of the blood and death, it ignited
the fury inside him, stoking the flames of vengeance.
'I will never forget what he did.'

'I understand,' she murmured. 'But surely there is
a way to compensate you for your loss. According to
the law—'

'The law will not bring back my father. Or Gilla.'
He pulled back from her and met her gaze squarely. He
could never be swayed from this course. He needed her
to understand that, but more than that, he needed distance between them. Her soft heart was weakening his
resolve. The closer he grew to Breanne, the more he
doubted his decisions. It was better to shut down any
thoughts of marriage.

'There can be no wedding between us. Not now or
ever.'

She closed her eyes as if his words were a physical
blow. 'I know you do not want me as your bride. But
so many lives could be saved. Including your own.'

He cared naught for his life. What good was he
to anyone now? He could barely fight, and he never
wanted to see a look of fear or loathing on Breanne's
face if he was unable to defend her. He had barely managed to save her from Oisin the first time.

He could not allow her to sacrifice her own future
for his, nor could he imagine another wedding—not
even to a woman he desired so badly. The memories of
bloodshed would never leave him, and he could not even

consider marriage. He didn't deserve happiness after his
first bride had died before he could save her. The gods
had punished him by allowing him to live as less than
a man with visible scars to remind him of his failure.

But he refused to accept that life. Better to die avenging those who had lost their lives than to go on with his.

Breanne was far too good for someone like him. He
had to cut her off and make her despise him. It was the
only way to protect her from being hurt. And so, he
delivered the cutting blow.

'You are only a slave to me, Breanne. It's all you've
ever been.' Alarr stood from the pallet, turning away
so he would not see her reaction. 'I bought you to get
close to Feann. And then, I always intended to kill him.'

He did not stay to hear her answer, nor did he want to
see her face. He wanted to sever all ties between them
and cause her to hate him. Only then, would it be easier
to leave her behind and enact his plans for vengeance.

Outside, the night air was cool, a welcome contrast
from the heat of his skin. Alarr strode across the fortress, the gates flanked by torches. Guards stood at intervals, and he nodded in greeting. He knew not where
he was going—only that he needed to escape the confines of the longhouse.

You did what was necessary, his conscience reminded him. *You had to let her go.*

And yet, he loathed himself for what he'd said—even
knowing that there was no other choice but to hurt her.

As he passed a shadowed corner, he heard a soft
laugh. There, he spied Caragh seated upon a low stool,
Styr kneeling before her. The leader was washing her
feet, and the act grew intimate when his wife's laugh
turned into a low intake of breath. Alarr kept walking,

pretending as if he hadn't seen them. But the image struck hard within him, of what it would be like to spend each day with a woman he cared about...of what it would be like to touch her and hear her sigh with desire.

The closest he had ever come to it was when he'd touched Breanne.

Chapter Five

In the morning, Breanne awakened and stared at the partition, feeling humiliated and broken.

'You are only a slave to me, Breanne. It's all you've ever been.'

Alarr's words had cut her to the bone, reminding her that she was worth nothing to him. She wanted to weep, but there were no tears, only the aching anguish within her. Not only from his refusal, but it was also because she felt abandoned by everyone.

No one wanted her. Not her foster family, not her betrothed husband, and not the man who had saved her. The shame burned within her that she had dared to offer him marriage.

It didn't matter. Alarr had made his point clear. There would be nothing between them. His intent was to use her and discard her.

But that didn't mean she would stand aside and let that happen. She had other ways of getting home, and she had no intention of becoming Alarr's pawn in a game of death.

She stood from her pallet and walked through the

longhouse, searching for Caragh. The young woman was nowhere to be found, but she saw Styr instead. The leader was speaking with one of his men about building another longhouse, and she waited quietly until he had finished. After the other man had left, Styr motioned for her to come closer.

'Was there something you needed, Breanne?' he asked quietly.

She nodded. 'I have decided to accept your wife's offer. She told me you could send several of your men as my escorts and return me to Killcobar without Alarr.' Breanne could see no other alternative than to return home in secret, before he could stop her. Then she would play no part in his attack. The harsh ache in her stomach returned along with her shame.

Styr hesitated before saying, 'You've decided not to travel with him, then?'

Breanne shook her head. 'He intends to kill my foster father. So no, I will not let him use me in his vengeance.' If words would not convince Alarr, she had no choice but to use actions instead.

Styr motioned for her to walk with him. 'Are you certain this is what he intends?' Although the *jarl* kept his tone even, she suspected he was probing for more information.

Breanne gazed at him squarely. 'He wants no ransom. His purpose is revenge.' From the look in Styr's eyes, she realised that he did not appear at all surprised. It made her wonder what else he knew.

'What happened between Alarr and Feann?' Styr asked.

She chose her words carefully. 'Feann slaughtered Alarr's bride and father on his wedding day. Alarr wanted to use me as a means of getting close to him. He planned to avenge the deaths of his family.' She paused and added, 'Rurik wanted to stop him. He thought if he brought me home first, then it would stop Alarr from his plans. But then we were attacked.'

'One man cannot avenge the deaths of so many,' Styr argued. 'He would die in the attempt.'

The ache deepened inside her at the thought. 'He would. But Alarr has said that it does not matter to him.' Nor did *she* matter to him. She should have been more guarded with her feelings, but she had allowed him to cloud her sense of reason. 'I would rather go home by myself. But he cannot know of this.'

Styr's expression was stoic, and he said, 'Let us go and speak with Caragh.'

He led her outside, past the other longhouses, until they reached the stables. Inside, the air was pungent, and the animals grazed in their stalls. Caragh was brushing a mare, speaking softly to her. When she heard them enter, she turned and smiled. 'I could not resist the urge to visit with the animals. I might go riding today if the weather holds.'

'Breanne wants to return to Killcobar today,' Styr said to his wife. 'Without Alarr.'

Caragh's smile faded. 'So you've changed your mind, then.'

Breanne nodded. 'I cannot be a part of his revenge.' She told Caragh of Alarr's plans and the young woman exchanged a glance with her husband. It was clear that the pair of them were deciding what to do, and in the meantime, Breanne distracted herself by rubbing the ears of a young stallion. The horse nudged her shoulder, wanting more affection, and she gave it.

'Alarr will pursue you the moment he knows you're gone,' Caragh predicted. 'He cares about you too much, Breanne.'

'I am his property, nothing more.' The words cut into her mood, darkening it. 'I will not go with him. Not if it endangers my family.' Or his own life, she thought. The worst part was that she could not deny that her own feelings for Alarr had gone past friendship. She needed to distance herself and remember that he was an enemy. He would not set aside his vengeance, no matter how she pleaded.

Styr regarded her and answered at last, 'I believe it's too late for me to send men to bring you home— especially now. Alarr would only pursue you and cause harm to my kinsmen.' He shook his head. 'I am sorry, but I cannot.'

'She could go if they leave in the middle of the night,' his wife suggested. 'If they ride swiftly, it may be possible.'

'No.' Styr was adamant in his refusal. 'The only thing I can do is send a messenger to Feann. If he wishes to come and claim her, I will allow it. That is the best I can offer.'

Breanne faced the pair of them and realised that she had no choice but to wait. Though she inclined her head and murmured her thanks, inwardly she feared it would not happen. Feann had sent no one to rescue her thus far. This message might have no effect on him, and she would still be forced to go with Alarr.

It bothered her deeply to know that she was alone, with no one to help her. She had relied on others to save her, and it had come to naught. If she wanted to change her circumstances, she would have to form her own plans.

But she would not allow Alarr to use her—not when it threatened the only family she had left.

Three days later

Rurik's wounds were healing, and Alarr was glad to see his brother walking once again. He needed his brother's advice about attacking Killcobar. During the past two nights, he had spent time apart from Breanne. She hardly spoke to him any more, and he regretted what he'd said. He had let himself get too close, and that was his own fault. Better to cut his ties now than to watch her anguish when he took Feann's life.

'How are you faring this morn?' he asked Rurik.

'Well enough.' His brother exposed the angry red flesh that was healing from his shoulder wound. 'Would that it had been my left shoulder that was injured. But I can still fight if I must.'

'Good. I will have need of your blade when the time comes.'

Rurik's expression twisted. 'We need to talk.'

He suspected that his brother would try to convince him not to fight Feann. But Alarr nodded and said, 'We should go outside the settlement to speak freely.'

Rurik agreed, and they walked past the outbuildings through the gates. When they were a short distance away from the tribesmen, Alarr said, 'Tell me why you are trying to avoid confronting Feann. You know what he did to our father.'

His half-brother paused a moment. 'I asked myself why Feann would travel so far to plot the murder of

Sigurd. Only a man trying to provoke a war would do something like that. Or someone who desired his own vengeance.'

'It doesn't matter why. It only matters that he and his men started the battle. I intend to finish it.' Alarr stopped when they reached the outskirts of the forest.

'My mother was from Éireann, Alarr. It was no coincidence that Feann's men travelled across the sea. There is a connection between Saorla and Feann. I believe that.'

'Possibly.' He conceded that there could have been a reason. 'But Saorla came to Maerr of her own free will. She bore children to Sigurd.'

'Was she truly willing?' Rurik questioned. 'Or was she forced?'

He didn't know, but he understood his brother's questions. 'You want to know about her past.'

Rurik agreed. 'And if you kill Feann, I may never have those answers.'

Alarr shrugged and offered, 'I could take him captive. After he confesses the truth, then I'll kill him.' He ventured a slight smile which Rurik returned.

'You and I both know that holding Feann prisoner won't give us any information at all. He's not a man who would admit anything to us. Especially when it concerns our father.' But Rurik's mood had lifted, none the less. 'I want to know about Saorla's past, if there is a connection. Danr will want to know also.' He hesitated and added, 'It would be better if I went alone, before you arrive, to learn what I can.'

The idea didn't sit well with Alarr, sending his brother off without anyone to guard him. 'No. We go together or not at all.'

But Rurik stared back at him. 'As you will. But know that I intend to learn Feann's reason for the killings first. And once I have my answers, he is yours for vengeance.'

He clasped his brother's hand in agreement. 'So be it.' Though he doubted if there was any connection between Feann and Saorla, he supposed there was no harm in asking.

They spoke of plans and possible ways to infiltrate the castle. Yet all the while, Alarr felt the sting of guilt for what he'd said to Breanne. He knew it had been necessary, but the sight of her stricken expression haunted him still. He had hurt her feelings, and he wished he could shut off his own response to her.

As they walked back towards the settlement, he caught sight of four riders approaching. They were dressed in the manner of the Irish, each wearing a long saffron *léine* and leather armour. They slowed when they reached Rurik and Alarr, eyeing them for a moment, but the riders did not stop. When they reached the gates, their leader spoke to the guards, and Styr's men allowed them to enter.

'Who are they?' Rurik asked.

Alarr's own suspicions were on alert. 'I don't know. But I intend to find out.'

Breanne followed Caragh towards the gates, after the young woman had told her about the visitors. To her shock, she saw three of her foster father's men. One of them she recognised as Darin MacPherson, captain of Feann's guards. He dismounted, along with the others, and tied his horse near a drinking trough. The moment he saw her, Darin smiled and bowed to her. 'My lady, I am glad to see that you are well.'

A blend of emotions washed over her, for the captain was behaving as if she had only been travelling instead of being brought out of slavery. She nodded to him and managed to greet him, 'It is good to see you once more, Darin.'

'I received word from the Hardrata tribe, a day ago, that you were here.'

He glanced around at the fortress, but Breanne felt numb inside. She wanted to ask, *Why did no one search for me?* But more than that, *Why didn't Feann come with you?*

It dug into her heart that her foster father had not searched for her. Finally, she asked, 'Where is the king?'

'He is travelling,' Darin said. 'He left just before you did. He has not returned yet.'

That lifted her spirits somewhat with the hope that perhaps her foster father *had* tried to find her. But she corrected Darin. 'I didn't leave. I was taken into slavery.'

The captain barely reacted to her words. She might as well have told him that she had gone to visit kinsmen. But he said, 'I am sorry to hear of it. We came at once to bring you home.'

Breanne knew she ought to be grateful, but instead, her thoughts grew guarded. She couldn't let go of her annoyance.

Before she could answer, another voice intruded. 'She is going nowhere with you.' Alarr stood beside Rurik, his hand resting upon the blade at his waist.

The silent threat was unmistakable. And she could almost hear the unspoken words: *She belongs to me.*

Anger flared up within her at his possessive behaviour. He had refused her offer of marriage and had treated her like dirt. Instead, she shot him a defiant look.

You hold no claim on me.

After what he'd said to her, she would not obey him. Her father's men had come for her, and she intended to accompany them home.

She suspected Alarr had heard every word Darin had said. Likely, he intended to alter his plans now that he knew Feann was not at Killcobar.

The captain moved his hand to his own weapon. 'Who is this, my lady? Is he a threat to you?'

Before she could answer, Alarr took a step closer. He placed his hand on the back of her neck in an unmistakable claim. 'I am the man who bought her in the slave market.'

Her face reddened at his words, and her anger rose hotter. His hand tightened upon her nape in a silent warning.

'Then we will repay you for her freedom,' the captain said. To Breanne, he added, 'Gather your belongings, my lady, and we can leave at once.'

Alarr's fury was unmistakable. She suspected that it would take very little to provoke a fight between them. It irritated her that he was treating her like an object.

Caragh came forward to intervene. 'I am certain that you and your men must be weary after your journey. We can discuss Breanne's release after you have had something to eat and drink.' There was a tangible strain in the air, but Caragh met the captain's gaze, saying, 'If you and your men follow me, that will give Breanne a few moments to gather her belongings.'

It was the opening she had been waiting for. Breanne reached back for Alarr's hand and moved it off her neck. He gripped her palm in response and walked with her back to the dwelling they had once shared. The moment they went inside, Alarr spoke a sharp order and the men stood and departed the longhouse, leaving them alone.

Her anger flared once again, and she turned to face him. 'I stayed with you because I believed you were taking me home. After all this time, I never felt like a slave in your presence. Until now.'

She moved towards the partition, but Alarr caught her by the arm. 'I don't trust the guards with you. Or any other man.' There was a note of jealousy in his tone, and she didn't know what to think of that. He had already claimed that she meant nothing to him. He had no right to interfere.

'They are my father's men,' she insisted. 'I know Darin, and he is one of Feann's strongest guards. I have the right to go home with them.'

'No,' Alarr insisted. 'I do not trust them.' He lightened his touch upon her arm and instead of a grip, it felt like a caress. She froze when he rested his palm upon her back, gentling his touch. 'You could be harmed, and I would not be there to protect you.'

She tried to steel herself against the warmth that washed over her with his words. He didn't mean what he was saying, and she had to stop herself from falling prey to idle feelings.

'Why does it matter to you if I leave?' The words came out as a whisper. 'We both know that I mean nothing to you.' She threw his own words back at him. 'I am only your slave. Isn't that what you said?'

But when she stared into his eyes, Alarr made no effort to hide his desire. His blue eyes held the fire of longing, and he looked as if he wanted to mark his claim upon her. Her skin tightened at his gaze, and she was caught up in wanting someone she could never have.

His hands moved up her spine, his hand cradling her nape. 'The truth is, I want you far too much, *søtnos*.'

The heat of his touch evoked a response she had never expected. Her head tried desperately to warn her, but her body savoured his caress. Her skin tightened, yearning for him, even as she knew he would not turn aside from revenge. Alarr was a *Lochlannach* warrior, a Norseman who would not yield to anyone.

And God help her, she wanted him, too.

The pieces of her heart crumbled when he cupped her face in his hands, leaning in to claim a kiss. His mouth coaxed her to kiss him back, and she melted into him, feeling as if her skin were blazing. Her brain tried to warn her of the danger, but Alarr's mouth silenced any protests.

'I won't let you go.' He spoke against her lips, drawing her body to his.

Breanne could feel the caged strength in his body, and she struggled to find her will power. 'I have to go back. Killcobar is my home.'

'And what if I refuse to let you leave?' he mused aloud. He drew her to their shared pallet and pushed her back against the furs. Gently, he pinned her wrists. 'What if I keep you here, bound to me?'

Alarr leaned down to kiss her again, and she suddenly understood what this was, beyond temptation. He wanted her to stay of her own free will by offering her the pleasure of his touch. A part of her hungered for the affection, as if he could push away the loneliness of the past few years. For so long, she had felt isolated, apart from everyone else at Killcobar. And Alarr was slowly taking apart the invisible walls she had built to shield herself from hurt.

His hands moved to her breasts, stroking them through the rough wool of her gown. Her nipples grew erect, and the sweet torment of his caress made her weak with desire. She wanted him badly, wanted to lose herself in him.

But it was an illusion, wasn't it? Alarr didn't truly want her. Had she not been King Feann's foster daughter, he would have left her in the slave market to become another man's possession. A harsh lump of disappointment pushed back the desire, and she turned her face aside.

'I don't want you to touch me,' she whispered. 'Please stop.'

He did, but the raw need in his expression made her falter. She sat up when he moved away, drawing her knees in. Right now, she wanted to weep, but she would not give Alarr the satisfaction.

'I am going home,' she told him. 'If you try to kill Feann, I will have no choice but to warn him.' She could not stand by and let her foster father be harmed.

Alarr's face turned grave. 'I cannot forget what Feann did to my bride and my family, Breanne. Justice must be served.'

She understood his desire for vengeance, and yet, she intended to confront her foster father first.

'He must have had a reason,' she said. 'Feann is not

a murderer. I believe what you say, but he would never act in such a way without purpose.' Though he had a ruthless side, she could not imagine her foster father attacking if there was no cause.

'And what purpose was there in killing my bride? Gilla was an innocent.'

She didn't know what to say to that. Innocent people died in battle all the time. But her foster father was not cruel in that way. She had seen him spare men's lives before. It was not usual for him to threaten a woman, and she had no answer for him.

'Did you love Gilla?' she asked quietly. Not that it mattered, but she wondered whether he grieved for her still.

'We were friends.' He sat beside her and admitted, 'I didn't love her, but we could have made a good marriage between us.'

It should not have made a difference, but she felt a slight sense of relief. As soon as the thought struck her, she pushed it away. Why should it matter if he was in love with his bride? Alarr was her captor and her enemy. He intended to murder the man who had given her a home and a family. She owed him nothing at all.

But she could not deny that he had spared her life and her virtue. It was difficult to reconcile the two sides to the man. And perhaps it was too late to change his mind.

'I should go back,' she murmured. 'The others will be waiting for me.'

'Let them wait.' He caught her hand, tracing the centre of her palm with his thumb. The caress reached beneath her defences, unravelling her senses.

'You will allow me to leave,' she said quietly. 'Because you are a man of honour.'

'Am I?' He reached out to caress her hair, sliding his hand down her spine. 'Because right now, all I want is your body beneath mine.'

A flame of desire took hold, drawing her beneath his spell. She could not deny the raw physical attraction she felt, but she gathered the shreds of her willpower and stepped back.

'Goodbye, Alarr,' she murmured. For a long moment, she stared at him, wondering if he could ever reconsider his revenge.

And then she walked away from him.

'I never thought you would let her go.' Rurik stood beside Alarr as Breanne rode away with the soldiers.

'I'm not letting her go.' He didn't trust Feann's guards at all. They had not found her until Styr had allowed her to send word to Killcobar. Had they ever intended to search for her? He was beginning to have his doubts, since Styr's settlement was only a day's journey away. It would not have been difficult to find her. Their negligence didn't seem right, and Alarr intended to follow them in secret—not only for his own purpose, but also to ensure that she was protected.

'You want to track them.' Rurik's gaze was knowing, and he crossed his arms.

Alarr didn't deny it. He wanted to ensure that Breanne made it safely home again, and if that meant following at a swift pace, so be it. 'I don't trust them.'

'You wouldn't trust any man with Breanne.'

'Especially not soldiers who would wait so long to

search for her. And I have not forgotten what I came here to do.'

That prompted a pained expression from Rurik. 'Feann isn't at Killcobar. You heard him say it. We have no reason to pursue Breanne.'

'We don't know for certain whether Feann is there.' He didn't trust their claims, and it was better to discover the truth for himself. 'Even if he is not, I think we should go and gather information. You were wanting to learn about your mother. I want to know about Feann's defences.'

'We might be recognised,' Rurik said. 'It's dangerous.'

His brother was right, but he still believed it was best to gather information. Someone might have the answers he sought.

'That may be true,' he said. 'But we can say truthfully that you have come in search of answers about your mother. And we may learn more about Feann while we are there.'

Rurik seemed to consider it. 'Has Breanne talked sense into you, then?'

'About killing Feann? No. But I agree that we should learn why he went to Maerr.' He stared out at the horizon to the riders that were no longer visible. Would Breanne be safe while he trailed them? It struck him as strange that the guards had barely questioned what had happened to her. Had Alarr been in their place, he would have demanded answers about how Breanne had been stolen away. He would have spent time ensuring that she was not injured—and never would he have allowed her to go off alone with a man who claimed to be her master.

'When do you want to go to Killcobar?' Rurik asked. 'And do you want escorts?'

Alarr thought about it and shook his head. 'Not at first. It would make us too conspicuous. Better to travel alone and let others believe we are searching for your family.' Only Feann and a handful of men might recognise them. And none of the tribe knew Rurik, since he was not at the wedding.

'I want to leave as soon as our belongings are prepared.' It was a risk to go alone, but he also understood Styr's reluctance to endanger his tribe. Perhaps the leader might be willing to visit Killcobar with his men, a few days from now.

He shielded his eyes against the sun, knowing it had been a mistake to let her go. Then he turned back to his brother. 'We are going to find our answers. No matter how long it takes.'

'And when Feann returns? Do you still intend to sacrifice your life for his? All to avenge a man who never cared about either one of us?'

'It's not only about our father. The king and his men slaughtered Gilla and her family. It was an act of war, and I intend to avenge our family's honour. The other tribes need to know that if they dare to attack, our retribution will be merciless. Already it has taken too long for us to respond.'

His brother fell silent for a time. 'And if you do kill him and lose your life, what will stop Feann from returning to Maerr?' He shook his head. 'Learn the truth if you will, but there are only two of us to fight. It's not enough.'

'It's enough for a slip of a blade between his ribs.'

Yet even as he spoke the words, Alarr recognised his brother's truth. He didn't know how to make Rurik understand his reasoning. His brother couldn't understand why he was willing to take such a risk. But in all honesty, he had nothing left to lose.

'Why do you want to die, Alarr?' Rurik asked quietly.

He thought about his brother's question for a time, choosing his words carefully. 'When I fought against Feann, he stole from me the life I was meant to have. I am no longer the fighter I was. No woman wants me the way I am. Hardly able to walk…barely able to wield a sword.'

'You survived wounds that would have killed most men. I am glad you are alive,' Rurik said. 'But I came with you to Éireann because I wanted answers. And because I wanted to stop you from doing something foolish, like murdering a king.'

'You cannot stop me, Rurik. I have chosen my path.'

'And what of Breanne? It will destroy her if you kill her foster father. He is all she has left.'

Alarr knew that, and yet, he could not turn from this path. Only after he had slain Feann would he believe that he had any worth as a man. Breanne might feel pity towards him, but that was all. If he somehow survived the fight, it would change naught. The thought of having to leave her filled him with regret. But there was nothing to be done for it.

'We will go to Killcobar and follow Breanne,' Alarr said. 'Until Feann returns, we will learn what we can and wait.' And in the meantime, he would protect her from harm.

Rurik met his gaze steadily and gave a nod. 'So be it.'

* * *

Breanne rode with the soldiers towards her father's lands, but inwardly, she could not shake the premonition that something was wrong. When they stopped to make camp for the night, Darin came to help her down from the horse.

She smiled at the captain. 'Thank you.'

He guided her towards a clearing where one of the men was attempting to build a fire. 'Come and warm yourself,' he offered. The night air was cool, and she was eager to rest. Her thoughts remained troubled, and although she knew she had made the right choice to go with them, she could not stop thinking of Alarr. He was handsome, and his dark hair and fierce fighting skills allured her. She had loved sleeping beside him at night, feeling his hard body nestled against hers. And his kiss haunted her still.

He was a man living in darkness, bound to vengeance. She didn't understand how he was willing to sacrifice his life in a fight with Feann. Did he really believe he had so little value? Even Rurik had tried to stop him from this path towards death.

An ache settled within her at the thought. She knew what it was to feel as if no one wanted you. The solitude held an oppressive weight, and she understood the feeling of isolation. But for a brief moment it had seemed as if there was a connection between them before he'd pushed her away.

You made the right choice, her brain reminded her. *He was only intending to betray you.*

And yet, she somehow didn't believe that. When she had ridden away from the Hardrata settlement, she had caught Alarr staring at her with longing. Despite his cruel words, it seemed as if he didn't want to let her go. Her own feelings had been torn and confused, for it seemed as if his words and actions were in conflict. He had claimed she meant nothing at all to him...but she sensed that it was a lie.

'Are you hungry?' the captain asked.

'A little.' She held out her hands to the fire, trying to warm herself. He went to his saddle bag and withdrew some dried meat. He gave her the venison, but it was tough to gnaw. She struggled with the meagre food, and he gave her a sip of ale from a drinking horn.

Darin sat nearby, and she waited for him to ask questions. Surely, he would want to know what had happened to her. But instead, he said nothing, only staring into the fire. For a time, Breanne thought she should begin a conversation or at least try to talk to him. But there was only silence.

It felt as if she had been forgotten by everyone...as if her disappearance meant nothing. She had wanted to believe that she was Feann's adopted daughter, to feel as if she belonged at Killcobar. All these years, she had tried to shape herself into the woman he wanted her to be. She had remained passive and obedient, quiet in the shadows. But now, it was clear that she had always been an outsider. No one had even noticed when she'd gone.

Breanne forced back the self-pity as her frustration rose higher. Though she wanted answers, did it even matter what they thought any more? They had abandoned her, and it was time to stop living her life to please others. No longer would she allow them to shape her destiny. This time, any decisions made would be her own.

At last, she spoke. 'Why did no one come for me during the past few weeks?'

The captain tossed a brick of peat into the fire and shrugged. Which was no answer at all. She waited again in disbelief, her anger rising. 'Am I worth so little to everyone?'

He hesitated and admitted, 'I know it must have seemed like this.'

'Then tell me what happened,' she demanded. 'Where is Feann now?'

Darin glanced over at his men, who quietly excused themselves to give them privacy. He stared into the fire for a long while, as if searching for the right words. 'He travelled to the west. King Cerball asked for his help with an escaped prisoner. We sent word to him after you were gone, but I know not if he received our messages.'

She stared hard at him. 'And you didn't think you should send other men to search for me?' Her irritation heightened at his lack of effort, though she realised that it was possible Feann hadn't known she was a captive—especially if he had been travelling. The flames flared against the peat bricks, a bright orange colour against the night sky.

'We should have,' he confessed. 'But then, Styr Hardrata sent word to Killcobar that you were at the *Lochlannach* settlement.' His expression turned guilty, and he said, 'I am sorry you felt abandoned, my lady. That was never our intention.'

She supposed she ought to feel relieved that soldiers had come to bring her home at last. But instead, she was starting to question all that had happened. Alarr had openly admitted that he didn't trust Feann's men, so why should she? Moreover, was it possible that one or more of them had conspired with the man who had sold her into slavery? For what purpose? She didn't believe Darin would do such a thing, but it made her wonder whom she could trust.

She had once believed she could trust Alarr. And yet, he had let her go.

Her heart gave a curious ache at the thought, and it made her suddenly think of his desire for revenge. Where was Alarr now, and was he still searching for Feann? She was afraid to imagine his intentions, and no matter what she said or did, she could not stop him. There was no choice but to warn her foster father.

Darin's face was shadowed, and he seemed preoccupied by something. He stood, walking towards the edge of the forest. Once again, his attention seemed to be elsewhere, and she could not guess why. It was almost as if he were waiting for something. Or that he had sensed someone approaching. Soon enough, Breanne heard the sound of a horse, and Darin went towards the clearing, reaching for his sword. He spoke quietly to his men, and all went on alert. Breanne couldn't say whether there was truly a threat, but her instincts warned her to hide. She backed away into the shadow of the trees, wondering if she was foolish for doing so.

A twig snapped from behind her, and she spun.

'Are you well?' came a low voice from the shadows.

Breanne bit back her surprise and suppressed a curse. 'Alarr?' He moved closer, and her mood tensed at the sight of him. 'What are you doing here?'

'I followed you to ensure that you were safe. I don't trust these men.'

'You don't trust anyone,' she pointed out. Though she ought to be irritated that he had tracked her, another part of her was startled that he would care. And despite her better judgement, she warmed to it.

He didn't argue with her but reached for her hand. His palm was warm, callused from fighting. She remembered the sensation of those fingers trailing over her skin, and she could not deny the thrill of memory.

When she walked back towards the campsite, he kept her hand in his, and she saw Rurik holding a sword and shield, staring at the captain and his men. Though he hadn't provoked a fight, it was clear that he was diverting their attention.

'Darin,' Breanne said.

He kept his weapon in hand as he turned back to her. When he saw her holding Alarr's hand, he froze and waited for her command. 'My lady, do you want me to send them away or let them stay?'

'It wouldn't matter, even if I did want them to go. Alarr would not leave.' Even so, her heart gave a sudden thrill of anticipation. She was unaccustomed to being followed, and she didn't know whether to be flattered or frustrated. 'They can stay.' To Rurik, she said, 'You may set up your camp over there.'

She wanted to maintain a distance between them to guard her wayward feelings. Alarr kept her hand in his, and his thumb was drawing lazy circles over her palm. The simple touch went deeper than she'd imagined, and she could feel the echo of the caress in other places.

'You didn't just follow me to ensure my safety,' she murmured. 'There was another reason.' Her brain warned her to strengthen the walls around her feelings. *He is using you.* It wasn't wise to imagine that he wanted her for anything other than to get close to Feann.

He leaned in close so that she could feel his breath against her ear. 'You are still mine, Breanne.'

Her mouth went dry, and she felt her restlessness brewing. Alarr gazed at her with undisguised interest, and every memory of his touch came back to her. She remembered the feeling of his heavy body pressed above hers, and the way she had melted into him.

But those memories wouldn't change the rift between them. She let go of his hand, rebuilding her self-defences. She could not trust this man, despite how he had already saved her life. Alarr had already admitted that he would not set aside his vengeance for her. And how could she care for a man who wanted to hurt someone she loved? It was impossible. The thoughts burdened her, making her wish she could simply lock her heart away.

The ache of regret weighed upon her, for she had let herself long for someone she couldn't have. *He doesn't want you.* No one did, it seemed. And it was hard to push back the loneliness when she had never had any true family or loved ones. Feann was the only person to show her kindness, and even he had abandoned her.

She needed to find the strength to live her own life without relying on anyone else. Although she would return to Killcobar with Darin and his men, no longer could she live a shadowed life where no one cared if she was there or not. And no matter what feelings she had towards Alarr, she would cut them off. It was better to be alone than to be used and discarded.

But for now, she would listen and watch.

Alarr led her towards the fire, and she sat on a fallen log. He took a place beside her, and then regarded Darin again. 'Where is Feann now?'

The man hesitated a moment. 'King Cerball wanted him to—'

'I asked where he is. Not what he is doing,' Alarr interrupted.

Darin eyed Breanne as if he didn't want to answer. At last, he said, 'I don't know where Feann is now.'

He wasn't going to tell Alarr anything, and she understood that. But he could tell her the truth if she commanded it. And perhaps she could confront Feann and end the vengeance between Alarr and him.

'But you do know where the escaped prisoner was being held,' she pointed out.

There was tension in his shoulders, as if he didn't want to reveal too much. She understood that he was trying to protect Feann, for her sake. His loyalty was commendable.

At that point, Rurik interrupted. 'Alarr, I can join these men and escort Breanne to Killcobar if you want to go in search of Feann and the prisoner.'

There was a silent glance exchanged between the men, and she wondered why Rurik would want them to split up. She was trying to decide what to say when Alarr's gaze narrowed upon Darin. 'There's something you're hiding from us, and it's not about Feann. It has greater importance, doesn't it? It's the reason why he didn't search for Breanne.'

The captain shifted his gaze back to Breanne but made no denial. 'My duty is to keep Lady Breanne safe.'

'But there is another threat,' Alarr guessed. 'And I suspect it has something to do with the escaped prisoner.'

The captain tried to keep his face expressionless, but

Breanne saw the way he averted his gaze. There *was* something Darin was hiding.

'Tell me,' Breanne insisted. 'I have the right to know the truth.' He refused to meet her gaze, so she stood and drew closer. Her senses grew heightened as she waited for him to answer.

At last, he lifted his head and regarded her. 'You do.' With a pause, he added, 'The prisoner that King Cerball exiled was your mother.'

Chapter Six

Breanne's heart was pounding with a blend of anxious nerves. 'They told me she was dead. My father was executed, and I thought Treasa was killed alongside him.' But now, she wondered if Feann had lied to her about everything.

The captain shook his head. 'Your father was executed for treason, and your mother was exiled. King Cerball has command of their lands at Clonagh.'

For a moment, she felt as if she had been turned to stone. Everything she had known in her life was a lie. A tremor of anger took root and slowly kindled into rage. 'And Feann knew she was alive. All this time, he knew.'

Darin nodded. 'Feann was trying to negotiate with King Cerball. He wanted you to reclaim your birthright by wedding a man loyal to Cerball. But Cerball denied him for years. Feann never told you because he didn't know if he would be able to bring you back again.'

She was already shaking her head. Right now, she felt as if her life had spun out of control, and she was struggling to grasp the truth. How could Feann have lied to her all those years about her family? The thought sickened her. She had believed that he cared for her like his own daughter. And now, it seemed that he had only been using her to solidify his alliance with Cerball and possibly gain command of Clonagh.

One moment, she had planned to leave Killcobar behind and begin anew with her own choices. Now, it seemed that kings were manipulating her life, pulling her in directions she'd never imagined.

There was only one person who could tell her the truth of what had happened. And she needed to understand all of it. She regarded Darin and asked, 'Where is my mother now?'

'If Feann was successful in capturing her, then likely she was returned to her exile at Dún Bolg,' the captain answered.

'What do you want to do, Breanne?' Alarr asked. His voice was quiet, almost gentle. 'You can go back with Rurik. Or if you want to go with me to Dún Bolg, I will escort you there. The choice is yours.'

At first, she didn't know whether to let him accompany her. But if Feann had already brought her mother to Dún Bolog, then likely her foster father was returning to Killcobar. It was better to keep Alarr away from Feann. 'I want to see my mother.'

She had so few memories of her past, and she didn't even know if she would recognise Treasa. Was her mother aware of what had happened to her? Would she care at all? A fervent longing prickled within her with the hope that she did have at least one person to call family.

'We can leave as soon as you are ready,' Alarr offered.

It surprised her that he wanted to travel by nightfall,

but perhaps it would be safer. The moon was bright, and most of the journey would be through open fields. Breanne had never been to Dún Bolg, but she had heard that the lands lay towards the west.

She gathered a few belongings, along with some food, while Alarr and Rurik spoke in the Norse language once more. Then the brothers bid one another farewell, embracing before Alarr brought his horse to her. He tied her bundle to the saddle and helped her mount.

To the captain, she said, 'I bid you and your men good fortune.' Then she turned to Rurik. 'Swear to me that you will not harm Feann.'

He nodded. 'I swear it. I only want information about what happened on the day we were attacked.'

She believed he would keep his word. 'I hope you learn the truth. Send word to me after Feann returns to Killcobar.'

'I will.'

Alarr swung up behind her and turned the animal westwards. Breanne leaned back against him as they rode. She said nothing, but during the ride, she was conscious of every line of his body. He was warm, his arms sheltering her from the cold. Her body ached from exhaustion, and in time, the swaying of the horse caused her to grow weary. Alarr seemed to sense her weakness, and he murmured against her ear. 'Sleep, if you wish. I won't let you fall.'

She closed her eyes, grateful for his presence. 'Thank you.'

As she succumbed to her exhaustion, she was confused by the feelings of security. This man had been her captor, and now they were travelling together as equals.

No longer did he seem like an enemy—instead, she grew aware that he had protected her at every moment.

His very presence made her want to lower her defences—just for a moment.

Alarr rested his cheek against her hair, and she indulged in the feeling of comfort, no matter that it was wrong. She told herself that it wasn't real, even as her wayward heart softened to his touch.

For the next few hours, they rode through the night along the edge of a winding stream, until the landscape shifted into rolling hills. Breanne slept against him, until at last, he came to a stop. The pale grey light of dawn creased the horizon, and she realised that they were in a part of Éireann she had never seen before. The green hills rose into a wooded area, but a road cut through the trees. In the distance, she saw mountains rising up, revealing a cashel atop the hillside.

'Where are we?' she asked.

'A few miles outside of Dún Bolg,' he answered. 'My father spoke of it during his travels, but I've never been there before.' He guided the horse up the hillside, and she then saw rock formations that provided natural shelter from the elements. 'We'll stop and sleep a while before we find your mother.' He didn't speak of Feann, though they both knew there was a chance that her foster father was still here.

Alarr chose a small indentation in the rock, not quite a cave, but surrounded on all sides. He dismounted and helped her down. Breanne started to gather supplies for a fire while he tended the horse and led it to drink at a mountain stream trickling down the hillside.

He chose a grassy place to tether the animal loosely,

so the horse could graze. When he returned to their shelter, he nodded in approval at the kindling and wood she'd gathered. Alarr tossed her a flint, and she used her knife to strike a spark. She fed the spark dry grasses, blowing gently, before she added dry twigs and sticks. Eventually, she added wood, and she warmed herself at the flames.

She hardly knew what to think of anything right now. Alarr had escorted her here, but she knew better than to imagine that it was for her sake. He wanted to confront Feann, whereas she wanted to see the mother she had never known. What could she even say to Treasa? Breanne had not seen her since she was two years old. The woman was naught but a stranger. Nerves gathered within her at the thought of seeing her mother.

Alarr spread out a sleeping fur on the ground and stretched out beside the fire. She knew he was tired from all the travelling, but he had not wanted to stop until now. Likely, he didn't want any of the guards at Dún Bolg to be aware of their arrival. It was too easy for them to be seen in an open clearing.

She wondered if she should remain on the other side of the fire, apart from him. Ever since she had left, there had been an unspoken tension between them. There was no question that he desired her…and yet, she knew the danger of drawing too close. Alarr allured her, and she could not deny that she wanted him too. If she lay beside him, all her defences would crumble. And then he would leave her. Whether he returned to Maerr or whether he died fighting Feann, the result was the same. It was not wise to let herself care about this man.

'There's no need to be afraid of me, Breanne,' he

said. Alarr leaned back on the fur and regarded her. 'I won't harm you.'

'I remember too well what happened the last time I was close to you,' she admitted. She didn't trust herself around him.

'I won't touch you unless you ask.' His voice was deep and resonant, as if he wouldn't mind it at all.

She drew close to the fire, holding out her hands. It was still cool in the morning, but she knew better than to get too close. For a moment, she gathered her thoughts, wondering if there was any means of dissuading him from his chosen path. She had asked him to give up his plans of vengeance before, and he had refused.

'Alarr,' she began, choosing her words with care, 'is there anything that would satisfy your need for vengeance that would allow my foster father to live?'

He leaned back against the furs, staring at the sky. 'No.'

She had expected this, but she was prepared to argue with him. 'Killing Feann won't bring your father back.'

He rolled to his side to face her. 'This isn't only about Sigurd. It's about me.'

Breanne came to kneel beside him. 'What is it?'

He sat up then and touched his legs. 'Feann took away more than my father's life. He took away the man I used to be.'

She sobered, but she wanted him to understand that he was not broken in her eyes. 'That's not true. Because of *your* actions, you protected me. Even when Oisin tried to take me.' She reached out to touch his knees. 'You are still a worthy fighter. You've overcome so much.'

Alarr captured her hands, holding them there. 'I have no balance, and I cannot run very far. When it rains, I feel the pain aching deep within. These are wounds that will never heal.'

She understood, then, why he believed he had to die in this battle. He did not believe he was a man of worth any more. His vengeance was not about hurting Feann—it was about ending his own pain of loss.

She leaned in closer and touched her forehead to his. 'Your wounds are not here, Alarr.' She lifted her hands from his legs and moved them to his heart. 'Your wounds are here.'

His face was a breath away from hers, and inwardly, she was trembling. His blue eyes were searing, his hunger burning within them. May the gods forgive her, she wanted him to touch her —even though she knew he would not stay.

She closed her eyes, trying to gather what little control she had. Beneath her palms, his skin was warm, but she did not pull her hands back.

'You are still a man of strength,' she whispered. 'He didn't take that from you.'

'He took away everything that mattered,' he said softly.

Her heart bled for him, for the losses he'd endured, and the dark frustration that shadowed his heart. And despite everything, she wanted him to live. Even if they could not be together, she wanted him to put the past behind him.

'He didn't take away everything,' she whispered. 'There are many who care about you.'

Alarr drew his hands around her waist and lay back on the furs, pulling her body atop his. She could feel the hard ridge of his arousal between her thighs, and it caused her body to ache. Beneath her gown, her breasts tightened, and it was difficult to catch her breath.

'What do you want from me, Breanne?' His voice was hoarse, as if he had no control remaining. The tension stretched between them, and her heartbeat quickened as she sat astride him.

The silence that fell between them was a chasm of unspoken words. He tightened his hold upon her body, and another flicker of heat licked at her skin. She hardly knew how to answer. At last, she said, 'I want you to let him live.'

Before he could refuse, she touched her fingertips to his mouth. 'I don't expect you to let go of your hatred or anger. But I am asking that you do this for my sake.'

He stared at her as if she had asked too much of him. Already she could see the refusal in his eyes. But this was about more than abandoning his vengeance. She didn't want him to die.

At this moment, she could not put a name to her feelings for Alarr, for they were tangled up in invisible knots. She knew he was wrong for her, an enemy. She knew he would leave. And yet, when she was in his arms, she felt alive. He had been both her warrior and her rescuer—a man who tempted her in ways she didn't understand.

But more than that, she wanted to close up Alarr's invisible wounds and make him see that he was more than a fighter. He was a man who deserved a new beginning.

Despite all the reasons why this was wrong…she could not suppress the longing that rose within her. And if she made Alarr believe that there was another way to avoid bloodshed, she could save them both.

'If you let Feann live, I will give you whatever you want.' Her voice was breathless, but she kept her gaze fixed upon him. Slowly, Breanne reached for the laces of her gown and loosened them. She knew it sounded as if she were making the ultimate sacrifice. But the truth was, she wanted Alarr badly. She hadn't lied when she had called him a man of strength. He had shielded her all these weeks, keeping her safe.

Alarr said nothing but distracted her by drawing his hand down the curve of her spine. He moved beneath her, and a shiver of anticipation slid over her. Her breath hitched, and she reached for his shoulders. He pressed against the juncture of her thighs, and a surge of desire prickled within. She grew wet between her legs, wanting something she could not understand.

'Feann must face justice for what he did.' His voice was like iron, rigid and unyielding.

Breanne drew her hands to his chest. 'I agree that he must atone for the attack. But grant me his life, I beg you.'

She leaned in and kissed him, hoping she could change his mind. Her action seemed to ignite his desire, and Alarr answered the kiss, devouring her with his mouth. His tongue slid inside, and she felt an answering ache between her legs. Her breathing grew rough, and she gripped his hair, meeting his needs with her own.

'He isn't worth your innocence, Breanne. Save that for a man worthier than me.'

She understood then, that he was granting her the choice. He wanted her, but he would not claim her body unless she gave her full consent. She could stop her actions now, and he would let her be. But she could not deny that his caress tempted her, making her want to be loved.

There was a strong chance that he would not agree to this bargain. But she didn't want to stand back without fighting for the lives of the men she cared about. 'You *are* a man of worth, Alarr.'

He lifted his hand to her face. 'When you left with those men, all I could think of was bringing you back.' He brought her palm to his heart, resting it there. 'I want more than your innocence, Breanne.'

She didn't understand what he meant. When she studied his face, she saw the man who had come for her, time and again. Alarr had been hardened by battle and the need for revenge. Yet, within him, she saw the same shadow of loneliness. He had lost everything— his father, his bride, and even his strength in battle.

His blue eyes burned into hers. 'If you give yourself to me, I will not let you go. Once you make this choice, we will be bound together by the gods.'

Her emotions softened when she realised what he was offering. This was not a man who was forcing her to bargain her virtue for Feann's life. It was much more than that. 'You want me to stay with you.'

'Of your own free will,' he said.

Her heart quaked at the thought, for she was afraid to ask for how long. He might intend for her to be his concubine...or perhaps his wife. She had never expected this, and it unsettled her. What was his purpose? Why would he ask her to stay?

It went against everything she had believed about him—that he would take what he wanted and then leave. Instead, he was reaching out to her, wanting her to remain with him. Never had she imagined this, and her defences came crashing down.

Of all the people in her life, Alarr was the only man she had come to depend on. He had never forsaken her, and that meant something. He was a man who had endured as much loss as she had. And perhaps they could fill the emptiness in one another.

'If I agree,' she said quietly, 'will you let him live?'

His expression never faltered, and he gave a single nod. Breanne studied him, trying to discern if he was telling her the truth.

In answer, she leaned in to kiss him again. Alarr claimed her mouth relentlessly, letting her know without a doubt how much he wanted her.

With shaking fingers, Breanne lowered her bodice, never taking her eyes from his. Then she took his palm and laid it upon her bare breast.

The scalding heat of his palm aroused her, and Alarr stroked her breast, lightly grazing the hardened nub. A bolt of heat made her moan, and he deepened the pleasure when he lowered his mouth to her nipple. Gently, he suckled the tip, his tongue driving her wild. She arched, unable to stop the surge of pleasure that filled her.

Against her skin, he murmured. 'You belong to me now, Breanne.'

She gripped his hair, his touch arousing her deeply. Then she added, 'And you belong to me.' To emphasise her words, she reached out to unfasten his tunic.

He helped her, stripping it away before he drew his lips back to hers. Against her mouth, he said, 'From now on, you will spend every night in my bed.'

With his hands, he drew back the edges of her gown,

exposing her naked body. She felt the heat of the fire against her skin and the fur beneath her body. Alarr removed the rest of his clothing and then pressed her back. 'I hated watching you leave with those men,' he said, trapping her wrists upon the furs. 'I didn't trust them to guard you.'

He lowered his mouth to her other breast, giving it the same attention as the first. She shuddered against him, threading her fingers through his hair. His touch was possessive, and it evoked a fiery pleasure she had never imagined. It was as if the years of loneliness had gathered up within him, and he needed her to fill the void inside.

Breanne framed his face with her hands. His blue eyes stared into hers, and she kissed him again. 'You always kept me safe.' She drew her hands down his muscled torso, feeling the rock-hard muscles beneath her palms. There was no trace of fat upon him, and his abdomen had several ridges. When her fingertips brushed against his ribs, he jolted with a slight laugh.

'You're ticklish,' she accused, and he did not deny it. Instead, he drew her hand lower, until her palm brushed against his large arousal. For a moment, her apprehension returned, and she closed her eyes. Alarr guided her to his manhood, and demanded, 'Touch me, Breanne.'

She curled her fingers around his shaft, understanding that he meant to empower her. Tentatively, she stroked him, and he hissed.

'Did I hurt you?'

'No.' He showed her how to touch him, and she felt his erection grow harder against her palm as she stroked. She marvelled at the sense of power that rose up and the heady pleasure of caressing him.

Alarr drew his hand between her thighs, and she grew embarrassed by her wetness. He seemed pleased, however. 'Do not be shy, Breanne. Your body knows what it wants. And I intend to learn what you need.'

He began rubbing gentle circles against her intimate opening. A shock of sensation flooded through her, and she gasped when he slipped a finger inside. In answer, she stroked his length, finding what made him groan with arousal. 'Don't stop what you are doing, *søtnos.*' He drew her hand higher, and she felt the answering bead of moisture at his tip.

Slowly, he began to penetrate her with his finger in slow strokes while his thumb moved in light circles. The motion wound her up tightly, and she found herself squeezing him, evoking a stronger sensation. He added another finger, stretching her and making her crave more. As the feelings rose up within, gathering into a fist of desire, he lowered his mouth to her stomach. He kissed her skin, parting her thighs and raising her knees. She did not know what he was planning to do, until she felt his warm breath against her intimate opening.

'Alarr?' she questioned, gripping the furs. Her skin was unbearably sensitive, and when he replaced his fingers with his mouth, she could not stop the cry mingled with a gasp. He was tormenting her, forcing her higher until she was sobbing. Over and over, he stroked her with his tongue, until she felt herself slipping over the edge. A shimmering eruption of release flooded through her, and she trembled hard as the pleasure claimed her.

Only then did he rise up, sliding the edge of his erection to her wet opening. She was still so overcome by the shocking sensations that she was barely aware of him entering her body. There was a slight discomfort as he breached her innocence, and then she welcomed the invasion that brought him deep inside. She tried to move against him, but he imprisoned her wrists again.

'Slowly, *søtnos.*' Alarr ground against her, and she quaked as an aftershock flooded through her.

He took her lips, kissing her as he began to thrust. She felt uncertain at first and a little sore. But gradually she found herself meeting him, lifting her hips as he caressed her deep within.

She arched her back, trying to get closer. Her breathing was hitched, but he kept his lovemaking slow, coaxing her passion higher. When she thought she could bear it no longer, he slid in deep and held himself there, gently stroking her hooded flesh. A shocking coil of desire struck hard, and she moaned as his caress evoked a powerful release that filled every inch of her body.

Her heart pounded, and she gripped the furs, trembling violently with the storm of pleasure. Breanne wrapped her legs around his waist, and he quickened the tempo, gripping her hips as he entered and withdrew. His breathing was harsh, and when she squeezed him with her inner walls, he lost control. Over and over, he took her, until she climaxed again, and he emptied himself inside. His breathing was laboured as he rode out his own release, and he collapsed on top of her.

She held him close, their bodies damp with perspiration. Never had any man made her feel this way. Her heart was thundering, her body alive in ways she'd never imagined. While he slept against her, she pushed back his hair, memorising the lines of his face. He would not let her go now, and she found that she *wanted* to be with him, whatever came next. Her feelings were vulnerable, and though she was wary of loving this man, she could not stop the emotions from gathering inside.

And as he drifted off to sleep, their bodies still joined, she prayed that she had made the right decision to stay with him.

Chapter Seven

Alarr made love to her twice more as the morning waned into afternoon. Though his conscience warned that he should not have taken advantage of her offer, he could not bring himself to hold regrets. The craving for her touch consumed him, and the knowledge that he was the only man who had ever claimed her body made him feel even more protective of Breanne.

She held an inner strength and bravery that he admired. But more than that, she had insisted that he was a man of worth. He didn't really believe her, but she had forced him to consider a decision beyond his thoughts of vengeance. It was still likely that he would die in battle, even if he did keep this vow. And for that reason, he had agreed to Breanne's bargain.

Alarr knew his fate, but before he breathed his last, he wanted to spend his remaining days with her. He wanted her bare skin next to his, just as it was now. And every time he pleasured her, he wanted to watch her tremble with release, welcoming his body inside hers. It was as close to a true marriage as he would ever have. And if somehow she conceived a child, a part of him would live on.

A hollow ache centred inside him at the knowledge that he would not share that with her. All he had were these last few days, and he wanted to savour them, searing them into his memory. He kept their bodies intertwined, feeling content as he had never been before. She was awake, but neither spoke. It was as if words would break the spell between them, bringing reality back. And he didn't want that—not yet.

But soon enough, Breanne's stomach growled, and at her soft laugh, he realised he could not keep her here for the rest of the day, much as he wanted to.

'Do we have anything to eat?' she asked, tracing his bare skin.

'I know what I want,' he answered, rolling her to her back and taking her breast into his mouth. He was rewarded with her slight gasp, before she sighed and moved her hips against him.

'Much as I love having you in my bed, we do need food.'

'Do we?' He reached to touch her and found that she was as aroused as he. Giving in to his desire, he slid inside her welcoming depths.

Breanne's swift intake of breath told him that she wanted him, too. He entered and withdrew slowly, and she raised her knees to take him deeper.

'When we approach Dún Bolg, we will tell them that you are my wife. It's safer to stay together.' But it was about more than protecting her—it was because he wanted no man to even look at Breanne. She was his for these last few days, and he needed her with him.

'I agree.' She pulled his face closer and kissed him.

He took her mouth, kissing her deeply as he continued to make love to her. Breanne met his thrusts, digging her fingers into his shoulders until she wrapped her legs around his waist, demanding more.

'If Feann is there—'

'Then I will stay with you and speak with him,' she interrupted. 'As you said, we will let him believe we are married.'

He didn't argue, but continued to love her, driving her close to the edge. If he dared to tell Feann that he had wed Breanne, the king would demand his life in return. Their battle might be this day. For all he knew, this might be the last time he could be with this woman.

He slowed his pace again, wanting it to last. Her breathing had shifted, and she tried to urge him on, begging, 'Alarr, please.'

But he continued to draw out her pleasure, sliding deep within as he lowered his mouth to her breast, stroking her with his tongue. He was starting to learn what she needed, and when she arched against him, he reached down to stroke her intimately.

She was shuddering against him, but he wanted her to remember this moment between them. Gently, he urged her higher, until she gave a keening cry and shattered in his arms. She was panting as he entered and withdrew. All around his erect length, he could feel her body spasming and embracing him.

By the gods, he needed this woman. And if this was the last time between them, at least he knew he had glimpsed the life he would never have. He penetrated her, grasping her hips as she clenched him, and when he emptied himself inside, he held her close, breathing in the scent of her hair. His heart was racing, and he never wanted to let her go.

But he had no choice in this. She had to face her past, just as he did. With great reluctance, he withdrew and kissed her again before he helped her put on her gown. He got dressed and they put out the fire.

Breanne picked up the furs and folded them, and he brought them over to their horse, binding the coverlet to the saddle. He lifted her on to the animal and then mounted behind her, guiding them back on to the path leading to Dún Bolg. The green fields spread out in the distance, and he took the horse towards the fortress. A high wooden fence surrounded it, and he approached the gates slowly.

His thoughts were troubled, for he was only waiting to learn if Feann was still here. He had made a promise to Breanne not to kill him, and yet, he still wanted justice for his father's death. The question was whether that could happen without bloodshed. He doubted if that was possible.

When they reached the entrance, two guards called out for him to halt. Every sense went on alert as Alarr dismounted, holding the reins of their horse. He kept his hand near his weapon to protect Breanne.

'Who are you, and why are you here?' one guard asked.

'I am here to bring my wife, Breanne Ó Callahan, home to see her mother.'

The guard spoke to the other and answered, 'We have no Ó Callahans here.'

Breanne muttered beneath her breath, 'He's lying.'

Alarr suspected as much, since the woman had gone

into hiding. 'May we speak with your king or your chief?'

'Wait here.'

One of the guards departed to ask, and Breanne kept her voice low. 'Why do you think she was exiled in this place?'

'I don't know. But Feann may have the answers if he's here.' Inwardly, the tension was stretched tight within him, making him suspicious of everyone.

A little while later, the guard returned and opened the gates to him. 'Follow me.'

They did, and Alarr saw that the fortress was organised and neat, with the thatched roundhouses evenly spaced. Outdoor hearths burned with bricks of peat, and an iron pot hung over another fire, redolent with the succulent aroma of stew. There was an air of peace and contentment here, not one of war or imprisonment. He didn't know what to think of that.

When they reached the largest dwelling, the guard stopped. 'Our chief will speak with your wife alone.'

'I will not leave Breanne alone with a stranger,' Alarr countered. 'I will remain with her at all times.' He pressed his hand to her waist to emphasise it.

'Iasan does not wish to welcome a *Lochlannach* in our midst,' the guard said.

He didn't care what the chief wanted. Breanne's safety came above all else. But then, she turned to him and touched a hand to his shoulder. 'The chief may know something about what happened to my mother. Let us compromise.' She regarded the guard and said, 'Tell Iasan that I will speak with him, but only if my husband can be present at the door or closer.'

The guard inclined his head. 'I will ask.'

Alarr wasn't convinced it was a good idea to let her speak to the chief alone, particularly if Feann was here. But he was starting to believe that his enemy was already gone, for there was no sign of visitors.

Breanne's mother might have answers about Feann, since she had chosen to foster her daughter with him. But when Alarr glanced at his wife, he saw her twisting her fingers together.

'What is it?' he asked gently.

She shook her head. 'Nothing, really. It's just that I'm nervous about seeing my mother for the first time in so long. I haven't seen her since I was a young child.'

Their upbringing had been vastly different, so it seemed. He had been part of a large family with many kinsmen in the tribe whereas she had been more isolated.

'Do you still want to see her, if she is here?' he asked. 'She might not have told them her real name.'

Breanne nodded slowly. 'Even if I don't know her, I would like to speak to her.'

The guard returned and said, 'Our chief has agreed to come and meet you here.'

Alarr understood that the leader wanted to ensure that there was no risk of an attack. He agreed, and within a few minutes, a man emerged from the roundhouse, leaning against a walking stick. His hair was a blend of grey and red, and though he was past his fighting years, there was no doubting the razor-sharp awareness in his eyes. When he studied Breanne, there was a visible discomfort, as if he recognised her somehow. He motioned for the guard to come closer and murmured a command in the man's ear.

'I understand you came in search of a Ó Callahan woman,' the chief said. 'Why?'

Breanne took a step closer. 'I was told that my parents were killed, years ago, and I lived with my foster father ever since. I learned only recently that my mother, Treasa, was exiled here. I was hoping to find her.'

The older warrior stared at her for a time, as if discerning something. Alarr met the man's gaze, and added, 'We mean no harm to her or to anyone of your tribe.'

The chief seemed full of distrust, and he said, 'That remains to be seen.' Then he added, 'You may stay the night with us. A few of our men are going hunting now, and you may join them if you wish. Your wife can stay with the women.'

Alarr was about to refuse, for he didn't like the idea of being separated from her. But then, Breanne leaned in close. 'I think he wants to learn if we truly are a threat. Go with them, and I will stay here. I have your knife, if there is a need.'

He was about to argue with her, when abruptly, he heard an audible gasp. A woman broke free from the others and hurried towards Breanne. Her hair was reddish gold, like Breanne's, and her face was an older version. There could be no doubt this was her mother.

Breanne stood motionless, in shock. For a moment, the two women stared at one another, until the older woman said, 'Breanne?'

When she gave a nod, the woman embraced her, openly weeping. Though Breanne did not push her away, it was obvious that she knew not what to do.

She appeared startled by the woman's presence and could not quite return the affection.

'I think I should remain with my wife,' Alarr said to the chief, 'while she becomes reacquainted with her mother.'

Breanne followed her mother across the fortress to another roundhouse. Treasa gripped her hand as if she never wanted to let go. There was no denying that her joy was real. Her cheeks were wet with tears, and her smile spread across her face.

As for herself, Breanne felt only confusion. She couldn't force herself to be happy at seeing Treasa, for she didn't know her at all. It almost made her feel guilty that she couldn't return her mother's happiness. All she could think of was how Feann had never once spoken of Treasa. Breanne had always believed that she was alone, never knowing that she had a surviving family member. More than anything, she had wanted to have that kinship bond with another person. Instead, she could hardly bring herself to feel anything. There was no sense of connection with her mother, and a slight flare of guilt troubled her. She ought to be overjoyed, instead of mistrustful.

Alarr followed her, and he appeared to be searching for any signs of danger. She was grateful for his presence, for she believed he would keep her safe. His hand remained at her waist in a silent warning to others, and the gentle touch brought her comfort.

Ever since she had given herself to him, he had remained close. Though she wanted to believe that he would keep his promise, she remained cautious. It did not seem that there was any trace of her foster father, and she was grateful that she had more time before the two men confronted one another.

An uneasy feeling settled in her stomach as she wondered if Alarr had been right about Feann. She had never seen a darker side to the king before. Had he exiled her mother as a means of controlling her lands at Clonagh? Or had he tried to save Treasa's life after her husband was executed? She couldn't understand why her mother would be a threat to anyone. But Feann's purpose remained unclear. Breanne didn't know what to think about a man who would lie about Treasa's existence for so long.

Her mother led her inside and bade her to sit down. Alarr joined them but remained near the doorway to give them a measure of privacy.

She braved a smile. 'I cannot tell you how glad I am that you came to visit me, Breanne. I've been in hiding for so long, I never imagined I would see you again.'

'Feann told me you were dead,' Breanne answered honestly. She hardly knew what to say or where to begin.

Treasa's expression grew pained. 'Sometimes I wished I were dead.' She took a steady breath and admitted, 'I lost everything. My home…my husband… even you.'

Breanne felt as if her emotions were in turmoil right now. She needed to put together the pieces of the past. 'I need to understand what happened to you and my father. Will you tell me how you came to Dún Bolg?'

And why you remained hidden for so long.

Even as a prisoner, someone could have told her that Treasa was still alive. But they didn't want her to know the truth, and she couldn't guess the reasons why.

Treasa rested her hands in her lap and glanced at Alarr. Breanne reassured her, 'Alarr can be trusted.'

Her mother hesitated for a moment as if trying to decide whether to believe it. Finally, she said, 'Your father, Dal, was a good friend and an ally of King Cerball MacDúnlainge. He is a powerful ruler, and there was a time when we thought of marrying you to one of Cerball's sons.'

Then her expression hardened at the memory. 'Dal thought we should send you to him for fostering, but I wasn't so certain. I knew Feann would protect you, and he was not as ambitious as Cerball.'

Against her spine, Breanne felt the light touch of Alarr's hand. Then he spoke, 'Where is Feann now?'

Treasa shrugged. 'He was here a few days ago. I suppose he returned to Killcobar.' Her expression revealed nothing about her failed attempts at escape. In fact, from her demeanour, Breanne questioned whether Darin had been telling the truth. Was she truly a prisoner in exile? Or were there more lies?

From the tension in his hand, Breanne knew that Alarr wanted to ask more, but he held back the questions.

'What happened to my father?' she asked Treasa.

Her mother's face tightened with emotion. 'Dal wanted to raise his own status by fighting Cerball's battles with our own men. I told him we should stay at Clonagh, but he refused. Instead, he went into battle against the *Lochlannach*, time and again, while he left me with Cerball. He believed I would be safe there, as an honoured guest in the household.'

Her face tightened, and she lowered her gaze, gripping her hands together. 'But I was Cerball's prisoner.'

Breanne sensed there was more that her mother did not wish to reveal. She turned to Alarr. 'Will you leave us alone for a moment?'

He drew his hand to her nape and nodded. 'If you feel safe here. I can guard the door.'

She nodded. Before he left, he pulled her close and kissed her. It was likely a mark of possession, to show her mother that they were bound together. But even so, the brief kiss made her savour the light pressure of his mouth. Breanne gathered her composure and after he left, she regarded her mother. 'How long were you his prisoner?'

'For three years,' Treasa answered. There was hatred within her voice, and Breanne suspected what else had happened.

'Were you his prisoner…in all ways?'

Her mother closed her eyes. 'Cerball told me he would send Dal to fight at the front of the battle lines if I did not give myself to him. I despised what he did to me, but I had no choice, if I wanted to keep your father alive. In the end, it didn't matter.'

'I'm so sorry for what you endured,' she whispered to her mother. The thought of being a king's prisoner, and being forced to share his bed, was horrifying. It evoked memories of Oisin and his attempt to take her into captivity. She could not even imagine her mother's pain—even worse because Cerball had still ordered Dal's execution. Breanne could see the suffering in Treasa's face, and she took the woman's hand, squeezing it.

Her mother tightened her lips and took a breath. 'It's over now, and I've made a new life for myself here.'

'They told me that my father was executed for treason. Was it because the king wanted you?'

Treasa stood and paced across the small dwelling. For several moments, she said nothing. Then she admitted, 'Cerball was a proud man, and he believed that I would love him more than my husband. He wanted me to set Dal aside and become his queen.' Her eyes gleamed with unshed tears, and she rested her hand upon one of the beams supporting the roof. 'When I refused, he grew enraged. He accused Dal of conspiring against him.'

'Do you think my father knew what was happening?'

Treasa nodded. 'Once Dal realised I was Cerball's captive, he did everything in his power to get me out.' She wiped a tear away and said, 'He helped me escape with one of his men but paid the price with his life. Cerball executed him and stole our lands.' She took a moment to gather control of her emotions.

'And you left me with Feann,' Breanne finished.

Her mother nodded. 'I was grateful that he promised to protect you until you came of age. Even if I was not allowed to see you.'

Breanne frowned, not truly understanding the reason why Feann had not wanted her to know that her mother was alive. Was it for Treasa's protection, or was it for his own reasons? She wanted to ask questions, but something held her back. Someone was lying, and she knew not if it was Feann or Treasa.

'Are you still a prisoner here?' she asked her mother.

Treasa gave a weak smile and nodded. 'This is where I have been exiled. After Cerball no longer desired me, he has kept me here all these years.' She added, 'I tried to visit Clonagh a time or two. Feann heard of it, and he brought me back.' Regret tinged Treasa's voice, but she could understand her mother's reasons for wanting to go home.

'What of our people?' Breanne asked quietly. 'What became of them?'

'They are under Cerball's rule. Feann was trying to arrange for you to reclaim Clonagh by wedding a man loyal to Cerball. I had hoped he would manage it.' Her mother's expression grew tense. 'But you are already wedded to this *Lochlannach*.' She appeared displeased by it. 'I don't know what can be done about an alliance now.'

Breanne thought about admitting to her mother that they were not truly married but decided against it. Instead, she rose from her seated position and went to the door to bring Alarr back inside. She had never thought about Clonagh in the past, always believing it was lost. But now, she wondered what to do.

Alarr came to sit beside her, and she took strength from his presence. Treasa eyed him and asked, 'Tell me how you came to be with my daughter.'

'I am Alarr Sigurdsson of the kingdom of Maerr,' Alarr replied. 'Breanne was in danger, and I wed her as a means of protecting her.' His tone remained neutral, the lie flowing easily. He slid his arm around her waist in a silent gesture to emphasise his claim.

Treasa's expression grew strained. 'Was it your wish to wed him, Breanne?' She appeared disconcerted by the idea of a union between her daughter and a *Lochlannach*.

Breanne caught his gaze and recognised that Alarr was trying to gain more information for both of them.

She would say nothing to dispute his claim. 'It was my choice, yes.'

Inwardly, she wondered if it had been the right decision to offer herself to him. She didn't know if Alarr would keep his vow not to kill Feann. But beyond her foster father's life, she could not bear the thought of Alarr's death. She wanted him to live, to recognise that he had a life beyond fighting. Would he truly set aside his plans for revenge? Or was he only saying words she wanted to hear?

His hand moved over her waist in a slight caress of reassurance. She glanced at Alarr, and in his eyes, she saw a man who would not let her go. His gaze was steadfast, and she wondered if the sudden intimacy between them would bring him out of his shadows and into a life where there was hope. For the first time in her life, it felt as if she had someone she could love. And though she was afraid to trust him, she wanted to believe that he would not betray her.

'How did you learn I was at Dún Bolg?' Treasa asked. 'Did Feann tell you?'

'No, it was another man,' Alarr responded. 'Breanne wanted to see you, and I agreed to bring her here.' He said nothing of Feann, and she knew it was a deliberate omission.

But Treasa would not be deterred. 'What other man? Was it Oisin MacLogan?' Her demeanour tensed, and Breanne stared in shock.

'Why would you speak of Oisin?' The very memory of the man made her skin crawl. Were it not for Alarr's rescue, she had no doubt that Oisin would have raped her or forced her to wed him.

'Oisin is one of Cerball's bastard sons. He was the man Cerball chose for you to wed.'

Breanne shuddered at the thought. But she was starting to realise that Feann had done all that he could to keep her from the alliance.

'Oisin was angry when I did not agree to wed him,' Breanne confessed to her mother. 'He tried to take me by force.' She explained how the man had tried to hunt her down, and Treasa's face blanched.

'Oisin had no lands of his own. He wanted to wed you, in order to claim Clonagh as his own.'

'But now, he cannot.' Breanne eyed Alarr, realising that they had destroyed Oisin's plans.It made her wonder about her future. Did Alarr intend to wed her in truth one day? Or was he only intending to keep her as his lover? Both possibilities made her uneasy. If she married him, he would want her to leave Éireann and return to Maerr. But if she was only his concubine, he might one day abandon her. The thought left an icy chill sinking within her mood. She didn't like the thought of being powerless to command her own future or being left behind.

Her mother reached out and touched his shoulder. 'Alarr, might I have another moment alone with my daughter?'

He hesitated, but Breanne nodded. 'I don't think there's any danger, and it's just the two of us.' She suspected that Treasa wanted to discuss her 'marriage' to Alarr.

'If you wish.' He rose and went to the door. Before he left, he glanced at Treasa and then back at Breanne. He was still wary, but she was glad for his overprotective nature. It had helped her to survive more than once.

When he had gone, Treasa sat closer, lowering her voice. 'Breanne, I must ask you this, in all seriousness. Would you consider setting aside Alarr as your husband? You could keep him as your consort instead.'

Her mother's question took her aback. 'Why would you say this?' She had no desire for a different man. She preferred to remain with Alarr, for he was a man of honour and strength.

'For the sake of our tribe,' Treasa continued. 'They are under Cerball's rule, and I know they are suffering. You need a husband who can help you take back our lands at Clonagh.' She glanced at the doorway. 'But we can never do this if you have a foreigner at your side. He is the enemy, Breanne.'

'Alarr protected me when no one else would,' she argued. And she saw no need to reclaim lands she barely remembered.

'I am not saying you must give him up,' Treasa insisted. 'Keep him as your lover, if you will.' She took both of Breanne's hands in hers. 'I do not ask you for a decision now. I ask only that you think about it. But we need an alliance with another Irish tribe if we are to reclaim Clonagh.'

We? Breanne thought. They had gone from being strangers, and now her mother expected her to tear apart her life for a birthright she didn't want? Her initial reaction was to refuse, but something made her hold her tongue.

Treasa seemed relieved by her silence. She squeezed her daughter's palms and added, 'I cannot tell you how glad I am that you are here now. I've not seen you since you were a child. It means everything to see you all grown up.' Her eyes gleamed with tears, though she smiled.

Breanne didn't know how to respond, for her thoughts were in turmoil. It had been years since she'd seen Treasa, and her mother had never attempted to contact her. She had not even sent word that she was alive. It was possible that the leader at Dún Bolg had refused to allow it, or possibly Feann had not wanted contact between them. But it seemed that only now, when she was of use to Treasa, did her mother appear to have feelings towards her. Though Breanne tried to suppress her suspicions, she couldn't bring herself to have any emotions of her own. There was a distance between them, a tangible rift that she could not quite bridge.

But Treasa did not appear to notice her discomfort. 'Let us go and join the others,' her mother suggested. 'The men may have brought back fresh meat from the hunt, and we can help them cook the evening meal.'

She followed Treasa outside and found Alarr standing at the doorway. He sent her a questioning look, and she nodded to reassure him that all was well. His gaze transformed as he watched over her. In his blue eyes, she saw the promise of another night in his arms. The thought only deepened her confusion, for she could not deny that she cared for this man. If she was not careful, she might grow to love him.

But her heart ached at the thought of leaving Éire-ann behind if Alarr wanted her to journey to Maerr. She wasn't ready to leave her home for a man who might one day set her aside. She didn't know what his feelings were towards her, beyond desire. She had indulged in a forbidden liaison, and she knew not what the future held.

Her mother had spoken of the suffering at Clonagh—suffering Breanne held the power to end, if she chose a proper alliance. It was what Feann had wanted, but she couldn't imagine taking another man as her husband or, sharing his bed. She wanted Alarr, despite all else.

As if in answer to her idle dreaming, he returned to her side. He drew his arm around her waist and leaned down to kiss her. Though she knew it meant to show his claim upon her, the heat of his lips rekindled her desires. She welcomed the embrace, bittersweet though it was.

When he pulled back, she fumbled for something to say. On the far end of the ringfort, she saw a group of hunters returning with a deer.

'It's good that they brought back venison,' she said. 'I am hungry tonight.'

'So am I,' he breathed, kissing her again. And there was no doubt what kind of hunger he was feeling.

Breanne answered his embrace, but it was still difficult to push back the uncertain emotions mingled with guilt. There were still so many unanswered questions. And she didn't know if Alarr truly wanted her—or if he was still using her for his own gain.

That night, they made their bed in a small storage chamber amid bags of grain. Alarr closed the door behind them and drew her close. He had held back his desire for most of the day and night, and he craved the touch of her hands on his body.

He had seen her apprehension around Treasa and the worry in her eyes. And although Feann was not here, he knew that the fight between them would happen soon enough. Alarr intended to make the most of whatever days he had left.

'Come here, *søtnos*. I've been waiting to touch you all day.' He kissed her roughly, and she met his lips with her own, winding her arms around his neck. At her sweet response, his desire grew hotter.

'Treasa wanted me to set you aside,' she confessed.

He wasn't surprised to hear it, but he tensed none the less. 'And what do you want, Breanne?'

She stood on tiptoe and drew his face down to hers. 'I don't want to think about her. Or anyone else.'

There was a desperate rush for both of them. He tore at the laces of her gown while she reached to pull his tunic off. He dragged her gown from her shoulders, below her breasts, baring them to his sight. By the gods, he needed her. The urge to mark her, to make her his, was burning through him. He took her nipple into his mouth and was rewarded by her groan.

Her hands gripped his face, and she gasped when he suckled her hard. There was no time for gentleness now. He lifted her up against a stack of grain sacks, and she pulled him close.

'Alarr,' she breathed. Her eyes were heavy with desire, her lips soft. He wanted nothing more than to take her now, but first, he wanted her to feel the bond between them. For whatever time they had left, he wanted her beside him. And he wanted her to know that he was hers, just as she was his.

He reached to touch her inner thigh, moving his hand higher. She arched against him, and at the touch of her opening, he could feel her wetness coating his fingers.

He bent to take her other breast in his mouth, and he caressed her intimately, ensuring that she was ready.

'Do you want me inside you?' he murmured against her skin.

In answer, she lifted her knees to offer herself. He pressed her skirts to her waist and cupped her hips. In one swift thrust, he filled her deeply, and she cried out at the pleasure. There was no resistance, only her silken wetness surrounding him.

She met him as he plunged deep inside, her body shuddering at his invasion. He lost himself in her, revelling as she squeezed him within her depths. 'There will be no other for you but me,' he demanded. At least, not while he lived. The thought of any other man touching her sent a roar of jealousy within him. With her body pressed against the grain, he thrust inside her, over and over.

But it was more than the need to claim her. He wanted her to remember him after he was gone. Breanne had somehow pushed away the all-consuming anger that fuelled his vengeance. In these moments with her, he forgot about the rest of the world. She made him feel something, and she didn't care that he was no longer the warrior he'd been. When she welcomed him into her body, he saw a faith in her eyes that he didn't deserve. And may the gods help him, he wanted to spend every last moment at her side.

Abruptly, she shattered in his arms, her body spasming around his length. The sensation of her pleasured response aroused him harder, and he kissed her to muffle a scream. Her legs tightened around his waist and he continued to grind against her, his own breathing harsh. But he slowed his pace, wanting to know more.

'What did you tell your mother after she asked you to set me aside?' he asked, tracing his fingertips over her bare back. Her hands dug into his skin in response, and she moved her hips beneath him.

'I said nothing.' Her voice was hitched as she tried to make him continue the lovemaking.

Her answer was a blow to his mood, for he'd wanted her to refuse. Yet, he had no right to demand that of her. She was free to make her own choices, even if she did not choose him.

With reluctance, he withdrew from her body and picked up the fallen furs they had brought with them. He arranged them on the ground and drew her to lie down beside him. He covered her with one fur, and drew her to her side, her backside pressed against him. His body was still rigid, but he held himself back.

Breanne remained still, sensing his anger. 'Treasa said that I owed it to our people to marry a man who could overthrow Cerball's rule. And she implied that I should not put my own personal desires above the needs of our family.'

The woman's proposition wasn't unexpected. Breanne was of noble birth. Her choice to stay with him was a decision born from her desire to save her father's life. She was never meant to be bound to a man like him.

He waited for her to say that she would not consider her mother's assertion, but her silence made him uneasy.

Breanne turned to face him, and her expression was troubled. 'She told me to keep you as my consort, and not to give her a decision about the marriage yet.'

Which meant that she *had* considered it. A tension rose up within him, that she would turn against him.

'No. I will not remain your consort on the side,' he said darkly. He would never allow another man to come between them.

'Isn't that what I am to you?' she countered. 'Your consort? Or am I a concubine?' To emphasise her words, she rolled to her back, pulling him on top of her. And he felt the need to possess her, to prove that she was more.

'You are mine,' he answered, leaning down to kiss her throat. He drew her so close, their bodies were skin to skin. He didn't want to put a name to their relationship, for in his eyes, they belonged to each other.

And yet, he knew that Breanne had not given up her innocence because she cared. It had been a negotiation to save Feann. A vain part of him had wanted to believe that she had enjoyed sharing his bed, for she had given herself willingly.

Breanne cupped his cheek with one hand and said, 'I feel as if I'm being blown around in a storm. Everyone wants to make decisions for my life. And I don't know what the answers are.'

He rested his hand upon her bare hip, and gooseflesh rose upon her skin beneath his touch. 'You already made your choice, *søtnos*. From the moment you surrendered yourself, I swore I would not let you go. You will never share another man's bed. Not while I live.'

His body was still aroused, and he needed her to know that she belonged to him. He wanted to claim her, to drive away all thoughts of anyone else.

'I don't want another man,' she whispered. 'But I

feel as if my life isn't my own any more. I feel as if the chains are still there, though I cannot see them.'

He drew his hand over her bare breast, and she inhaled as the nipple grew erect. 'In what way?'

'I thought I was Feann's foster daughter with no living family. Now I find out that my mother is alive, but she's in exile. And she wants me to take back a homeland I don't even know.' She covered his hand with hers, straining at his touch.

Though he understood her dilemma, he wanted her to recognise that she did have control of her choices. 'You have the power to say no.'

She turned to meet his gaze. 'A woman holds no power at all. She is at the mercy of others.'

Alarr thought of his mother Hilda and his aunt Kolga, both of whom held a great deal of power in Maerr. 'The women of my tribe are equal to men. If anyone tried to tell my mother Hilda that she was at the mercy of others, she would strike them down.' A faint smile caught his mouth at the thought. Then he turned serious. 'You can make whatever choices you want, Breanne. So long as you stay with me.'

Alarr bent down and suckled her breast, moving his hand lower. She inhaled sharply, as he was learning just how to touch her, to draw out her pleasure.

'I want to stay with you,' she whispered.

He guided his shaft to her damp opening. Although she tried to welcome him inside once again, he held back, resting his body weight on his arms. 'Your life. Your body. Your very soul is mine, Breanne.'

He thrust deep inside her, marking her as his own. She gave a cry and gripped his hair, embracing him. As he took her, she rose to meet his hips with her own.

'If that is true,' she whispered, her face revealing her desire, 'then you belong to me as well. Your life.' She squeezed his length within her depths, and he hissed at the dark pleasure that filled him.

'Your body.' She kissed him hard, lifting her mouth to his. He returned the kiss, claiming her lips, welcoming the soft intrusion of her tongue.

'Your soul.' She moved him until he was on his back, buried deep inside her. Breanne rose up on her knees, riding him. He let her take her pleasure, watching her face tighten with rising desire. Her breathing rhythm shifted, and he sat up, lifting her hips and plunging inside hard. This was no longer simple lovemaking. Instead, it was a battle for control—and he gave it to her.

She met him, thrust for thrust, until her face transformed with raw desire, and she shattered around him. Alarr could feel the pulse of her release, but he would not stop. The sight of her coming apart was his own undoing. He penetrated her, over and over, until he erupted deep inside and his own shout joined hers. It was brutal, passionate, and his heart would not stop racing.

He remained inside her, bringing her gently to the side. 'Did I hurt you, *søtnos*?' He had been so caught up in the moment, he had lost control.

'No,' she breathed, smiling at him. 'I liked it.'

He kissed her, sliding his hands over her body. He could not stop touching her, marvelling that this woman was his. But then came the clouded reality that she would only be his until he faced Feann. He knew not if they would have any life together afterwards, especially if he kept his vow not to kill Feann.

He had never promised not to seek revenge—only to grant the king his life. But a gnawing suspicion took root that he could still die in battle. His time with Breanne might only be brief, though he would savour every moment.

It was sobering to think of losing this woman, and he pushed away the thought. Or worse, the idea of betraying her.

Chapter Eight

'Have you thought about what I said?' Treasa asked. Her mother had an expectant look upon her face, along with a slight smile. Undoubtedly, she believed Breanne would follow her wishes and wed a different man.

'I have,' Breanne answered. 'And I have decided to remain with Alarr.' After the night she'd spent in his arms, she believed that he would let her make her own choices. But more than that, she believed that he cared about her. This morn, they had lain in each other's arms, and he could not stop himself from touching her. The light caresses were an unconscious gesture, and she warmed to the affection. She didn't want to be with another man—not now.

Her mother sighed. 'I was hoping you would understand, Breanne. This is about more than your personal needs. It's about our home and our people.'

Treasa's unspoken message was: *You're being selfish.*

But Breanne refused to be manipulated by guilt. 'You cannot expect me to sacrifice myself for a home I do not remember and people I have never seen.'

'It is your duty,' Treasa said. 'You are all we have, Breanne. It must fall upon your shoulders.'

Frustration and irritation brimmed inside her at the woman's expectation. 'That isn't true. Why don't *you* marry an ally and restore our lands?'

'I am too old, and no man would have me.' Treasa's voice grew weary. 'I am sorry if I have asked too much of you. I had hoped that you would agree, knowing that you could keep Alarr with you.'

'No. I would never use him in that way.' She understood his pride, and Alarr would not allow her to go from another man's bed back into his. Nor would she consider such a thing. She had honour and loyalty.

Treasa's gaze narrowed. 'Was it Alarr's intent to take command of Clonagh? Is that why he wed you?'

He never wed me, she thought to herself, but sidestepped the question instead. 'Of course not. Why would you think that?' It was as if her mother believed Alarr intended to conquer their lands. 'He wanted to protect me. And he has his own lands in Maerr.'

She spoke with confidence, but the truth was, she knew little about Alarr's lands or even his family. They had hardly spoken about his life back in his homeland.

Treasa drew her hands together and sat down. 'I do not know your *Lochlannach* well enough to understand his intentions. But you are my only child, Breanne. I love you, and I want to ensure that you have a home. I cannot let Clonagh remain part of Cerball's kingdom.'

Though her mother's words sounded sympathetic, something did not ring true. She understood her mother feeling responsible for the fate of her people, but Breanne was unwilling to become Treasa's pawn. 'Then ask Feann to help you take it back.' She squared her shoulders and faced Treasa. 'Clonagh is not mine.' She had no memory of their lands, and Killcobar was the only home she'd known. She felt no obligation towards Treasa.

Her mother took a deep breath. 'I am sorry, Breanne. I suppose I should not have put so many of my hopes on you. But... I think you should see Clonagh before you make your decision. It has been a long time since you've been there. I could make arrangements for your travel.'

'No, thank you,' she said. She saw no reason to create ties with her past. Clonagh had never been her home, and she doubted if it ever would be. The true question was where would she live now? Alarr had sworn that he would stay by her side; yet, they had never spoken about what they would do next. She knew he had planned to remain here for a short time and then go back to Killcobar to confront Feann. But after that? She didn't know. Did he want to return to Maerr, after Feann paid the *corp-dire* for his father's death? She decided to ask him when they were alone.

To her mother, she said, 'I hope you find a way to win back Clonagh.'

'So do I,' Treasa answered.

There was a bitter tone to her voice, but Breanne refused to feel guilty about it. She would not sacrifice her life for strangers. She'd made her choice, and it was enough. She excused herself and walked outside.

She found Alarr among the men who had returned from fishing that morn. They had baskets filled with fish, and when he saw her, he set his own basket down.

'You look pale,' he said. 'Are you well?'

'I'm just restless,' she said. 'Will you walk with me a moment?'

He did, and she told him of her conversation with Treasa. 'I refused to submit to my mother's wishes,' she admitted. 'I see no reason to give myself up for land I've never seen and people I do not know.'

Alarr took her hand in his, leading her back to the privacy of their shelter. Inside, it was dark, with only a few rays of sunlight piercing through the crevices in the wood. 'I would not have let you go to another man, Breanne. You know this.'

He leaned down to kiss her, and she felt the familiar ache of longing. When had this happened? The thought of being parted from this man was a physical pain, and it confused her. She had given herself as part of a bargain, but with each moment she spent at his side, she wanted more.

'What will we do now?' she asked.

He cupped her cheek, tilting it up to meet her gaze. 'We have unfinished business with Feann.'

'You swore an oath,' she reminded him.

'I swore not to kill him. That does not mean he will not face justice.'

'You will do nothing to endanger yourself,' she insisted. 'We must consult the *brehons*. They will pass judgement, and Feann will accept their wisdom.'

'Will he?' He leaned down to kiss her throat, and she threaded her hands in his hair. 'You seem convinced that all will go according to your plans.'

'It will,' she answered. She saw no choice but to believe it. She knew Feann would be angry with her for choosing Alarr, but she didn't care. Her *Lochlannach* had captured more than her body—he had stolen her heart.

He kissed her deeply, his hands moving over her.

He laid her back against one of the large piles of grain sacks, so that he would not have to lean down. She welcomed the familiar rush of need and the rise of desire. Somehow, he knew exactly how to touch her until she craved his lovemaking.

'I will have my answers from Feann, Breanne.'

'You will.' She trembled as he caressed her, and whispered, 'Then we will go back to your lands in Maerr.'

Though she was afraid of leaving Éireann, she realised that if she stayed, she would be pressured into obeying the commands of Feann or Treasa. Here, she had hardly any freedom. The idea of starting over was a welcome thought, to travel with Alarr to a place where no one would use her for their own gain. Her life would be her own again. And while she was afraid of the unknown, she knew she would be happier with him than if she were left behind.

He kept his eyes locked upon her. 'You would give up your home for me?'

She lifted her hips to meet him, cupping his face between her hands. 'I will go wherever you go.' Her emotions grew heavy as he kissed her again, his tongue tangled with hers. She was starting to love this man. And though it made her vulnerable, she realised that she wanted a home with him and children.

Alarr murmured against her mouth, 'We will travel back to Killcobar in a few more days. Then we will take our ship back from Styr and return to Maerr.'

A tremor caught her as he continued to stroke her with his fingers. She came apart, her breathing a sharp moan as her body embraced him. Liquid desire pulsed in a fierce eruption that made her shake, crying out as the pleasure climbed higher. His tenderness was her undoing, and she could hardly breathe from the sudden release.

'You've bewitched me,' he admitted, a lazy smile coming over his mouth. 'I cannot stop touching you.'

'I don't want you to stop,' she whispered, pulling his mouth to hers and kissing him deeply. He invaded her mouth, his tongue tangling with hers until she felt the delicious echo in her womb.

Alarr remained within her for a few more moments before he said, 'While I would love to stay here with you, we need to rejoin the others.'

'At least until tonight,' she promised, stroking back his hair. She intended to give him the same pleasure he had given to her, until he could no longer bear it.

When they emerged from the shelter, she saw her mother staring at them. The look in Treasa's eyes held regret, as if her plans had shattered apart. And though Breanne understood her mother's desires, it was not her task to fulfil them. She had made the decision to leave her old life behind and begin anew.

And no one would stand in her way.

Alarr rode back towards Killcobar with Breanne and the six escorts sent by Iasan, the chief of Dún Bolg. Along the way, he thought of the older woman's discontent and her last words to him. 'Breanne is giving up her birthright and her kingdom for you. What kind of a life will she have in Maerr? Will she be queen there, as she would have been in Clonagh?'

'I will provide everything she needs,' he'd said. 'It will be enough.' But in truth, he didn't know if he could keep that vow. After he and his brothers had been declared outlaws and sent away, he knew not if he had a home, much less if he would survive the fight with Feann. If he died in battle, Breanne would be forced to remain with her foster father. It bothered him, for she didn't deserve a life where Feann would tell her who to marry. She was fighting for her freedom, and she deserved to choose her own path.

Were it possible, and if his life were different, he might have asked Breanne to marry him. The thought of waking beside her and watching her grow round with an unborn child was a welcome vision.

You cannot wed her, a voice inside him warned. *You don't deserve happiness with her.*

As one of the survivors of the massacre, he owed it to Gilla and Sigurd to seek vengeance. He could not set aside the past or even dream of a future until he had settled that promise.

Although he had decided to keep his vow to Breanne, he fully intended to wound Feann—even at the risk to his own life. He knew that the moment he struck down the king, the soldiers would attack. While they would not harm Breanne, Alarr knew better than to believe he could escape unscathed. And if Rurik was still there, his brother would face the same threat. More likely, his brother would fight at his side and die at the hands of their enemy.

He needed to send Rurik away. His brother would not stand by and let him face the battle alone. But Alarr didn't want him to die because of the choices he'd made. Somehow, he had to convince Rurik to go, in order to protect him.

They would reach Killcobar in the early evening. Breanne had guided them there throughout the morning and afternoon, and as they neared the fortress, he saw the sudden worry in her eyes.

'It's going to be all right,' she said quietly. 'I will speak to my father and see what can be done. But keep your face hidden for now.'

Although he knew she wanted to try, he knew better than to believe that this confrontation would result in peace between himself and Feann. The Irish king would never admit to wrongdoing, and Alarr fully intended to seek restitution. He raised his hood in the hopes that no one would recognise him.

'Wait here,' she said, dismounting from her horse. She walked to the gates and spoke with the guards for a few moments. Then she returned and took the reins of her mount. 'I told them that you are my escorts. Stay behind me when we go inside.'

The guards held their spears as Breanne led the way, allowing them to enter the fortress. She guided them towards the stables, and Alarr dismounted, ordering Iasan's escorts to take the horses and remain apart from them. Breanne took his hand in hers, and said, 'I could meet with Feann alone first, if you wish.'

'No.' He wanted her at his side at all times. 'We remain together.' Alarr glanced around and asked, 'Do you think he's here?'

'I don't know.' She continued walking towards the largest dwelling. It was rectangular in structure, and the roof was made of thatch. Breanne pushed the door open and brought him inside. Several stone oil lamps were set out, providing a dim light. On the far end, he saw a dais with wooden chairs, but no one was seated in them.

'Alarr!' came a man's voice.

He turned and saw his brother Rurik. He removed his hood and embraced his brother. 'Are you well?'

Rurik nodded. 'Come and join me. I have much to tell you.'

'Where is Feann?' he asked.

'He has not yet returned, but he sent word that he will be back within a few days.'

'So, you've not seen him yet.'

His brother shook his head. 'But I learned a great deal about my mother from the men here.' He beckoned for Alarr and Breanne to sit at a low table. They did, and Rurik poured them cups of mead. 'She was Feann's sister.'

His brother's revelation was not entirely a surprise. Saorla had always carried herself like a noblewoman. Alarr barely remembered her, since she had died years ago, but he knew she'd been angry with Sigurd.

'Sigurd led her to believe that they would be married. She went away with him when she learned she was with child, and he brought her to Maerr. Then she discovered that he already had a wife.'

Alarr eyed his brother and said, 'So you and Danr are Feann's nephews.'

'We are. Though I doubt if it means anything to him.' Rurik took a long drink of mead. 'Feann travelled to Maerr after he learned of Saorla's death. He intended to avenge her by killing Sigurd.'

'And they did,' Alarr said.

But Rurik surprised him by saying, 'No. Sigurd was already dead before Feann could reach the longhouse. There were other enemies there.' His blue eyes were serious when he said, 'Feann was furious that he was unable to kill him. The men told me of his plans, but he was unable to achieve them.'

'Who else was there?'

Rurik shrugged. 'They didn't know the men. But one was from Glannoventa in Northumbria. They heard his men call him Wilfrid.'

'Why would Feann's men tell you anything?' He wouldn't trust them at all. They were strangers with no reason to confess the truth.

'I never told them who I was,' Rurik said. 'Remember, I speak the Irish tongue better than you. I asked questions, but I gave them no information about me.'

'Will you tell Feann the truth about your mother?' Alarr questioned whether it was wise to reveal it, since the king might not believe him.

His brother inclined his head. 'If the moment is right.' He paused a moment and said, 'Alarr, we will have our answers. But Feann was not the cause of his death.'

'He intended to kill Sigurd.'

'But he didn't. And neither did his men. We need to find out who our other enemies were. Feann may be able to help us with more information.'

A soft touch on his arm caught his attention, and Alarr turned back to Breanne. She ventured, 'Let me talk with my foster father after he returns. He may trust me more than both of you.'

Rurik's gaze fixed upon her and then he turned back to Alarr. From the knowing look in his eyes, it was clear that he was aware of their connection. 'What happened after I left?'

Alarr knew exactly what his brother was asking, but he feigned ignorance. 'We found Breanne's mother. She was exiled after her husband turned traitor. She wanted Breanne to reclaim their lands at Clonagh by wedding a man loyal to King Cerball.'

His brother's eyebrows raised, and he straightened. 'And what does Breanne think of that?' He turned to hear her answer.

She squared her shoulders. 'I care not what Treasa or Feann think I should do. This is my life, and I intend to remain with Alarr.'

'That wasn't what you said a few days ago when your father's men arrived to take you home.' Rurik refilled their cups, and Alarr distracted himself by drinking.

'Leave her alone, Rurik.' He sent his brother a hard look, warning him not to question her further. For a long moment, they stared at one another. He knew that Rurik was only trying to protect him, but he wanted his brother to back down.

'It's all right,' Breanne intervened. 'He can ask me his questions. I will answer.'

At that, Rurik's expression grew tense. 'What agreement did you make with my brother?'

'We made a bargain between us,' Breanne answered. 'He promised not to kill Feann.' She kept her tone even, but Rurik was not fooled by it.

'And what did you receive in return?'

Alarr did not want to dishonour Breanne by implying that she had traded herself. Instead, he said, 'She swore that she would seek justice on our behalf.'

His brother did not appear convinced. He took a step closer and his gaze hardened. 'If you betray my brother to Feann, you will answer to me.'

Before he could say a word, Breanne released his hand and stepped forward. 'I will never betray Alarr.

After everything I faced, he is the only man who ever fought for me.' The iron in her voice was unyielding, and her fierce tone made his brother smile.

'Good.'

Alarr moved to her side, resting his hand upon her waist. 'Breanne will return to Maerr with us, after this is all over.'

Rurik hesitated and said, 'I do not think Feann will allow her to go. It would be safer if you do not tell him your plans.'

'You may be right,' she agreed. 'While I don't think he will seek to harm Alarr, we should all be careful.' To Rurik, she asked, 'Who do the clansmen believe you are?'

'I told them I was from the Ó Callahan clan.'

At that, she smiled. 'They think you are one of my kinsmen?'

Rurik shrugged. 'It seemed like a good idea at the time.'

Breanne thought a moment and then said, 'Do you think anyone will recognise you, Alarr?'

He wasn't certain. 'I don't think so, since it was over a year ago. But it is likely that the king might remember me.' As for himself, he could never forget the man who had caused his injuries. His legs would never be the same again because of it.

Breanne eyed them both and then said, 'I do not wish to lie to Feann. But if he does not remember you, that might be for the best. I could tell him that Alarr rescued me and brought me home again.'

Alarr exchanged a look with his brother but said nothing to ruin her dreams. Feann would never believe such a thing. But he only squeezed her hand and silently warned his brother not to speak. 'We will make that decision when the time comes.'

Breanne immersed herself in the familiar tasks of Killcobar. The activity filled her days, but she was aware that her people were wary of her friendliness with Alarr and Rurik. She and Alarr had decided not to avoid raising suspicions until Feann returned, and for the past week, she had not shared his bed. The strain was growing between them, and she knew he craved her body as much as she longed for him.

A few days ago, she had tried to send her mother's escorts back to Dún Bolg, but all had refused. She couldn't understand why. There was no need for them now, but each time she asked, they declined. She was beginning to believe that the men were spying on her with the intent of bringing back news to Treasa.

This morning, she had gone to meet with the captain of the guards. Darin had informed her about Feann's imminent return and the talk of invasion.

'Our men train each day,' he said. 'They are prepared for any battle or raid.'

'Good,' she said. She believed him from what she had seen thus far. And yet, another question abraded her mind. 'Has there been a recent threat that called Feann away? I thought he intended to return to Killcobar sooner than this.'

'There have been many threats,' Darin answered. 'Not only from other kings, but also from our alliances.'

A sense of foreboding caught her, and she wondered if he meant a threat from Oisin. More and more, she wondered if it had been a mistake to leave him alive. She tried to push back her apprehensions, and she thanked him quietly.

The captain returned to the other soldiers who were training outside. Among them were Alarr and Rurik, though they remained apart from the others. They sparred against one another, using dulled swords. Both men had stripped away their tunics, bared from the waist up. Though it was not a warm summer day, their bodies gleamed with sweat from exertion. Breanne stopped to watch, and she was not alone. Several women found reasons to stop their tasks and observe the sword fight.

Alarr swung his weapon hard, and Rurik blocked it with his shield. Over and over, he struck, and his brother met each blow. Then Rurik took the lead and wielded his weapon against his older brother. Their movements were smooth, like a dance, and their expertise was evident. But after a while longer, she saw Alarr's movement beginning to change. No longer was it an easy deflection, but instead, she saw the slight limp in his step. His brother seized the advantage and struck harder, forcing Alarr to retreat. His limp grew more pronounced, and Rurik continued to wield punishing blows against him.

Abruptly, Alarr stumbled and dropped to the ground. Rurik moved in for the kill, but before he could do anything, his brother tripped him and sent him sprawling. A moment later, he stood over Rurik with his sword against his brother's throat.

With a wry grin, he offered his arm and pulled Rurik to stand, while some of the men applauded. Some exchanged coins, revealing that they had gambled on the fight. Alarr waited until the others returned to their sparring, before he walked towards her. Though he tried to disguise it, she could still see his limp.

His gaze was heated, and Breanne stood her ground, watching him. Other women eyed him with interest, but he strode past them until he reached her side. Without a word, he took her hand in his and led her away. She knew his leg was bothering him, but he continued walking towards the stables.

'Are we going somewhere?' she asked, but he didn't answer.

The moment they were inside the stable, he pressed her up against a horse stall and kissed her hard. She wound her arms around his neck, answering his kiss with her own. His tongue threaded with hers, and she felt the answering pull deep inside her.

'I've been needing to touch you,' he said. 'This has gone on long enough.'

'I agree,' she said. His mouth moved to her throat, and she touched his bare chest, tracing the ridged muscles.

'I want you,' he growled. 'Here and now.'

'Anyone could see us,' she whispered. 'It's not safe.' But the idea of being taken like this was arousing in a way she hadn't expected. Alarr was already reaching beneath her skirts when she felt a warm tongue against her ear. She started laughing when she realised that the horse was peering over the stall, licking the salt from her skin.

'Ugh.' She started to pull away, and the horse whinnied, shaking its head.

Alarr was grinning, and he drew her away from the stall. 'This wasn't my intention, *søtnos*. It was an impulse.'

She stood on tiptoe to kiss him again. 'Impulse or not, I promise you this night you may have me in any way you wish. Wait for me in your tent, and I will come to you.'

He took her lips, gripping her hips so she could feel his rigid staff. Then he lifted her up, and she drew her legs around his waist. 'Or I could have you now.'

'I'd rather have hours with you,' she murmured. 'I don't want to stop. And the others will wonder where I've gone.'

He cupped her breast, toying with her erect nipple. 'Swear it, Breanne.'

'I will find a way. I swear it.' She ground herself against him, and he inhaled sharply at the contact. He held her there a moment, until at last, he let her down. She drew her hands over his chest, loving the feeling of his body beneath her palms.

No sooner had they left the stable, when there was a commotion from the gates. Breanne released his hand when she saw the horses approaching. Behind the first two riders, she spied Feann. His gaze narrowed when he saw her, but it was not the look of a man who was happy to have her home. There was tension there, and it sharpened when he stared at them. Alarr rested his palm upon her spine in a possessive manner, raising his chin in defiance.

Although she ought to be overjoyed at the sight of Feann, her heartbeat began to quicken. For she suspected that he would not approve of them being together. It was more likely that he would attempt to sever their relationship entirely.

Feann dismounted and crossed past the others to

stand before her. His face was a hard mask asserting his dominance.

'You've returned, I see. And brought enemies among us.'

Chapter Nine

Alarr met Feann's gaze, and there was no doubt that the man remembered him. Fury brewed in the king's eyes, especially when he saw their joined hands. His own anger was barely in check, for the very sight of his enemy evoked the memory of the swordfight. He recalled Feann's fury when the blade sliced through skin and muscle, nearly ending Alarr's ability to walk. The past rose up between them, and were it not for his promise to Breanne, he would have claimed his vengeance this very moment. The man's life meant nothing to him.

'Alarr and Rurik are not our enemies,' Breanne said. 'And this isn't a conversation I wish to have outside. Come and join us for food and drink. We will talk about what has happened.'

'I will speak with *you*, Breanne,' Feann said. 'But not them.'

'Come inside,' Breanne repeated. 'We will dine alone, the four of us.' She did not wait for her father's agreement, but instead led the way, holding Alarr's hand in hers while Rurik trailed them.

The interior of her father's home was warm from the

heated stones set all around the room. Breanne gave orders for food and busied herself with preparations. Alarr stood with Rurik, noting the number of guards who joined them. The king was not a fool, and he spaced out his guards in a circle all around the room.

Feann took his place at table, in the centre of the dais. He motioned for Breanne to come and sit beside him, but she hesitated. With a look towards Alarr, she picked up another stool and brought it with her, nodding for Rurik to do the same.

It took an effort to hide his smile. Breanne was eliminating any chance of Feann presiding over them. After she set down the stool, she stood before her foster father, but he noticed that she did not embrace the man. 'Did you have a good journey?'

Feann only grunted and sat. Breanne joined him, and Alarr chose the seat on her opposite side. Rurik also sat, but he kept a wise distance from the king.

'Why have you brought them here, Breanne?'

Alarr felt her fingers reaching beneath the table for his hand, as if she wanted the security. He squeezed her palm in reassurance.

She straightened, raising her chin. 'A better question might be, why didn't you send men to find me when I was taken away into slavery? Alarr saved me and brought me home. And yet, you treat him like an enemy.'

'His father *was* my enemy,' Feann said. 'After what Sigurd did to my sister, Saorla, he deserved to die. Why should Sigurd's sons be any different?' His eyes blazed with fury, as if he already suspected the intimacy between them.

'Because they did nothing to you,' Breanne argued.

'And yet, your men attacked on Alarr's wedding day. What you did was wrong.'

'You have no right to judge my actions, Breanne. What I did was justice.'

'Many innocents died that day,' Alarr said. He could not hide the rage in his voice. 'Your men killed dozens of my kinsmen. And my bride.'

'So you came here to kill me, is that it?' Feann's rigid stare held no empathy. 'You used Breanne for your own purpose.'

'At first, that was my intent,' he admitted. 'But she bargained for your life.'

There was a faint surprise in the man's face, as if he'd not expected Alarr to confess the truth. 'Is that supposed to make me feel better about dining with you?'

'We need to talk about what should be done,' Breanne started to say, but Feann cut her off.

'Do you really think I would believe any words spoken by a *Lochlannach*?' He shook his head in disgust. 'My men will escort you out. I give you the gift of your lives, for Breanne's sake. Go now, before I order my men to cut you down.'

'No.' Breanne stood, her face pale. 'Alarr will remain at my side.'

At her declaration, Feann's face grew thunderous. 'Why would you dare such a thing, Breanne?'

Alarr stood beside her, still holding her hand. He didn't trust the man's rage, and he intended to guard Breanne from all harm.

'Because Alarr took care of me when I needed help. He rescued me from the slave market, and he protected me from Oisin.' Her voice was tremulous, but she slid her arm around his waist to emphasise her words. Alarr

pulled her close, watching as Feann's mood darkened.
Against his body, he could feel the tremor of her fear.

'I will not let you remain with a *Lochlannach*,' the
king insisted. 'Especially one who wants me dead.'

She faced him boldly, and admitted, 'I would rather
have a man willing to fight for me than one who treats
me as if I am worth nothing at all.'

Feann's face turned stony. 'I knew nothing of your
captivity until recently. And by then, my men had found
you.' There was no sympathy in his tone, and Alarr
sensed that the man was holding something back. There
were secrets the king was keeping, though he could not
guess what they were.

'I want you to leave Killcobar,' Feann commanded
Alarr. 'Take your brother with you, and do not return.
Breanne, you will remain here.'

Her face turned scarlet with her own anger, and she
levelled a stare at Feann. 'I brought these men here because Alarr deserves justice for the murder of his bride
and his father. I told him that the *brehons* would treat
them fairly. But I never imagined you would behave
in this way. I believed that you were a man of honour.'

'I owe nothing to these men,' Feann countered.
'They are lucky I didn't kill them that day.'

Before Breanne could respond, Rurik stepped forward. 'There is more you should know about your sister, Feann. I believe you will want to hear my tale.' He
paused a moment, then added, 'Or perhaps I should
call you Uncle.'

At that, Feann froze. He stared hard at Rurik, but
his emotions were unreadable. It was a risky move,
but Alarr understood why his brother had spoken. The

question was whether the king would recognise Rurik as his nephew.

'Saorla was my mother,' Rurik continued. 'She gave birth to my twin brother Danr and me after she reached Maerr.'

'You have no proof of that,' Feann started to say. 'Why would I believe this?'

'She told me stories about you,' Rurik continued. 'Though she refused to speak any names from her past, she told me that the two of you were close. And that you gave her a blade when she was young.' He unsheathed the knife and held it out hilt-first.

At that, Feann's expression transformed. He took the blade and examined it, running his thumb along the curved antler handle. He glanced back at Rurik for a long moment, his gaze passing over him. There was an unreadable emotion in his eyes, a flare of grief mingled with distrust.

Rurik asked, 'Why did you come to Maerr to attack my father? It was twenty years since Saorla left. If you wanted to kill our father, why wait that long?'

'I did not know that Sigurd had set her aside,' Feann said. 'I believed Saorla made the choice for her own happiness, to wed a man she loved.' He shook his head in disgust. 'But I was wrong to let her go with him. Once I learned the truth, I sailed across the sea to kill Sigurd for what he did to my sister.'

It made Alarr wonder who had informed Feann about his sister and why. Saorla had died years ago, and no one had known that she was a king's daughter, save Sigurd. After all these years, why would anyone bother to send word across the sea to Éireann? His first thoughts went to his mother. He wouldn't put it past Hilda to do such a thing. Or perhaps his aunt Kolga.

'Saorla sailed to Maerr of her own free will,' Rurik reminded him. 'When she learned she was with child, she remained there.'

'Likely she was ashamed,' Feann answered. 'She fought everyone for the right to abandon her responsibilities and run away with him. But I don't understand why she didn't come home after he set her aside.'

'I heard them fighting, years ago,' Rurik answered. 'Sigurd would not let her go unless she left my brother and me behind. She refused.' He turned sombre at the revelation, as if he blamed his father for imprisoning her.

Feann's expression tightened with unspoken emotion. 'Our father was furious with her for leaving her responsibilities and our kingdom. But Sigurd was only using her, wasn't he?' While he spoke, he kept his eyes fixed upon Alarr. There was no doubt of the hidden meaning in his words.

'Sigurd was already married,' Rurik answered. 'And while his actions lacked honour, he did give Saorla a home of her own, and he provided for Danr and me.'

'My sister deserved better than to be treated like a whore,' Feann shot back.

'Then why did you not come earlier to see her for yourself?' Rurik asked. 'If you cared about her welfare so much, why did you never visit while she was alive?'

'Because we argued the day she left. Saorla swore she would never speak to me again. I was angry with her for choosing a *Lochlannach* instead of obeying our father. I told her she was welcome to return, but I would never set foot in Maerr.'

Breanne took a steadying breath before she turned to look at him. 'I think it would be best if I spoke with my foster father alone now. Will you leave us for a moment?'

Alarr touched her face, understanding that she wanted a private conversation with Feann. She was more likely to gain what she wanted if he allowed it. 'So long as you are safe.' He beckoned for Rurik to join him. Then he leaned down to kiss her, knowing it would irritate the king. She embraced him, and then he stepped back. 'We will await you near the stables.'

Breanne waited until they were gone, and the soldiers followed. Her foster father paced across the dais without speaking, but she could read his frustration in every step. Her mood matched his own, but she waited for him to speak.

'You cannot give yourself to a *Lochlannach* enemy.' He faced her, his expression forged in anger. 'He cannot be trusted any more than Sigurd could. He will use you and set you aside.'

She took a breath and chose her words carefully. 'I trust him.' Her answer was a silent defiance, and she stood her ground.

He looked as if he wanted to fly into a rage, but he gathered his control and regarded her. 'What is it you want, Breanne?'

'I want justice for what was done to Alarr and his family. You must pay the *corp-dire* for your vengeance. You killed his *bride*,' she shot back. 'An innocent woman died at the hands of your men, as well as his father.'

A thin smile stretched across his face. 'But I did not

have the honour of killing Sigurd. When I reached the longhouse, he was already slain.'

'You caused Alarr's injuries,' she continued. 'It took him over a year before he could walk again.'

'I could have taken his life,' Feann answered. 'Instead I allowed him to live. Which was a mistake, now that I look back on it.' Her foster father steepled his hands. 'Had I cut him down, you would not believe yourself bound to him.'

Breanne fell silent, wondering what to say to him now. He would not listen to reason, and he was behaving like an overprotective father.

But he had lied to her, letting her believe her mother was dead. Treasa was her only living blood relative, and he had kept that knowledge from her, all these years. She wanted to confront him over it, but something held her back. Right now, she didn't trust him, and she decided it was better not to reveal that she had met with her mother.

Feann stood, his face a mask of stiff rage. 'Breanne, let him go. You can never wed a *Lochlannach*.'

'Why not? Because then I cannot wed a man of your choosing?' A look of guilt flashed in his eyes at her accusation, and she pressed again.

'Or is it because your only claim to Clonagh is through me?' she ventured. Perhaps Feann wanted to choose a weak man as her husband, one whom he could control. She was beginning to wonder if greed had played a role in his secrets. If so, he would not want a *Lochlannach* on the throne beside her.

'Clonagh is under King Cerball's rule,' Feann said. 'The lands became his by right of conquest, after your parents' treason. I have only governed them on his behalf.'

'Treason according to whom?' she demanded. 'It sounds as if King Cerball accused them of treason in order to gain possession of my father's kingdom.'

Feann sighed and sat down once again. 'You're wrong, Breanne. Cerball did not seize the land with the intend of keeping it. I was asked to protect Clonagh until you came of age. You were to marry a man loyal to Cerball. But now, your actions have changed that. What man will want to claim you now?'

She was beginning to realise the far-reaching implications of staying with Alarr. Both Feann and Treasa wanted to use her for their own gains.

'You must leave him,' her foster father said. 'If you do, it is possible that you may regain all that was lost.'

'And what of Alarr? He will never regain all that he lost.' Her voice cracked, revealing her own frustration. 'But that doesn't matter to you, does it?'

'No.' Feann drew closer to her, his eyes hardened into stone. 'His fate means nothing to me.'

Breanne was beginning to realise the depths of his hatred. Once, she had believed that Feann had held affection for her, that he had thought of her as his true daughter. She had done everything to please him, trying to shape herself into the person he wanted. But now, she could no longer deny the truth.

'I don't matter to you either, do I?' It broke her heart to realise that all these years, he had never thought much of her. He truly didn't care that she had been sold into slavery. Her only use to him was for a marriage alliance.

For a moment, his steel gaze seemed to relent, but he said only, 'Think of your duty, Breanne.'

'I have,' she whispered. And duty be damned. She would no longer allow her life to be twisted as everyone else wanted. This time, she would make her own decisions and be herself, not the woman others wanted her to be. 'I only wish I had seen you for what you are sooner.'

With that, she walked away, tears filling up in her eyes. She crossed past familiar faces, people she had once believed were her friends. But they, too, were controlled by Feann. A true friend would have greeted her, welcomed her home. And although she had worked among them during the past few days, she realised that there would always be a distance between them. She was not a MacPherson and never would be.

When she reached Alarr, he seemed to sense what she wanted—an escape before she released the hold on her emotions. Without asking he led her mount forward and helped her atop the saddle.

'Where are we going?' Rurik asked.

'*You* are staying here,' Alarr answered. 'I am taking Breanne away so we can speak alone. We will return later.'

She was grateful, for he seemed to understand that her feelings were hanging by a single thread. The tears and anger were so tightly intertwined, she didn't know if she wanted to weep or rage at the world.

'If you have need of protection,' one of the guards offered, 'we can join you.'

'No.' Alarr swung up behind her and said, 'I can defend Breanne on my own. We won't go far.'

With that, he nudged the animal forward and outside

the gates. She took comfort from his arms around her and let the tears fall freely. No one would see them, and no one would judge her for them. But it hurt so deeply to recognise that Feann had never loved her as a daughter.

Alarr took the horse into a hard gallop, and the wind caused her hair to stream behind her. They rode for several minutes, until he found a small outcropping of limestone. Then he slowed the mare's pace to a stop and dismounted, helping her down.

Breanne dried her tears, grateful to be away from Feann and the others. Her heart ached with the sadness of loss. And through it all, Alarr had been steadfast.

'You kept your word,' she said at last. 'Though I know you wanted to kill him.'

His face tensed. 'I did.' Then he paused and added, 'I still do.'

Breanne couldn't stop herself from pacing from one stone to another. Restlessness pulsed in her veins. She wanted to rage at Feann and at herself for believing that he had ever cared about her. To his credit, Alarr said nothing but let her be.

At last, she stopped to face him. 'I know I promised you justice. But I do not know what I can do now.' The thought of Feann made her stomach clench. She had defended him for so long, but he had only wanted to use her.

'Do you still want him to live?' Alarr asked.

Breanne closed her eyes, pushing back the pain. Even though she despised the king right now, it wasn't possible to push away the years of memories. He had cared for her, and when she was a little girl, there were nights when he had comforted her after bad dreams. In spite of everything, she didn't want him to die.

'Yes, he should live,' she answered. 'But I don't want to stand by and let him get away with what he did to your family. It isn't right.' Her cheeks were still wet from her tears, but she needed his arms around her. She went to Alarr and pressed both hands against his chest. His arms came around her, and she drew comfort from his embrace.

'Then we must take away something that has value to him. Does Feann have sons?'

'He does, but they are still being fostered elsewhere. They are not yet of age.' She drew back and said, 'I know what you are thinking, but I don't want to harm my foster brothers. I would rather take away his power.' She thought a moment, an idea starting to form in her mind. There was nothing that would irritate Feann more than to have a *Lochlannach* claim the Irish throne he was protecting.

'We should go to Clonagh together,' she suggested. 'And…if we married, you could take possession of the land as my husband.' It was a risk to mention it to him, for she had already agreed to travel to his homeland. Even more, she did not know if he wanted her to become his bride after all that had happened.

Alarr was already shaking his head. 'I cannot stay here in Éireann. I belong in Maerr. You know this.' He traced the edge of her jaw, and her skin tightened at his touch.

She covered his hand with her own and stared back. Did he feel the same as she did, this sense of longing? Or was it only her loneliness that made her crave a deeper connection with Alarr? She closed her eyes, forcing her attention back to the problem at hand.

'I wanted Feann to grant you compensation for your

losses. But silver is not enough to bring your loved ones back, is it?'

He shook his head. His expression was stoic, devoid of emotion. She wanted to reassure him, to somehow make him see that she would find a way to grant him justice.

'Feann will face the consequences for his choices,' Alarr said. 'I promise you that.' The coldness in his voice unnerved her. 'And then I will find the man who murdered Sigurd and avenge my father's death.'

Breanne studied him closely, and then wondered aloud, 'Why do you think it was a man?'

Alarr paused, wondering what she meant by that. 'There were no female fighters at that battle, Breanne.'

'A woman does not need to swing a sword to be responsible for a man's death.' She squeezed his hands and prompted, 'What of your mother? I imagine that she was not pleased about Sigurd's infidelity. Or his bastard sons.'

Alarr had considered this, for Hilda's jealousy and resentment of Saorla had been no secret. But would she truly go that far? 'I don't know.' But he could not deny the possibility.

A coldness settled inside him at the thought. His mother had sent Brandt away on the morning of his wedding, claiming that there was a raid. Was that true? Or had she known something about the impending attack? She might have been trying to protect her eldest son.

Hilda had forbidden them to carry weapons that day, which had left them unarmed in the presence of enemies. Alarr had been fortunate to have two ceremonial swords, but others had no means of defending themselves. He didn't want to imagine that his mother had enacted such a brutal attack…but she had played a role in it, whether or not she had intended to do so.

'What do you think we should do now?'

Alarr hesitated, considering it. Breanne had given him the chance to confront Feann, and in return, she had asked him to spare her foster father's life. But he had no intention of sparing the king from his retribution. 'Feann stole my ability to fight. The wounds he left will always be there. I want him to suffer as I did.' He intended to attack the king, even knowing the risk to his own life.

Her face held a flicker of fear. 'And what of our agreement? Do you intend to go back on your word?'

'I will spare his life,' Alarr answered. 'But after all he has done, he must face the consequences.' At the very least, he wanted to wound Feann, to make him understand how he had suffered. His anger rose hotter, and in this he would not yield.

Her face grew troubled. 'Anything you do will not change the past. And while I will ensure that he pays you *corp-dire*, that is all we can do.'

'I don't want blood money for what he did.' He didn't bother to hide the edge of his rage. And Breanne took a step backwards, wary of his mood. She could never understand his anger, and there was nothing he could say to change that.

'Alarr, there are better ways to gain your vengeance,' she said softly. 'I don't want you to endanger yourself.'

Though he supposed she was trying to show him that she cared, it made him realise that she had no faith in his fighting skills. And why should she? He had nearly failed her once before. Though he tried to push away his resentment, he was starting to see the truth. Though he desired this woman and wanted to be with her, she deserved better. One day, she might face a threat, and if he were unable to defend her, he could never forgive himself.

She had spoken of sailing away from her homeland, never to return. But she didn't belong in Maerr any more than he belonged in Éireann. It was wrong to ask her to stay with him. And when she rested her cheek upon his heart and embraced him, the guilt only deepened.

If you truly cared for her, you would let her go, his conscience warned.

And though the very idea caused a wrenching ache inside, he knew it was the right thing to do.

'Breanne, I think you should know the truth about what happened when you were taken from Feann as a slave. I owe you that much.'

'Go on.' In her green eyes, he saw compassion. She would despise him afterwards, but he could not keep it from her. Breanne deserved to know everything. And so, he started at the beginning.

'I travelled to Killcobar and watched Feann for a time. I realised that I could never get into the fortress without a good reason. And when I saw you, I saw an opportunity.' He stood and turned away from her, gathering his thoughts. 'I bribed one of your father's men to take you from Killcobar. I wanted him to imprison you and bring you to me. Then I planned to use you to get close to Feann.'

'But Feann had already left in secret.'

He nodded. 'I didn't realise it at the time.' Which

was fortunate for the king, since it would have been a simple matter to end Feann's life, if he had caught him.

Breanne's expression grew clouded. 'I never saw the soldier's face. He blindfolded me and gagged me on the night I was taken. It was in the middle of the night, and he sold me to the traders before dawn. I don't even know who it was.' Her mouth pressed into a tight line when she confronted him. 'If you paid him to take me, why didn't you rescue me from the slavers sooner? Why would you allow them to hold me captive for so long?'

Her accusation only deepened the burden of guilt. He knew he should have kept a closer eye upon her. 'It took some time before I discovered your whereabouts,' Alarr admitted. 'I didn't know he'd sold you. I thought he was holding you somewhere for ransom.'

Her gaze never wavered, the resentment filling up her expression. 'How did you find him?'

'He went hunting boar with a group of men. I separated him from the others and…questioned him.' After he'd learned of the man's betrayal, Alarr had shown no mercy. 'It took another day to track where the slavers had taken you.'

Her face winced when she realised what he was implying. 'Is he dead now?'

Alarr gave a nod. 'The others thought he was hurt by the boar. I made certain his injuries appeared accidental.' He held no regret for what he'd done. Any man who would sell the king's foster daughter into slavery deserved to die.

Then he continued. 'We tracked you to Áth Cliath, and I intended to outbid any man who tried to buy you. But then, you tried to escape.' He crossed his arms and said, 'You already know the rest.'

For a time, she remained quiet. 'So, *you* were the reason I was taken from Killcobar.'

'Yes.' He refused to deny the role he had played. 'I don't want you to think of me as the man who saved you. I was the man who caused your suffering.' He remained apart from her and confessed, 'It was my fault.'

She didn't move but clenched her hands together. Her expression held doubts. 'I need time to think, Alarr.'

He could see the uncertainty in her eyes, but he said, 'You deserve the truth, Breanne. I cannot pretend to be a good man. I'm not.'

'And you told me this, because you want me to hate you,' she finished. 'So you can walk away from me and it will be easier for you to end what is between us.' Her green eyes turned stormy. 'You don't want me to go back to your homeland.'

He didn't argue with her. It was better to break the fragile bond between them and let her go. Then she could be free to love a man who would give her the life she deserved.

'You should hate me,' he agreed. 'I paid to have you taken from your home, and I stole your innocence.'

'No.' She crossed her arms as if to ward off his words. 'I gave you my innocence.' A flush suffused her cheeks, and she confessed, 'I am glad it was you.'

He didn't know how to respond to that, so he answered, 'You were trying to save Feann's life. I had no right to claim you.'

Her anger rose up higher, her face scarlet with anger. 'Do you truly believe that was the reason? Do you deny that there are feelings between us?'

Her words stopped him cold, for he hadn't wanted to believe it. He didn't want ties that bound him to this life. He had sailed this far for vengeance, fully intending to sacrifice himself. As a scarred, wounded man, he had no value as a warrior.

But Breanne was undermining his plans. When he looked upon her face, he saw a woman who captivated him. She had woven her way into his life without him realising it. And when he made love to her, she made him feel as if there was nowhere else he'd rather be, save in her arms. He craved her, and it was killing him to be apart from her at night.

Yet he knew he could not give her the life she needed. He *did* care about her, and for that reason, it was best to let her go.

'We don't belong together,' he answered. 'Once I have settled the matter of my father's death, I will return to Maerr alone.'

Tears rose up in her eyes, and he felt like an utter bastard for hurting her. 'So you'll just avenge yourself against my foster father and leave me behind.'

He avoided answering her, but admitted, 'I intend to question him first. Feann claims that he did not kill Sigurd. I need to know who did. Whether it was Wilfrid or someone else.'

She took a breath, shielding her emotions. 'And once you have your answers, you will go.'

'If I survive the fight, yes.'

She waited for a time, choosing her words carefully. 'I think you're afraid to stay. You always planned to end your life while bringing Feann down. You would rather die than face a life where you are not the man you once were.' She shook her head in disbelief. 'But you are so much more. Your wounds made you into the man I care about.'

Her words were a sharp blade, cutting into his heart. She was right, that he had never intended to survive the fight against Feann. Nor had he intended to intertwine his days with Breanne. For the first time in years, he found that he had someone to live for—and yet, he didn't feel that he had earned that right.

Even so, he wanted her. From the moment he awakened with her beside him, to the moment he lay down to sleep, she filled the emptiness inside him. But if he admitted his feelings, it weakened him. He had sailed across the sea for vengeance—not to fall in love and allow Feann to escape with no consequences. He had no right to seek his own happiness, especially when he had not achieved his goal of punishing Feann.

Breanne moved in closer, regarding him. She rested her hands upon his heart, and the touch of her fingers blazed through him. 'Look into my eyes and tell me you want to leave. That you don't care about me.'

He knew she wanted a life he couldn't give to her, but he took her hands in his. 'I cannot stay here, Breanne.'

She released his hands, and he could see her trying to regain her composure. 'Then I don't have a choice any more.' Her voice grew softer, more vulnerable. 'I'm not going to stand aside and let others decide my fate.'

'What are you going to do?'

Her green eyes were filled with tears, but she said, 'I'm going to return to my mother. And then I won't have to watch you fight the only father I've ever known.'

Chapter Ten

They did not dine with Feann that night, as Rurik did, but instead took food to share in Alarr's shelter. Rurik had wisely left them alone, and Breanne had been careful to slip into the shelter unnoticed. Her heart was raw with unspoken pain. A part of her had hoped that Alarr would argue with her and try to stop her from leaving. But he had said nothing at all.

Now, more than ever, it was clear that his vengeance meant more than his feelings for her. And there was nothing she could do to change his mind.

'When will you go?' he asked.

'At dawn. I will take my mother's guards back with me.' She now understood why Treasa had insisted that the men remain with her. It gave her a means of protection on the journey back to Dún Bolg.

'Good.' Alarr's tone was dull, devoid of emotion. 'It's better this way, Breanne. I will fight Feann on the morrow, after you're gone. He consented to the match.'

His statement took her by surprise. 'Alarr, why would Feann agree to this? What could he hope to gain?' She knew his guards could cut Alarr down in moments, without warning. There was no reason for her foster father to seek one-on-one combat.

'Because he wanted to defend your honour.'

She winced, for it meant Feann was fully aware that she had given her body to Alarr. 'You told him about us?' These past few days, she had been careful to sleep alone to suppress idle tongues.

'He guessed the truth. I didn't deny it.'

A sudden fear took hold of her at the thought of them battling against one another. She couldn't bear to be caught in the middle any more. 'And you think this will somehow grant you the vengeance you seek? Will you hurt him?'

'If he doesn't defend himself, then yes. I won't hesitate to wound him. We will fight until the other can no longer fight.' He stared at her, and she saw only distance and ice in his gaze. 'My honour will be satisfied.'

She didn't know what to say, but it bothered her deeply that Feann had agreed to fight Alarr. 'I am glad I won't be there to see it.'

He reached out to cup her face between his hands. 'No matter what happens to me, I hope you find the life you deserve, Breanne.' She memorised the lines of his face, the dark hair that fell to his shoulders, and the piercing blue eyes that were watching her. Never had she felt like this before with any man, as if the rest of the world could fall away.

But until he set aside his revenge, there could be no life for them.

'I wanted a life with you,' she confessed. 'I wanted a husband and a home. Perhaps one day a child.'

His face softened, and he stroked back her hair. 'You will have that one day. I believe it.'

'But not with you,' she finished. She closed her eyes, holding back the rising anguish. Though she did not want to think of it, one of the men she loved would be injured on the morrow. One might die. And yet, both were too stubborn to stand down.

Alarr leaned in and murmured, 'Will you kiss me goodbye, Breanne? Give me a memory before I fight Feann.'

She didn't want to, for it would only remind her of the nights they had shared in each other's arms. Her body ached for his, but she held herself back. In the end, he ignored her silence and claimed her lips.

It was a gentle kiss, coaxing her to respond. His mouth was warm and seductive, his tongue sliding against the seam of her lips. Her body responded with heat and desire, and between her legs, she grew damp. Alarr continued kissing her while he drew her down. He sat upon a low stool and pulled her to straddle his waist. Against her womanhood she could feel his hard length.

Though he did naught but kiss her, she craved more. She ached to have his body inside hers, and she wanted to remember every part of this moment.

He pulled back, and her lips felt numb and swollen. She needed him badly, and her heart raced within her chest.

'Breanne,' he said quietly. 'I want you to know that I never wanted any woman as much as I want you.'

'Then let go of your vengeance,' she offered. 'Leave with me, and turn your back on the past.'

He held her waist, and answered, 'You know I cannot.'

'Will not,' she corrected. 'You're making a choice.'

'I can't let it go,' he said. 'Feann changed me. He

took away my ability to fight, and I will have to live with this weakness for the rest of my life. He must pay for what he did to me.'

'You are still the same man as before.' She reached out to touch his heart. 'Your strength of will is greater than any man I've ever met.'

'It does me no good if I lack balance or the ability to run.' He tightened his grip around her waist. 'Because of him, I cannot defend you the way I once could. I would never forgive myself if someone hurt you.'

And she sensed that this was the true reason. No matter what she said, he did not believe he could protect her. Rather than try to make the best of his skills, he had chosen to walk away. There was nothing she could do to change his mind.

Instead, she extricated herself from his embrace and stood. 'You may not believe you are the same man as before. But I believe you are stronger now. I pray that you will abandon this vengeance and leave with me at dawn.' She bent down and kissed him. 'Goodbye, Alarr.'

As she left his shelter, her heart broke. But she had no other choice than to walk away from a man trapped by the past, unable to look towards his own future.

Alarr hadn't slept at all that night. His furs had felt empty without Breanne in his arms. And though he'd told himself that he had done the right thing, a part of him didn't believe it.

Breanne had left at dawn, as promised, with the guards her mother had sent. She'd spoken no farewell to him or even to Feann. But as she'd ridden away, it had torn a piece of himself away. The emptiness flowed through him, and he realised that she had given him a gift by leaving. There would be no distractions during the battle, nothing to stop him from fighting with everything he had.

Feann had arranged for the battle to take place at sundown. Alarr had spent the day with Rurik, sparring and preparing for the fight. His brother had said little about the upcoming contest, but there was no doubt that he did not approve.

At twilight, Alarr walked towards the inner part of the fortress. His emotions were calm, and no longer did he fear death. Breanne was gone, and it made it easier to face her foster father. This was the day he had been waiting for, the moment when he would face his enemy and prove that his fighting skills were not lost. Vengeance belonged to him.

In one hand, he held a wooden shield and in the other, his uncle's sword. Rurik had given him the weapon, and when he held it, the weapon brought back a flood of memories. He remembered training alongside his uncle, watching as Hafr had taught him how to lunge and parry a blow. And he remembered the clang of iron and how his arm had gone numb from the force of each strike.

Watch over me, he prayed to the gods. *Let my sword be strong. Let me give honour to my ancestors.*

He walked closer, and the memories shifted to the memory of the wedding massacre. He remembered offering the sword to Gilla and her smile as she had handed him another weapon. Her face had been filled with hope, and yet, it had all ended in death.

But the ache in his heart at this moment was not about losing her, he realised. It was about losing Breanne.

She had made a wise choice not to witness the fight. But her absence was a chasm in his chest, an emptiness that filled him with doubts. He knew that he might never see her again, might never hold her. And it bothered him more than he'd ever imagined it would. She was unlike any woman he'd ever met. Brave and kind, she saw past his physical scars to the man he was inside. When he was with her, he felt as if he were the man he used to be.

Feann was donning leather armour, and his servant held a large wooden shield with an elaborately wrought-iron boss in the centre. The tangled iron reminded him of serpents, and Alarr was eager to begin the fight. At last, this was the moment he had anticipated, and he intended to win.

The clansmen and women of Killcobar were lined up in a circle, surrounding the fighting arena. Alarr approached, and Feann stared hard at him. 'Where is Breanne?'

'She had no desire to watch.' He gripped his shield and took his position opposite Feann. She had not wanted anyone to know of her departure, but he was confident in her safety. Her mother's guards would let nothing happen to her.

Feann reached for an iron helm. He held it a moment and asked, 'What is it you hope to accomplish with this fight, Alarr?'

'Justice,' he answered. He knew that wounding Feann would not eradicate the past. It would not bring back his loved ones. But it would make him feel as if he'd done *something* to fight for them.

Feann's face remained rigid and unyielding. 'And

I fight for Breanne's honour. She deserved far better than you.'

Alarr did not argue with the man over that. It was why he had let Breanne go. Feann donned the helm, which covered his forehead and nose, leaving his eyes, cheeks, and mouth visible.

His brother offered him a helm of his own, but Alarr declined. He wanted nothing to hinder his view of the enemy.

He kept his shield up, his sword at the ready while Feann circled. The older man was wiry, his dark hair greying. A thin scar on his cheek had whitened over time. Alarr waited, never taking his eyes from the enemy.

Without warning, Feann struck, and Alarr deflected the blow with his shield, slicing his blade towards the king's head. His enemy sidestepped, and the sword met only air. A slight smile tightened Feann's mouth.

Once again Alarr charged forward and struck, only to come again at a different angle. The king kept circling him, slashing at all different points. He was trying to make him lose his balance.

It was a strategic tactic, but Alarr was careful to keep his footing. The longer he lasted, the more the king would tire.

'For someone who wanted vengeance, you're not fighting much,' Feann taunted. 'Are your legs bothering you?'

He countered by swinging his sword hard and slashing at his opponent. It felt good to fight, to unleash his raw frustration. Not only because of the wounds Feann had inflicted years ago, but also to avenge the deaths of Gilla and his father. Over and over, he swung. When his sword struck Feann's shield, he let his mind go empty. The weapon became an extension of his arm, and he poured all his rage into the fight.

Feann renewed his attack, and this time, he used his shield to shove him back. Alarr stumbled, and the king swung his weapon lower. He dived to avoid the blade and rolled through the dirt. Alarr caught the flash of the weapon and raised his shield, scrambling to rise from the ground.

But then Feann's sword plunged downwards. He tried to avoid the slice, but pain ripped through him as the blade met flesh.

Breanne dismounted from her horse and trudged towards her mother's dwelling. She had ridden at a swift pace all morning and afternoon. Her body ached, but she was glad to have reached Dún Bolg. More than anything else, she wanted to fall asleep and forget about Alarr.

She pushed the door open, ducking into the small hut. 'Treasa?' she murmured. It was dark inside, save for the faint light of an oil lamp.

'Breanne?' Her mother rose and approached with a smile. 'I never expected to see you. Are you all right? What happened to the *Lochlannach* with you?'

'We decided to part ways,' was all Breanne could say. Her heart was still battered from the loss of Alarr. The ache of loneliness weighed upon her, and she struggled to let him go.

Her mother came to embrace her. She gave no judgement, but only held her in sympathy. For a moment, it felt good to forget about the loss and take comfort in

Treasa's arms. The kindness made it hard to fight back the tears, but she did not want to reveal her feelings.

'I am sorry,' her mother murmured. 'I know how you cared for him.'

I fell in love with him, she wanted to say, but didn't. 'It's hard,' was all she could manage.

'Well, I am glad you came back to me,' Treasa said, embracing her hard. 'Are you hungry? Have you eaten?'

She was, but the thought of food turned her stomach. When her mother offered a piece of dense, fresh bread, Breanne took it. Though she didn't truly want to eat, she tried a little, and it did seem to help.

'I still would like you to visit Clonagh with me, if you will think about it,' Treasa said. 'You could see the place where you were born. There are some things that belonged to your father that he would want you to have.'

A sudden tightness caught her suspicions. 'I thought you were in exile and were not allowed to leave.'

Treasa's face softened in the lamplight. 'What I am supposed to do and what I choose to do are not always the same. If I travel with only a guard or two, I can usually visit my people in secret. They are usually glad, because I bring them supplies or do what I can to help. Iasan does not mind, so long as I return within a day, and King Cerball has no need to know. I am only a woman, so what harm is there?'

Breanne thought it was a risk, but if Treasa was only bringing small gifts and then leaving, perhaps it was not so dangerous. 'I will think about it.'

'Good.' Her mother held out her hand. 'Why don't you rest for a while? You must be weary from the journey, and there's time enough to talk about it in the morning.' She led her to a pile of sleeping furs near the heated stones that provided warmth within the hut. Breanne curled up and closed her eyes. But it did nothing to diminish the longing within her. The familiar scent of wood and straw conjured up the memories of lying in Alarr's arms.

Had he fought with Feann this night? Was he alive? Silently, her tears fell, dampening her cheeks. Why couldn't he give up his plans to fight her foster father? It tore her apart to imagine either one of them hurt.

She wanted to believe that he had spared her father's life, but she didn't know what he had done. Silently, she wept, wishing she could push aside the raw feelings.

She heard her mother get up and walk outside. Dimly, she heard Treasa speaking to someone in a low voice before she returned inside.

'I am sending one of my men ahead to Clonagh at dawn, so that our kinsmen will know of our arrival, Breanne,' she whispered. 'They will make a place for us to sleep where no one will know we are there.'

Breanne didn't answer, feigning sleep. Perhaps it was best to return to Clonagh and see for herself what had happened there. She was not about to let Feann arrange a marriage for her—that is, if he had survived the fight with Alarr. Her mood turned bleak as she wondered what had happened to them.

She loved both men, and neither would stand down. And choosing one meant abandoning the other. Because of it, she would have to give up both. It broke her heart, being caught in the middle.

Breanne shifted her thoughts back to Clonagh, and she tried to imagine making a home there. It wasn't the life she had envisioned, but it was time to make her own choices.

Even if that meant being alone.

Alarr gasped as the blade cut into his shoulder, but he managed to shield himself before Feann could strike again.

He pushed back against the king's blows, rising to his feet. Blood dripped down his arm, but he didn't care. Instead, he poured himself into the fight. His mind blurred, and he used his strength to strike his hardest blows. It was time to end this.

He released a battle cry, using all his strength to catch his enemy off guard. But Feann was a skilled warrior, despite his age. He met Alarr's blows with his own force. They circled one another, and despite it all, there was no doubting that they were equally matched.

Feann lunged, striking a low blow. But as Alarr side-stepped the attack, he brought his blade to the king's throat.

Then, beneath his own neck, he felt the cold kiss of metal. Across from him, he saw his brother staring. Rurik shook his head slowly, as if in warning.

'Enough,' Feann said. 'This fight is over.' To one of his men, he ordered, 'Bring Breanne to me.'

'She's gone,' Alarr admitted. 'She left this morn to go back to her mother.'

At that, Feann pressed the blade against Alarr's throat until blood welled. Alarr answered with his own pressure, never taking the blade from the king's neck.

'You let her go back to Treasa?' Feann said with incredulity. 'Why would you send her there?' He drew his blade back, and Alarr did the same. Feann cursed and swung his sword again. 'She is a conniving viper who will only betray her.'

Alarr didn't know what the king meant by that. Treasa had appeared harmless, hardly any threat at all. But now, the king's emotions caused him to fight recklessly, and Alarr seized the advantage. He allowed Feann to rail with his anger, waiting until the right moment to strike. Iron struck iron, and he kept his patience, until the moment the king crossed his sword, leaning in.

At that, Alarr reached for Feann's wrist and twisted the sword away, disarming him. With both weapons in his hands, he drew the blades on either side of the king's neck. It would take only a single blow to behead him.

'Kneel,' he ordered.

The king's men started to surround Alarr, but Feann commanded, 'Stand down. This is between us.'

The soldiers took a step back, though they appeared ready to fight. Then Feann met Alarr's gaze. 'Swear to me you will go after Breanne. Her mother is not to be trusted.'

He ignored the man's warning and pressed the blades into his neck. 'I said, "Kneel".'

'Swear it first. You must find her and protect her from Treasa.' The king's eyes met his, and he said, 'Breanne is all that matters. You know this.'

There was true fear in Feann's expression, but it was for his foster daughter, not himself. Alarr didn't understand why the man had abandoned her, if he truly wanted her safe. Something didn't ring true. 'If you care more for her than your own life, why did you not save her when she needed you?'

'Because I thought Treasa had taken her!' the king

retorted. 'After I heard she had escaped from Dún Bolg, I searched for them, only to discover that I was wrong.' He took a breath and knelt. 'Seize your vengeance and end my life, if that is what you want. I thought avenging Saorla would heal the guilt I felt over her death. But I know it won't ever bring her back. And it won't mend the past.'

The king's words resonated within him. It was true that killing the man would never bring back Gilla or Sigurd. Feann wasn't even the one who had struck the blow to end their lives. Nor had he begun the fire.

'If you care for Breanne, then you must save her,' Feann insisted. 'Treasa will stop at nothing to get Clonagh—even putting her own daughter in danger.'

He hesitated, and the king met his gaze. 'Please.'

In his heart, Alarr tried to summon up the resentment and rage he'd felt after losing the ability to walk. He thought about striking Feann down, wounding him so he would know the same pain.

But hurting Feann would do nothing. This man was on his knees, not begging for his own life, but pleading for him to save Breanne.

What would she think of him now? He could imagine the fragile hurt in her eyes, the worry and the fear. Breanne was a woman who put others before herself, despite having been abandoned by so many. And he had told her he would leave her too, after he'd avenged himself against Feann. At the time, he had thought it was the right choice, to let her go.

Now, he realised that he could no more give her up than he could cut off his own arm. He wanted her eyes filled with love and faith, not the pain that he had caused. He wanted to spend each day with her, loving her.

Hurting Feann wouldn't make him a stronger man, but it would break Breanne's heart. He had promised to let her foster father live. And now that he had proven his strength, it was time to keep that vow.

'Alarr,' came Rurik's voice. He saw his brother's gaze and understood the unspoken message.

He lowered his swords and sheathed one, keeping the other in his hand. 'I swore to Breanne that I would not end your life. And I will keep that promise.'

The king stared at Alarr, and he never took his gaze from Feann. For a long moment, the tension remained between them. Although he had won this fight, it was too soon to smooth the sharp edges of their distrust.

But if Breanne was in danger from Treasa, he would need an ally—someone who would put her safety first. Though it was a grave risk, Alarr extended his hand. 'If I'm going to find Breanne and protect her, I will need help.' With an army of men, they could easily defend her. And despite the years of hatred, they shared a common bond in wanting Breanne to be safe.

The king hesitated a moment but then clasped Alarr's palm and stood. 'So be it.'

He handed Feann his sword back, hilt first. Though he didn't trust the man, it was the first step towards mending the breach.

The king called out to his men to gather nearby. He chose a dozen men to go to Dún Bolg, and he asked Rurik to remain at Killcobar. Another dozen men would accompany Feann and Alarr.

'Aren't we returning to Dún Bolg with the others?' Alarr asked.

Feann shook his head. 'There is only one place Treasa will bring Breanne. She wants dominion over Clonagh. That's where she will go, and that's where we will find them.'

Chapter Eleven

Two days later

It was afternoon by the time they arrived at Clonagh.
Breanne and her mother had travelled north-east with
only two men to guard them. As they drew near, she
glimpsed a small fortress enclosed by a wicker fence.
It surprised her, for her mother had spoken of Clonagh
as if it were a vast ringfort. She frowned, wondering
what else Treasa had exaggerated.

They left their horses with their two guards, and
Treasa said, 'It is safe to go through the gates.'

Breanne was still wary of walking alone, but her
mother remained cheerful, as if she was delighted to
be home. They walked uphill, and Treasa smiled at the
guards standing at the entrance. They opened the gates
without question, and Breanne followed her mother
inside. Inside the ringfort, she saw very few people.
As Treasa had said, there was a sense of hopelessness
and loss.

Her mother took her by the hand and led her to an
old man standing outside one of the roundhouses. He

wore a long grey *léine*, and his expression was sombre. When they reached his side, Treasa said, 'This is Father Bain.'

She didn't know quite what to say, except, 'I am glad to meet you, Father.' She was surprised to find a priest here, for they were nowhere near a monastery.

The priest ventured a smile that didn't quite meet his eyes. 'And you, my child.' He glanced towards the gates, and it was then that Breanne became aware of more guards gathering at the entrance.

Treasa's face grew uneasy. 'I think we should go inside, Breanne. It might be best to remain hidden, in case there is a threat.'

'I thought they were our kinsmen,' she replied.

Her mother shook her head. 'We have a few men loyal to us, like those who met us when we first arrived. But King Cerball has his own forces here, mingled with ours. They know I am only a woman and there is no harm by my presence. But it doesn't mean they will let me come and go freely.'

'Are we prisoners now?' Breanne asked. She was aghast at the idea, wishing she had heeded her instincts. Without knowing King Cerball, she had no idea what she had done by coming here.

'No, no. Nothing like that,' Treasa reassured her. 'But, let us say, we are well guarded.' Her mother took her arm in hers and bid the priest farewell. She guided her to the far end of the ringfort where there was a smaller roundhouse. 'Let us go somewhere we can talk freely.'

With no other choice, she followed her mother. Even so, she grew aware that several soldiers were watching. An older woman risked a gaze at Breanne and shook her head.

What did that mean? Something was very wrong at Clonagh, and already she was regretting her decision to come here. She could not make her home in a place like this, heavily guarded by a neighbouring king who had executed her father for treason.

Her mother pushed open the doorway and waited at the entrance. 'Come inside. There is someone else I've been wanting you to meet.'

Breanne risked a glance back at the soldiers and the old woman. Every part of her felt the invisible threat. She knew it wasn't safe here, but no longer did she have strong *Lochlannach* warriors to guard her. Instead, she would have to defend herself.

You've done nothing wrong, she reminded herself.

These men had no reason to harm her. Unless they did not want her or her mother to dwell here. Clonagh felt like a graveyard, filled with spirits haunting the air.

'Breanne?' her mother prompted. 'Go inside. It's warmer there, and we can talk.'

With a sigh, she decided to obey. There was no reason not to. She ducked her head inside the low opening and stepped inside the space. The ceiling was tall, supported by heavy beams, and the roof was made of thatch.

The door closed behind her, and she turned to where her mother had been standing. But Treasa was gone.

'Mother?' she asked. She tried to open the door, and when she did, she saw the face of Oisin.

'Hello, Breanne,' he said. His smile held malice as he pushed his way inside. 'I've been waiting a long time for this.'

* * *

They journeyed with all haste, for which Alarr was grateful. He had never imagined that Treasa was a threat to Breanne, and he cursed himself for letting her go. Feann had insisted that they take his fastest horses, and when night fell, they stopped briefly to let the horses drink. Alarr held the reins of his mount. 'Why do you think she brought Breanne to Clonagh? Why not Dún Bolg?'

'Because Treasa wants to rule over Clonagh. She won't hesitate to use Breanne for that purpose. Whether that means another arranged marriage to a weaker man or she'll choose a man who will die sooner, leaving Treasa in command.' Feann rubbed his horse down, tending to the animal.

'What happened to Breanne's father?' Alarr asked. He had heard murmurings about treason, but it made him wonder what the truth really was.

'Treasa lied to Cerball. She tried to seduce him and failed. Then she told him that Dal was cruel and beat her. She claimed that Dal was raising an army against Cerball. But the men Dal brought to the gates were men who had planned to swear an oath of fealty to Cerball. Dal was trying to bring their families together.' Feann let out a breath and lowered his gaze. 'Treasa betrayed him, and he was executed before anyone recognised the truth.

'When Cerball learned that he had killed an innocent man, he had Treasa exiled. Were it me, I would have executed *her* for what she did to Dal.'

Alarr had never suspected that the matron had

caused so much trouble, and he hoped they could reach Breanne in time. 'What will Treasa do to her daughter?'

'I don't know,' Feann admitted. 'But we're going to find Breanne and bring her home.'

Alarr nodded in agreement. But this time, he wanted to offer her a different choice. She had begged him to set aside his vengeance, and now, he had come to an understanding with Feann. No longer did the bitterness of revenge burn within his veins. Instead, he saw a man who loved his foster daughter as his own blood, who would stop at nothing to save her. Alarr had found a grudging respect for the king, in the way he had gathered his forces and planned their strategy.

'Do you need to rest?' Feann asked.

'Only when we have her back,' Alarr answered.

At that, the king's face relaxed somewhat. 'If you were not a *Lochlannach* who tried to kill me, I might like you, Alarr Sigurdsson.' He mounted his horse once again and led the animal back to the pathway.

Alarr climbed on to his own horse. 'If you were not the man who took away my ability to walk for a year, I might like you, Feann.' He shrugged, making it clear that it was still unlikely. Though he had bandaged his shoulder, the cut still burned from their earlier fight.

There was a slight lift in the older man's mouth, as if he were suppressing a smile. They rode in silence for a time, and finally Feann asked, 'Why did you let Breanne leave that night? Especially with so few men to guard her?'

Guilt pressed upon his conscience, for Alarr regretted it. But a part of him had known that if he didn't let her go, she would talk him into giving up his vengeance. She held a power over him that he didn't understand. And the only way to overcome it was with distance.

'She wanted to go, and I don't believe in imprisoning women. Since I hold no command over your men, I couldn't send them with her, could I?'

'You should have told me of her plans to leave.'

'It was her decision to make. And she wanted to leave quietly.'

Feann tightened his grip on the reins, his expression a harsh mask of anger. 'You wanted her to go, didn't you?'

He didn't answer the king. Because both answers were true. He'd wanted Breanne to leave because he didn't want her to witness the fight. He had needed the chance to fight Feann, to drive out the demons of his past and strike back. In the end, the battle hadn't given him the resolution he'd wanted—but he held no regrets.

'I didn't want her to watch our fight,' he admitted. 'And I knew I wasn't worthy of her.' But he'd missed waking up and seeing her each day. He missed the warmth of her mouth and the touch of her hands upon him. She had healed a part of him he hadn't known was broken. For so long, he had lived for his vengeance, never daring to imagine a life after his injuries. He'd believed that he didn't deserve to live after he'd failed his family.

Before Feann could speak, Alarr added, 'But I will find her and protect her from all harm. And I will do everything I can to be the man she needs.' The loss of her was an emptiness he needed to fill. And if she would have him, this time he would not let her go.

Feann studied him for a time, as if discerning the truth. Then he shrugged. 'That remains to be seen.'

Alarr wasn't surprised at the man's reluctance and he turned the conversation to their plans. 'What do you want to do when we arrive?'

'I don't want Treasa to know you are here,' the king answered. 'It's better if you remain hidden. Then if there is trouble, you can get Breanne out.'

Alarr understood that they needed an alternative plan, in case there was an unforeseen danger. And yet, he wasn't about to let Feann go in alone. 'I will disguise myself among your men, if that is what you want. But I won't remain outside the fortress.'

Feann met his gaze steadily. 'Do not let her see you.'

Alarr privately agreed with the king. He was there to ensure Breanne's safety, and he did not want to alert Treasa's suspicions. He would support Feann's quest to bring her to safety, but he would not reveal his presence unless it was necessary.

It was early morning, and Breanne jerked to a seated position when she heard footsteps approaching. She had spent the night locked inside one of the dwellings, hardly able to sleep at all. Her mother had left her alone after she'd refused to speak with Oisin.

When they started to lift the bar that held the door shut, she stood, searching for some sort of weapon—but there was nothing. Instead, she stared at the door, squaring her shoulders in preparation for the fight to come.

Her mother entered first and smiled at her. Oisin followed behind her, and the knowing look on his face made her stomach clench. Fury blazed through her that her mother would dare to invite Oisin into their ring-fort. He was an enemy whom she had barely escaped the last time.

'Why would you bring him here?' Breanne demanded.

Though his injuries were somewhat healed, she noticed that his shoulder was still bandaged. Even so, she could feel the threat of his presence.

He was standing tall, his expression filled with gloating. 'I came for you, Breanne,' he answered. 'Your mother was kind enough to make the wedding arrangements.' He turned to Treasa and added, 'Go now, and leave me with my bride.'

Her mother only nodded and closed the door behind her.

'I will never wed you,' she told Oisin. But worse than this situation was the clarity of her mother's betrayal. Though she had known Treasa wanted Clonagh, she had never imagined the woman would stoop to such depths for her own ambitions. Her own daughter was nothing but a pawn, just as Breanne had feared.

She had no intention of obeying Treasa's wishes. She would fight back against a forced marriage, even if there was no one to come to her aid now. The bleak feeling of isolation threatened to drown her, but she tried to steel her courage. If no one could save her, then she would have to save herself.

Oisin drew closer, and she took a step back, trying to keep distance between them. He smiled at her. 'King Cerball ordered that you should wed a man loyal to him. Who better than his own bastard son?'

'The only loyalty you hold is fealty to yourself,' she countered. 'You do not want to wed me.' Oisin only wanted to control her, to mould her into his imagined wife.

'You're wrong,' he answered. 'I wouldn't care if you had the face and temperament of a shrew. Marriage to you will bring Clonagh under my dominion.' He took another step, and when Breanne tried to move away, he seized her arm and pressed her against the wall. 'But as it is, I do desire you, Breanne.' He leaned in, and his hot breath fanned her cheek. She was repulsed by him, for he appeared to delight in her inability to fight him. When she tried to shove him back, he pinned her with one arm.

'I am going to enjoy claiming you with my body,' he said. 'I'll enjoy it more if you fight me.' To underscore his words, he pinched her nipple roughly.

This time, she used all her strength to push against Oisin, but he only laughed. Panic flooded through her at the realisation that he could easily subdue her, and she could do nothing to stop him. She struggled against him, fighting to break free, but it was like trying to push back a stone wall.

'Do you see how weak you are? You cannot fight me.' Oisin reached for the hem of her gown and lifted it while he continued to hold her against the wall with his arm and shoulder. He started to reach between her legs, and fear shot through her. He intended to claim her now, to assert his body over hers.

She had to fight back, to protect herself somehow. But there was nothing she could use as a weapon, and she lacked the strength. Breanne screamed as loudly as she could, but he seemed to delight in her terror.

'I'm going to enjoy taming you,' he said. To emphasise his words, he kissed her roughly, biting her lower lip until he drew blood.

Her heart pounded, and she realised she was in a state of shock. Her mind went blank, her limbs frozen as she trembled.

Don't surrender, she warned herself. *You have to fight. There is always a way.*

Her gaze fixed upon his bandaged shoulder, and when he tried to touch her intimately, she rammed her head against his wound. Oisin roared at the sudden pain and released her. Breanne raced for the door, but before she could reach it, he grabbed the length of her hair and pulled her back. With his fist, he backhanded her, and the pain exploded against her mouth. 'You're going to regret what you did,' he swore. 'And you'll stay here until you willingly agree to wed me.'

Breanne tasted blood, but before she could run again, he closed the door and secured it behind him. She was alone in the darkness, imprisoned within the dwelling.

Her teeth chattered, and it was only then that she realised how badly she was shaking. Slowly, she sank against the wall until she was sitting on the ground. Silent tears ran down her face, and she realised just how dangerous Oisin was. He was not a man who would listen to reason. He delighted in hurting her, and marriage to him would be horrifying.

But you're not going to wed him, she reminded herself.

No one could force the vows from her lips. She might be at the mercy of her mother and a man she despised, but that didn't mean she was powerless.

She could try to send someone from Clonagh back to Killcobar. Or seek help from the people here. Though she lacked the physical strength, she had intelligence. There had to be a way to free herself from this prison.

She lay down upon the furs, wishing she had not left Alarr. If he were here, he would hold her until she stopped trembling. She would draw strength from him, and he would break down the door, freeing them both. The thoughts brought her comfort, though she knew they were only an illusion.

She loved him, in spite of everything. Though she could not bear to watch him fight Feann, it cut her deeply to be without him. Whether he was dead or whether he had returned to Maerr, the aching emptiness was consuming. She could hardly bear it.

In her heart, she believed that he had kept his vow not to kill Feann. The only question was whether her foster father had granted him the same mercy.

Breanne swiped at the tears, gathering her emotions and pushing back against her fear.

You're going to escape, she told herself. *No matter what happens, you will find a way out.*

And once she did, she would find out what had happened to Alarr and learn whether they could be together.

Hours passed, and afternoon faded into evening. Breanne had calmed her terror, forming a plan, despite her earlier fears. A knock sounded at the door, and a woman's voice said, 'May I come in?'

Breanne rose to her feet, and an older woman came inside, holding a loaf of bread, a small flagon, and a bundle of clothing. 'I brought you food and wine.' The matron set it down, but before she could leave, Breanne ran to the door.

'Wait. Please.' She blocked the woman's exit. 'I need your help.'

'I can do nothing,' she insisted. 'Do not ask me to let you go. They will hurt my family.'

Breanne didn't bother to ask who *they* were. Instead, she said, 'How many guards are outside this shelter?'

The matron glanced at the doorway as if uncertain whether to answer. But at last, she mumbled, 'Six.'

Then any attempts to flee would be futile. There was no means of escaping six men. She needed to find a different way, perhaps a hidden way out of the shelter. But there were no windows and no other exits from the dwelling.

She redirected her question. 'What are they planning to do with me?'

The woman bit her lip, as if wondering whether to answer. She looked down at the bundle of food. 'They will come for you on the morrow. The priest will hear your vows, and you are to marry Oisin MacLogan.'

So she had only one day left. Breanne sat down with the bread, her mind turning over the problem. She drew up her knees against her chest and closed her eyes. 'Do I have until sunset for the wedding?'

'No. They have planned it a few hours after dawn,' she answered. With a glance at the door, the older woman withdrew a small eating knife from her waist. Without a word, she hid the dagger inside the bundle of clothing. It was an unexpected gift—and a chance to free herself. For a moment, the older woman met her gaze with understanding before she departed.

Breanne didn't know how she would use the weapon, but it offered a slight glimmer of hope.

You can save yourself, she told herself. *Be strong and use your wits.*

But even so, she was afraid that her time was running out.

Chapter Twelve

It was late at night when they arrived at Clonagh. Rain pounded against them, soaking Alarr to the skin. The harsh weather offered an advantage, for it meant that no one would leave their shelter unless commanded to do so.

'Are you certain you won't remain outside?' Feann questioned. 'We need someone beyond the gates.'

'Let it be one of your men,' Alarr countered. He had no intention of being left behind—not while Breanne was in danger.

The king eyed him with annoyance but relented after a time. 'Fine. But you must remain hidden.'

They approached the gate with stealth where one man guarded the entrance with a spear. To his surprise, Feann signalled to the guard. For a brief moment Alarr wondered if the king would betray him. He wouldn't put it past Feann, for neither of them fully trusted the other. Instead, the king spoke quietly to the soldier, and they were allowed to enter.

'Let no one see you,' the guard warned. He pointed

towards a grain storage shed. 'When the next guard comes to take my place, I will come to you.'

The rain continued to pour in punishing sheets, but they made their way to the shed. Though it was cold, Alarr was grateful to be out of the harsh weather. He found a place to sit, and he wondered if Breanne was safe. It tempted him to leave the shelter and find her, for he knew not what Treasa had done.

'We will make our plans tonight,' Feann said in a low voice. 'Nevin is one of my men. I sent him to Clonagh years ago, and no one knows of his loyalty to me.'

Alarr gave a nod, recognising it as a sound strategy. Yet, he questioned what the king would do now. 'What is Breanne to you? A political pawn for your own alliances?'

Feann leaned back against the shed. 'She is a daughter to me, in all but blood. I have cared for her since she was two years of age.' There was a softness in his voice as he spoke of her.

'But you intended to wed her to one of Cerball's men,' Alarr ventured.

'It would have kept her safe from Treasa. I needed a strong man to marry her, one who would protect her and ensure that she would not be killed for her lands. A warrior.'

In the darkness, Alarr could not see Feann's expression. He knew that the king had no wish to see Breanne with a man like him, though he didn't say it. Even so, the thought of giving Breanne to another warrior filled him with a surge of possessive anger.

Another man would not understand that despite her façade of bravery, she had a tender heart and a fierce loyalty to her family. One day, when she bore children, he had no doubt she would fight to protect them. She was a strong woman, and she had faced threats that would have made others weep. Instead, she had risen up to meet those challenges.

Yet, he had turned her away for the sake of vengeance.

He closed his eyes, recognising what a mistake he had made. Although Feann wanted her to wed an Irish nobleman, Alarr knew he could not give her up a second time. She belonged to him and he was hers. Somehow, he would find a way to be with her.

The door swung open, and both of them unsheathed their weapons. 'It's me,' came the voice of the guard, Nevin.

'What can you tell us about Breanne?' Feann asked.

The guard answered, 'She is being held captive in the shelter at the far end of the ringfort. In the morning, Oisin plans to wed her and seize command of Clonagh.' From the man's tone, it was clear that he did not support Oisin's leadership.

Alarr's mood darkened, and he regretted not killing the man when he'd first had the opportunity. He would not hesitate a second time. He gritted his teeth and asked the guard, 'Did he harm her?'

The guard's silence weighed heavily. Then, after a time, he admitted, 'Everyone heard her screams.'

Alarr felt his rage gather into a tight ball of hatred. He never should have let her leave. 'I will see Oisin dead for this.'

Feann caught his arm. 'Take your vengeance upon him. And I will see to Breanne's safety first.' In a low voice, he ordered the guard to leave.

At first, Alarr wanted to be the one to save Breanne. He blamed himself for what had happened, and he should be there for her.

And yet, he remembered how Breanne had felt abandoned by her father. She had gone into slavery, believing that Feann had left her, when the truth was, her father had tried to search for her. Moreover, if he sent the king to fight Oisin, Feann might not survive.

The decision weighed up on him as he tried to decide what was best. Breanne had left him, not wanting to witness their fight. She might not want to see him again, and he knew he would not be able to stop himself from embracing her.

Gods help him, he was in love with her. And he didn't know if he had the strength to let her go. He could not force her to stay with him, nor was it right. She deserved the choice.

'As you will,' he told the king. 'Go and save Breanne. I will face Oisin.' If he placed his focus on killing his enemy, it would be a strong distraction.

The thought of being without Breanne was a physical ache inside him. If she did not want to see him again, it was best to leave Éireann and never look back.

There was a slight ease in the man's tension. 'And after he is dead? What then?'

'I don't know the answer to that yet.' It depended entirely on Breanne's wishes. But after she had left him once, he doubted if she would change her mind.

The king's expression darkened. 'I was right about you. You were only using her for your own gains. Breanne never meant anything to you.'

At that, his temper exploded. He took Feann by the throat and shoved him against the wall. 'Breanne meant *everything* to me. But I know I'm not the man she needs.

I cannot ask her to turn her back on her homeland. I will do the right thing by her, even if it means walking away.'

He released Feann and stepped back. The king appeared startled by his outburst, but his demeanour turned thoughtful. 'And what is it you think she needs?'

'A powerful warrior who can love her and protect her. One who is whole.' He hadn't meant to voice the last part, but it was true. He had let her go, fearing he couldn't fight for Breanne the way he wanted to. He never wanted to see her broken or hurt because of him.

'You defeated me,' Feann pointed out. 'But I agree with you. Breanne should not wed a *Lochlannach* and abandon her kingdom. They need her now, more than ever.'

Alarr said nothing, though he was startled at Feann's reminder. He *had* defeated a strong fighter, in the end. He might not have the speed or balance that he'd once had, but he had been a warrior all his life. Perhaps it was time to stop dwelling on the possibility of failure and live his life for her. Breanne had wanted him to leave the past behind, and he'd refused.

But now, he realised that he didn't want any future without her in it. He would sacrifice everything to save her and give her the choice of becoming his wife. He wanted that, more than all else. If she refused, then after he killed Oisin, he would accompany Rurik to Northumbria. There, they could search for the other fighters who had slaughtered his kinsmen in Maerr.

For now, he hoped he could convince her to stay. In the meantime, he needed to find Breanne and free her from captivity.

'What should we do about Treasa?' Alarr asked.

'She is dangerous,' Feann admitted. 'Ambitious, and I blame her for bringing this threat to Breanne.' With a slight laugh, he suggested, 'You could take her back to Maerr with you where she could do no harm.'

There was a slight lift in the tension between them, but Alarr shook his head. 'Her fate should rest in Cerball's hands.'

'I agree.' The king paused again as he regarded him. 'What will you do afterwards?'

'What I want to do and what I will do are not the same,' he admitted. 'I want to take Breanne back with me to Maerr. I want to wed her and keep her at my side.' He saw the grim look of fury in Feann's expression. 'But it is her choice to make.'

'You cannot ask her to surrender her kingdom. It's better if you leave her behind, even if she grieves.'

He met the king's gaze. 'We both know she is worth more than any kingdom. I will do what is right.'

Breanne had spent most of the night making her plans. It was far better to feign surrender, for then, the others might let their guard down. She had tied the blade and sheath to her thigh beneath her shift. Though she didn't truly know how she would use the weapon yet, she intended to leave Clonagh by any means necessary. A knock sounded at the door, and a woman's voice called out, 'Breanne, may I come inside?' It was her mother.

She bit her tongue to keep from stating the obvious, that she was heavily guarded, and the door was locked. Instead, she answered, 'Yes.' This might be a chance to seize her escape, especially if her mother left the door unlocked.

Treasa lifted the bar and came inside. She was dressed in a crimson gown, and her hair was neatly braided and concealed within a cap. 'I brought this for you to wear.' In her arms, she held out a gown of soft yellow, the colour of morning sunshine. It was beautiful, and for a moment, Breanne imagined herself wearing the *léine* while marrying Alarr instead. The thought made her throat close up with emotion, for he was gone. She had left him of her own free will, and there was no one to save her now.

Her mother helped her change into the *léine*, and when she finished lacing up the gown, Treasa turned to look at her. 'You are so beautiful, Breanne. I could not be prouder.'

'And yet, you are handing me to the enemy,' she countered. 'You brought me here under the pretence of seeing my homeland. But all along, you intended to force this marriage.'

Treasa's face turned pained. 'Sometimes sacrifices must be made for the greater good.'

'But you are not the one making the sacrifice, are you?' She crossed her arms. 'Oisin is not a kind man. He is not one you can manipulate to do your will.'

The expression on Treasa's face never changed. 'Oh, my sweet girl. You are so very young. Did you believe I would choose a man like Oisin without ensuring that you would be safe from him?'

Breanne didn't understand. 'What do you mean?'

Her mother drew close and lowered her voice. 'Oisin is Cerball's bastard son, but he is not a favourite. We will make the marital alliance and prove our loyalty to Cerball. But Oisin will not live long enough to be a threat.'

Treasa spoke of murder as if she were discussing food to prepare for an evening meal. 'Wed him willingly, and I will see to it that he does not survive the wedding night.'

Breanne said nothing but only stared at her mother. Treasa folded her hands together. 'Unless you want to lie with him?'

The thought made bile rise to her throat. 'No.'

'Good. Then I will bring you a potion to slip into his wine. He will fall asleep and never awaken.'

Breanne still could not bring herself to speak. Not only was her mother planning a murder, but she intended her daughter to carry out her plans. No matter that she despised Oisin, she was not a killer.

Treasa continued, 'Let everyone believe that the marriage is consummated. I will bring your *Lochlannach* to you later, and you can attempt to conceive a child. We will claim it is Oisin's, and the alliance will be finished.' It was clear that her mother had no qualms about taking another man's life if it served her purpose. And her lack of emotion was utterly chilling.

Breanne decided it was better to behave as if she were ignorant. She lowered her head, wondering how much time she had remaining.

Her unspoken question was answered when her mother asked, 'Are you ready?'

No, she wasn't. But it was far better to leave this chamber than to remain a prisoner. Before she could say anything, she heard the sound of a battle cry outside. Treasa pushed the door closed and blocked her path. Breanne peered through a crack in the door, and outside she saw a group of armed men charging forward. One of them was Alarr.

He was here. And from the looks of it, so was her foster father. Her emotions gathered up and spilled over as she could not stop her smile of joy. They had come for her, and both were alive.

When she glanced at Treasa, her mother's face had turned furious. 'Wait here,' she said. After she closed the door, Breanne heard the sound of the wooden bar locking her inside.

Damn her for this.

She tried to stare through the cracks in the doorway and saw Oisin facing off against Alarr. Feann barked a command and then left with a group of his men. He was stopped by other soldiers, and she watched as the men fought one another. Fear pulsed inside her veins, but she forced herself to watch. Her gaze fixed upon Alarr. His sword moved with speed, and he struck Oisin hard. In his left hand he held a shield, and he used it to protect himself from his enemy's punishing blows.

Over and over he attacked, and she found herself breathless, watching her warrior. He moved with confidence, and she knew he was fighting for her. She didn't know how he had learned of the threat, but at the sight of him, she felt a surge of love.

No matter what had happened, he had always been there for her. She had complete faith that he would protect her. And she would fight alongside him.

A shadow crossed her door, and she heard Feann's voice. 'Breanne, are you there?'

She called out, 'I'm here.' There was a noise of him lifting the wooden bar, and he threw the door open.

'Are you all right?' he asked. His face was creased

with worry, and her emotions welled up at the sight of him. 'Did anyone hurt you?'

'I'm fine,' Breanne murmured. She was in his arms a moment later, and he stroked her hair back, gripping her in a fierce embrace.

'We will get you out of here,' he assured her. 'I swear it.'

'What about Alarr?'

'He is fighting Oisin.'

Breanne clung to him, and her foster father escorted her from the shelter. They walked outside, and she froze at the sight of six guards surrounding them. Feann unsheathed his sword and faced them. 'Go back inside, Breanne.'

She hesitated, for her foster father was badly outnumbered. With six men, they could easily kill him, and she could do nothing to stop it.

Don't be a coward, she warned herself.

If she stood back and did nothing, he would die. And despite the danger, she didn't believe they would kill her. She took a breath and stepped forward. 'Stop!' she called out to the soldiers. 'Leave him. I will surrender without a fight.'

'Breanne, no,' Feann insisted. He appeared furious that she would refuse his protection. But she knew better than to let him face so many men. There was a greater chance that Alarr could help her, with her father's support.

She moved another step, standing between them. One of the men seized her arm, while another kept his sword pointed at Feann. Her foster father glared at her. 'Don't do this. I can defend you long enough for you to escape.'

But she would not let him make the sacrifice. 'I'm not going to stand aside and watch you die. Not when I can stop it from happening.'

Two of the men pressed her father back while the others surrounded her. She pushed back the rising fear and forced herself to leave with the men as they retreated.

But as they escorted her to the far end of the ring-fort where Oisin was fighting Alarr, she was afraid to wonder what would happen now.

Alarr's arm was numb from the sword fight, but he ignored the pain and continued to strike hard at his enemy. He could see the sweat running down Oisin's face. The man was growing weary, and that gave Alarr an advantage. He lunged with his blade and nicked Oisin's side before the man could dodge the blow.

This was about more than winning a sword fight. It was about protecting Breanne from a man who wanted to possess her. Never would he allow her to marry a man like Oisin, who would subjugate her to his will.

Without warning, Oisin changed his pace. He struck hard, swinging the sword at Alarr's knees. He had to leap to get out of the way, and when his feet landed, he was off balance. Oisin took advantage and shoved his wounded shoulder, causing Alarr to gasp at the pain before he fell to the ground. He rolled out of the way and raised his shield just as his enemy struck a downward blow.

His pulse thundered, and he forced himself to centre his rage. He needed to remain calm and not allow his body's weakness to betray him. But he struggled to push back the frustration of his lack of balance. He could not doubt himself, or it would only lead to failure.

'You cannot win this fight,' Oisin taunted. 'And when you're dead, I'm going to claim her body. You'll die, knowing that she will be mine to do with as I choose.' A thin smile curved at Oisin's mouth.

Not if I can help it.

Alarr knew the man was trying to incite his rage, to make him careless. He used all his strength to push back with his shield and managed to stand up from the ground. His legs were still unsteady, but he feigned a strength he didn't feel.

Oisin pressed back, and when Alarr stared into the man's eyes, he saw no mercy. He had no doubt that his enemy would hurt Breanne, given the opportunity. This time, he would not stop until Oisin was dead and could no longer threaten Breanne.

With a surge of strength, he shoved Oisin back and swung his sword. He saw a slight smile as his enemy dodged the blow, but Alarr ignored the mocking stare and continued to fight.

Out of nowhere, a searing pain struck the back of his knees, and he crumpled to the ground. He spied another man attacking from behind, and Alarr barely avoided the killing blow. It was dishonourable, and he should have expected it from Oisin. The second man struck him with a club, and Alarr bit back a roar of pain as he tried to defend himself from both fighters.

A soft exclamation caught his attention, and he saw Breanne being held by two men, with two others nearby. She wore a yellow gown, and when she caught sight of him on the ground, he saw the fear in her eyes.

'Alarr,' she called out, struggling to free herself from their grasp.

It burned his pride that she had seen him like this, crouched on the ground like a wounded animal. The second man struck again, and his shield reverberated from the vicious blow as he deflected it. But Breanne's presence renewed his resolution to win. He would do anything to defeat his enemies.

Oisin was gloating, and he held his sword aloft. 'Would you like to witness his death, Breanne? I could make you watch while I sink this blade into his heart.'

Alarr struggled and nearly managed to break away. But at a signal from Oisin, two more soldiers came to restrain him. They bore their full weight upon him, and he fought to free himself from the men.

'No,' Breanne said. 'Let him live.' Her tone was quiet, tinged with fear. 'I will do as you command.'

Alarr was about to voice a protest, but he saw her give a slight shake of her head. She had done this on purpose as a distraction. And he needed to take advantage.

Oisin seemed pleased by her response. 'Good.' He reached for her wrist and pulled her closer. 'Look at him.'

Alarr knew that his enemy was trying to demean him in her eyes. Although he ought to feel humiliated, instead he was determined to save her. At that moment, Oisin leaned in and kissed her hard. His mouth was bruising, possessive, and there was no doubt of the message he was sending. The man intended to claim Breanne, forcing her to do his will.

At that moment, Alarr wanted nothing more than

to bury his blade in the man's heart. But first, he had to free himself from his captors to reach his weapon.

'Oisin!' came a man's voice. It was Feann. His face was swollen, his lip bleeding as he held out his sword. 'Let her go.'

Oisin turned, and Alarr used the moment to push back against the men holding him down. He rolled away and managed to rise to his feet, though his knees were burning from the pain. He refused to give up and would willingly sacrifice his life for hers. Never would he allow Oisin to claim her.

Despite the pain, Alarr held his weapon and charged forwards, heedless of the soldiers. His only concern was reaching her before his enemy could harm her. Before he got very far, the other fighters flanked him. King Feann rushed forward with his sword and joined at Alarr's side. It was strange to realise that the man he'd tried to kill was now defending him and fighting alongside him. The clanging sound of iron resounded as the king blocked an enemy's sword. They moved back to back, facing off against their common foes. Breanne's face still held worry, yet she appeared startled by the sight of them together.

Oisin's mouth tightened, and he gripped her arm, moving towards the back of the ringfort. Alarr doubled his efforts against his opponents. He wasn't about to let him take Breanne.

'Go after her,' Feann commanded. 'I'll hold them off with our men.' Just as he'd predicted, several of the Killcobar soldiers joined in. And then, to his surprise, some of the Clonagh men joined at Feann's side.

Alarr didn't argue but hurried towards Breanne. Oisin stopped in the centre of the ringfort in a silent challenge. He held Breanne around the waist, and with his left hand, he reached under her skirt.

No. He would not stand by and let his enemy defile Breanne. Alarr raced towards them, but Oisin withdrew a hidden blade that had been strapped to Breanne's thigh. He held it against her throat and gave a mocking smile. 'Let her go, *Lochlannach*. And I might let you live.'

He pressed the blade against Breanne's skin until blood welled. The sight of her suffering ignited Alarr's fury, but he didn't dare move again for fear that Oisin would cut her throat.

'I don't think you want to come any closer,' his enemy continued. 'Or it will be your fault she died. Just like your first wife, wasn't it?'

Alarr didn't know how Oisin had any knowledge of Gilla, but he remained motionless. His mind tried to think of another way to save her, and he glanced back at Feann. The king and their men had pushed back the other fighters, but he held his sword and shield in readiness.

'If you harm Breanne, you will lose Clonagh,' Alarr warned. 'Her people will defend her.' He had already witnessed that, when the men of Clonagh had joined Feann in the fight.

'These people have never seen her before,' Oisin scoffed. 'They care nothing for her fate.'

'And what of me?' came a voice. Treasa emerged from one of the dwellings, and she pulled her hood back to reveal her face. 'Do you not think my people would defend me?'

Oisin's gaze turned mocking. 'If they cared, they

would have brought you out of exile.' He surveyed the lands and added, 'They need a strong leader to guide them.'

'They don't need a tyrant,' Breanne countered. She stared at Alarr in a silent message of her own. She appeared poised and courageous in the face of danger. But he worried that she would fight back. He didn't want to risk her being hurt.

'Oisin, do not do this,' Treasa pleaded. 'There is no need for fighting.' She stepped between them and pleaded, 'Put down the blade. Breanne has already agreed to wed you.'

Alarr tightened his grip on his weapon. He knew the woman was lying, but he couldn't guess what she was trying to accomplish.

Yet Oisin did not lower the knife. Instead, he addressed the crowd. 'I want everyone to know that I will always guard Clonagh from outsiders.' He stared at the people, and many looked away, out of fear. 'No one will threaten me or those I protect.'

'This isn't protection,' Breanne said quietly. 'This is cowardice. You are using me as a shield because you know this is a fight you cannot win.' She tried to pull his hand back, but his grip remained firm.

Alarr studied the man closely, wondering if he could somehow disarm him without hurting Breanne.

Oisin called out to his men and ordered them, 'Take her to my dwelling and bind her. I will come to her later.'

Breanne met Alarr's gaze with a quiet steadiness. He didn't know what her plan was, but it was clear that she had no intention of behaving like a meek woman.

There was an aura of determination about her, and he questioned what she would do now.

Without warning, Breanne slumped forward, her body going slack.

It was easy to behave like a helpless woman, for Breanne had behaved as such for all her life. But she'd had her fill of being a man's victim. It was time to act, time to free herself from this prison. The blade was still pressed close to her throat, but Oisin had lightened the pressure after she had let herself fall into a dead weight. Distraction was her aim, and the moment he pulled back the weapon, she shoved him backwards. She regained her footing and ran hard towards Alarr. He caught her in his arms and asked, 'Are you all right?'

She nodded, and he pressed her back. 'Go to Feann. He will get you out.'

'I'm not leaving you.' She knew, without a doubt, that he would stay and fight—even at the cost of his life. But this time, she had no intention of running away. Not any more. She would rather stand by his side and face the worst than abandon him to his enemies.

'Breanne, no.'

Before he could stop her, she turned and addressed the people of Clonagh. 'These men do not belong in your fortress. They have no right to lay claim to your land or your homes.'

She saw her mother take a step forward, as if she wanted to say something. But then, she faltered. Breanne stood at Alarr's back, heedless of the danger. There were dozens of men surrounding her father's meagre forces. Yet, she didn't believe that they wanted to live like this.

'Oisin is not your ruler. Stand together, and drive him out.'

The men of Clonagh appeared uncertain. It was a grave risk, but one worth taking if it meant saving the man she loved.

'These men are not fighters,' Treasa intervened. 'They know they cannot succeed against his forces. They know what will happen if they betray King Cerball and his son.' She returned to the centre of the ringfort and faced all of them. 'Is it not better to be protected by Oisin than to be his enemy? He will guard you and defend you.'

'He will imprison you,' Breanne countered. 'And I have no intention of wedding him.' She turned to stare at Oisin. 'You have no place here. I want you to leave.'

'You may want to reconsider that,' Oisin responded. Then he looked up towards the guard tower and gave a signal.

Within an instant, arrows descended upon Alarr and Feann.

Chapter Thirteen

Alarr barely reacted in time. He pushed Breanne out of range and raised his shield. 'Stay back!' he warned. One arrow grazed his leg, leaving a line of blood on his calf. Feann took an arrow in his shoulder and grunted with pain.

But in that moment, Alarr's rage erupted. Oisin had threatened the woman he loved, and intended to kill anyone who stood in his way. He moved back from his enemy, out of range of the arrows. But instead of running away, Breanne joined him.

'This isn't your fight,' he cautioned. 'It's not safe.'

'It is my fight more than yours,' she shot back. 'Oisin threatened me, my foster father, and the man I love.'

He reached out to take her hand and squeezed it in silent reassurance. 'I will not let anything happen to you, Breanne.'

'No,' she agreed. 'But Oisin is not going to live.' Her tone was hardened, as if she had nothing to lose. But she had no experience in fighting, and if she tried to face Oisin, she could die.

'Let me fight this battle on your behalf,' he said. 'Let me be your champion and defend your honour.'

She hesitated, as if she did not want to risk his life. Her eyes gleamed with unshed tears, and she squeezed his hand again. 'All right. But after you win, I am staying at your side. Wherever you go, I will go.'

Alarr leaned in and kissed her hard. 'So be it.'

The battle wounds of the past might have weakened his strength, but he would not stand down in this fight. She was his reason for fighting, but more than that, she was his reason to live.

No longer was his life shadowed by the need for revenge. Instead, he would fight to protect the woman he loved.

He moved back towards Oisin, and two of Feann's men joined Breanne to bring her to her father's side. The others were with the king, tending his injury. He embraced his foster daughter and spoke quietly to her.

When Alarr glanced back at the archers, he saw that the men of Clonagh had disarmed them, tossing the weapons aside. It surprised him, for it revealed that the people had no interest in Oisin winning this fight.

Then he turned back to face his enemy. 'Only a coward would send a man to attack from behind or use archers at a distance. You're afraid to fight me. Because you know you will lose.'

Oisin raised his own shield and sword. 'I am not afraid of a crippled warrior. You're going to die, *Lochlannach.*'

'Not by your hand.' He swung his weapon hard, and it struck Oisin's wooden shield. Alarr knew this was about more than defeating an enemy. It was about protecting Breanne and earning the right to wed her.

As he circled Oisin, more of the people gathered around to watch. They appeared intrigued by the battle, and their presence kept Oisin's men from joining in. Alarr centred his focus on his opponent. He knew not to trust Oisin if he revealed any sort of vulnerability, for it was always a trap meant to lure him closer. But the warrior's weakness was pride. If he could somehow humiliate Oisin, his temper might erupt and bring about carelessness.

His enemy fought like a man who had spent his entire life trying to be perfect...like one trying to please his father. And Alarr knew how to press that weakness.

'Your father never noticed you, did he?' he asked. 'Because you were only a bastard.'

He understood that emotion, for his father hadn't noticed him either. He was the second-born son, hardly worthy of notice. Sigurd had given Brandt his full attention, while Alarr was an afterthought, often forgotten.

When Oisin gave no answer, Alarr continued. 'I suppose you thought that by wedding Treasa's daughter, you would have your own lands and become chief.'

'I *will* be their chief,' Oisin answered. 'We will become one of the strongest fortresses in Eireann.'

Alarr lunged and tried to find a weak point, but Oisin only parried the blow. He circled again. 'Your father never believed you would become anything, did he?'

'He will soon think differently. And one day, I will have his lands as well.' The arrogance of the statement revealed his illusions of victory. But they would never come true.

From his peripheral vision, Alarr saw Treasa drawing nearer. She was gripping her hands together and muttering to herself. Worry creased her forehead, and he warned her, 'Stay back, Treasa. This is our fight, not yours.'

'It shouldn't be,' she mumbled. 'I arranged all of it. The priest, the wedding. Breanne is supposed to marry him.'

'Oisin will never be her husband,' Alarr insisted. 'Do as you will for Clonagh, but Breanne is coming with me.'

He continued to strike out at his opponent, but Treasa's hysteria was rising. 'No,' she moaned. 'My daughter must wed the son of a king. She must restore our lands. And I will be the one to guide her. I will be queen here until I have breathed my last.'

She took another step forward, and Alarr cursed under his breath. 'Stay back, Treasa.'

He increased his speed, their swords clashing again and again. Oisin was growing tired, and Alarr saw the perspiration on the man's forehead. He continued to fight, but Oisin barely avoided a death blow when he aimed for Alarr's legs.

The time to finish the fight was now. Alarr moved with swiftness, and all around him, he heard the sounds of encouragement from the people. It was unnerving to feel their support, but it aided him in a way he had never expected.

And then Treasa bolted between them, her knife raised high. 'She will never wed a *Lochlannach*.'

Alarr barely stopped his sword's motion, but Oisin's never ceased. It sliced through Treasa's flesh and bone, and he stumbled backwards. The people around him inhaled with shock as Treasa fell forward, knocking

Oisin to the ground. Her body lay in a pool of blood, and beneath her was Oisin. His expression held shock, and when Alarr pulled Treasa back, he realised that her blade had pierced Oisin's heart when she had collapsed atop him. His enemy was grasping at the weapon, but he could do nothing. He was choking, blood spilling from his mouth. Within moments, both of them were dead.

Breanne came running to him, and Alarr embraced her hard, heedless of the blood. He was dimly aware that one of the blades had cut him, but he cared not. All that mattered was being in her arms.

'I love you,' she whispered, kissing him. 'Thank the gods you are all right.'

Alarr held her close, and in that moment, all that mattered was holding her in his arms. It didn't matter about the people of Clonagh or the bodies of the fallen. All that mattered was her.

'I love you, Breanne,' he said. 'And I want you to be my wife.'

He hadn't meant to blurt out the words so suddenly, but it was the truth. He didn't want to awaken without her by his side. She had never perceived him as less than a man, and with her, he was whole. He didn't care where they lived, so long as they were together.

Breanne's face transformed with a blend of relief and joy. 'Yes,' she wept. 'I promise.'

He buried his face in her hair, feeling gratitude that she would share her life with him. When he pulled back, he saw Feann watching, and a look of understanding passed between them. The king knew that he would guard her with his life and defend her.

For so long, he had lived for vengeance, never realising that it was a hollow emotion. In the end, death would not heal the wounds of loss. Only love could do that.

When he took Breanne's hands in his and faced the people, one of the men approached. The man had dark hair with threads of silver, and he regarded both of them. With a glance at the others, he spoke only a few words. 'Our council of *brehons* would like to speak with you both to discuss the future of Clonagh.'

Alarr didn't answer at first, though he knew it was a grave concern for them. King Cerball wanted Breanne to govern her own lands with a loyal man at her side. But Alarr would never let anyone take her from him now. And that left him questioning what was right.

'I would like to speak to them as well,' came the voice of Feann. 'And I would like to propose that Breanne should become your queen.'

She was already shaking her head in refusal. 'I know nothing about ruling over a clan. And I will not wed another man for an alliance of your choosing. The only one I will take as my husband is Alarr.'

He held her close, feeling her tension rise higher. But the older clansman surprised him by nodding in agreement. 'Having a *Lochlannach* as your husband may prove to be of value. There are several settlements nearby. It would be an advantage to have someone who could intercede on our behalf and prevent raids.'

Alarr sobered as he realised what they were asking. They wanted him to stay at Clonagh with Breanne. Only a man of honour and strength could rule over a small kingdom. He held Breanne close, and though he had never imagined such a life would be possible, he would do anything to remain at her side.

Four days later

Breanne stood beside her father, the immense joy swelling up within her. Feann's expression held a tight emotion and he ventured, 'You're certain that wedding this man is what you want.'

She nodded, and smiled, feeling as if her heart would soar out from her chest. 'It is.' Her only regret was that Alarr's brother Rurik was not here, though she had sent a message to Killcobar. Likely, he was on a ship already, journeying to Northumbria, in search of answers. But she hoped he would return to visit.

Breanne wore a gown of deep green with a golden torque around her throat. Her hair was braided back with flowers, and the thought of her wedding brought a surge of emotions brimming up within her. Alarr meant everything to her, and she could hardly believe that they would be married this day.

'King Cerball will not like this union,' her father warned. 'He wanted you to wed an Irish ally.'

'But you will intercede for me, won't you?' She met his gaze with her own fervent hope.

'I will speak with him,' Feann promised. 'But I cannot say that Cerball will approve. If you allow his soldiers to stay for a time, he may relent and call them back, once he is certain there is no threat.'

Breanne didn't like the thought of the ringfort remaining occupied by Cerball's guards. And yet, she also understood that it was a means towards peace and a compromise was necessary. In time, perhaps she could convince the king to send them away.

'I hope that will not take long. The people feel uneasy with so many outsiders.'

Her father nodded with understanding. 'It will take time for them to accept the changes. But so long as you remain queen and appoint a small council of advisors, it will suffice.' One of the terms of their marriage contract was that Alarr had sworn to let her rule over Clonagh. He had admitted to her privately that he agreed with her father. It was easier for the people to accept an Irish queen than a foreigner. In the meantime, Alarr intended to oversee their defences and protect the ringfort from harm.

Breanne reached out to take her father's hand. Feann walked with her from the small dwelling and led her outside. Alarr was waiting for her, but she could see the apprehension on his face. Not from the marriage, but likely from memories of his previous wedding ceremony. His gaze shifted around the ringfort as if searching for invisible threats.

He wore his *Lochlannach* attire of a woollen tunic, leather armour and dark leggings. She was not at all displeased, for she was about to marry a warrior. This was his custom, and she was proud of his physical form. His dark hair was wet, and his face held the stubble of a dark beard. Around his throat, he wore a bronze necklace with small hammer pendants. It gave him a wild appearance, and a rush of desire filled her up inside. Later this night, she would welcome the chance to feel his hardened muscular form against hers.

But when Alarr caught sight of her, his expression transformed. There was wonder in his eyes, as if he could not believe she was standing there. She smiled at him, and he gave an answering smile. When he took her hands, she squeezed his in reassurance.

'I love you,' she whispered.

'I love you,' came his answer. 'And Freya herself could not be more beautiful.'

Before the ceremony could begin, there was the sound of an approaching horse. To their surprise, the gates opened, and a single rider drew near.

He dismounted and pushed his hood back. Alarr's face held surprise and happiness when he caught sight of his brother Rurik. The younger man hurried towards them. 'Did I miss the wedding?'

'Not yet,' Breanne answered. 'I am so glad you were able to be here.'

'As am I.' Alarr gripped his brother's forearms and smiled.

'Your bride sent a message, and I could not refuse.' He drew back and nodded. 'I wish you both joy in your marriage.' Then Rurik returned to stand by the other guests.

Happiness overwhelmed her with emotions, and she struggled to hold back happy tears. The priest began the words of the marriage rite, and at last, Alarr spoke his vows. 'In the sight of the gods, I take you as my wife, Breanne. I grant you my protection, and I will provide for you and our children. With Freya's blessing, I swear to honour you.'

The tears did fall, then, although she was smiling in the midst of them. The thought of Alarr becoming her husband brought a tender ache to her heart.

Breanne met his gaze and spoke. 'In the sight of the gods, I take you as my husband, Alarr. I will make a home for you and give you children, with the blessing of your gods and my own.'

He gripped her hands tightly, and when she finished her vow, she could see the intense love in his eyes. He would never abandon her, and she had complete trust in him.

The priest gave his blessing and then instructed Alarr to give her a kiss of peace. He did, and she embraced him fully, so grateful to be wedded to this man. But more than that, she was thankful that he had turned aside his vengeance and had learned to live in peace with Feann. She turned to her foster father, and whispered, 'Thank you.'

Alarr led her to the centre of the ringfort and leaned in to murmur at her ear. 'It is time for you to address the people as their queen.'

She kept his hand in hers and smiled at the people while they gathered around. 'I invite all of you to share in our wedding feast and celebration. Know that you are welcome here, and it is our promise to protect this clan. In time, Clonagh will be yours once more.'

At that, she saw tentative smiles among the people. Many raised their knees as a gesture of respect, and several cheered.

Alarr brought her a horn of ale and gave her the first drink before he drank from the same place her lips had touched. He covered the horn and then kissed her in front of everyone. It was a kiss of promise, and it kindled her desire.

Over the next few hours, there was feasting and dancing. She lost track of all the people, and there were so many names she would have to learn. But her happiness soared until she could scarcely contain her joy.

The air had turned cooler, and Alarr drew his cloak around her after he saw her shiver. She turned to him, pressing her hand against his heart. His arms tightened around her. 'Are you afraid, *søtnos*?'

She shook her head. Afraid wasn't the right word. She felt the deep pull of anticipation, and she drew her fingers lightly over his face. Alarr's skin was darker from the sun, and his cheeks were rough with his beard. He took her hand in his and led her to the dwelling that would be theirs. She ducked her head beneath the doorway as she went inside. The air was warmer here, heated by the hot stones around the room. There was a bed of furs in one corner, and someone had laid out food and drink for them to share.

'Is it right to leave the people alone at the feast?' she wondered aloud.

'I care not,' Alarr answered. 'I intend to spend the remainder of this day with you, my bride.' He drew a low table nearby and bade her to sit down. He chose a selection of roasted fowl, boiled goose eggs, honeyed cakes, and almonds for her. He broke off a piece of meat and drew it to her lips. She ate and did the same for him, bringing her fingers to his mouth. He sucked one finger inside, and she felt the answering pull of desire.

'Alarr,' she murmured. 'I find that I'm not very hungry right now.' She drew her arms around his neck, hoping he would understand her meaning.

'That's too bad,' he responded. 'For I am starving.' He lifted her into his arms and carried her to the furs.

After he lowered her to standing, he unlaced her gown, sliding it from her shoulders until it pooled at her feet. He kissed her hard, his callused hands moving to her bare skin beneath her shift. She gasped when he cupped one breast, his thumb caressing the erect nipple.

Alarr leaned in and kissed her, sliding his tongue

over the rosy tip while he stripped away the rest of her clothing.

He laid her back against the furs, and she could hardly breathe as he feasted upon her, tonguing one breast and then the other. His mouth was hot and hungry upon her skin, tasting every inch. His warm breath brushed over her navel, and he lifted her knees, spreading her open.

She was trembling at that, feeling utterly vulnerable to him. He cupped her bottom, lifting her until he drew his mouth to her inner thigh. She was already aroused, but the tension of his mouth so close to her womanhood was driving her wild. He slid his tongue so close, and then moved to the opposite thigh, kissing her gently.

She was desperate to have his mouth upon her, and her fingers gripped the furs tightly. 'Alarr,' she moaned. 'I need you so badly.'

In the darkness, she could see his head bent between her legs, and his hands gripped her hips, lifting her to him. With his tongue, he tasted her intimately, and she could not stifle her cry. His mouth tormented her sweetly, and she felt herself rising higher. He invaded her with his tongue, nibbling against her hooded flesh while a white-hot fire of need claimed her. She could barely gather her thoughts while he suckled against her most sensitive place.

When he used his thumb to caress her, she could bear it no longer. Her body was alive, the release gathering tightly inside, and when he slid two fingers inside, she lost control. A thousand shudders broke over her, and she arched hard, gasping as the pleasure flooded through her skin. Alarr entered and withdrew with his fingers, and she reached for him, guiding his hard flesh inside. He invaded her in one swift penetration, and she gloried in the feeling of his body joined with hers. She met him, thrust for thrust, wrapping her legs around him.

He deepened the sensations when he suckled at her breast once more, and she squeezed him within her depths. No longer was he gentle, and she revelled in his claiming.

'Take me,' she whispered. 'I am yours.'

He pinned her wrists to the furs, and she released her grip around his waist. Instead, she bent her knees to allow him a deeper angle. This time, his slick shaft rubbed against her, and she could not stop the release that erupted within her. There was only joy in making love to the man she adored, and she gave herself over completely. In his blue eyes she saw love, and when his face contorted, she watched as he took his pleasure, filling her with his seed. He entered and withdrew a few more times until he drew her legs to tangle with his.

She smiled, feeling the heat of their joined bodies. When she touched his chest, she could feel his heart racing. 'I am glad you captured me that day in the slave market,' she murmured. 'I cannot imagine a life without you.'

He kissed her, tracing the skin of her back. 'There is no life for me, without you.' He hugged her close, and she slid her hands down his back, over the curve of his hip, until she reached the scars on the backs of his knees.

He opened his eyes and stared at her while she traced them. 'I am also grateful that you did not kill Feann. And that you made a truce between you.'

'I did it for your sake,' he admitted. 'You are like a

true-born daughter to him. He would do anything to protect you. And that is something I understand.'

She brought her hands back to twine around his neck. 'Will you be happy with me at Clonagh? Or do you wish we would return to Maerr?'

'I want to visit Maerr,' he confessed. 'But that kingdom does not belong to me. It is my brother's, if he can reclaim it once more.' He kissed her mouth, and against her lips, he murmured, 'There was a time when I would never have considered staying here. Éireann is not my home.'

'But you belong with me,' she answered.

He leaned in to kiss her. 'You will be my queen, and I will guard you. Whatever we may face, we face it together.'

'Do you want to be a king one day?'

He shook his head. 'Only if there comes a time when the people ask it of me. Until then, I will be your protector.'

'And my husband,' she added. 'Perhaps one day, you will become a father.'

His expression softened, and she realised that he did want that as much as she. 'I will do my best to make you happy, *søtnos*. In whatever life the gods grant us, with any children we may have.' With a wicked smile, he caressed her sensitive breast once more. 'It may take some time before that happens. We will have to keep trying.'

She laughed and embraced him hard. Never had she imagined it was possible to feel so much happiness or love for a man. With Alarr, she became whole and beloved, and her eyes filled up with tears of joy.

'I love you,' she whispered, welcoming him into her

arms. And as the afternoon drifted into twilight, he did indeed try again.

And there was only the sweetest pleasure of knowing that she would awaken in this man's arms for the rest of her life.

Epilogue

R̲urik stared out over the dark-grey waves as the village of Glannoventa slowly came into view. The fierce wind rippling the sails of the ship assured him that he would reach it by nightfall. Boats bobbed in the sea along its coast. Further up, a fortress sat back on a hillside, the sinking sun turning the stones shades of orange and red. No doubt Wilfrid sat inside those walls, drinking ale and deceiving himself into thinking that he was safe. The man had no idea that vengeance was coming for him before the night was out.

Rurik did not seek revenge for Sigurd's sake—he had his own reasons. He despised his father for what he had done to Saorla. Sigurd had made promises to her that he had broken, and the past could not be healed of its scars. But Rurik intended to seek his own justice for his mother's sake and his brothers. After speaking to his uncle Feann and the others, piecing together what had happened on the day his father was murdered, Rurik had concluded that Wilfrid was the one responsible for the slaughter—and he would pay the price.

He glanced behind him towards the shores of Éireann that had long since disappeared. Alarr had found his own peace with his new bride and would stay there and guard Clonagh. As for the kingdom of Maerr, they both knew it was not theirs. Now that it was ruled by his uncle Thorfinn, no one knew if Brandt would try to reclaim it. Their oldest brother had gone cold with rage, isolating himself from everyone. Sandulf and Danr had their own demons to battle.

This battle was his.

When Rurik looked back at the approaching village, the setting sun had slid from behind a cloud, casting a glimmer on the sea that reminded him of blood. A fitting prophecy of what was to come.

No one would attack Maerr without retribution—he and his brothers had sworn it. Justice was coming for Wilfrid and anyone who stood in Rurik's way.

* * * * *

Marrying Her Viking Enemy
Harper St. George

Harper St. George was raised in rural Alabama and along the tranquil coast of northwest Florida. It was these settings, filled with stories of the old days, that instilled in her a love of history, romance and adventure. In high school she discovered the romance novel, which combined all those elements into one perfect package. She lives in Atlanta, Georgia, with her husband and two young children. Visit her website, harperstgeorge.com.

Books by Harper St. George

Harlequin Historical

To Wed a Viking

Marrying Her Viking Enemy

Outlaws of the Wild West

The Innocent and the Outlaw
A Marriage Deal with the Outlaw
An Outlaw to Protect Her

Viking Warriors

Enslaved by the Viking
One Night with the Viking
In Bed with the Viking Warrior
The Viking Warrior's Bride

Visit the Author Profile page
at millsandboon.com.au for more titles.

Author Note

I have always been fascinated by the Viking Age and the millions of dramas that must have turned up in ordinary life because of the melding of cultures that era produced. The strong women and men who found themselves forced together by circumstance and the way they dealt with the fallout is fodder for countless tales. My Viking stories are my hopes of how some of those could have played out with a happily-ever-after.

I'm so thrilled to be setting off on yet another Viking adventure with my new series, To Wed a Viking. As the name suggests, all the books will feature heroines who, one way or another, find themselves wed to Viking husbands. I hope you enjoy reading how Elswyth finds her way to falling in love with her Viking enemy. Look for her sister, Ellan, to find her own happily-ever-after soon.

Thank you for reading.

DEDICATION

With sincerest thanks to Laurie Benson,
Nathan Jerpe and Tara Wyatt for their friendship
and guidance while I was writing this book.

Prologue

'Traitors will be punished.' Rolfe's words rang out over the gathered crowd, punctuated by the roar of the newly set fire at his back.

A black cloud of smoke rose high in the air, filling the village of Banford with its acrid scent as tongues of flame licked hungrily at the hut's thatched roof. It was engulfed like kindling, half-burned to the ground by the time a blaze flickered to life on a second one. Tightening his hold on his stallion's reins to be ready should one of the Saxon warriors dare to attempt to fight him, Rolfe ignored the sharp ache in his shoulder from yesterday's battle. He refused to show weakness before these people, especially when he had to make certain that his words were heard.

'We found one of your neighbours among the Scots we battled yesterday. Durwin was there as a friend to them, giving information to our enemy, and he raised his axe to us in battle.' Durwin had been a simple farm worker with no sword to his name. He'd had no cause to meet with the Scots. No cause save the wounded pride that many of the Saxons seemed to share when it came to the Danes. On his cue, his men cut Durwin's blanket-wrapped body down from a horse and laid him respectfully on the ground.

Rolfe and his men had come directly from that confrontation to this village on Alvey lands where the traitor lived. Cnut, Rolfe's man in charge of the Saxon village, had quickly led them to Durwin's house. Thank the gods that it had been empty. Rolfe didn't relish the task of making women and children homeless.

'But what of his brother Osric?' An old woman's voice rose from the people who had come from their homes to watch. They all stood huddled together, a few with blankets over their shoulders to guard against the snow that had started to fall. The flakes hissed when they touched the flames that engulfed the second hut. 'Was he there, too?'

Cnut stepped forward. 'They've been suspected of fraternising with the Scots for months. Osric hasn't been seen in days. Can anyone vouch for his whereabouts?'

Of course no one could. Rolfe knew in his gut that Osric was fraternising with the Scots. Everyone in the village knew it, but no one would give up that information. It was why Rolfe had given the order to burn both of their houses. It was the only way to send the harsh but necessary message that traitors would not be tolerated.

'You are people of Alvey.' It was a simple fact that should need no reminder. 'You were born here and your loyalty should lie with your lord and lady.'

A few in the crowd nodded along with his words, but

many only stared at him. Pockets of rebellion had broken out since his Jarl, Vidar, had married their Saxon lady, Gwendolyn. Rolfe was hopeful that the melding of their people would continue, but it was inevitable to face some resistance. Their only choice was to catch it early. It was particularly disconcerting in this case because the village of Banford was the closest to the Scots who lived just north of their border. A rebellion here could have devastating consequences should they join with the Scottish army, which was why it was particularly important that he squash any seeds of uprising now. 'Lord Vidar and Lady Gwendolyn will not tolerate traitors. Anyone known to be giving information to the Scots will have their belongings seized and risk execution.'

A grumble of unease ran through the gathered crowd, prompting his dog, who had been lying beside the horse, to get to his feet, his ears forward. 'Easy, Wyborn.' Rolfe kept his voice low and the mongrel settled while still keeping alert to the possibility of danger.

'Consider that we Danes have not butchered your people. We have not taken your land from you. Will the Scots, who have haunted you for generations, be so fair? Will the Scots allow your women to choose their own mates? Will the Scots extend silver to the families who marry their warriors?'

He paused to look over their faces, hoping that his words rang true for them. The people murmured, but not one of them stepped forward or offered comment. This brooding rebellion was merely misplaced pride. If sense prevailed, they would come to understand that.

For real peace to be fostered and to thrive, they would have to accept that the Danes were here to stay.

'Your lord and lady have offered you all of these things. We have come to live in peace and to unite our people. The Scots will not offer you that. They will befriend you, only to enslave you.'

Rolfe gave a final nod and swung his horse around to walk to the edge of the village. Cnut and Wyborn walked beside him. 'Are any other men missing besides Osric?'

'None from the village.' Cnut nodded in the direction of the fields and the farmhouse set with several outbuildings on the outskirts of the village. 'I couldn't say about the farm. Since I've been here Godric keeps most of his people to himself, but I will question him.'

The wheat field was fallow now with the arrival of winter and, though most of the trees were bare, a hill hindered a clear view of the house. Godric was known to dislike the Danes, but so far had done nothing that would cross the line to outright treason. However, Rolfe had been gone from Alvey all summer—first visiting Jarl Eirik to the south and then Haken up north where he'd come across Durwin meeting with the Scots—and things might have changed. He'd need to speak with Vidar before doing anything in that quarter.

'Thank you, Cnut. Send word if Osric returns or you have more information.'

'Aye, immediately.'

Rolfe set his heels to his horse and led the way from the village, some of his men falling in line behind him. The rest of his army had been left to return home in the longships, while he detoured to Banford. Wyborn ran out front as if he sensed they were going home. The wound from the spear Rolfe had taken to his shoulder the day before ached with every jolt of the horse. It would take over a day of hard riding to make it home to Alvey. He'd been gone for months and was ready to be home. He only hoped this show of treachery wasn't a sign of things to come.

Chapter One

Bernicia, northern Northumbria—winter 872

'The Danes are a fearful sight, are they not?'

Elswyth could not find the breath to answer her sister's question. It had lodged in her throat where it held until her lungs burned. The Norsemen came out of the forest on horseback, filtering into the clearing in a stream of warriors that didn't seem to have an end. There were thirty…forty, but even more followed behind. Several mongrels in various shades of brown and grey ran in their midst. She imagined them as blood-thirsty wolves from the tales she had heard growing up, with teeth dripping the blood of their enemies and snapping jaws clamouring for more.

The sun hung low behind the trees, a stray beam glinting off their armour and the hilts of their sheathed swords, casting their faces in the shadow of a cold night-fall. The earth rumbled from the beat of the hooves as the horde moved closer. Her heart echoed that beat of distant thunder. It knew that the days of calm were over. These men were why her father had sent her to spy on Alvey.

It was an objective she meant to carry out, not only to prove her loyalty to her family, but also to bring hope to their small village of Banford. Banford needed hope that a reprieve from the Danes would soon come. She was to bring that hope to them in the form of information about the Danes' plans for the future.

'Aye,' she finally whispered when she could draw breath. 'They are quite fearful.' The frigid stone of the fortress wall bit into her palms as she stared down at the men approaching. The warriors were merely coming home and not here for battle, but her instinct was to reach for the short-handled axe at her belt as fear pounded through her veins. They were Danes, which meant they were her enemy.

''Tis good they are attractive, then.' Ellan grinned, her eyes calculating as she looked them over.

Elswyth smiled, for once grateful that Ellan was never serious about anything. Though only scarcely more than a year separated their births, Elswyth sometimes felt far older than her often frivolous younger sister. 'Why do you care if they're attractive?'

'Because I would not care for an ugly husband.'

The horde forgotten for the moment, Elswyth swung her head around to stare at her sister in shock. 'You are not seriously considering marriage to one of them?' Ellan surely wouldn't, especially after the way their mother had run off with a Dane, abandoning the whole family to take up with the heathen. But something in her sister's expression made Elswyth's breath catch.

'And why wouldn't I?' The wind caught the cloak covering Ellan's hair, forcing her to take it in hand. Her cheeks were pink from the frigid air, while her eyes were fierce with challenge. 'What husband is there for me once we return home to Banford? Shepherd? Farmer? I'd much prefer a warrior.' Her gaze returned to the Danes below. 'You have to admit they're far more attractive than the men at home.'

Still in shock at her sister's blasphemy, Elswyth's gaze found the man leading the warriors. He sat proudly on his stallion with broad shoulders. His shirtsleeves had fallen back as he rode to reveal the defined muscles of his forearms flexing as he held the reins. His fur cloak hung low behind him, exposing the strong sweep of his cheekbones and his bearded jawline to the light cast by the wall's torches. She couldn't make out details, but she could tell—with some regret—that it was a handsome face. Much to her surprise, his gaze was fixed on the two of them. If she wasn't so accomplished at keeping her thoughts to herself, she might've reacted, giving away how her heart pounded against her ribcage. Instead she levelled her gaze and stared back at him, too proud to let him know how afraid she was.

'Rolfe!' A boy near the gate called out to him and he forgot her, his mouth splitting in a grin as he surged forward, clearly happy to see the caller.

The warrior was attractive, but she would never admit that to her sister or anyone. It felt deceitful to acknowledge that attribute in her enemy. So instead, she focused on his hair. Ropes of the dark blond mass had been pulled back from his forehead and were secured at the crown of his head and left to fall well past his shoulders. No self-respecting Saxon man wore his hair in such a barbaric fashion. Her father would say that it was proof of their deviltry. She didn't think it was quite so sinister, but neither was it civilised.

Pitching her voice low so she wouldn't be overheard, she said, 'I would be careful what you say, Ellan. You wouldn't want word getting back to Father that you're thinking of aligning yourself with our enemy.'

The ever-present mischievous spark in her sister's eye glowed when she said, 'What will Father do precisely? Come and take me back?' Her arms widened as she indicated the thriving fortress around them. 'The great and terrible Godric may rule Banford, but we are in Alvey now and this is where I plan to stay. Besides, the Danes are not our enemies any more. Lady Gwendolyn has made certain of that with her marriage to the Jarl. Father is only bitter because of what Mother did. He lives in years that have long since passed. You can go back home if you want. You always did enjoy work on the farm more than I did.'

Elswyth refrained from pointing out that she didn't enjoy it as much as someone needed to care for the family after their mother's abandonment. Instead the sight of the Danes flooding through the gates, filling the yard of the fortress as friends and loved ones came out to greet them, held her captivated. Lady Gwendolyn had married the Dane Vidar nearly two years ago. Since then the pair had been doing their best to make certain the Saxons and Danes in their corner of Northumbria lived peacefully together. There was no doubt that the Danes only allowed the peace because they had taken lands, silver and women in return.

Saxon lands, Saxon silver and Saxon women.

The Saxons were slowly being replaced by the invaders, or so her father claimed. She could understand his fear as she looked down at the powerful warriors below. They were formidable.

Elswyth and her sister had spent the autumn in Alvey at the request of Lady Gwendolyn, helping with her household. Elswyth had seen first-hand how the people co-existed within these walls. The Danes and Saxons could get along, but only here. Outside in the farms and villages there was still strain. Every week brought more stories of the Danes' brutality to the south of England. Even in Alvey lands there were stories of men fighting over the women, who numbered too few to meet the demands of every Saxon and Dane warrior. Then there were women like Ellan—women like their mother— who willingly chose the Danes over the Saxons. Many Saxons were bitter about that.

A fight was likely to happen soon. Lady Gwendolyn might refuse to see it, but Elswyth had heard the discontent with her own ears. Her own family, with the exception of Ellan, it seemed, would champion a fight.

'You speak blasphemy. Father would never agree to you marrying a Dane.' Elswyth crossed her arms over her chest and met her sister's eyes which were green like the waters of the lake back home. Sometimes it seemed their eyes were the only thing they had in common. Instead of hair as dark as her own, Ellan's was striped with honeyed tones. Her sister had always been happy and free from the worries that plagued the rest of the family, while Elswyth had assumed the mantle of responsibility. Ellan was like their wayward mother in many ways and it was worrisome.

'As I said, Father doesn't have to agree. I'll choose my own husband, thank you very much.'

While Elswyth was certainly fine with Ellan choosing her own husband, their father and brothers would not agree to a Dane. Danes were not to marry.

'I think it best to get below,' she said, giving her sister a dubious look. 'Lady Gwendolyn will need extra hands for tonight's feast.' Elswyth led the way along the rampart to the steps set into the corner of the wall. The fires had been burning all day in preparation for the men arriving, so that the air was filled with the aroma of roasting meat and vegetables.

Ellan's eyes were alight with an infuriating glow as she looked over the crowd below. 'I wonder which of them I shall marry.'

Elswyth rolled her eyes. Tired of arguing, she said, 'You've had months to ponder that with the Danes left behind while these were out raiding or whatever it is they were doing. Why haven't you chosen one of them?' She had known that a large group of warriors led by a warrior named Rolfe were due to winter here, but she had not been able to find out what they had been doing over the summer months. She was certain it was information her father would covet.

Ellan giggled. 'Because these are *new*. Why limit myself when there are so many to consider?'

'You haven't the faintest idea how to choose a proper husband, Ellan. I fear for your future,' Elswyth teased and stepped on to the hard-packed ground to make her way to the great hall, careful to stay near the wall and away from the arriving warriors. They were creating such an uproar with their celebratory shouts and bellows that they seemed as wild as the beasts in the forest.

'You make it sound difficult. You simply pick a man with a pleasing look and a disposition to match and there you have a good husband,' Ellan explained.

'Ah, well then, I pity the task ahead of you. None of these wildlings have good dispositions.' As if to lend weight to her words, a man was thrown free from the crowd to land with a crash against the stone wall before them. He settled on his bottom with a hard thud before standing and shaking the wild mane of dark hair from his face. Muttering something in his harsh language that made his friends howl with laughter, he tackled one of them and the two rolled on the ground in a skirmish. The rest of their group shouted encouragements and circled around them. Elswyth resisted the urge to roll her eyes again. She would never understand the Danes.

Ellan hurried to catch up as Elswyth stepped around the group. 'Certainly not one of *those*. But there are some. Lord Vidar is acceptable. I thought I might make a search through the men closest to him.'

It was true. Lord Vidar was acceptable, as Danes went. In the months they had lived in Alvey, Elswyth had come to greatly admire Lady Gwendolyn. Where her family saw Lady Gwendolyn as a traitor to the Saxons, Elswyth had come to see how well she and Lord Vidar got along. He was crude and sometimes boorish, but he treated his wife well and had gained the respect of the people in Alvey, even the Saxons. She'd seen how he could be fair and reasonable. Their marriage had brought two groups of people together while avoiding the bloodshed of battle. Elswyth still pitied Lady Gwendolyn, but perhaps in this one instance marriage to a Dane had been necessary.

Still, the subject hardly bore considering for her and Ellan, but there was no use arguing with her sister. The girl did what she wanted and always had. Elswyth had no doubt that an ill-considered marriage with a Dane would send her running back to the farm within a year. 'I wish you luck sorting through that madness. As for me, I'll remain unwed for the time being.'

Ellan snickered, but she took Elswyth's hand to soften her words. 'Father won't like that any more than he'll like me with a Dane. You know he'd see you wed to Osric.'

'Osric?' Elswyth laughed.

'Aye? Why is that funny?'

'Osric is… Osric. He's a dear friend, but I'd never marry him.' Though she had to admit that it would be the natural choice. He was her father's trusted man on the farm and they had been friends since she was born, but he wasn't what she wanted in a husband. She couldn't name what it was that she wanted from a marriage except that it was to be more than a farmer's wife.

'I expect Father will disagree.' Ellan sniffed and took the lead.

'Nay, he won't like it, but he cannot force me to wed.' Lady Gwendolyn would never stand for it.

'I haven't found proof, but my gut tells me that Godric is in league with the Scots.' Rolfe tightened his grip on his tankard of mead and tossed back a swallow, savouring the honeyed sweetness. The stench of treachery might have soured his homecoming, but at least there was mead.

Vidar cursed under his breath and shook his head. 'Godric has that entire village in his grip. Either he knew of Durwin's treachery or he won't believe it. The only certainty is that he will demand blood in return for the man's death.'

Rolfe ground his molars as he remembered the fight with the Scots, anger at the Saxon's presence there still burning hot within him. 'They *have* blood in return. I wanted to take Durwin alive, but he fought, cleaving two of my men before he was felled. He'd gladly have killed us given the chance.'

'Are they well?'

'Aye, one will bear a nasty scar, but they'll both recover.'

Vidar nodded and leaned back, turning his tankard absently between his palms. 'We'll keep Durwin's death quiet for now. I'm certain the news will make its way here in time, but there's no sense in announcing it.'

Rolfe was in firm agreement. Many of the Saxons within Alvey's walls had already made peace with

the Danes, but there were some holdouts. He wouldn't
have them using this whisper of rebellion as a reason
to fight. 'I've already talked to my men. They'll hold
their tongues about him.'

'Good. How were the talks with Haken?'

'He has agreed to align with us should the need arise.
He has nearly two hundred men on Alba's west coast.
Says there were a few skirmishes, but he rarely sees
more than twenty Scots at once. I doubt we'll have need
of his men.' Rolfe took another long drink.

Aside from the matter of Durwin and his brother,
Osric, the summer campaign had been a success. After
spending most of it to the south with Jarl Eirik, Vidar's
eldest brother, Rolfe and his men had taken their boats
north for the autumn. The meeting with Haken, the
Dane Jarl to the north, had gone far in creating an alliance between his camp and Alvey.

Vidar nodded, but his eyes were troubled. 'We cannot underestimate the Scots. They've been a nuisance to
Alvey for ages and with our numbers increasing, they're
bound to be agitated. In the morning, after you've had
time to refresh yourself, we'll discuss plans for what
to do with them. It's time we meet and end this once
and for all.'

'You think a meeting is necessary?'

Vidar gave a short nod of his head. 'The rumours
of Banford turning to them get stronger and this could
very well push Godric into it. I'd like to think they are
only rumours, but we can't take that chance. Godric is
difficult. I fear we have no choice but to put an end to
any potential alliance before it gets worse.'

'You two look serious. Is there news?' Lady Gwendolyn approached with baby Tova in her arms. Wyborn rose from his place at Rolfe's feet, tail wagging as he greeted them both, giving the baby an enthusiastic sniff that made her babble gleefully.

'Aye, some,' Vidar said, shifting on the bench so that she could sit beside him. He indicated the sacks of coin on the table that Rolfe and his men had lifted from the Scots. 'Rolfe encountered the Scots and this is what we have for the trouble.' A smile lit his face as he took the baby and sat her on his knee.

Rolfe grinned, always happy to see the woman who had given Vidar his much-needed comeuppance. She, along with Tova's chubby cheeks, were enough to brighten his mood. Now that Wyborn had moved back to his place at Rolfe's feet, the baby stared at him, her blue eyes round in curiosity. 'I see you've had a busy summer. She's grown.'

Lady Gwendolyn settled herself on the bench beside Vidar, a soft expression on her face as she glanced over at her husband and child. 'Very busy. Not yet a year old and she's already trying to walk.'

'Ah, she's a determined one, like her mother.' Lady Gwendolyn smiled, so he shifted his gaze to Vidar as he said, 'I feared the babe would look like her father, but the gods have smiled on her and only given her his wheaten hair. She looks more like you now, Lady. She is beautiful.' And indeed she was. Her cheeks were plump and rosy, her eyes bright and inquisitive.

Lady Gwendolyn gave him a playful glare while Vidar chuckled and the babe looked away, the sound of her father's deep laugh drawing her gaze. An unexpected ache swelled in Rolfe's chest at the scene. There was no doubt that his homecoming was victorious. Despite the traitors in their midst, he should feel pleased and content for a job well done. Instead, watching the little family before him made him aware of what was missing from his own life. It was a peculiar feeling, when he'd been content with his life for a while now.

To distract himself he reached forward and stroked Tova's silken hair, stifling a grunt of pain as he pulled at the wound on his shoulder. 'She'll rule this place soon.'

'You're hurt, Rolfe!' Lady Gwendolyn exclaimed. She rushed around to his back and pulled at his tunic. He grimaced as the blood that had dried to the linen under-tunic pulled at his wound and looked across the hall to distract himself as she prodded.

He'd been vaguely aware of the woman he'd seen atop the wall working across the hall this whole time. He found her now, trying her best to not appear as if she was curious about him as she filled cups with mead, all the while she kept stealing glances at their small group. Her expression was filled with the same wariness and grim determination he'd seen on her face outside. A thick braid of dark hair fell over her shoulder, across her lush breast and nearly down to her waist. She hadn't been in Alvey when he'd left and he couldn't help but wonder who she was.

'There's a good amount of blood,' said Lady Gwendolyn and he grimaced as she poked the tender edges of the wound. The woman had many skills, but sensitivity to his pain didn't appear to be one of them.

'A spear tip, compliments of the Scots. It's fine. It wasn't very deep.' It burned like fire, but a fever had yet to set in.

'What happened?' she asked and he gave her an abbreviated version of events.

'A minor skirmish.' He shrugged when he'd finished. 'There were less than twenty of them.' He'd leave it to Vidar to tell her about Durwin's betrayal.

As she moved back around him to retake her seat, she followed his gaze to the girl across the hall. Giving him a knowing smile, she said, 'Go upstairs and I'll send someone to tend you.'

He thought about objecting, but the idea of possibly having some time alone with the girl was too pleasing to pass up. Grabbing a bag of loot that would be his portion from the stash on the table, he rose to his feet and sought his chamber.

Chapter Two

Elswyth hadn't thought that she would be attending the warrior named Rolfe in his bath. Yet there he sat in a tub of steaming water. His chest was thick and broad, roped with muscle above the rim of the tub which was too short for his large frame. His knees were bent, sticking up out of the water so that she could see the cords of muscle that shaped his powerful thighs. Water clung to his hair, making it a few shades darker than the blond it had been earlier. It hung free from its constraints, but had been pushed back to better reveal the chiselled planes of his face. His nose was a bit too prominent, his brow line too defined, his lips too hard, but somehow taken altogether those features were almost pretty on him. A masculine pretty that took her aback.

And that was before he looked at her. His eyes were the purest blue she'd ever seen. Not piercing, but intense and so vivid the colour almost didn't seem real. There was a kindness lurking in their depths that helped her to step farther into his chamber and draw the door closed behind her. Lady Gwendolyn had made it clear to all when they'd arrived that she and Ellan were not here for the men's pleasure. But this man was new and she didn't know if he'd been advised. Wounded or not, he was powerful enough to do what he wanted with her and, though she could fight him, her axe was best thrown from a distance.

A soft growl from the corner warned her to proceed with caution, as a large mongrel with grey fur rose to his feet. 'Down, Wyborn.' The dog responded immediately to the warrior's command and lay back down, but his ears were standing up as he watched her.

Casting her wary gaze from the mongrel to his master, she said, 'I've brought herbs for your shoulder, Lord.'

'I'm no lord.' His voice was somehow smooth and rough all at the same time and pitched so low that the timbre of it was quite pleasing. She was surprised at how easily he spoke her language with barely any accent at all. His gaze dropped to the axe on her hip before he turned back to the task she had interrupted and splashed more water over his head, though he only used his right hand.

His chamber was larger than she'd thought. Shelves and chests lined one wall and a table and bench occupied the corner. Behind the dog, a bed was set into an alcove that could be curtained off from the rest of the room. It was larger than the one she shared with Ellan and piled high with thick furs. In the middle of those furs a red stone set amid pieces of silver and gold glinted back at her in the candlelight. She carefully averted her eyes from that treasure. It was stolen from a Saxon, no doubt. The thought gave her the surge of anger she needed to rediscover her courage.

'What's your name, girl?'

She set the tray holding the poultice, linens and herbs down on a chest a little harder than she'd intended to. So hard that he paused in his administrations and looked over at her. 'I'm no girl,' she said, mimicking his words to her. Whenever men wanted to keep her in her place they liked to throw that word around. It made them feel stronger and she found herself disappointed that a warrior such as him would feel the need to use it.

She expected him to let those unnaturally vivid blue eyes sweep down her body. To take in the curves of her breasts and hips. To make it clear that he understood that she wasn't a girl after all. Her body could only belong to a woman who could only be here to please him with those very same curves. But he didn't break eye contact except to take in her expression. Finally, he gave a brief nod and a tiny smile lurked around the corners of his mouth, hinting at a dimple in his cheek.

'Nay, you are no girl. I can see that now.'

Those words felt like a compliment. In a life that had been short on compliments of late, it was most welcomed. Her cheeks burned and she looked down at the tray to make herself appear busy.

'What are you called?' he asked.

'Elswyth.'

'I'm Rolfe,' he said and held out his hand.

She stared at it, half-expecting it to hold some danger, which was silly. It was simply a hand, calloused and rough looking with a complement of various nicks and cuts. However, men did not generally offer a hand to her, especially in her current capacity as servant. It was suspicious for its eccentricity alone. With a glance at his bare chest and the water lapping at his hips, she gave him her hand in a brief touch before quickly turning to secure a scrap of linen for a bandage. This man had unsettled her from the first. The sooner she could be done with this task the better.

'You weren't here when I left in the summer. Who are you?' He, too, seemed content to go back to the task at hand and continued to sluice water on his body.

'My mother was a distant relation of Lady Gwendolyn's mother. My sister and I have served here for the past few months at the Lady's invitation.'

With a gentle hand on his shoulder, she pushed him forward to take a closer look at his wound. His hair nearly covered it, so she was forced to take the thick mass in hand and move it aside. It was wet silk against her palm, smooth, yet strangely rough, too. The heaviness of it sliding against her skin seemed too personal. Everything about this seemed too personal. She should have very little to do with this man who was her enemy, yet here she was tending to him in his bath. He was naked beneath the water and her entire body burned in awareness of that fact.

Forcing a deep breath, she leaned in closer to examine the puncture. He was lucky that it hadn't festered yet. The edges were slightly pink, but they weren't swollen and angry. It was clear that someone had tended it after it had happened. Plunging the linen into the water, she gently ran it over the gouge to clean out the dried blood. 'Sorry,' she whispered, though he hadn't flinched.

The mongrel came forward, curiously sniffing around her as she worked on his master. She tried to ignore him, somewhat confident that the warrior would intervene should the mongrel overstep his bounds. Reassured that she meant his master no harm, the mongrel went back to his spot beside the bed and plopped down. Putting his front two paws out in front of him, he dropped his muzzle on to them and watched her, his deep brown eyes glittering in the candlelight.

'Are you a healer?' Rolfe asked.

'I know enough to clean wounds and mix common poultices. It is one of my tasks back home.' Satisfied that she'd done her best to remove the dried blood, she grabbed a bit of soap from the bowl that sat on the floor beside the tub. He clearly wasn't able to use his left arm well, so his back was still marred with smudges of dirt and old blood from the wound that he hadn't reached. With gentle strokes, she washed his back, the linen moving over his skin in a soft caress that allowed her to feel just how hard he was beneath his skin. His strength was powerful and could have been intimidating, but he merely hummed softly in approval of her touch and dropped his forehead to his knees, lending an odd peace to the moment.

When she was finished cleaning, she laid the linen across the rim of the tub and dipped a dish into the bucket of steaming hot water that had been left beside the tub, careful not to burn her fingers. 'This may hurt a bit.'

He smothered a groan as she trickled the hot water over his wound. The water left streaks of reddened skin down his back. 'I'll need to do it once more to make certain the wound is clean. It helps the healing.' He nodded, leaning forward a bit more to give her better access. This time he didn't make a sound save for a swift exhalation of breath as the scalding water slid over him. 'There. It's done.' The wound had reopened, but only a little blood seeped from it. It was a good sign that there would be no festering.

'You've been sent to exact Saxon vengeance. Admit it.' His blue eyes gleamed at her over his shoulder, that same almost-smile hovering at the edges of his mouth.

'I'll admit nothing,' she quipped, squeezing out the linen and indulging this strange urge to tease with him. 'But if a Saxon gave you this scratch, 'tis my duty to make it hurt more.'

He laughed and sat back against the rim, his eyes stroking her face. 'Then I'm forced to disclose the truth. It was no Saxon, but a Scot. Are you under the same allegiance to the Scots?'

She had to force herself not to take in a breath or show any sort of reaction. He was teasing, but it was as close to the truth as anyone had come in the entire time she had served Lady Gwendolyn. *She* was not in league with the Scots, but her father very well might be by now. There had been rumours that he'd met with them before she'd left.

'Not to my knowledge.' She gave a shrug, hoping the comment sounded flippant and a part of the game.

'That's good to know. Otherwise I would worry about your axe.'

'You're not worried about it regardless? Saxon vengeance, as you said.'

His eyes fairly sparkled with merriment and she found herself unable to look away from them. It was as if someone had found a way to dye them the most vivid shade of blue she had ever seen. He slowly shook his head, a drop of water running down the side of his face. 'It's an interesting choice of weapon.'

She stared down at the axe attached to her belt because she had to look away from him. 'It's more tool than weapon. It's useful on the farm and I've grown accustomed to wearing it.' She didn't mention that she was more accurate than any man when it came to hitting targets with it. 'Lady Gwendolyn has been kind enough to give me archery lessons while I'm here. Perhaps you should worry about that tomorrow on the practice field.'

This made him grin and that dimple in his cheek shone. He was so handsome when he smiled that she had to look away again. He was likely to think she was a fool like Ellan with how she seemed suddenly unable to hold his stare. There were many ways that this man unsettled her. What was happening? Was he flirting with her? Was this teasing usual for the warrior?

Enemy, enemy, enemy, the mantra repeated in her head.

'I'll look forward to seeing that.' Something about the way he said that, so firm and exact, made her believe it. It also made her chest swell with pride. Despite herself, it pleased her that a warrior of his renown wanted to watch her skill.

'Is that where you were all summer?' She busied herself by sorting the items on the tray and preparing the poultice. 'Fighting the Scots?' She told herself that she was asking out of curiosity, but the words of her father wouldn't leave her. They made that feeling of unease churn deep in her belly. Any news about the relations between Danes and Scots would be useful to him.

'Not all summer, but a fair bit of it. They've been active, but are so far no threat to Alvey.'

'My home is to the north. Should I be worried about them?' It was a fair question. She had spent many nights in her bed worrying about the Scots to the north and the Danes to the south, and her tiny village caught between them.

'Nay, no need to worry yet. And, Elswyth...' She nearly dropped the poultice when he reached out to touch her shoulder. His eyes were deep and solemn with concern. The warmth from his touch moved down her back to settle deep in her belly, wrapping itself around that knot of unease. 'We'll protect you from them if the time comes.'

And what if we are the reason the Scots have come? What if Father has done something that has brought them to our door?

She didn't ask those questions, though. She would not give her family away. 'How do you know they won't be too powerful?'

He smiled again and let her go. His teeth were straight and white, making his smile far too pleasing for a warrior such as him. He should be fierce, with a fierce smile to match. His expression turned to pure masculine arrogance when he answered, 'They'll never be too powerful for the Danes.'

She scoffed and made a show of finishing her work with the poultice, mixing the herbs in the bowl before readying a bandage with a length of folded linen. However, deep in her heart, she feared that he was right. She'd been impressed with the Danes who had spent the summer in Alvey. She'd been even more impressed by the sheer power of the army that had marched into Alvey hours ago. Tomorrow she would see them in practice, but she really had no need to see them to know that they would be fierce. Their reputation preceded them there.

'You Danes are all alike. Too full of yourselves for your own good.'

'It's not conceit if it's true. I've never lost a fight.'

She found it very easy to believe him. He sat in that humble tub like a king, his powerful arms stretched along the rim, his eyes shining with confidence. In that moment she had to wonder if it was possible for anyone to best him.

His eyes had gone slightly hooded as he watched her, an indolent quality coming over his face. 'I toured the north after Lord Vidar married Lady Gwendolyn. I don't remember meeting you.' He said it as if he would've remembered.

God knew that she would have remembered him had they met before. He was too vibrant and too formidable, equal parts terrifying and fascinating.

'Nay, we never met.' She remembered their visit well, though her father had kept her and Ellan hidden away inside so that she'd never actually seen Rolfe. It was no secret to anyone that Father distrusted the Danes. She suspected it had been one of the reasons Lord Gwendolyn had sent for her and her sister. The woman was ever trying to make peace, but it seemed no matter what she did, Father wouldn't approve.

He despised the fact that his own wife had run off with one of them. It ate at him constantly. Before it had happened, he'd always been stern and quiet, but something had changed in him in the years since. He brimmed with anger and bitterness. Lady Gwendolyn marrying a Dane had brought it all to overflowing. He hated that she'd married Lord Vidar and he hated all the Danes in Alvey that came as a result of that marriage. There would be no peace as far as he was concerned.

Elswyth had been surprised that Father had agreed to Lady Gwendolyn's plan, but his reasoning had become clear on the morning of their departure. He had approached her horse where she was saying goodbye to her younger brother Baldric. Ellan had followed their older brother, Galan, out of the yard, giving them a brief moment of solitude.

Pitching his voice low, he'd said, 'Keep your eyes open, Elswyth. We need to know what these Danes are really up to. I'll expect your account upon your return.' She'd stared at him in shock, but he'd only slapped the horse on the rump and called after her, 'I'm depending on you!'

He had meant for her to spy. A lump of unease had

been present in her belly ever since. Rolfe's presence only made it worse. While everyone knew that Lord Vidar was in charge, he would not dare to lead warriors against people he was sworn to protect. Should an uprising occur, it would be Rolfe sent to dowse it. Rolfe commanded the warriors. Rolfe would raise his sword against her village and her family if it was ordered.

Knowing all of that, she couldn't understand why he fascinated her so. She should despise him. Because of men like him, her mother had abandoned the family. Elswyth had been forced to take over her duties when she'd scarcely been able to carry a pail of water on her own. She had spent the formative years of her childhood wondering how she could have prevented her mother from leaving, questioning if she had been a better daughter would her mother have stayed and even secretly thinking that perhaps she herself was unlovable.

Yet, even with that history giving her plenty of reasons to hate him, she couldn't keep her eyes from him. From beneath her lashes, her gaze swept over his broad shoulders and the cords of muscle that defined his arms. 'You'll need to get yourself dry so that I can put the poultice on your shoulder. It shouldn't get wet.'

Without giving her a chance to prepare herself or even avert her eyes, he stood in the tub. Water sluiced down his strong body in rivulets, reflecting gold in the soft glow of the candles. The solid muscles in his back tapered down to a narrow waist and a pair of buttocks that might have been carved stone. His thighs were corded in muscle, thick as tree trunks and just as strong from the looks of them, with a light sprinkling of dark blond hair. In the slit of light visible between them, the weight of his manly parts hung—a gasp tore from her throat when a sheet of linen blocked her view, making her realise that she had been staring. Not once had she even attempted to avert her gaze. He had been decent enough to not ogle her the entire time she'd been in his chamber, his eyes had never left her face as they'd talked, but she couldn't find the decency to look away from his nakedness. Her face burned in shame as she forced her attention to the poultice.

He stepped out of the tub on to a rug made of rushes and tied the sheet around his waist. Grabbing another sheet of linen, he wrapped it around his shoulders, though he did it awkwardly with one hand while keeping his left arm against his torso. She would have helped him had she not been too astonished at her own bad behaviour. Instead, she waited for him to get settled on the bench before bringing the tray over to set it on the table next to him, her face—indeed her entire body—still flaming with embarrassment. Slowly and with as little touch against his bare skin as possible, she used the sheet to dry off his back.

Working with efficiency, she managed to apply the poultice on to his wound and wrap linen around his shoulder. The light sprinkling of fur on his chest teased her fingertips on the first pass, sending cinders of curious sensation running down her arm. This man was nothing like she had imagined. He wasn't a monster, or even particularly unpleasant. He was simply a man, made of warm, solid muscle and bone. Yet, that realisation somehow made him more dangerous to her. Tying off the end of the bandage, she stood back, making minor adjustments to the wrapping. 'I'll make you a sling. You should wear it to keep your shoulder braced until it starts to heal. You don't want it to break open again.'

'I'll try.' Wearing only the linen slung low around his waist, he walked to a chest at the foot of his bed and pulled out an under-tunic. 'Would you help me put it on?'

With a wordless nod, she took the folded linen from him. She was tall for a woman, but he was so much taller he had to stoop down for her to put it over his head. A tightening of his jaw was the only indication he gave that he experienced discomfort as he shoved his left arm through the sleeve. She didn't even give him time to rummage through the chest for trousers, knowing that she couldn't handle the embarrassment of watching him discard the linen sheet to put them on. Instead, she immediately grabbed the material for the sling and stepped up to him.

He smelled good. Clean like the soap, but also like evergreen needles in the forest mixed with a rich masculine scent that was very pleasing. He was quiet as she fitted it, knotted it and then slipped it across his chest, but she could feel his eyes on her face. They seemed curious and that damnable kindness lurking in their depths made it impossible for her to summon the anger and hate that she meant to feel towards him.

'When do you go back home?'

The question made her heart stutter. Satisfied with the sling, she lowered her arms from his shoulders and forced herself to take a step back from him. Distance seemed very good at the moment. 'My father is meant to come before the next full moon.'

'A fortnight, then.' He nodded as if the information pleased him somehow, as if he was mulling something over and that worked nicely into his plans, when she shouldn't fit anywhere into his plans.

Her heart picked up speed and she turned to quickly gather up the tray of medicinals that she'd brought. Never mind that her hands shook for some odd reason or that her knees were so weak she felt certain they would follow suit. *Distance*. The single word replaced the 'enemy' mantra in her head because she no longer believed that to be true. Or worse. It was true, but it was no longer enough to keep a wall between them.

'Good evening.'

'I look forward to seeing your aim on the practice field in the morning.' His voice followed her out.

Chapter Three

'That's twice I've bested you. If these swords weren't wooden, you'd be dead by now.' Aevir deftly swung away, leaving several feet between him and Rolfe.

Rolfe doubled his assault, ignoring how his arm smarted where Aevir's training sword had hit as he pushed his friend even farther back in an attempt to wipe the smug smile from his face. Rolfe had spent the entire morning running the men through their paces and taking playful digs from some of them about his sling. It was time they realised that having his left arm in a brace wouldn't slow him down. 'You must be jesting. You've yet to best me once.'

Aevir scoffed, 'I would've drawn first blood had the sword been metal.' He lunged forward again and Rolfe rolled to the side, leaving Aevir off balance.

'And when do we ever battle to first blood?' Rolfe asked.

'Had the blade drawn blood, you would have cried out in pain and broken your stride, leaving yourself open so that I could skewer your gullet.'

'You live in your fantasies.' Rolfe laughed and renewed his attack. The truth was that he *had* been distracted in their sparring match, but it hadn't been because of his wound. Elswyth had come out on to the other side of the field with her bow and a quiver of arrows and was currently shooting at targets. His gaze had been caught by her form in profile, equal parts slim and lush as she had notched an arrow and pulled back the string. He'd been waiting to see if she'd made her target when Aevir had hit him.

'Go easy, Aevir.' Vidar's voice interrupted their sparring. 'He's an injured man. I wouldn't have you making his injury worse.'

Rolfe groaned silently. Vidar meant well, but he'd only make the teasing worse.

Aevir grinned and lowered his sword. 'The Jarl has saved you, my friend.'

The sling on Rolfe's left arm restricted his balance a bit, but his wound was hardly in any danger. 'Nay, let's finish.'

Aevir raised his sword to accept the challenge, but Vidar stepped between them. 'We have other things to discuss this morning, now that you've both had some rest.' The three of them walked to the edge of the practice field. The clang of steel on steel and splintering wood as the warriors continued to practise filled the air around them.

'As long as it's the Scots and not wives we're discussing again,' Aevir said in a dry tone.

'Wives?' Rolfe asked.

Vidar gave him a telling glance before looking towards his own wife, who had made her way to them across the sparring field where she'd been leading a group of archers in practice. Lady Gwendolyn was quite possibly the most accomplished archer Rolfe had ever seen. She smiled at them as she approached, but trepidation lurked in her expression, a rare moment of uncertainty for her.

'Good morning. How is your shoulder?' Lady Gwendolyn asked.

After assuring her that he was on the mend, he asked, 'Am I being offered up as a husband?'

She had the grace to look sheepish. 'I admit the lack of marriages among the Danes and Saxons concerns me. We've had a few families take us up on the offer of coin in exchange for marriage to the Danes, but most are reluctant.' It had been their hope that after their marriage others would follow suit. They wanted to unite the Saxons and Danes in Alvey through marriage and avoid as much bloodshed as possible.

'It will take time.' Vidar ran a hand down her back in silent support.

She nodded before continuing. 'We would like it to be known that our highest warriors…including you… are looking for wives. I think an offering of higher-status marriages would ease some reluctance.'

Rolfe laughed, but it was a hollow sound. The very thought of marriage made the skin on his neck tighten uncomfortably. 'You *are* offering me up as husband.'

Her cheeks reddened, but she didn't back down from her stance. 'You have to admit that many would say you are a desirable husband. Your word among the Danes is

second only to Vidar's. You are known as a great warrior with great wealth.'

'It's true,' Rolfe said, mulling over her words and
making Vidar laugh out loud.

'It's good to see you're still humble, Brother.'

Ignoring him, Rolfe said, 'I can see how this would
be helpful for harmony.' It would not, however, be helpful for his peace of mind. He tried not to think of the
woman he'd nearly married back home, but her face
came to mind anyway. Hilde had been beautiful. He'd
convinced himself that she was kind and generous,
everything he'd thought he'd wanted in a wife. He'd
learned too late—after her thievery—that her beautiful
outside had hidden a traitorous core. She'd only used
him for her own gain.

Lady Gwendolyn's smile brightened, encouraged
by his words. 'I resisted my father's way of thinking,
but I understand now how marriage to further peace is
best for everyone.' Vidar smiled at her, his eyes full of
gentleness and admiration.

Rolfe wasn't entirely surprised by the plan and it certainly spoke to that odd longing for a family he'd felt
upon his homecoming last night, but he didn't relish the
idea of marrying. The amount of trust inherent in such
a union was not something he was comfortable with.
Of its own volition, his gaze landed on Elswyth. The
same short-handled axe from last night was hooked on
the belt around her waist, leading him to wonder if she
wielded it as well as the bow and arrow.

Glancing back to Lady Gwendolyn and then Vidar,
he could practically feel the noose of matrimony tight-

ening around his neck. He wouldn't shirk his duty, but neither would he welcome it. His only choice was to make certain of the only thing he could control. 'I would choose my own wife.'

'Of course,' Lady Gwendolyn was quick to acquiesce. In a softer voice she added, 'But you would have to choose someone beneficial to uniting our people.'

He gave a nod, his gaze once again shifting over to Elswyth of its own volition.

The victorious glance that passed between Vidar and his wife wasn't lost on him. They had already discussed his marriage, it seemed.

'Thank you, Rolfe,' Vidar said. 'You'll be well-rewarded for your duty. With things to the north unsettled, it goes without saying that sooner rather than later would be best.'

'Aevir will be called to marry as well?' Rolfe and Vidar had known Aevir for several years. He was a renowned warrior who had fought in the south as the battle had been waged for East Anglia. He'd gained a reputation there for his fearlessness in battle and had gone on to fight for Jarl Eirik for the past couple of years. Yesterday when he'd ridden in with Rolfe had been the first time he'd set foot in Alvey. Rolfe knew the man had vowed never to settle down because of some trauma from his past, so he lived a life that was never settled, always moving from place to place looking for the next fight. Rolfe liked him and respected him, but he found it hard to believe the man was ready for marriage.

'For the right woman it could be well worth it.'

Aevir shrugged. 'But it's too early in the day to speak of women.'

'The right woman?' Rolfe asked, unable to believe his ears. Aevir was actually considering marriage.

Still smiling, Aevir shrugged. 'The right lands and riches to be more specific.'

That sounded more like what Rolfe had expected. Still, the idea of marriage without affection was hard for him to accept. He had pledged his loyalty to Jarl Vidar and would do it if his duty called for it, but it wasn't what he would choose for himself. Aevir had no such pledge holding him here. 'And what of the woman herself? Her face?' *Her heart.* Rolfe didn't say that part, but he could not imagine sharing his home and future children with a woman who was cruel or less than honourable. Someone like Hilde.

'What does a face matter in the dark of night?' Aevir laughed, but when he glanced away there was a hollowness in his eyes. It was the same empty resolve he brought to battle that made him a great warrior. Rolfe didn't think it would work so well in marriage. 'Her lands and wealth will suit me much better than a fine face.'

Rolfe shook his head, but he hadn't expected anything else from Aevir. The man would sell his hand like he sold his sword, it seemed. He wouldn't be the first man to do so. Once more he found Elswyth across the field. This time he watched her arrow fly and stifled a smile at her hoot of triumph when her aim proved true. She fascinated him and their banter the night before had come easily and naturally. She wasn't afraid to challenge him. He had no idea if she'd be suitable based on Lady Gwendolyn's requirements, but she was the only one who had stirred an interest in him in a while.

'Do you need to find your nursemaid to check your wound?' Aevir teased, following Rolfe's line of sight.

'I'd forgotten how insufferable you were,' Rolfe growled, which resulted in Aevir's bark of laughter.

Vidar had walked away to speak with his wife, but stepped up to them now, his gaze roaming across the field to where his wife's charges practised. 'Godric will arrive in about a fortnight and I hope to negotiate his blessing for a marriage. I've already allotted the silver needed.'

Elswyth had just landed another arrow in the target while a girl he assumed to be her sister cheered her on. Aevir's face shone with interest as he watched her, and Rolfe felt the hair on the back of his head bristle in warning. Aevir's interest in Elswyth alone would have raised his ire, but to have Godric's name spoken in regard to her did not bode well for Rolfe's intentions.

'The sisters will be available?' Aevir tipped his head towards Elswyth and her sister.

'Aye, but only one of them need marry... Elswyth is the eldest. I'd prefer it if one of you marry her. The match will go far to ease our troubles in Banford,' Vidar added in a low voice.

Rolfe froze, his hand clenched tight around the hilt of his sparring sword. The girl was Godric's daughter. When she'd said she was from the north, she meant Banford. She meant the very village he'd put a torch to only two days ago. The very village that seemed to turn out traitors one after the next.

'You would give the traitor silver and allow him to keep his lands?' asked Aevir.

Vidar's brow furrowed. 'Traitor may be harsh. Remember that we only have rumours that Godric's been in contact with the Scot King. We've seen no evidence. We *do* know that it will be in our favour to tie him to Alvey with his daughter's hand. We need him on our side.'

The very idea of giving tolerance to the man who was likely at the centre of every conspiracy with the Scots didn't sit right with Rolfe. 'You can't deny that Durwin's presence with the Scots is strong evidence. Everyone knows how close he and his brother were to Godric.' He knew in his gut that the connection was there. Rewarding Godric's tricks with a fortuitous marriage for his daughter would not solve their problems. Indeed, such a marriage could be disastrous for all parties involved.

'Aye, it's a strong indication, but not evidence. We'll see how he feels soon. He'll arrive in a fortnight and give his permission for Elswyth's hand unless he'd prefer to insult his Lady,' said Vidar.

'Is that why his daughters are here?' Rolfe asked. Now that he knew who Elswyth was he was shocked to find Godric's daughters within the confines of Alvey. Shocked because if the man had truly gone against Alvey, his daughters would have been locked within her walls and at the mercy of the very Danes he claimed to despise. The man had to be a fool and she had to be a spy. There would be no other reason for Godric to allow their presence here.

'They're distant relations of Gwendolyn's on her mother's side. Gwendolyn hoped to gain the girls' co-operation by inviting them here. I'd hoped that since he allowed them to come here, he had accepted that we are here to stay. She hasn't mentioned marriage to Elswyth yet, but she will now that you're both here.'

Both. Thinking of her with Aevir didn't sit well with him, but he pushed the thought aside to consider the issue of Godric. Sending his daughters to work for his Lady could have been a very solid offering of truce. Or it could have been a very clever way of appearing con-trite while using them for his own gain. If Rolfe had to guess, he would assume the latter.

'Which other brides are we to consider and which lands come with them?' Aevir asked.

'We'll discuss the properties and dowries tonight. It's only fair that you know beforehand to help you de-cide which girl to win over.'

Aevir shook his head and laughed. 'Is enticing her necessary? The girl will marry who her father says she will marry, will she not?'

Vidar grinned. 'That's not how Lady Gwendolyn would prefer the marriages to happen. She wants the women to have a say in their choice of groom.'

'It's only a bride, Jarl.' Aevir shrugged. 'What does it matter if she approves or even if I approve of her? Isn't it merely an arrangement for loyalty and coin?'

Rolfe and Vidar exchanged knowing glances. They'd had a very similar conversation when it was Vidar arriving to wed Lady Gwendolyn. Vidar had been of a similar opinion.

'The girl must approve of her groom,' Vidar said again and, like lightning drawn to the highest point on a plain, Rolfe found Elswyth again with his eyes.

He tried to see her through the eyes he'd had the night before. Eyes that hadn't known her parentage. The belt around her waist emphasised her lean figure, and the curve of her hips. She was soft in all the places a woman should be soft. The blush on her face last night when she'd gazed upon his nudity confirmed her interest in him as a man. If she *was* a spy, perhaps he'd have better success seducing the admission out of her.

Once realised, the thought took up residence in his head and refused to leave. As arousing as the idea of having her beneath him was, the task left a bitter taste. If she were a spy for her father, then it would confirm Godric's intention. And Rolfe would have lost the only woman to challenge him in a long time.

She let another arrow fly and this time hit the target dead centre. Despite himself, pride swelled in his chest. It was unreasonable that he should feel anything for her already, but there it was. He told himself it was lingering affection for the woman who had tended him last night, the woman who had sparked his interest before he'd learned her true identity. The wind tugged at the hair in her loose braid, sending a few dark strands to fly free across her face. It was actually a very lovely face, with soft lips and gently sculpted cheekbones. When she brushed the strands back, she looked up and caught him watching her, but the distance was too great for him to discern her thoughts.

Lady Gwendolyn had walked back to the sisters and started working with the other, drawing Elswyth's attention. Free from her stare, he caught Aevir watching the sisters. 'Leave her be, Aevir.'

'I rather like looking at the pair of them.' His friend grinned.

'They haven't the land or the riches you desire.'

Aevir stared at him in shock. 'You're declaring yourself already, man?'

Rolfe shrugged. 'Nay.' The word sounded weak. He had enough riches from his years of fighting at Vidar's side to see him well into his old age and he didn't particularly need or want lands. For whatever reason, he'd liked Elswyth last night before he'd found out who her father was. If she was here with honourable intentions instead of as an emissary for her father and he had no choice but to wed…why not let it be to her?

'Let's not quibble over women,' Vidar said. 'There are more than enough to go around. Besides, Aevir, I need you to go north. Watch Banford. Our skirmish with the Scots is bound to have an effect. If Banford is co-operating with them, they'll be communicating now.'

'I can go,' Rolfe offered. He felt responsible for the situation and he would see it through.

'Nay, stay and recover. Right now we're only watching. You need to be well for the fight, if there is one,' said Vidar.

Aevir nodded. 'Of course.'

'You'll leave tomorrow. We'll talk more tonight.'

Aevir agreed and then left them to finish sparring with some of his warriors.

Vidar chuckled when they were alone. 'It's good that you want her. I only hope she feels the same.'

Regret twisted inside him. He liked her well enough, aye, but why did she have to come from Banford? Some men married and were able to keep their hearts out of it. Rolfe didn't think he was one of those men. A few moments with Elswyth last night had already touched him far too deeply. Rolfe knew himself well enough to know that if he allowed himself to become infatuated with her, then his judgement could be compromised. If it had happened with Hilde, it could happen again. 'Do you not suspect her of being a spy?'

Vidar was quiet as he pondered that for a moment. 'Until last night she had barely deigned to speak to a Dane—aside from me—the entire time she's been here. It seems her father's attitudes have indeed been ingrained in the girl. I pondered early on in her visit that he'd sent her to poison us with the meals she helped prepare and was gratified when that didn't come to pass.' Then he shrugged as if her being a spy was nothing. 'Let her tell him of our warriors and our power. Perhaps the information will spur him to our side.'

'I would find out the truth of her intentions before marrying her.'

Vidar was quiet for a moment before finally nodding. 'How would you do that?'

Rolfe hardly thought Vidar would agree to seduction. Elswyth was his wife's relation and under his guardianship, spy or not. 'I'll ingratiate myself to her…see if I can get her to open up to me.'

'She'd hardly be a good spy if a little kindness gets her to spill her secrets,' Vidar said as if he suspected Rolfe's plan.

'She's a farm girl. She'll hardly be experienced enough in spying to mislead me.'

'And if she's innocent?' Vidar's voice was even and quiet.

Rolfe paused, nearly choking on the words he was about to say. 'Then I'll marry her. But if she's not, then we have proof of Godric's treachery.'

'It's a solid plan.'

'I'll have your word that she'll be mine and you won't offer her to Aevir.'

Vidar grinned. 'She will be yours, though you'll have a fight on your hands if she ever finds out about your actions in Banford.'

Vidar was right. If her loyalty to her family and village was even half as fierce as Rolfe suspected, then she would hate him for what he had done. 'Then we have no choice but to make certain she never finds out.'

Chapter Four

Notch the arrow. Pull back. Focus on the target. Let it fly.

It was a ritual that quieted Elswyth's mind and one that she'd come to appreciate. It allowed her to ignore the very real possibility that, with threats from the Scots and possibly the Danes, she'd have to use her newly acquired archery skills in the near future. Lady Gwendolyn and Ellan had moved farther down the field to work on her sister's aim, leaving Elswyth to her ritual. Ellan was enthusiastic, but lacked the interest required for hours of daily practice. Elswyth, on the other hand, loved losing herself in the steady rhythm of repetitive training.

She wasn't surprised that Rolfe came to a stop near her after the women had drifted away. He'd been watching her from across the field for nearly the entire practice. Her traitorous arm trembled at his nearness, forcing her to take in a deep breath to steady herself. He had a large presence and it wasn't simply due to his size, though that alone would have been intimidating.

There was something about him that announced his arrival without him even having to say a word, as if he commanded the very air around him the way he commanded his men.

She let the arrow fly and it landed just to the left of the centre of her target. It wasn't perfect, but it was good. She had placed the sack fifty paces out, so she'd count it as her furthest success so far. 'Good morning, Dane.'

'Saxon.' She didn't look at him, but the smile was evident in his voice. 'You're very good. How long have you been an archer?'

The next arrow made a soft whooshing sound as she drew it out of the quiver on her back. She took her time notching it, letting her thumb brush over the roughly carved wood as she pondered his question. It was simple enough to answer, but she couldn't help but wonder why he was asking. Did he suspect something of her? What exactly did he want with her? Had she imagined the way he'd talked with her last night had been a sign of something more than benign friendship he was offering? Was she even capable of leading him down that path in the hopes of gathering more information from him? She wanted desperately to prove her loyalty to her father, but she wasn't very good at artifice.

Last night Rolfe hadn't come out and said anything inappropriate. If anything, *she* was the inappropriate one. But there had seemed to be something more. Even across the field this morning, when he'd looked at her, there had been an intensity there that hinted at an interest that was more than friendship.

Why her? Pulling the arrow back, she let it fly to land in the sack, but still outside the target. Evidence of how he unsettled her.

Dropping her arm, she finally turned to look at him. He was dressed casually today in trousers with a simple tunic, leaving his muscled arms revealed even though the morning air was quite brisk. His dark blond hair was pulled up again in the barbaric style he'd worn yesterday with ropes of it pulled back from his face and secured at the crown of his head. The dimple in his cheek shone when he smiled at her and it nearly hurt to look at it. How could a man so potentially dangerous to her family appear so attractively virile? The ever-present knot of unease tightened in her belly. 'I've been practising archery only since Ellan and I arrived in Alvey.'

He raised his chin a notch and gave her an approving nod. 'You're a quick learner.'

He said it as if the trait met with his approval and that approval filled her with pride. Instead of commenting on his statement and facing that emotion, she asked, 'How is your shoulder?'

Part of her had wondered in anticipation if Lady Gwendolyn would direct her to tend to him again that morning, while another part of her had been busy coming up with a bevy of excuses that would get her out of the task. In the end it hadn't mattered, she'd left the little alcove she shared with Ellan at the same time a serving girl had emerged from his chamber. The white hot flair of jealousy she'd experienced had been quickly extinguished and tucked out of sight. What did it matter to her if someone else tended him? It particularly did not matter that the girl had emerged with mussed hair, making Elswyth wonder exactly how long she'd stayed in Rolfe's chamber and to which part of him she had attended.

'It's sore but improved.' His honesty impressed her. Most men she knew would not admit to any ailment. Her older brother Galan had once walked on a broken foot for three whole days before it had swollen so large that his shoe had to be cut off. Only then had he admitted he 'might have twisted it a bit'.

'Is there any inflammation? Heat?'

He gave a quick shake of his head. 'Not any more than there was, but I'm nearly out of the salve you left. Can you can bring more tonight?'

She stared at him, weighing the risks of agreeing to help him again. There was no denying the fact that helping him would give her a chance to gather information for Father, but her sense of self-preservation warned her away from him. He unsettled her, making her feel interest when she shouldn't. Yet, she understood that to refuse would rouse suspicion, so she nodded and said, 'I'll prepare more for you.'

'Do you wield the axe as well as you do the bow?' The abrupt change in topic startled her, prompting him to nod towards her hip where her axe was secured.

'Better. I've been using it for years.'

'Would you show me?' He gestured towards the piles of wood a bit farther down the field past where Ellan and Lady Gwendolyn were practising.

'Do you not know how to use one, Dane?'

Through his close-cropped beard she could see the dimple in his cheek when he smiled and shook his head. 'The sword is my weapon. I can swing an axe in battle, but I can see how a smaller one for throwing could be useful.'

No man had ever asked her to show him how to do anything before. At the farm, she and Ellan ran the household and helped with the animals when it was needed. No one asked them for advice or sought them out, though that hardly deterred her from offering her opinion on matters when she saw that it would be beneficial. Still, she couldn't stop the pleasure that welled in her chest that this warrior would ask her for a demonstration. Unable to find her voice, she nodded and set down her bow before unstrapping the quiver of arrows from her back. When she was finished, he stepped back to let her lead him farther afield.

Finding a nice, round stump, she rolled it to a clearing farther away from the practising warriors and set it in place upright. Satisfied with its position, she walked back to him and withdrew the axe from her belt. 'As with your sword, I imagine, the trick is to keep your blade well tended. It need not be so sharp that it nicks your clothing, but it shouldn't be dull.'

'Do you sharpen your own blades?' He took the axe from her and held it up, running the pad of his thumb across the edge of the blade.

'Aye, it was necessary at home. Father didn't approve of my use of it so forbade anyone to help me. Of course, here the blacksmith has been kind enough to see to the task.'

Grinning, he handed it back to her handle first. 'But you didn't let your father's disapproval stop you.'

'Nay, of course not.' In some ways his censure had spurned her onwards. Her father was a difficult man, equal parts kind and stubborn. After her mother's abandonment, he had seemed to look upon both her and Ellan with suspicion, as if they were somehow waiting to betray the family as well. That suspicion drove her now to prove to him that she could be relied upon. Growing up, it had meant that she had been forced to grab at her every freedom. Fortunately, he'd allowed her to keep them once she'd wrested them away.

'I can tell you're related to Lady Gwendolyn. Independence must run in your line.' He said it with pleasure, as if it was something to be celebrated instead of criticised. An opinion in direct opposition to her father's... and most of the men in her life, now that she thought about it. Lord Vidar was the only man she'd known to tolerate his wife's eccentricities as he had.

Still, for all the delight it gave her, it made her feel rather like a horse. Her attributes weighed and measured against the line of her ancestors. 'Does independence run in your line as well, Dane?'

He laughed, a deep and rich sound that was entirely more pleasing than it should have been. 'You could say that. I have four older sisters, each one more independent than the next.'

She tried to imagine a young Rolfe with four older sisters badgering him about, but she couldn't do it even though she liked the idea of it. She could only see him as the powerful man that he was. Every man in a position of power over women needed at least one woman in his life to answer to.

Instead of responding, she gripped the axe by the handle and held it high over her head. Aiming for the centre of the stump, she let it go, hitting her mark dead on with a smooth popping sound as the tip of the blade embedded itself in the wood.

'That's good. Do it two more times and we'll call it skill and not luck.'

He was teasing her, and she couldn't help but laugh. Twice more would be no trouble at all. She had been throwing axes since she was a child. Retrieving it, she went on to show him two more times how accurate she was. Each throw landed within a finger width of the one before.

'Now you try.' She grinned as she walked back to him, holding the axe out. 'Let's see how *lucky* you are.'

'The difference, Saxon, is that I never claimed to be skilled.'

'Now you're retreating? Interesting. I took you for a man of courage.'

He chuckled and took it from her, his fingertips grazing her palm and making goosebumps move up her arm. Only when she stepped back to give him space to throw did she realise that they had drawn a small crowd. Being with him had made her forget everyone else and she would have sworn it was the same with him. He didn't seem to care that his warriors watched them. In fact, he only seemed to have eyes for her. When she spoke his gaze never strayed from her face and, every time she'd thrown the axe or shot an arrow, she had felt his study of her. Being the centre of his attention was a heady thing, but no matter how important or valued he made her feel, she must remember that he was the man who would be sent to destroy her family if the need arose.

He finally looked away from her to study the stump, bringing the axe up to gauge the distance. She worried that he wouldn't get leverage without the use of his left arm for balance, but when he threw it the axe sailed through the air, easily reaching the stump. He probably could've thrown it much farther. It sliced into the wood deeply, landing roughly a hand's width below the gouges she had left.

'Not bad,' she said as he walked to retrieve the axe, and she couldn't stop her treacherous gaze from roaming down his backside when he bent over to pull it out of the stump. The sight of his nude body, muscled and unquestionably masculine, was still vivid in her mind. A tiny flicker of awareness joined the tension in her belly. It gave her pause, because she'd never felt that for a Saxon man.

Had she been secretly harbouring a core of wickedness like her mother all this time? Last night she'd been able to assuage her guilt by convincing herself that her feelings had been a natural result of seeing her first nude male body. But that wasn't precisely true, she realised now. It was him. The Dane clearly made her feel wicked things.

His next throw was a bit wide, barely clipping the stump on its right side. His third attempt was true and hit where her first blade had touched to the cheers of the small group of warriors watching them. He gave a simple nod of acknowledgement to them.

'You're very good for someone who doesn't know how to throw an axe.' Honestly, she would have been amazed had he been terrible. The man was probably good at everything he tried.

'Not as good as you,' he said, bringing the axe back to her.

'Nothing a little practice won't cure.'

Holding it out for her, handle side out, he said, 'You've mastered the axe. You're progressing at archery. How would you like to try learning the sword? Or am I wrong and you mastered the blade as a child?'

She smiled at his question and shook her head, taking the axe to affix it to her belt. 'I've never held a blade. My father forbade it and a sword was too costly for me to acquire on my own.'

'Do you want to learn?' He asked it as if it were a simple thing.

'From you?' Why did her heart pounce in anticipation?

He nodded. 'Unless you're afraid of disobeying your father.' There was a challenge in his eyes as he said that. 'But you never let that stop you before, have you?'

Actually, she had let that stop her. Since her mother left, she'd been doing everything she could to prove to her father that she wasn't like the woman. That meant that, aside from a few indiscretions such as the axe, she had done everything to find his favour. Father would not want her spending time with this man, yet she was very tempted to accept the offer.

Rolfe's voice had been pitched too low to be over-heard, but she still took a look around to make sure. Lady Gwendolyn casually glanced over at them from where she was still instructing Ellan, curiosity burning in her features. The warriors, assuming correctly that the entertainment was over, were slowly going back to their own sparring. That more than anything decided her. She couldn't bear their audience as she practised. Slowly shaking her head, she said, 'I cannot. I'm afraid that my pride couldn't bear the scrutiny of an audience.'

'There's a clearing to the south. It's not far from the walls of Alvey, but far enough for privacy. I could teach you there in the mornings.'

He spoke so earnestly that she almost forgot to be suspicious. Almost. 'Why would you teach me?'

He took in a breath, his chest expanding with the ef-fort as he thought over his answer. 'Because you want to learn and I can see that no one else will teach you.' She didn't know what she had expected from him, but it wasn't that.

She did want to learn. Every day at home felt like a threat with the Scots and the Danes on each side. The more she learned the better chance she had of protect-ing herself and her younger siblings. Of course, she also had purely selfish reasons. She was good at learning how to fight. She liked the training. 'What would be the point if I'm to leave in a fortnight?'

'You're right. It's not nearly long enough to master the skill, but it's enough to give you basic knowledge.' He paused, but she sensed that he wasn't finished. 'Al-though I understand if you're too afraid.'

'I'm not afraid,' she said before she realised that he'd baited her.

Grinning, he said, 'Then I'll see you in the morning.' He walked away and she was curious enough about him and what the morning would bring that she let him go without arguing. One morning with him wouldn't change anything.

Chapter Five

'What are you smiling about?' Ellan surprised Elswyth by following her outside the great hall later that evening.

They had finished the evening meal, so Elswyth had come out for a bit of fresh air and to clear her head. The warriors were crammed inside to capacity, but despite the crowd, she'd been aware of Rolfe's gaze on her all evening. 'Was I smiling?' Elswyth frowned.

'Aye. It was quite strange watching you all night because you hardly ever smile. What has you so cheerful?'

'If I was smiling—' which she really didn't think she had been '—it's because we'll be leaving soon.' Her thoughts of Rolfe were so new and unexpected that she wanted to keep them to herself for a while. Maybe for ever. Nothing could ever come of them.

Leading the way, she meandered with no particular destination through the various cook fires that flickered in the yard. Several men huddled around each one, talking and not paying the sisters any attention. It seemed that Lady Gwendolyn had mentioned to the newcomers that they were to be left unmolested.

'Hmm… I thought you were smiling because a certain Dane couldn't keep his eyes off you all night.' Ellan grinned and, even in the deep shadows of twilight, her eyes sparkled with merriment.

'He couldn't, could he?' The words were out before she could stop herself. Once she said them it was a relief to have someone know. 'I must admit that these warriors are different than I thought they would be. I suppose I was expecting barbarians and, while some of them fit the description, most of them are…tamer than I anticipated.' Would her father believe her if she told him that? Even saying the words felt like some sort of betrayal to him.

Elswyth had never met the group of Danes that her mother had run off with. They had camped along the coast, a little bit north-east of Banford. Her mother had come across them on one of their trips inland. That trip had led to several others until one night Elswyth had heard her parents arguing. She'd heard enough to realise that Father had found their mother in a compromising position with one of the Danes and had fought the man. At home that night he'd given her an ultimatum: repent and face punishment or be banished. She had chosen banishment. The next morning she'd left to meet her Dane and they'd never seen her again.

To this day, Elswyth didn't understand what could prompt someone to leave their family behind. She had struggled with the question for years, but wasn't any closer to coming to an answer. The only conclusion she'd come to was that she needed to try extra hard to prove her loyalty. If that meant despising the Danes, then that's what she did. Only now that didn't seem so simple to do.

A Dane at the nearest cook fire threw back his head and laughed at something his friend, a Saxon warrior, had said. Father would have her believe the Dane and Saxon warriors were constantly at each other's throats, but that didn't seem to be the case. Not here.

'You *like him*, don't you?'

Elswyth's ears burned. 'Shh.' She glanced around to make certain that no one had overheard her sister's dubious claim. 'I don't like him, not the way your tone implies.' *Liar*, a tiny voice in her head accused. 'I merely think he is kind and not nearly as ruthless as I had thought.'

Ellan didn't believe her. She wore a smug smile that made her eyes gleam victoriously. 'Time will tell.'

Elswyth opened her mouth to argue. She didn't quite understand her need to argue, she only knew that she needed to emphatically deny any interest in the warrior so that her sister would understand that in no way did she favour the man. She was not like their mother and she would not abandon her family for one of them.

'Elswyth!' The voice came from nowhere, but it drew every eye in the area. The men at the nearby fire briefly stopped talking to look around, but went back to their meal when no culprit could be found.

Her heart clamoured, taking a moment to gather itself before trying to beat free of her chest when her gaze landed on a flurry of movement in the shadow of the granary. Someone stood there motioning to her, the hand white in the inky black that surrounded it.

'Who is that?' Ellan asked, following her gaze.

'If I didn't know better, I'd think it was Galan,' she whispered. But that couldn't be. Their older brother was at home on the farm, not here sneaking around among their enemy, especially not alone.

The longer she stared into the shadows, and the more urgently he waved her over, the more convinced she became of his identity. If it was he, it could only mean that there had been trouble at home. Father! Dear God, what if something had happened to him? 'Stay here. I'll go see what he wants.'

She made her way around the perimeter of the open area, not going directly towards the granary. No one seemed to notice her as she turned in that direction. Galan—or who she assumed to be her brother—whirled when she approached and retreated farther through the fortress, moving with ease through the night. His cloak was up around his head to shield his identity. He could have been any number of the Saxon men who wandered through the village at this time of night. But he wasn't and her heart pounded from that knowledge as she followed him. He finally stopped in the shadow of the wall—the gates were swung wide open which is probably how he'd got inside.

A small village made of tents had been set up outside because Alvey wasn't big enough to hold all the warriors within her walls. A sea of fabric fluttered in the cold winter gusts as far as the trees. This was the first time she'd seen them and the sight nearly stole her breath. More of the warriors had returned from the south than she had anticipated. Despite what she'd said to Ellan and how she felt about Rolfe, the spectacle of them made her shiver with the reminder of how precarious this all was. War could come any day. If her family chose the wrong side… She couldn't even allow herself to finish the thought.

Stepping carefully into the shadows, she approached her brother. The white of his smile was barely visible in the twilight and she was seized by the need to hug him and shake him all at the same time. She decided on hugging, closing her eyes in thanks for his safety when his arms went around her. It only lasted a brief moment, but it was enough to reassure her that, aside from being thinner than she remembered, he was whole. She released him when he pulled back, but only to grip him by the shoulders and look up into his dirt-streaked face. 'What are you doing here? Have you come alone?'

'Aye. I'm by myself.'

Between the Scots, the Danes, unknown Saxons and travellers, it was foolish to travel alone. 'But why? It's too dangerous. Any number of catastrophes could have befallen you on the way.'

His smile fell to become a scowl. 'I can take care of myself, Elswyth. Besides, I didn't come all this way to have you scold me.'

'Why are you here? Has something happened to Father?' In her excitement it was hard to keep her voice low so that any of the Danes coming in and out of the gates wouldn't hear.

'Nay, Father is well, or at least I assume he is. I haven't been home yet, I've come straight here.' He hesitated and her chest tightened. 'It's Baldric. He's been taken by the Scots.'

'What?' That was the last thing she had expected him to say. Their younger brother was only fourteen winters and he had no interaction with the Scots, or he hadn't when she'd been home. Galan had been their father's accomplice in advocating for joining their ranks. He'd ridden with Father last spring to their secret meetings with the warriors. She had hoped that the winter would bring an end to that, but it seemed her hope had been in vain. 'How is that possible?'

Galan had the grace to look guilty. The cloak had fallen back a bit and he ran the heel of his hand over his brow and couldn't seem to meet her eyes. 'He went with me to our meeting with them.' Ignoring her gasp of outrage, he continued, 'While we were there a group of Scots met up with some Danes who were on their way to Alvey, we believe. They destroyed them, Elswyth. Every last one of the Scots were killed.'

She tried not to imagine the carnage that sort of battle involved, but the images flashed behind her eyes anyway. Rolfe had taken a Scot's spear a few days ago. Could it have been him and his group of warriors? She shuddered at the violence she had known him capable of. 'You were not involved in the battle?'

He shook his head. 'Nay, we were at their camp. The group of Scots were on their way to us, but obviously they never made it. A scout found the carnage left behind and came to let us know. The Scots suspect that Father was somehow involved in revealing their location to the Danes.'

'That's preposterous! Father would never betray their location.' Whether or not she agreed with his madness in attempting to drive the Danes from their land, she knew that he was an honourable man. He would never betray anyone he considered a friend or ally.

'We both know that. They, however, want proof of our loyalty.'

'How does kidnapping a child prove anything of loyalty?'

'Baldric is hardly a child. He will be fifteen winters very soon.'

She sniffed in disagreement. The weight of Baldric's hand in hers was still vivid from all the nights she had lain in bed with him after Mother had gone, telling him stories when he couldn't sleep or was ill. He wasn't old enough to be brought into this madness. 'He is a child and he should never have been there. How could you have taken him with you?'

'He demanded to come and he's old enough to make his own decisions now.'

She strongly disagreed with that, but arguing that now wouldn't get them anywhere. 'What does Baldric have to do with proving Father's loyalty?'

'Because the Dane bastards…' He paused to spit as if the word was foul on his tongue.

'Shh.' A quick look around assured her that no one had overheard him.

'They stole a small fortune from the Scots they attacked. It was a stash of coin and jewels meant for the mercenaries at our meeting.'

'Mercenaries!' This time it was Galan's turn to shush

her. 'Have things progressed so far already? They're hiring mercenaries to attack the Danes?'

Galan took her arm and led her farther away from the gates. In a whisper he explained, 'There are Danes on their western coast. They are preparing to fight those. At the moment there are no set plans for Alvey.'

That was a relief, but it was only a matter of time, she feared. Somehow in all of this, hating the Danes had come second to keeping her family safe.

'I don't know the details,' he continued, 'but one of the jewels that was taken with the coin was a bloodstone. It belongs to King Causantín's family and has some ceremonial importance to them. That is what they want us to recover. If we can deliver it to them, then they will consider Father's loyalty proven and release Baldric. Do you think you can do it?'

She still didn't understand their idea of loyalty. Wasn't it possible for Father to despise them and yet return the stone to free Baldric? Sometimes she failed to comprehend the logic of warriors. 'You want me to find the bloodstone?'

'Aye. They believe that Rolfe led the band of Danes that took it. He's here?'

She nodded, because her mouth was suddenly too dry for speech. Last night Rolfe had sat with Lord Vidar and Lady Gwendolyn in the hall, sacks of coin between them. Later, when she'd patched his wound, she had noticed a red stone on his bed set amid some silver. Could that be the one?

'Good. Then the stone is likely here as well. You must find it, Elswyth. It's the only way to save Baldric.'

'But how will I know which one it is?'

He shrugged. 'All I know is that it is the size of a walnut and is set in gold on a chain.'

'I may have seen it.'

Galan grabbed her shoulders in his joy. 'Have you truly?'

'Aye.' She nodded. 'I saw the warrior Rolfe with a red stone. I don't know if it was set in gold or on a chain. I only had a glimpse.'

'Do you think you can find it and relieve him of it?'

Shaking her head, she said, 'I'm not certain. It's possible.' It would mean she'd have to make a search of his chamber, because he hadn't worn it on his person today.

'But you will try?'

'Aye, of course I'll try. We must save Baldric.'

'Thank God.' He let out a breath and pulled her close, his shoulders slumped in obvious relief. 'Can you make a search tonight or tomorrow? I must get back to Baldric soon.'

'If I hurry, I can make a search of his chamber tonight before he retires.' As she spoke, the reality of what she was about to do set in, making her heart pound. Dear God, war really was coming and their family could be right in the middle of it! With a hand on her chest, she took a step back from Galan and struggled to take a deep breath. The air raced through her lungs as quickly as her thoughts raced through her mind.

Sensing her panic, Galan touched her cheek. 'You can do this, Elswyth. I believe in you.'

Stories of the Danes haunted her. They were ruthless and brutal when crossed. There was one story that her father liked to tell of a man who had stolen a coin from a drunken Dane in some unnamed southern village. He'd gone about his evening, thinking that he'd got away with the crime, only to wake up as his hand had been cleaved from his body. They gave no quarter or mercy. What would happen if they found out she'd stolen something as precious as a jewel?

Rubbing her wrist, she held her hands against her belly. Would Rolfe be that brutal and unforgiving? She was having a difficult time reconciling the gentle Rolfe from last night in the bath with the warrior who had cut down an entire troop of Scots. Even this morning, he'd been kind and teasing with her. How could he be a ruthless Norseman as well?

'But what if he finds it gone before morning? What will happen?'

'They'll make a search for it, I'm sure, but no one will be able to connect you to the crime. Keep it hidden. You'll need to bring it to me as soon as you can.'

She had to do this for Baldric. He needed her right now more than she feared for her future at the hands of the Danes. 'I'm due to go south in the morning with Rolfe. There's a clearing there where he's to teach me swordplay.' She didn't have to see Galan clearly to sense the tension in his body that her words had caused.

'You will be alone with him?'

'Aye, we'll be alone. If I'm able to find the stone tonight, I'll bring it and leave it for you at the base of a tree.'

'But why would he teach you swordplay?'

'To be honest, I'm uncertain. He seems to have taken

an interest in my axe. I demonstrated my skill with throwing it and he offered to teach me the sword.' He was quiet for so long that his very silence lent a significance to her words that wasn't really present.

'Be vigilant with him,' he finally said, letting out a disappointed breath. 'I would tell you not to be alone with him, but we must do this.'

'Oh, Rolfe wouldn't hurt me…not yet, anyway.' She knew that Galan's fears were unfounded, but that would change if her thievery was ever exposed. 'Once we have Baldric back you and Father must stop this madness. No more secret meetings.'

In an instant, his ire was back. 'The Danes need to be run out of here once and for all. We were once the proud people of Bernicia.'

'You sound like Father.' His eyes flashed with hatred that was so familiar to her. Her father ate that hatred with his porridge every morning and spent his days with it coursing through his blood.

He drew himself up taller, shoulders back and his voice a harsh whisper. 'Northumbria has given herself over to the Danes, but we won't follow suit.'

'So you'd rather we join the Scots? Give our homes over to them?'

He shook his head. 'It won't come to that. They only want things to go back to how it was with Alvey a buffer between the north and the Danes to the south.'

'You must tell Father to stop this madness. The Danes cannot be defeated so easily.'

He stared at her as if she'd become the lowest of traitors. 'How can you say that? They must be!'

'Shh!' she again warned him to keep his voice low. 'Do you see the warriors in their tents? The warriors walking around Alvey? There are even more in the great hall. He is wrong to think that the Saxon warriors will rise up and defeat them. I've seen with my own eyes how they work together with the Danes. They will join forces with the Danes and together there are too many of them.' She knew her words bordered on treachery, but she needed him to understand the truth of the situation.

Galan shook his head manically. 'There are still loyal Saxons in the villages who would take our side.'

'Our side? We don't have a side. They would be forced to take the side of the Scots and the Scots have been our enemies in the past just like the Danes.'

'Not like the Danes,' he argued. 'The Danes are worse.'

Taking a deep breath so the argument wouldn't escalate, she clenched her jaw and spoke through her teeth. 'Be that as it may, they are still too powerful. Tell Father that he needs to stop this madness at once. We could all die if it comes to war.'

'Some of us would rather die than make peace with them.' He glared at her and his body stiffened. She knew that he was about to make a run for the gates, so she put a hand on his arm to stop him.

There was no use in arguing at the moment. Perhaps Father was right, or perhaps they had no choice but to accept the Danes. Whatever the answer, it wouldn't be decided between her and Galan tonight. 'This arguing

won't get us anywhere. I'm sorry.' Only slightly mollified, he shrugged out of her grasp.

Closing her eyes, she forced herself to swallow past
the lump in her throat. It did nothing to dispel the heaviness of her heart or her disdain for what she was about
to do. 'In the morning try to hide near the clearing so
you can see where I leave the jewel. I'll try to leave the
ground disturbed just in case you can't see me hide it.'
She had no idea how she would accomplish this task
she'd set for herself, but she'd figure that out in the
morning.

'You won't even know I'm there, unless he tries to
hurt you. If he does, I'll kill him.'

His crooked smile softened the harsh words. It was
the same smile she always remembered when she
thought of him. A wave of affection washed over her
and she pulled him into an embrace. He put his arms
around her again and squeezed. 'I've missed you,' he
whispered.

An ache swelled in her throat, making speech impossible for a moment. 'I've missed you, too,' she said when
she could speak. 'Please be careful. Please take Baldric
home safely and don't venture north again. Please.'

He pulled back and grimaced and she knew that he
had no intention of following her order. With a nod of
goodbye, he disappeared into the deep shadows cast
by the wall. Dread made her steps heavy as she walked
back towards the great hall. She had no choice but to
steal from Rolfe, a man who had been nothing but kind
to her. Baldric's life was worth more than a blasted
bloodstone. For a moment she imagined telling Rolfe

why she needed the stone and in her fantasy he was understanding and gave it to her. But it was only a fantasy. If she confessed all to Rolfe, then she'd have to confess what Father and Galan had been up to. Somehow she didn't think he'd be so understanding about their dallying with treason.

She told herself that it didn't matter she was stealing from him. He was their enemy. He'd have no qualms about doing what must be done if he found out about Galan's talks with the Scots. Besides, hadn't he merely stolen the jewel from the Scots anyway? It wasn't even really his to keep.

None of those arguments seemed to make a difference to the guilt gnawing at her.

She would have to steal from Rolfe.

Chapter Six

The tray felt heavier in her arms than it had the night before. Or maybe it was the weight of her intentions making it seem that way. She had tried to talk herself out of the plan at least a hundred times in the past hour, but Baldric's life was worth more than her misgivings. Putting her body against Rolfe's door, she nudged it open with her shoulder. The bowl on the tray wobbled, but she managed to right it before any damage was done. Once inside, she pushed it closed with her toe and waited there in the dark silence, quite certain that someone would come in and know her for the thief that she was.

After a moment, the pounding of her heart in her ears settled enough that she was able to hear the revelry still going on below. The men had finished their supper, but the deep voice of a skald could be heard, regaling them with some adventure in their own language, his words punctuated by cheers and heckles at various times. Elswyth had only picked up a few words of their language, not nearly enough to follow along. Because her own Saxon tongue was important to Lady Gwendolyn it was the one spoken the most; the Norsemen only spoke their own language among themselves or on nights like this when a story must be told.

She hoped the entertainment would keep Rolfe below for now. When she'd left the main hall, he'd been deep in discussion with the lord and lady and some warrior she thought was named Aevir. Wyborn had been busy chewing a bone under the table. She only had a few moments to herself before they would both come up to retire for the evening.

Placing the tray on the small table, she set a taper to the single candle burning low on the table and lit several more so that she could study his room. Her gaze immediately went to his bed where she had last seen the stone, but of course it wasn't there anymore. Her steps were slow and shaky as she walked over to run her hand over the furs just in case. Rolfe's scent rose from them and she couldn't help but think of him lying beneath them. The flutter in her belly at that thought was so visceral that she jerked her hand back.

She had to get on with this or he would surely find her. A chest was set against the wall near the end of the bed, but she recognised it as the one he'd pulled his under-tunic out of the night before. Probably not that one. There was a smaller one next to it, so she made quick work of tossing open the lid. A cloth-wrapped bundle lay on top. She unwrapped it gently so that he wouldn't know she'd disturbed it to find that it was a child's doll. It seemed rather old and worn, but it clearly meant something to him if he had kept it with him these years. Bringing it to her nose, she confirmed that it, too, bore his scent. She imagined him taking it out from time to time and the image did not match the ruthless warrior that Galan had described. It did match the man who had smiled at her with his kind blue eyes and a single dimple.

Suddenly she felt worse than a thief. Who was she to have access to this man's memories? She had no right to set her eyes upon something so personal to him, yet she wanted to climb into the chest and stay there. She wanted to savour any knowledge she could find about this man who was so mysterious and fascinating to her.

Wrapping the doll back up very carefully, she set it aside. No matter how she chastised herself, she couldn't help her curiosity when it came to him. The things in this chest were little pieces of him and she found that she wanted to know more about him—not for Father's sake, but for her own reasons. Underneath the doll, she found several things that she imagined he'd brought home from his travels over the years: a wooden coin with the crude carving of a nude lady on it, a volume of strange writing wrapped in leather, a piece of amber. At the very bottom was a bottle of wine laid on its side, but no jewel. Something gleamed at her from the darkened corner, the flicker of candlelight picking up the trace of metal. Cool iron met her fingertips and she lifted the slight weight. It was a key. Her heart gave a slight leap of joy. Reverently, she placed everything back inside except for the key and closed the lid.

Her gaze made a search through the rest of his room, looking for the lock that it matched. His shelves proved fruitless as did another large chest which was unlocked in which she discovered some of his chain-mail and leathers. She was beginning to despair, having almost decided that he kept his valuables locked in the armoury, when she fell to her knees beside his bed and put her cheek to the floor. The light barely reached there, but it was enough to reveal the latches of two small chests, the metal of the clasps winking at her.

Stifling a hoot of triumph, she pulled the first one out. It was heavy and what sounded suspiciously like coins tinkling against each other met her ears. The key slid in easily and turned. The lock released and the lid popped open. There was a small fortune of sacks filled with coin inside. Along with the coin she suspected to be in the other chest, there was enough to buy an entire army of mercenaries if he needed them.

She couldn't stifle the shiver that ran through her body as she reverently touched the sacks, the coins hard and cold beneath the coarse fabric. This was only Rolfe's personal stash. It didn't include the larger chests in the armoury and whatever else might be hidden. The Danes were never leaving. This confirmed it, but she knew even with this knowledge Father wouldn't reconcile himself to their staying. She knew that with a certainty that was a physical pain through her body.

Footsteps walked briskly past the door outside, making her remember how tenuous her current position was. She made quick work of searching the chest, feeling the contents of each bag through the fabric. Finally, one of the sacks on the bottom seemed to hold something other than coin. It was heavy and there was a bulge larger than a coin, so she dumped the contents into her hand. She could hardly believe her eyes when the bloodstone sat in her palm, winking at her in the candlelight. It was set in gold filigree and attached to a golden chain which hung down through her fingers. It had to be the jewel Galan had told her about. It was about the right size and she was almost certain that it was the one she'd seen on Rolfe's bed.

Deciding it would have to do and that she didn't have the time to search through the other chest, she put everything else back inside and dropped the key into the corner of the chest where she'd found it. Then she pushed the entire chest back under the bed before tucking the stone between her breasts. Briefly, she considered staying and applying the poultice to his shoulder again so as not to rouse suspicion, but she knew that there was no way she would be able to keep her composure with his blue eyes staring her down. If she didn't crack under the strain and admit everything, she'd make a fool of herself as her fear got the better of her. She honestly didn't know if she'd be able to look the man in the eyes, knowing the stone rested against her skin.

It was best to leave and let him make of that what he would. It was better than her giving herself away. She wasn't made for thievery and deceptions. Opening the door, she glanced out to make certain that no one noticed her and then made her way to the alcove she shared with Ellan. Once inside she let the curtain fall down, hiding her away from the world.

* * *

The next morning a harsh shake woke her. She opened her eyes to see Rolfe staring down at her. He was a shadow above her, the only light coming from the fire below in the hall, but there was no mistaking his powerful form. She gasped. Her first thought was that he had found his bloodstone missing and come directly to her. It had to be obvious that she had stolen it. Her hand immediately went to her waist where the bloodstone rested against her stomach. She had tied a purse there beneath her clothes and around her waist where she kept the stone hidden.

'Please understand that it was necessary.' Her voice was husky with sleep.

He knelt down, balancing on his heels and leaned close, presumably so that he wouldn't wake Ellan who was snoring lightly next to her against the wall. 'Wake up, fair lady. It's time for your sword lesson.' There was laughter in his voice.

He didn't know. The relief that overcame her was so powerful that it left her muscles weak, her body sagging into the straw mattress. She couldn't speak, couldn't move.

'You don't wake easily.' The smile stayed in his voice.

'I never have,' she said, though it was in no way an explanation for what she had almost confessed, and it came out rather garbled. Pushing herself up, he moved back to give her space.

'Come, I'll be waiting outside for you with the horses. I have food you can eat on the way.'

She nodded, too surprised for speech as he turned and left, his broad shoulders nearly filling up the opening of their little alcove. She was caught off guard that he would see to those things for her. She was essentially a servant. She had served the lord and lady last night and he had sat next to them, politely taking the food and drink she'd brought. Before he and his men had arrived, she had often sat to take her own meal with them after serving them, but there had seemed no place for her and Ellan at the crowded table after they had arrived—not to mention the fact that she didn't particularly want to sit with the Danes.

Yet he'd arranged for food for her this morning as if she were his equal. Or as if she were someone with whom he was attempting to court favour. Her throat went dry at that thought. What would he stand to gain from her favour? She might have the advantage of sharing Lady Gwendolyn's bloodline, but she didn't have a dowry to speak of, not one that a warrior such as Rolfe could command. He could take a wife who would bring an estate to the marriage, or at least a hefty amount of silver. Why would he want *her*? And why did the idea of him pursuing her in that way send pleasure spiralling through her?

It was too early to figure out those things, so she shook her head and looked for her shoes. He was a puzzle she wasn't quite able to work her way through just yet. She had slept in her clothes precisely so that she wouldn't have to dress this morning and risk exposing the jewel, so at least there was no need for her to dress. Shoes found, she ran a comb through her hair and quickly plaited the length of it in the near darkness. Grabbing her thickest cloak, she made her way downstairs.

The entire hall seemed to be asleep, so she trod carefully lest she wake one of them. Now that it was colder at night, more of the warriors had begun to sleep inside so she wound her way around them as she walked to the front door. When she opened the door, Wyborn approached, tail wagging, to sniff her palm. She gave the fur on his head a quick pet and he walked back to stand beside his master. Rolfe held the reins of two great horses. Their hooves pawed the ground anxiously. Twin puffs of steam floated up from their nostrils to dissipate in the morning darkness.

'This is Sleipnir.' He stroked a hand down the neck of the stallion that he'd ridden into Alvey. His coat was a deep grey that darkened to midnight around his legs. 'You'll ride Gyllir. She's very gentle. I wasn't certain if you were an experienced rider.'

'I've ridden some.' Only while travelling occasionally to neighbouring villages or to Alvey. At home there was hardly a need for it.

The mare gave a soft whinny and Elswyth couldn't resist touching her velvet nose. Her coat was golden and seemed to glow in the pale moonlight of early morning. She rooted in Elswyth's hand for a treat, prompting a soft laugh from Rolfe. 'She's a greedy one.'

Despite the massive beauty of the horses, it was Rolfe who held her in her thrall. Silver moonlight painted him in her generous light, touching his chiselled features with a soft hand so that she was struck anew by his masculine beauty. There was no room in her life for how her stomach fluttered in his presence or the way her gaze was reluctant to leave him. She refused to become what her mother had been.

'Come, I'll help you.' His low voice moved right down inside her to settle deep in her chest. When he moved around his horse to stand beside Gyllir, he held out his hand to her. She took in a deep, wavering breath as she touched his palm with hers. His long fingers closed around hers and he tugged slightly, bringing her to stand before him. There was no explanation for how protected he made her feel. In one easy movement he put his hands to her waist and lifted her to sit astride the horse. She tugged her tunic upward, leaving her leggings exposed from the knee down.

'I thought you might need this.' He tossed a thick fur up and around her shoulders before she could say anything. It smelled like him and she had to close her eyes for a moment to savour it. She should push it away and give it back to him, but it was deliciously warm in the morning's bitter cold. Her own cloak was no match for the frigid air without sun.

'Thank you,' she muttered, tying the thick folds closed around her body.

'You're welcome,' he said and pulled a small sack from Sleipnir's back, pulling out a honeyed cake. Her mouth watered at the sight. How had he known they were her favourite? Lady Gwendolyn always made certain that they were filled with the most deliciously gooey mixture of honey and walnuts. 'To break your fast.' He smiled as he held it up to her.

She took it, hardly able to find the words to thank him, but he didn't wait for her to say anything. He turned and pulled his powerful frame easily atop his horse, the perfect balance of power and grace.

He offered her a nod as he set his heels to the horse and led the way out of Alvey. She followed with Wyborn trotting along at her side and they rode in silence for a while as they both nibbled their honey cakes.

Finally they moved past the small city of tents and made their way into the forest. The silence was broken by the happy calls of the migrating thrushes beginning their day. Their songs were filled with a cheeriness that Elswyth was far from feeling. That blasted stone burned against her belly like an ember that only roused her guilt.

She needed to know something about him, something that would make her feel better about what she'd done. Something that would remind her that he was a ruthless Dane. Of course she wouldn't go back and not take the stone—Baldric needed to be saved from the Scots—but if Rolfe was really a ruthless warrior, then the knowledge would help to soothe her conscience.

'Why are you taking up so much time with me? Why teach me the sword and bring me honey cakes and be so nice to me?' That wasn't precisely what she'd meant to say when she'd opened her mouth, but that's what had come out and she couldn't take it back now.

The path was wider here, so when he looked over at her he slowed his pace to allow her horse to come abreast of his. He wasn't smiling, but his eyes were soft. 'Why shouldn't I do these things for you?'

Infuriating man. 'You know very well why. You are the commander of one of the most powerful armies in the north.' It nearly choked her to say those words, but they were true. 'I am the daughter of a farmer.'

He was quiet, so after a few moments passed she dared to glance over at him to see that he was studying her. His eyes were intense, but she couldn't begin to fathom what he was thinking. 'You sell yourself short, Elswyth. You are far more than that. Besides, your father's farm is the largest in Alvey. He produces enough food and wool to feed and clothe an army. Without that farm, Alvey is weak.'

She had never considered their farm that important to Alvey, but she knew that he was right in his assessment. She'd simply never viewed it in such mercenary terms before. It had always simply been her home. Slightly mollified, she said, 'Is that it, then? You want to align our farm and village more closely with Alvey?' It made sense. It was no secret that her father didn't care for the Danes.

'It's what Lord Vidar wants. He and Lady Gwendolyn both want to align all the villages with Alvey. They can see the potential risk in losing your farm.'

Her breath caught in her throat. 'You've spoken to Lord Vidar about me…about us?' They must have spoken of marriage. Had anything been decided? Did she even have a say in the matter? Her mind whirled with a hundred questions, only stopping when Rolfe reached over and touched her shoulder through the fur.

'Only for a moment. He plans for me to wed this winter and he mentioned several names for consideration. Yours was merely one of many.'

One of many. Somehow she hated that even more than she hated the fact that they had spoken of her. Rolfe would wed this winter and it might not be her. She could only sit for a moment as that thought washed over her.

Unreasonably, that cold fist of jealousy tightened in her chest the same as it had the previous morning when the servant had left his room. Someone else could be the recipient of those breathtaking smiles very soon. Someone else could lie upon those warm furs in his bed alongside him, touching and...she couldn't let her thoughts go so far. But she did recall very vividly how he had looked when he'd stood from the tub. Nude, his skin golden in the candlelight. In her mind's eye, she imagined him walking towards his bed, only the woman waiting for him wasn't her and she hated it.

The bitterness with which she hated it surprised her. This was absolute madness. She would not allow herself to be seduced by a Dane, but somehow she was having these thoughts and they were far from pure.

Realising that it had been some time since she'd spoken, she forced herself to nod, not caring that it was a bit jerky and ungraceful. 'Did you plan to let me know that I was being considered?'

He shifted at her side, but she couldn't bring herself to look at him. 'I thought it best to allow you to get to know me before approaching the subject. If it turned out that you hated me—' the smile was evident in his voice as he said it, as if she couldn't possibly hate him '—then there would be no need to talk further about it.'

'I suppose I should feel grateful that you planned to consider my wishes.'

He laughed. 'The truth is that you had already lured me in before Lord Vidar mentioned your name.'

With wide eyes she looked over at him and he said, 'I noticed you on the wall the evening I returned. You looked so fierce and resolute, I took you for a lady warrior like Lady Gwendolyn. Then later when you came to my chamber you spoke to me so boldly as if you had no fear.'

'That's hardly—'

'Nay, it's true. This may seem insignificant to you, but hardly any woman has spoken so boldly to me since I was a boy.' The dimple shone in his cheek as he explained. 'I grew up the younger son of a farmer with no prospects.'

She had to stop her chin from dropping. If what he said was true, he'd grown up much like she had. He was a fierce and respected leader, and she had rather blindly assumed that he always had been.

'It took dedication and years of relentless training to become the leader I am today. I'm told that many find me intimidating. But not you. You're honest about your feelings, Elswyth, and I like that about you.'

But she wasn't honest. She wasn't honest at all. The bloodstone seemed to warm against her as if it had its own internal heat meant to remind her of her duplicity. 'Do you miss home?' she asked, because it was the only thing in that entire speech that she could latch on to without feeling even worse about what she had done. Baldric needed the stone, she had no qualms about saving him. Only she despised that she had to lie to Rolfe to do it.

'Aye, sometimes. I had a happy childhood…for a time, then I left to join with Jarl Hegard, Lord Vidar's father,' he supplied.

'Why did you leave home?' she asked, sensing he'd left something out.

'There was nothing for me there. My older brother was married with children of his own and he stayed to work the farm. There were six of us and my parents needed the silver I could send home to them. I craved adventure, anyway. Leaving suited me.' A thread of bitterness had entered his voice before he went quiet for a moment. Finally he added, 'For a while now I've found myself remembering my childhood and all the trouble I caused my parents. I once thought it was homesickness, but I have no particular desire to go home. I like Alvey. Now I realise that it's the desire for my own family that's calling to me.'

She was struck by two things. The first was that he was being more honest with her than she ever thought he would be. The second was that he was being so honest with her because he wanted her to share the life he had made for himself. She could hardly fathom that they were having this conversation when she hadn't even known him two days ago. He had been but a faceless warrior who would brutally end her people's struggle for independence. Now he was real and kind and not at all what she'd expected. She had to put a stop to what he was thinking before things went too far.

'I cannot wed a Dane.'

The words settled between them with a thud, making the silence seem louder and more obtrusive until he finally said, 'It's true, then, that you share your father's feelings about us?' His voice was low and even, making it impossible to tell his feelings. She couldn't bring herself to look at him again.

'Not precisely…' She realised that those words at least were true. She didn't hold the hatred for the Danes as she might have had she not spent months in Alvey. 'But neither do I welcome you here.'

He was quiet as he mulled that over. Finally the silence became too much and she had to look over to see what he was thinking. She was surprised that he didn't seem hurt, angry, or even confused by her words. There was a slight heat in his eyes, but it wasn't fury. 'Lord Vidar believes that our joining could bring peace. What do you think?'

Would it bring peace? 'Father would never agree to a marriage, so, nay, there could be no peace from our joining.'

Chapter Seven

Rolfe didn't respond to her, so they rode the rest of the way in silence. Elswyth had been chastising herself for turning him down with such finality, afraid that he would take them back to Alvey immediately. After all, if he was not attempting to win her favour, then what was the need to spend time with her? She was certain now that's what this sword practice was about, but when he made no move to turn around she kept quiet, afraid that to displease him further would mean she wouldn't be able to finish her task.

The sun began to crest the horizon, throwing the world into shades of grey as she followed him to the edge of the clearing where he stopped his horse and dismounted. Her gaze immediately took in the trees nearest them, looking for one large enough to hide behind so that she could rid herself of the bloodstone. A tall poplar stood about forty paces away. It was easily large enough to shield her and the evergreens crowded around it would help as well. Her palms were sweaty as she dismounted and made sure to lay his fur over the back of her horse. She missed its warmth already as a shiver ran through her.

Rolfe was busy lashing the reins to a tree so the horses wouldn't wander off to look at her. Thank goodness, because she could imagine how guilty she looked standing there, shifting from foot to foot, already breathless because her heart was pounding so hard. He must have noticed her stare, because he glanced over his shoulder at her. She said the only plausible thing she could think of to explain her fidgeting, 'I'm sorry. I wasn't able to use the... Do you mind if I take a moment before we start?' She glanced towards the tree.

He nodded, turning back to start unstrapping the wooden swords from his horse. She breathed a sigh of relief and hurried off in the direction of the poplar. It wasn't nearly far enough away to put her at ease, but her fear of discovery only made her move faster. Lifting her skirt once she was safely behind it, she reached beneath to untie the leather purse and breathed a sigh of relief when she pulled it free. At least now she could drop it beneath the limbs of a nearby tree if he came over. Just to make certain, she peered around the trunk of the tree, spying on him through the limbs of an evergreen to make sure he was still busy. He had finished untying the swords and was swinging one, she assumed to loosen his muscles, with his back to her.

Satisfied that she had a few more moments to herself, she brushed the leaves and needles aside with her foot and looked for a stick with which to dig a hole. If she came back with dirty fingers, she didn't know how she would explain that.

'Elswyth.' The harsh voice spoken so close behind her nearly made her scream in panic.

She turned with her arms raised to strike an attacker, but it was only Galan. 'Are you mad? He could see you,' she whispered.

Galan scowled in Rolfe's direction, but didn't leave her. 'Did you find it?'

'Aye. I think this is it.' She held out the purse and Galan took it, peering inside.

'It matches the description,' he confirmed. 'How did you get it?'

Her face burned as she answered him, 'I had to sneak into his chamber. It was hidden in a chest.'

Galan stared at her with a mixture of horror and anger shining from his eyes. 'Does he force you to share his bed?'

Somehow her blush deepened and spread to the rest of her body. She frowned, resenting the fact that Galan was questioning not only her methods, but her chastity as well. 'Nay. I was sent to tend his wound the first night. That's how I saw it. I sneaked back in last night after we spoke while he was below at the evening meal.' She glanced behind her, but couldn't see around the tree to tell what Rolfe was doing. 'What does it matter? You have to go.'

Galan glanced from her to the clearing where Rolfe was no doubt wondering what she was up to. He scowled and his eyes were fiercer than she'd ever seen them. 'Are you two alone?'

She nodded. 'But he won't try anything like what you're thinking. He's…he doesn't strike me as the sort to take advantage of a woman.' It was true. The Dane she had spent so much time fearing and even hating seemed to be honourable. She wouldn't have believed it herself had she not met him.

'Do not let yourself be fooled by a handsome face. I'm certain Mother thought the same thing and look where that got her. The Danes have no notion of honour. He wouldn't think twice about taking you here against your will.'

She flinched at the comparison. Would she spend her entire life proving to her family that she wasn't like her mother? 'He wouldn't do that,' she whispered vehemently, beginning to despair of ever finding peace between their people if everyone was like Galan and kept insisting on something that was plainly not true.

Galan didn't seem to be paying attention to her. He was staring between the evergreen needles, watching Rolfe. 'I could shoot the bastard right now if I had my bow.'

Despite herself, a wave of fear for Rolfe swept through her. 'You wouldn't kill an innocent man from behind.'

That made him look at her, his gaze seeming to see far more in her than she wanted to share. 'He's far from innocent, Elswyth. Don't ever forget that.' He looked back through the needles and his hand went to the handle of the axe strapped across his back. 'But you're right. I should kill him now, face to face, man to man.'

'Nay, Galan!' She gripped his arm to stay him, struggling to keep her voice low. 'You must go. Someone has to save Baldric. They could kill him if you don't return.'

He wavered, but finally lowered his arm and turned to face her. 'You're right, Sister, as usual.' The moment of madness over, he gave her a brief smile and pulled her close. 'Take care of yourself. I vow to you that I will do all I can to save Baldric.' She didn't even have a chance to respond before he had disappeared into the depths of the forest.

Rolfe couldn't shake the feeling that something was wrong. There had been a wariness about Elswyth this morning that hadn't been present the day before. When he'd gently shaken her awake she'd looked upon him as if he'd come to do her harm. He could believe that was because it wasn't every morning a warrior came to pull you from your bed, except that her wariness had hardly changed as they rode to the clearing. Something had happened between their banter on the sparring field yesterday and this morning to put that caution in her eyes. Perhaps she had learned about what he had done in Banford.

He wanted to ask her. His nature was to be direct, but a subtle approach would work so much better, even though he despised ploys and artifice. If he could take them back to that place—the one they'd found the night of his bath before he'd known her identity—then he'd get further with her.

To do that, he'd have to forget who she was and he wasn't certain that was something he wanted to do. Something about her got under his skin so easily that she was dangerous to him. She could be a very big distraction. Wyborn picked his way around the trees, nosing through the dead leaves and foliage on the ground. A sound or movement that Rolfe wasn't aware of pricked his curiosity. The dog lowered his head towards the ground, his ears tilted forward as he faced the direction Elswyth had disappeared.

Something *was* wrong. Rolfe stared, unable to shake the feeling that someone was out there in the depths of the morning forest watching him. The hairs on the back of his neck raised in warning, so he dropped the wooden swords against the trunk of a tree and pulled his own sword from the sheath strapped on to his horse. Its familiar weight set heavy in his hand as he turned a slow circle, taking in the silence of the trees. Nothing moved. The weak rays of early sunlight that managed to penetrate the clouds and hazy fog showed him only grey.

For one tense moment he wasn't certain if Elswyth was in danger or if she was the one who had brought danger. Already his fascination with her was distracting him. Perhaps his instinct had been correct and she had found a way to bring her father and his men here to this clearing. He cursed himself for a fool for underestimating her as he listened for any sound to betray the danger. Just as he parted his lips to call to Elswyth, she stepped through the trees on her way back to him. He was struck motionless by the sight of her beauty. The dark smudges of her gracefully arched brows and long eyelashes stood out against the nearly ethereal glow of her face in the silver morning mist. Her eyes shimmered a depthless green in the grey light and the delicate curve of her cheekbones seemed emphasised beneath the smooth satin of her skin. Her mouth was a red swatch of colour that dropped open as she stared at him.

How had he only realised at just this moment how beautiful she was? He'd had a glimpse of it two nights ago in his chamber, but there she'd been turned golden and delectably human with the candlelight. Here the silver light made her look like a goddess stepping through the trees.

He swallowed thickly, shaken by the thought. She broke the spell when she looked over her shoulder to check the path behind her as she stepped into the clearing. Her gait had altered, not smooth and confident, but halting and worried. It was apparent that she was upset about something. Her eyes swung back around to settle on his sword, sliding along its length before coming up to meet his.

'Are you all right?' he asked into the growing silence. His thoughts turned to Hilde and how she had seemed gentle, all the while plotting behind his back. Was he doomed to only be attracted to women who would betray him?

She swallowed, her throat working before finding her voice. 'Aye.' She glanced back once more in the direction she'd come and he stepped closer. Wyborn hurried over to her, sniffing around the hem of her skirts as if he'd found new smells. She buried her fingers in his fur and knelt down to pet him, murmuring softly. From her place at his feet, she looked up at Rolfe. Her face seemed paler than was natural against the rich darkness of her hair.

'Are you ill?'

She shook her head and her gaze moved back to his sword. 'Are you planning to cure me with that if I am?' Her lips quirked upwards in a brief attempt at a smile as she rose to her full height, leaving Wyborn sniffing around her heels.

Appreciating the fact that the sword was menacing, especially to a Saxon woman who distrusted him, he slowly lowered it to his side. However, he didn't put it away, because he couldn't quite dismiss the feeling that something was wrong. Attempting a smile, he shook his head. 'It's more of a remedy than a cure.'

Her face went blank for a moment, but then she let out a burst of laughter as if she hadn't expected the humour. Colour rose in her cheeks and she wasn't quite so pallid any more. 'You're not what I expected, Dane.' Then as if the moment hadn't even happened, she stepped lightly around him to retrieve one of the wooden swords where they rested against a tree trunk. Turning towards him, she swung it out so that it was pointed right at him. With a nod towards the sword at his side, she said, 'I expect you'll have an unfair advantage if you're practising with the real thing.'

For the first time since she emerged from the forest, Rolfe found himself smiling genuinely and that feeling of unease drifted away in the face of her humour. 'Fortunately, I don't need a sword to hold the advantage. I already have it.' Stepping across the blanket of pine needles, he returned his sword to the sheath fastened to his saddle and retrieved a wooden sword.

'I'm surprised to hear such arrogance from a man who will be fighting with only one arm.' She nodded pointedly towards his left arm which was without its sling, though he still held it tucked against his side.

'It's much better.'

'But not healed. Perhaps we should postpone the sparring until you won't risk reopening the wound.' Her brow furrowed with concern and he found himself believing it to be genuine.

He swung the sword around with his right arm, loosening his wrist as he walked a slow circle around her. 'I apologise for my lack of a sling. My nurse was abed this morning and not able to help me.'

She smirked as she turned with him, her feet too close together and her posture far too rigid for proper combat. 'You're teasing me. You managed quite well yesterday morning without my help.'

Could that be jealousy flashing in her eyes? Probably not, but he couldn't help but goad her to make certain. 'Do you mean Claennis?' She was one of the girls brought from the villages to work at the great hall since the Danes had taken residence in Alvey. She'd dogged him relentlessly the previous winter and his absence had seemed to change nothing in regard to her intentions. The girl was free with her favours, but Rolfe was careful never to take his pleasure with a house servant. It led to bad feelings that close proximity didn't help when the girl eventually expected more than the occasional lay. Nevertheless, Claennis hadn't given up hope and had presented herself to him the morning after he'd returned home, before he'd even managed to pull himself from his bed. Instead of accepting her offer, he'd asked her to help him with the sling.

Elswyth raised her chin a notch. She probably didn't even realise that she had done it, but the movement revealed the long, smooth column of her throat and the soft, silken skin that disappeared beneath the high neck of her underdress. The urge to put his mouth there and taste her gripped him with a near-visceral force and refused to let him go. Across the sparse distance, he could see the flutter of her pulse and the way she swallowed hard. She *was* jealous. A flare of satisfaction moved through him, urging him to go to her. His boots scraped over the rough ground as he took a step away, not trusting himself in the grip of this sudden madness.

'Claennis does not share my bed.' He didn't know why the words came. One moment he was thinking of ways to prod her jealousy and in the next he'd admitted to the truth. 'She helped me with my sling.' He added that last as if it somehow erased the first.

Her full bottom lip dropped open the slightest bit, but enough to draw his gaze to settle on the lush curve. Fuller than its counterpart on top, it looked as soft as a flower's petal. He wanted to draw it into his mouth and scrape his teeth across it until she gasped in pleasure. Then he'd dip his tongue into her. She'd probably taste like honey from the cake. The knowledge sent a rush of blood to his groin.

He swallowed hard, bemused by his own thoughts. Elswyth was a challenge, a woman whom he was meant to seduce and here he was being seduced by her. And all she had done was hold a wooden sword on him and look at him as if he'd betrayed her in some way.

'I don't particularly care what you do with Claennis.

It's no business of mine,' she lied. He could tell by the way her eyes dipped to the side as she spoke. He should be gratified that he had this hold on her—and a part of him relished it—but he found himself wanting to comfort her.

'I've brought the sling. Come help me with it?'

'Why didn't you say as much before now?' Her eyes flared with annoyance. 'You could have harmed yourself.'

He forced himself not to smile as he walked to his horse and retrieved the cloth from the sack tied to the saddle. She tossed the wooden sword to the side as she took it from him, drawing it out in lengths that she measured between her hands.

'Is Claennis the reason you left the poultice for me last night instead of seeing to my wound yourself?'

She hesitated. He probably wouldn't have noticed how her hands faltered in their manipulation of the linen if he hadn't been so intent on her every movement. The slender fingers paused, twisting the material, before picking up their previous rhythm and smoothing it out again. 'You seem far more concerned with Claennis than I,' she murmured. 'Last night I was tired and, anticipating the early morning, I went to bed rather than wait for you.'

She'd kept her eyes downcast so he couldn't tell if she was lying. When he opened his mouth to prod her further, she said, 'Lean down', and held the sling up so that she could put it over his head. He obliged and she set it against his right shoulder and held it down so that he could tuck his elbow into it. She made herself appear extraordinarily busy smoothing out the fabric and turning the edges so it sat just so against his chest.

'There, I only hope you haven't set yourself back in healing time. The more you reopen the wound the longer it will take to mend.'

Her eyes were depthless pools of the deepest green when she looked up at him. An intoxicating mix of innocence and strength swirled within them. He could feel them tugging at him like a siren in a story he had heard once, tempting him to dive in and give himself over to her. At that moment he would have sworn that his instincts lied and she had no part in her father's crimes. It was proof that he lost his sense of right and wrong and duty when he was around her. Her hand had come to settle on his chest and the heat from her palm sank into him, seeping through the layers of his clothing.

The touch was so unexpected that he had to look down to make sure he hadn't imagined it. She jerked it away, curling her fingers towards her palm as if she hadn't realised what she'd done until he drew her attention to it, and he was sorry that he had moved at all. She looked stunned, her eyes wide and her lips parted.

'You don't have gloves?' he asked to break the strange awareness that had settled between the two of them. To bring attention to anything else except the way his heart pounded and his blood flowed thick and heavy through his veins.

She shook her head. 'Nay, I don't own a pair.' He wasn't surprised. Leather gloves were expensive and, while not destitute, he was under the impression that despite being important to Alvey, either her farm didn't produce much wealth, or her father was a miserly sort.

As gently as if he were approaching a serpent, he took her wrist. She was fine boned so his fingers slipped around it effortlessly. She watched him without breathing, her chest still and her lips slightly parted. Bringing her hand to his, he placed their palms together. She had long graceful fingers, but he could still have closed the last joint of his fingers over the tip of hers. 'How did you ever make it through the winters?'

'My friend Osric made me a pair once, though they were more like wool sleeves that fit over the end of my fingers. They only lasted a couple of winters. Perhaps I'll request a new pair.' He released her as soon as she said the name and she gave him a hesitant smile as she took a step backwards, putting space between their awkwardness.

He didn't know why the name startled him. She was from Banford and it had been almost certain that she knew Osric, yet he hadn't expected such a personal connection between them. 'Osric?' he asked, because he couldn't let the name settle between them without comment.

She nodded and walked back to where she'd tossed her wooden sword. 'He works on my father's farm and is a good friend to me.'

Swallowing, he bent to pick up his own sparring sword while forcing himself to remember they were probably all traitors, including her. 'How good a friend is Osric?' he asked before he could stop himself.

She swung on him and would have hit him across his

right shoulder had he not seen the movement from the corner of his eye and swung to block her. She seemed stunned, but ultimately impressed that she had been thwarted. A smile lightened her features. 'Not as good a friend as Claennis is to you,' she said with honeyed sweetness.

Osric had not bedded her. Rolfe knew that there were a hundred things he could have taken away from that statement, but somehow the most important was that they were not lovers. 'Claennis is not my friend.' The words came out as a grumble that made her laugh. The sound of her laughter unexpectedly tugged at some long-hidden knot within him, pulling at the tightly intertwined string until it loosened and he felt lighter than he had in a long time.

'He's only a few years older than I and he's worked on the farm as long as I can remember. He's like an older brother to me, only nicer, because Galan is frequently insufferable.' She kept her voice light and he didn't know if that was intentional or an indication of her affections for them both.

What would she think of him once she knew that Osric's brother was dead because of him? That he'd burned Osric's home? The significance of a battle that had been hardly more than a skirmish to him suddenly grew by a hundred. It settled like a weight on his chest, threatening to slowly squeeze the air from him.

'Loosen your stance. Your legs are too stiff and your knees too straight. One strong blow will knock you over.' His voice was coarse and harsh. Her eyes widened at the change, but she immediately tried to adjust her stance. He kept his voice more even as he explained, 'You must keep your limbs loose so that you can absorb the jolt of an impact.

'Good,' he praised when she complied. 'Hold the sword here.' He demonstrated with his own grip. 'Any lower and you can easily lose your grip. Higher and it will limit your range of motion.'

He made certain that there was no room for idle talking for the rest of the lesson. The rules of his seduction had suddenly been changed and he didn't like it. He had known that she would despise him for his role in what had happened in Banford, but he had soothed himself with the knowledge that her anger would be rooted in misplaced pride. There was no wrong in his actions, no personal affront to her.

Only now he understood that she *would* take it personally. She would hate him for what he'd done.

Chapter Eight

'How was the sparring lesson this morning?' Lady Gwendolyn asked from her bath, giving Elswyth a sly smile as she ran a cloth over her shoulder.

Elswyth tried not to react, but she could feel her cheeks warm at the woman's tone. It was the same tone with which Ellan had asked her as soon as they'd returned that morning. Somehow she didn't think a hastily mumbled, 'It was fine', would suffice here. The range of emotions she'd experienced this morning had left her quite drained and unable to fully understand what she felt towards Rolfe. She'd gone from absolute terror that the warrior would find out about the stolen bloodstone, to jealousy about Claennis, to an awareness of him as a man that she hadn't been able to shake. The lesson with the sword had hardly signified after all of that.

She sat with baby Tova on the floor of the chamber Lady Gwendolyn shared with her husband, playing with the baby who crawled around her. She delighted in pulling a soft, thinly woven wool blanket over her head so that Elswyth could find her. 'Where is Tova? Wasn't she just here?' she said with a lilting voice. Tova pulled the blanket down to reveal herself, grinning widely to show several white milk teeth. Elswyth pretended to be surprised and the girl fell over with laughter. Her laugh never failed to make Elswyth laugh along with her.

But Lady Gwendolyn expected an answer. Though she smiled indulgently at Elswyth and her daughter, when the moment had passed, she looked at Elswyth with a raised eyebrow. 'It was fine.' A quick glance confirmed that the lady did indeed expect more in the way of an answer. 'I'm merely sceptical of how much I can learn in less than a fortnight.' She busied herself with folding up the blanket. Tova liked it better when she could unfold it before hiding under it.

Lady Gwendolyn went back to her washing, but the pregnant silence let her know that the conversation wasn't over.

'What do you think of Rolfe?' Lady Gwendolyn finally asked.

There was a question rife with difficulty. 'He's a fine teacher. Patient and not too demanding, especially when I do something wrong.' Much to her chagrin, the sword didn't seem to come to her as easily as the axe or the bow and arrow. Or perhaps she'd been too distracted by Rolfe to concentrate properly on her lesson.

'That's good to know.' There seemed to be a sliver of impatience in her voice, but Elswyth wasn't certain if she had only imagined it. 'Anything else?'

Elswyth shrugged as she set the blanket aside and watched Tova start to unravel it. 'He seems to be a great warrior. I've been impressed with the men under his command. They respect him and he respects them.' That was saying a lot actually. Her own father frequently became impatient with his men and was given to bouts of shouting at them. She had yet to see such behaviour from Rolfe. Of course his men were well trained and hardly needed the admonishment.

Lady Gwendolyn laughed. 'You know that's not what I'm asking you, Elswyth. What do you think of him… as a man?'

Not only were her cheeks flaming now, but the heat had spread to her neck and chest. Nevertheless, she made herself answer, because she knew that Lady Gwendolyn wouldn't be put off as easily as Ellan had been. She'd keep asking, because it was likely that she was in on this whole marriage idea. Besides, she liked Lady Gwendolyn. They'd developed an easy friendship in the time Elswyth had been here. 'He's powerful… and kind…and an impressive warrior. His men respect him—oh, fine.' She rolled her eyes at her lady's narrowed gaze. 'He's very handsome.'

The woman smiled knowingly. 'And you find favour with him?'

'Aye.' She was surprised to find her voice hoarse. A knot of guilt tightened in the pit of her stomach as she thought of her mother and what her attraction to a Dane had caused. Nothing good would come of this.

'That's good.' The relief in the woman's voice was so evident that it made Elswyth look away from the blanket-covered Tova to meet her gaze. 'I think he finds favour with you as well.'

'Why does that matter, my lady?' She swallowed against the tightness in her throat. She wanted to hear the woman give voice to the idea of their marriage, to confirm or deny the intention.

Tova peeked out at her from the blanket, so Elswyth went through the motions of trying to find her until the baby yanked the blanket off. The entire time her heart pounded as she wondered what this line of questioning meant. Was she being given to Rolfe? In some deep dark place inside her the thought appealed to her, which left her terrified.

'Come attend me, Elswyth.' Finished with her bath, Lady Gwendolyn stood and Elswyth walked over to wrap a light piece of sheeting around her. Tova was tired of her game by this time and crawled over to the edge of the rug to play with her wooden spinning figures on the hard floor.

After drying her body, Lady Gwendolyn secured the end of the sheet between her breasts and surprised Elswyth by taking her hand and leading her to the bed. She sat at the corner and indicated that Elswyth should take a seat next to her. 'I'd like to talk to you about marriage, Elswyth.'

With those words her heart began to beat in double its normal rhythm.

'Do you know how Lord Vidar and I have offered coin and gifts to Saxon and Dane couples who marry?' At Elswyth's nod, she continued, 'We've had some success with this, but we'd like even more success. For that reason, we've asked some of our best warriors—

including Rolfe—to take Saxon wives. We feel this is the best way to foster peace between our people.'

'I understand. I don't think I did until I came here, but I've seen how your own marriage has helped bring peace to Alvey. My father would have me believe that peace isn't possible and I confess that I once thought that was true, but you've opened my eyes to how well it can work in certain circumstances.'

Lady Gwendolyn smiled at that. 'It warms me to hear you say that. You've become a friend to me, Elswyth, and I couldn't bear it if you harboured ill feelings for me and my husband.'

Elswyth was shaking her head before she'd even finished speaking. 'Nay, my lady. I could never harbour those feelings for you. I admit that Lord Vidar, being a Dane, is a bit rough for me sometimes, but he treats you well and I can see the affection between you both.'

'Good.' She bit her lip in a rare moment of uncertainty, but then pushed on. 'I'd hoped to hear you say this, because it is my belief that Rolfe could be a good husband to you.'

Those were the words Elswyth had expected all along, but hearing them was far more potent than she'd imagined. In an instant she saw herself with him…sitting at the long table at his side, riding with him across the plains near the sea, walking hand in hand with him in the forest…in every imagining he was smiling at her as he had that first night in his chamber. He was smiling because she knew that he would be kind and gentle with her as he had always been, not the monster that Galan and Father made him out to be. And just like that her imaginings disappeared, thoughts of her family chasing them away. She couldn't betray them. She wouldn't.

Thoughts of her mother, her father's meetings with the Scots and her own duplicity in taking the blood-stone swept through her. She sucked in a breath, but it moved in jerks and starts over the serrated edges of her regret. 'I believe that you're right. Rolfe would make a good husband…but not for me.'

The light in Lady Gwendolyn's eyes dimmed and her shoulders slumped as if Elswyth's rejection had taken the air from her. 'But why ever not?'

'He…' The word had no sound, so she cleared her throat and tried again. 'He is a Dane, my lady. I could never marry a Dane.' Had this conversation taken place before she'd met Rolfe those words would have come out strong and high with the full force of Elswyth's conviction behind them. As it was, she was forced to say them now…after she had met Rolfe and knew how honourable he was. It didn't matter that she'd said the same thing to the man himself this morning. The words didn't come any easier.

'Because of your father?' Lady Gwendolyn prodded.

It would be so easy to say aye and end it there, but it wasn't the complete truth. She had worked too hard since Mother's abandonment to show everyone in Banford that she wasn't like her. Her mother might have been faithless and vain, but *she* was good and noble and would put her family first. She wasn't a silly girl to allow a handsome face to sway her. What would the people who had been her entire world since birth think of her if she turned her back on them now by marrying a Dane?

'Nay, my lady. You have chosen a Dane for a husband and I can respect your choice. I, however, cannot overlook what they've done. They are our enemy and I cannot marry one of them.'

A hand rose to Lady Gwendolyn's chest. She was clearly unprepared for the harsh declaration. 'I'm sorry, Elswyth. I had no idea that your feelings were so strong. Do you hate them, then? All Danes?'

Elswyth nodded.

'What of Tova?'

The question brought Elswyth head up sharply. 'Nay, my lady. Never could I hate Tova.' Hearing her name, the baby made her way over to them with an adorable smile on her face.

'She has as much of her father's blood in her veins as she has mine. Many would say that makes her a Dane.'

'Nay. I didn't mean that. I do not hate Lord Vidar or even Rolfe.' It was true. She'd been genuinely afraid for Rolfe when Galan had threatened him. Tova reached for her skirt and pulled herself up, smiling proudly as she stood holding on to Elswyth's knees. Elswyth took the child up into her lap and hugged her close. The soft golden curls on top of the baby's head tickled her chin. 'I only meant that I despise their actions.'

'What do you despise?' Lady Gwendolyn kept her voice soft, but Elswyth knew that she had hurt her.

'That we are forced to do their bidding or face death.'

'I wouldn't say it with such dramatics, but we are all at the mercy of someone. Had I married a Saxon man to be lord here, the same rules would need to be followed.'

'But there's the crux, my lady. Forgive me, but if you

had married a Saxon man then he would be one of us. Not one of them.'

Lady Gwendolyn was silent for a moment, a myriad of emotions crossing her features. Elswyth wondered if she might have gone a step too far and ruined the friendship she had come to hold dear. Finally, Lady Gwendolyn said, 'They are not so different than us, Elswyth. Rolfe may be the leader of the warriors, but he's a gentle man. The choice is yours, but do not discount him as an option so quickly.'

'I fear that Elswyth isn't quite as amiable to a wedding as I had hoped,' said Lady Gwendolyn later that evening at the long table in the hall.

Rolfe tried to hide the smile tugging at the corners of his mouth, but he failed miserably. How anyone who knew Elswyth could assume that she would be agreeable to marrying a Dane was beyond him.

'We knew the girl held a dislike for us, love. It's no secret.' Vidar matched Rolfe's smile as he looked adoringly at his wife.

'Of course we knew, but she seemed so reasonable. I thought—naively, it seems—that she would agree to a marriage.'

'Has she told you nay?' Rolfe asked, curious about the details of their conversation. He wasn't surprised at her refusal, since she'd told him as much this morning, but he wondered what Lady Gwendolyn planned to do about it.

'In so many words.'

Vidar frowned, his glance moving to the newly constructed gallery above them where Rolfe's chamber was along with the alcoves. The woman in question had disappeared to the space she shared with her sister after the evening meal. The heavy curtain that hid their sleeping alcove was closed. 'What of Ellan? She seems agreeable to taking a Dane warrior as husband. I've seen her talking with quite a few of them.'

Lady Gwendolyn nodded. 'I've thought of that, but you remember when we approached Godric with the offer to bring them here. It was Elswyth who has his respect, as well as that of her people. Ellan is a charming girl, but the alliance wouldn't have as much consequence with her.'

Something inside him revolted at the idea of exchanging Elswyth for Ellan. Rolfe and Vidar shared a glance, their earlier conversation about forcing an alliance weighing heavily on Rolfe's mind. He liked Elswyth well enough. This morning had made him admit exactly how much he desired her. However, nothing had changed with respect to how he felt about marrying a spy.

'Have you mentioned an alliance with her father?' Rolfe asked. 'This whole discussion could be inconsequential if he opposes it.'

Vidar and Lady Gwendolyn exchanged a look that set Rolfe on edge. The look clearly said that they had been plotting. 'It's time for me to confess,' Lady Gwendolyn said. 'I had hoped to have Elswyth agree to the marriage without consulting her father. With her on our side, I assumed that the wedding was a certainty. She'd either get his agreement, or marry you anyway and damn the consequences. No one—aside from her father—in Banford would oppose the union if it's what she wanted.'

The table was silent for a moment. Many of the men had settled down to sleep on the benches at the perimeter of the room, but some still huddled around tables, playing dice games. After a while, Vidar said, 'We may have no choice but to force her.' It was stated with quiet conviction, but it made Lady Gwendolyn take in a sharp breath.

'I could not,' she said.

'Not even if it would save lives?' Vidar asked.

She looked uncomfortable, but she didn't say anything as her concerned gaze trailed off to the curtained alcove above them. Rolfe swallowed thickly as he renewed his commitment to his quest to prove or disprove her guilt. 'It's not a question we have to answer now,' he began. 'Give me a few days with her and we'll revisit the dilemma.'

He'd come to a grim conclusion. He'd bed her if that's what it took to get her to confess. If she confessed to being a spy, then the question of marriage was moot. If she was innocent, then bedding her would almost assure her co-operation in a marriage that would benefit everyone. He'd have an entirely new problem on his hands—how to take her as his wife while keeping his distance from her—but he'd deal with that when and if the time came.

Duty would always come first.

Chapter Nine

Rolfe stared down at the face that was quickly starting to take over his every spare thought. Thick, sooty lashes laid in a crescent over pale cheeks, drawing his attention to her near-perfect skin. It was smooth like the ivory handle of the knife he'd bought in Hedeby years ago. Only he knew that unlike the knife that was perpetually cool to the touch, her skin would be warm and soft. His fingertips ached to touch her, to feel the difference in the textures of the smooth skin covering the curve of her cheek and the silken heat of her lips. Her pink lips were parted as she took in deep, sleeping breaths. They looked soft and inviting, making him ache to cover them with his own and wake her with a kiss.

He shook himself from that fantasy before it could take root. He couldn't be seduced by her or any woman. Infatuation made him weak and he refused to allow the emotion to wreak havoc with his life again. He had so much more to lose this time. It was imperative that he kept control.

The woman slept like a child. He'd called her softly from outside of the curtained alcove to no effect. She and her sister both slumbered on, lost in dreams. He'd been forced to come inside as he had the previous morning and shake her awake, only she hadn't responded to his first attempt, which had given him ample time to become distracted by her.

'Saxon.' He raised his voice to slightly higher than a whisper and gave a gentle nudge to her shoulder.

She sighed and smiled in her sleep, turning on to her side to face him. Her warm breath feathered across his wrist, causing an uncomfortable stirring deep in his gut and a tightening farther down that made him crouch to hide any indication of what she had done to him. Surrendering to temptation, he allowed the tip of one finger to trace across her cheekbone. It was as warm and smooth as he'd expected. What he hadn't expected was how that warmth slid across his palm and up his arm in a low flame that burned hotter and faster than he'd ever experienced. He drew his hand back almost as if she'd burned him.

'Wake up, Saxon.' His voice was rather ineffectually hoarse and low, but she managed to hear him this time none the less.

'Rolfe,' she whispered in a voice husky with sleep. Her eyelids fluttered, but didn't open, lost as she was in that dream-filled place between wakefulness and sleep. The sound of his name in her mouth made him bite back a groan as it brought his body to full awareness of her. If they were in bed together, he'd have rolled her beneath him and found that sweet place between her thighs with his fingers, parting her to receive him. He'd kiss her awake as he nudged inside her.

As it was, he was nothing but a lecher, desiring a sleeping woman who had no idea he was here. He forced himself to swallow down his lust. There were better ways to use this unexpected gift of sleep, if only he could focus on his mission with her and stop behaving like a besotted fool. The way she affected him was nothing short of extraordinary. All his life he'd known control and discipline, but she brought something out in him that he'd rather forget existed. Hilde was the only other woman to do this to him.

As a simple farm boy turned warrior, he'd not been nearly good enough for the beautiful daughter of a jarl, but he'd wanted her anyway. In the two years he'd worked under her father as a warrior and oarsman, he'd kept every bit of coin he had earned in the hopes of having enough to be worthy of her. Rolfe had worked harder than any other man and in that short time had gained enough to earn the Jarl's grudging respect. Hilde had noticed him as well.

Eventually, she had begun to welcome his attentions, sneaking away to meet him when she could. Soon they had become lovers and she'd agreed to be his wife. Knowing that her father would never agree to their marriage, they planned to sneak away and come back in a month when her father would have no choice but to accept. Rolfe had no doubts that he would have, because Rolfe had proven himself and had double the required coin for her bride price.

But on the night they were to meet, she walked into

the clearing cwith several of her father's men at her back, one of them a man named Bjorn who Rolfe had fought with before. She'd very calmly told him that she'd had another offer of marriage. Bjorn had smiled broadly as he stepped forward and put his arm around her, but it was her smile that had wounded Rolfe. She'd turned and left, leaving him to defend himself against Bjorn and the others. It was hardly a fair fight, eight against one, and they had beaten him until he'd blacked out.

Rolfe had awakened early the next morning with his coin and sword missing. Bloodied, bruised, and left with nothing, it had taken him several days to make the trip to his family's farm. On that long and agonising trip, he'd vowed to never let a woman deceive him again. As soon as he was able, he'd left to join with Jarl Hegard, and then Vidar, vowing to himself that he would become a warrior with whom to be reckoned. Now, years later, he commanded an army of warriors, yet one slip of a girl was on the verge of reducing him to the fool he had been.

Nay, he wouldn't allow it to happen, especially not with Elswyth, who was almost certainly a traitor. Pushing those useless thoughts from his mind, he forced himself to focus on the task at hand. 'Why are you here, Saxon?'

'Hmm…' was her completely useless reply. The sound of her voice whispered pleasantly over his skin.

Appreciating the fact that this was a very inept way to get information, he decided to try again as his usual methods of physical force and violence were unavailable to him. 'Are you here to obtain information?'

'Information,' she repeated, though the end of the word was rather garbled in her sleep.

'Aye, information about us.' He kept his voice gentle so it sounded coaxing rather than accusing. 'About the Danes... Lord Vidar...me...'

'Only you, Rolfe.' Her lips curved in another smile.

He frowned. Her father had probably wanted to know where they'd gone over the summer. It could be no secret that a large contingency of warriors had ridden out at the beginning of summer. Understanding that he would probably only get basic answers from her now with no detail, he decided to change subjects. 'Have you met with the Scots?'

'No Scots...just you.'

His frown deepened. What was he supposed to make of that? As he was trying to make sense of it, she surprised him by taking his hand in hers. It was the hand he'd touched her with and, instead of putting it away from her as he should have, he'd curled his fingers into the edge of her mattress where she'd found it. Scarcely daring to breathe, he tracked the movement as she set his hand to her cheek, settling his fingers there and covering them with her own. Despite his intentions, he allowed them to stay and even savoured the feel of her, warmth and velvet, beneath his fingertips.

'I would marry you, Rolfe.'

The words had been so distinct and clear, his gaze flew to her eyes, expecting to find her awake and watching him. However, she slept on, though she turned her face more fully into his hand until her mouth nearly brushed against the heel and her nose tickled his palm.

She was stroking herself against him, he realised with a start, and an answering smoulder started deep in his belly. His breaths came heavy and harsh.

'You will marry me,' he repeated. He didn't know if the words were a promise or a hope as his thumb traced over the silky curve of her lips. She hadn't been talking about spying or information all this time. She'd been talking about him and this strange bond they seemed to have.

She smiled at the sensation of his touch and her hot breath caressed him when she whispered, 'Aye.'

Guilt that he had expected something far worse from her dropped into his stomach and settled there like a stone. A wave of fierce protection washed over him, as he saw her as the girl she was the night she had come to tend his wound. Nothing more. But he didn't know that for certain and the warrior in him couldn't let go of the idea that she could be a spy until he knew for certain.

Gently drawing his hand back, he called to her in a firmer voice, 'Elswyth, we must go.'

The sound of her name finally roused her. She sat up halfway, resting on her elbows. Her gaze wandered over the small alcove disoriented until she set her eyes on him. They widened slightly, but her face was still slack with sleep. 'Rolfe?'

He tried not to notice the way her breasts pressed against her linen nightdress, the only clothing she appeared to be wearing. Even in the deep shadows, he caught a glimpse of a pebbled nipple pushing against the fabric. 'You sleep like the dead.'

'What are you doing here?'

'Waking you so that we can continue your lessons.'
When she looked at him with a question in her eyes, he
clarified, 'The sword.'

The last remnants of sleep left her as her mouth
dropped open in understanding. 'I didn't think you
would want to continue…after yesterday.' After she'd
told him in no uncertain terms that she didn't plan to
marry a Dane, including him.

The blanket shifted as she sat up fully, falling farther
into her lap. The laces of her nightdress were supposed
to be tied at her throat but had come apart during the
night so that it gaped open, revealing the soft swells of
her breasts, but stopping just short of exposing her nipples. He sucked in a fierce breath and turned his head
away from the sight as hot lust poured through him. He
wanted to forget the lesson, take her in his arms and
carry her back to his bed. Determining if she was a spy
had very little to do with his desire.

'Meet me downstairs if you still want to learn. I have
the horses waiting.' He left before he could make his
thoughts a reality.

Elswyth hurried to get dressed, making Ellan grumble in protest as she turned her back and pulled the blanket over her head. She had assumed that Rolfe had only
offered to teach her the sword because he'd hoped to
soften her to him so that she would agree to marriage.
The last thing she'd expected was for him to wake her
this morning. As she'd stared at him beside her bed,
she had realised exactly how pleased she was to see
him and how much she wanted to learn from him. It

was the only way she could explain how her heart had leapt to life in her chest at seeing him next to her bed. It wasn't fear of discovery as it had been the day before when she'd worried he'd found out his bloodstone was missing. It was excitement.

It had to be eagerness to continue her lesson. It could *not* have anything to do with how she had lain awake last night, tossing and turning as she had relived her conversation with Lady Gwendolyn in her head. Once, she had closed her eyes and allowed herself to imagine what it would be like to be his wife. Those thoughts had inevitably made her think of all the tender and good things about him. The dimple when he smiled…how often he seemed to smile at her…the gentle but firm way he instructed her with the sword. He was patient but commanding in his instruction, which were attributes she greatly admired. A few times his hand had gone to her waist, or better yet, touched her hand to adjust her grip and his touch had been very nice, warm and firm, but gentle. Always gentle.

Her Viking warrior was the most gentle man she'd ever met.

If he were Saxon she was afraid that she'd have eagerly agreed to wed him. Even now the thought of that sent a thrill shooting through her belly, because it made her think of his nude body. She'd probably see much more of it if they were wed, perhaps even his front side. She giggled to herself, much to the annoyance of Ellan who mumbled from under the blanket.

Tying the end of her braid off with a piece of linen, she hurried out the curtain and down the steps to the front door. She felt as though she was floating and barely noticed the men sleeping in the hall. Rolfe was waiting for her as he'd been the day before with Gyllir and Sleipnir saddled and ready, and Wyborn in tow. As she stepped up to him, aware of the embarrassing way her face was glowing, he put the fur cloak around her shoulders. She went to mount, but he stopped her and pulled out a pair of leather gloves. The kid skin looked soft and supple. Without asking, he took her left hand as if he intended to place the glove on her hand.

So this was why he had held his palm up to hers yesterday. He'd been measuring her hand against his to size the gloves. 'Is that for me? I cannot accept such a gift.'

He seemed surprised when he glanced at her. 'Why not? It's cold and you'll need warm hands to grip the sword.'

'The expense…they're too fine.'

He shrugged and reached for her fingers again. 'It's nothing. I had the leather anyway. They're not that fine, they were made very fast.'

She knew that he spoke the truth because she'd seen a few different bolts of leather when she'd searched his chamber. The guilt of accepting his gift after having stolen from him, combined with her suspicion of him, made her draw her fingers away from him again. 'Nay, I cannot accept.' His brow furrowed deeply in question. 'It's…it's been my experience that men only give gifts when they expect something in return,' she explained.

He met her gaze, those vivid blue eyes staring right into her as if to pull out all of her secrets. 'Did Osric expect something from you in return?'

Shocked that he would bring up her friend again, she paused to stare at him. His handsome features were solemn as he stared back. Some small part of her wanted to believe that she had heard jealousy in his tone, but she knew that couldn't be true. He had no reason to be jealous. They hardly knew one another. But then she'd had no reason to be jealous of Claennis, yet the fire of her jealousy had burned through her veins.

His gaze dropped to her mouth and she took in a ragged breath. When she'd awakened, she had felt the soft remains of a weight on her lips, as if he'd stroked over them. The remembered heat left behind from his imagined touch warmed her now, coming to life even though she knew that she had made it up.

'I believe that he also wants marriage,' she whispered.

His eyes jerked back to hers, this time with a fire burning in their depths. 'Are you promised to him?' The skin over his cheekbones tightened as he clenched his jaw.

'Nay. My father might wish it, but he's not the one I want.'

'Even though he's Saxon?' he surprised her by asking the impertinent question.

She might have taken offence had the sparkle of humour not returned to his eyes. Instead, she found herself shaking her head. 'It's not my only requirement for a husband.'

He raised an eyebrow in question and proceeded to help her put on the glove. This time she let him. 'But it is the most important one.'

She took in the breadth of his shoulders as she answered him. 'Nay, he must also be a fine warrior, strong and kind, generous and noble. Brave and patient.' It was only after she said those things that she understood she had described all the attributes she had come to associate with Rolfe.

'You find me lacking in those qualities?' He gently took hold of her other hand and helped her with the glove. Her palm tingled with warmth as his fingertips stroked over it. By the time he'd finished helping her put the gloves on, all traces of cold were gone.

'Nay, you're not lacking.' She honestly couldn't say that he lacked any one of those.

'Then it's only that I'm a Dane?'

He stood so closely that she should have felt dwarfed by him, or at least intimidated. He didn't make her feel either of those. She felt alive in a way she never had before and safe when he was near. 'You have to admit that it's a very large shortcoming.'

He laughed and the white puff of his breath brushed across her cheek. 'If I were Saxon…would you marry me?'

Even though she had known the question was coming, nothing could have prepared her for the way she felt when he asked it. The words asked too much, were too probing and personal, yet she could feel the truth begging to come out. It was as if she needed to compensate for the lies of omission she was forced to tell him by being completely honest with him in every other way. No other man had ever made her want to entertain marriage before. No other man had ever excited her in any way. Only Rolfe. Only the man most unsuitable for her.

'Aye.'

It was little more than a breath, but he heard, his vivid blue eyes widening slightly. His own breath sucked in sharply and his body seemed to vibrate with something he was trying desperately to contain. It felt right to say it and acknowledge what was between them. A weight lifted from her chest and she felt a moment of near euphoria as she allowed herself that brief instant to imagine, out in the open, how it could be with them.

'You understand that you've just issued me a challenge, Saxon?'

The slight hitch in her breath was only from the cold, she tried to assure herself. It had nothing to do with the excitement flooding her veins. His brows had narrowed, his gaze had gone intense with hunger and become slightly proprietary. For all that, she still felt safe, because there was a gentleness beneath it all. The way his gaze stroked her features was as tender as a caress. She might have stoked the beast inside him to life, but he'd never hurt her.

'Challenge?' She smiled, drawing strength from her certainty.

'To make you say aye, even though I will always be a Dane.'

'Have I?' Her smile widening, she shrugged and left him standing there as she went to mount the horse he had brought for her.

Chapter Ten

'Keep your weight centred here.' Rolfe's hands settled on Elswyth's hips and tightened as he moved her slowly from side to side. 'Your knees should stay loose so that you can move about freely, but your middle must stay solid.' One hand slipped around to her front to rest on her lower belly. Her muscles there instinctively tensed even more, drawing as taut as the string of a bow. Her grip on the hilt of the wooden sword tightened as pulses of awareness shot through her core. 'Now try again,' his deep voice wafted past her ear just before he stepped back to give her space.

She blinked furiously, trying to make herself focus on the grooves he had carved into the tree she was currently battering. Her task was to hit each one of them in a series of rapid whacks with the blunt wooden sword. Unfortunately, his touch had wrecked the little bit of concentration she'd been able to scrape together. After the question of marriage had been raised again, she'd had a difficult time thinking of anything else all morning.

'Better,' he praised her and walked around so that she could see him from the corner of her eyes. 'Try it with more force this time.'

She whacked, but the impact vibrated painfully up her arm.

'The trick is to move with the blow. Hit from your middle, not your arms. Keep them loose. It might help if you imagine the tree is a Dane.' The smile in his voice nearly made her smile as she swung again. This time she hit the marks with less effort and more force.

'Perfect.'

She couldn't hold back her smile and affected a mock bow. 'I'm glad to have met with my lord's approval.' Straightening, she added, 'Ah, I forgot, you're no lord.' He laughed when she teased him with his words from their first meeting. The deep sound suffused her with pleasure.

'Come and take a rest. You've earned it.' He walked to the nearby tree where he'd placed the packs which had contained their breakfast. A skein of water sat beside the pack, along with Wyborn who had grown bored with watching their antics and laid napping. He awoke when Rolfe retrieved the skein, unstoppered it and held it out for her. She drank gratefully as she watched Rolfe rub Wyborn's head in affection. Stray snowflakes had begun to fall as the morning had worn on and a few of them rested in the mongrel's dark coat.

Finished slaking her thirst, she handed it back to Rolfe and took a seat on the pine needles. Wyborn gave her hand a sniff so she held it still for him, only petting his head when he'd nosed her palm.

'He's warmed up to you quite fast,' Rolfe observed.

'I'm fond of dogs. We have a few at home. They help tell the sheep what's what.' She made the mistake of looking up into his eyes. Their colour never failed to strike her. To distract from the way he affected her, she asked, 'How old is he?'

'Almost three winters. I found him as a pup. We were south, outside York, driving the Saxons back and I came across a muddy lump of fur howling pitifully in a field. Sleipnir nearly trampled him. There were no litter mates around and no mother that I could find.'

'So you kept him.' She finished the thought for him. It was so easy to imagine this tender giant of a man showing kindness to such a pitiful creature. 'It explains why he's so devoted to you. He follows you endlessly.'

The ghost of a smile shaped his mouth, drawing her gaze to the well-formed ridge of his top lip. The short bristle of gold hair there held her attention as she wondered if it would be hard or soft against her skin if they were to kiss.

'He refused to leave me even after he was old enough to be on his way.' Rolfe stroked the dog's thick coat in obvious affection. 'But I've found he can be quite useful at times. He's saved my hide more than once.'

'You were kind to take him in when you found him.'

He shook his head, meeting her gaze again. 'It wasn't kindness. There is nothing noble in leaving an innocent to suffer needlessly.'

He said it with such quiet conviction that she knew he spoke true. His sense of honour was one thing that had attracted her to him from the beginning. It wasn't kindness that had made him do it. It was duty. As much as she admired that about him, it was making it difficult to keep herself away from him. This would all be much easier if he was abhorrent and easy to hate. Honestly, it was becoming easier and easier to forget that he was a Dane. Perhaps if Father met him, he would understand that Rolfe was nothing like the Danes they despised.

'What are you thinking?' he asked, his perceptive gaze picking up her unsettled thoughts.

Caught up in the relentless need to be as noble as he, she answered honestly. 'That I wish you weren't a Dane.' If he was a Saxon, she'd have never been put in the awful position of plotting against him. Would he look at her so gently if he knew she'd stolen from him? That she'd been sent to spy on him? Beneath it all was a deep-seated insecurity that had been present since her mother's abandonment: How could he want *her*? She was no one important.

He sensed there was more to her words and his gaze dropped down to her mouth before gliding back up to her eyes. 'Perhaps if you close your eyes you can pretend.' His voice held a dry edge of humour, but his eyes were fathomless and intense.

Somehow in the next instance, they were leaning over Wyborn, so close together that she could smell the sweet honey from the morning cake on his breath. She had no recollection of moving, but his mouth hovered over hers and she let her eyes fall closed. The butterflies in her stomach leapt for joy when his warm breath caressed her lips. In the next instance, his mouth pressed tenderly against hers. She'd never dreamed that his lips could feel so soft. They moved over hers in a gentle caress, searching and slow, but it wasn't enough for either of them. A sound she didn't recognise came from her throat and he moved to touch her neck, cupping the back of her head in his large hand and tilting her slightly.

His lips became searching, moving in gentle brushes along the rim of hers and taunting her with the promise of more. She'd never been kissed before and had only once or twice come upon Ellan kissing some boy, but she'd never thought that it could feel this way. It was lovely and gentle. The soft bristles of his short beard occasionally rasped against her smooth skin, but the sensation was pleasant, exciting even, scattering bolts of awareness that seemed to shoot all through her body with each touch. Even her fingertips and toes tingled with the pleasure.

This is why Ellan kisses boys. It was heavenly.

'Is it working?' he whispered against her lips.

She was so lost in the moment she barely knew what he meant, but a mumbled, 'Aye', tumbled past her lips none the less. Saxon or Dane, all that mattered was that Rolfe was kissing her. Before she could stop herself or think better of it, she chased him, her mouth finding his and searching for more. Much to her delight, he obliged her, pushing his hand up farther on her scalp so that he cupped the back of her head to hold her for his pleasure. An animal sound came from his throat, low and rough, but exciting her. It sent a pulse of excitement to some place deep between her thighs. She put a hand on his chest to steady herself and was pleased to feel his heart pounding as fast as her own.

Something wet and smooth touched her bottom lip. The feeling was so strange and unexpected that she jumped back slightly. His fingers tightened in her hair, pulling pleasurably as he brought her back to him. 'Shh…' he soothed, his lips brushing hers as he spoke. 'Open to me.' The harsh rasp of his voice was her undoing. The need and textured longing made her want to do anything to please him, so she complied with his request and parted her lips, though she had no idea why he'd want her to do such a thing.

The hot wetness stroked her again, sliding across her bottom lip before dipping inside, the contrast between the smooth and rough texture revealing to her that it was his tongue. His tongue! The first thought that went through her mind was that no Saxon would ever kiss this way. It was barbaric and it served her right for ever thinking for a moment that she could convince herself that he wasn't a Dane.

She should stop him…she meant to stop him. Only his tongue chose *that moment* to brush against her own. The slick glide was pure wickedness that left embers of heat crackling where he'd touched her. She made a sound of surprise, but he must have taken it as assent because it made him brush his tongue against hers again. This time he moved in a soft and silky rhythm, in and out, parrying with the tip of her tongue.

He might have been giving the bulk of his attention to her mouth, but her entire body throbbed to vibrant life. Every skilful thrust of his tongue caused a reaction some place else. Her breasts swelled and tightened, her stomach fluttered and farther down her body turned molten, slickening, aching for him in a way she'd never felt before.

Hesitant but somehow wanting more of the delicious torment, she touched him back, chasing his tongue with hers and delighting in the friction of their tongues sliding against each other. Shifting her weight to better reach him, she tightened her grip on his tunic and apparently displeased Wyborn, because he made a sound of discontent and shoved out from between them. They broke apart, her gaze falling to the dog who came to his feet and stretched, one paw sticking out behind him, before he trotted off to the opposite side of the clearing, sniffing the ground to look for a good spot to relieve himself.

Only when he'd sniffed his way around the trunk of an oak did she become aware of the rather large male next to her. His breaths came in deep, heaving pants that made his chest move up and down. His eyes were alive with a fierce hunger she'd never seen in him before. He'd always been so reserved and controlled with her. The pupils of his eyes had expanded, making the vivid blue appear darker. The way he looked at her made her feel like prey and he was the predator waiting to eat her up. By some perversity she couldn't begin to fathom, she liked that feeling, wanted to savour it. It made her think that she might enjoy being devoured by him.

As soon as the wicked thought crossed her mind, her face flamed with shame. This. This was the wicked temptation that had led her own mother astray. He was her enemy and for those few moments it hadn't mat-

tered that he was a Dane. She'd have given him anything he wanted.

Was this how Mother had felt? Had this strange
pleasure turned a once loving woman into someone
who could turn her back on her entire family? With a
clarity often born of experience, Elswyth understood
that this was exactly what had happened. Her mother
had traded her dreary life at home for the excitement
of a Dane who had tempted her beyond her resistance.
Worse…Elswyth could feel that same allure snaking
itself around her, digging its roots into her and pulling her to the man at her side. She was just like her
mother, maybe worse in some ways, because she had
known of this temptation and had allowed it to happen anyway.

Shaking her head to deny it, she asked, 'How could
you kiss me like that?' It was as sharp as an accusation.

The space between his brows became very small as
he looked down at her. 'Like what?'

'Like…like a heathen. I am a Saxon and I won't be
treated like a…a…'

'Dane?' He filled in the silence with the only obvious answer.

She shook her head, unable to reply.

The sardonic humour in his voice was unmistakable
when he asked, 'Do you truly believe that a Saxon man
wouldn't kiss that way?'

She had, but the way he asked the question had her
wondering if she'd been wrong.

'Or is the problem really that you enjoyed it too
much?' His voice was back to being soft and tender

with the husky edge that she was coming to crave. 'And you were aware that I was a Dane the entire time.'

She closed her eyes as the truth of his accusation washed over her. That was exactly the problem. She very much feared that she was ready to allow him to do whatever he wanted with her and the fact that he was a Dane would matter very little.

The faint sound of a horn back at Alvey saved her from answering. It signalled the end of morning chores and was the call to the morning meal. It also meant the end of their sparring session. He rose and began to gather the wooden swords without another word.

'Ellan, what is kissing like?' That night after they had retired to their alcove for the evening, Elswyth finally got up the nerve to ask the question that had been burning through her all day. Ellan stopped with the comb halfway finished with its journey through a lock of her long hair. The lock shimmered with notes of honey and sunlight in the glow of several tallow candles set across the bench at the end of their shared bed.

'Have you never been kissed?' Ellan asked.

The air was heavy as even it seemed to await her answer. She'd already determined to not lie any more than she had to—the theft of the bloodstone and the fact that she was supposed to be spying on these people she was coming to respect sat heavy on her. She wouldn't compound her sins by becoming more of a liar. She couldn't look at Ellan's face, so she stared at the lock of hair as she answered, 'Not at the farm.'

Ellan took a moment to mull that over before her hands resumed working the comb through a small knot. 'You mean to say that Osric never...'

Elswyth shook her head, her brows furrowing as she finally met her sister's gaze. She was so tired of hearing about Osric. 'Nay! I told you that I had no plans to wed him.'

'Apologies,' Ellan said without any regret evident in her tone. 'He followed you around enough that I assumed he'd stolen one or two.'

'Well, he didn't.'

'That explains a lot actually about your lack of kissing. No other man could get close to you with the way he hovered.'

Elswyth held back a groan at the turn in the conversation. She had known that asking the question to her sister wouldn't be straightforward, which is why she'd put it off for as long as she had. For a time she had even considered going to Lady Gwendolyn, but had put that thought aside as soon as she'd had it. She didn't want to explain to her what had happened with Rolfe. Not that she wanted to explain it to Ellan either, but she needed to talk to someone.

'But wait!' Ellan's exclamation made Elswyth startle, nearly dropping her own comb. 'You said not on the farm... Does that mean you've been kissed here? In Alvey?' Her eyes narrowed as her lips turned up in a shrewd smile.

Elswyth swallowed once...twice. It didn't help to moisten her dry mouth at all. 'Could you just answer the question, please?' she finally asked.

Ellan waited until Elswyth had almost decided she shouldn't have asked, before she said, 'I presume you know the general way it's done.' Her eyes softened along with her tone, and she moved across the bed to sit beside her sister, the comb forgotten. 'What is it precisely that you want to know?'

'Is it more than a touching of lips?'

Ellan's eyebrow rose slightly, but she didn't seem to think the question completely foolish. 'It can often lead to more than kissing,' she answered with a smile.

'Nay, I mean the kissing itself. Is…?' Her cheeks burned with what she was about to ask, but she needed to know so she closed her eyes and forced out the words. 'Is the tongue involved?'

She had known it was a wicked deed, but Ellan's swift inhale of breath only confirmed it. 'Someone kissed you with his tongue? Who?' She gave a shriek that she quickly covered with her hands. 'It was Rolfe! Is that what you've been doing every morning?'

'Shh.' Elswyth was tempted to poke her head out to make certain no one had heard them, but decided it would only rouse suspicion. 'Aye, he kissed me this morning, but it's not what we've been doing *every* morning.' The muscles in her arms were sore from the sparring sessions over the past couple of days. They were making progress, despite getting diverted today.

'And he used his tongue?' Ellan prodded her.

If it was possible, she managed to blush harder. She could feel the heat all the way up to her ears. Why was she making her say it again? 'Aye. Is that…normal? Do Saxon men kiss like that?'

'Ah, I see.' Ellan nodded, assuming the look of a wise elder as she straightened her shoulders. 'In my experience, the Danes are much more...what's the word to use here? Knowledgeable.'

'In your experience? Ellan, how many of them have you kissed?'

'Only two. Don't look at me like that. How else am I to choose a husband?'

Elswyth scoffed, 'I didn't even realise kissing had anything to do with choosing a husband.'

'Oh, Elswyth.' She shook her head. 'Of course it has something to do with it. He must do it properly. If he doesn't it could go very badly when it comes to bed-play.'

Elswyth rose and put her hands to her flaming cheeks. 'I don't believe Father meant for this to happen when he allowed us to come here.'

'Nay, I'm certain he didn't. He wants us to be proper little puppets who will marry and produce babies as he chooses, but we are not puppets. I won't have just any husband and neither should you. Sit and let's finish our talk.' She reached up and gently took Elswyth's hand and tugged her back down. 'I'm sorry this is shocking to you. I think if you had spent more time with the women in the village and less time at home with the chores, this would all be much clearer. I should have realised that there are things you don't know. I apologise for not speaking with you sooner.'

Somewhat overcome by this whole trove of information she'd known nothing about, Elswyth gave a quick nod.

Ellan relaxed and set her comb aside. Taking both of Elswyth's hands in hers, she said, 'I didn't mean to imply that kissing was the only way to choose a husband, but it is very important. Men like to pretend that it doesn't matter, because it goes easier for them that way. If they don't have to try to make it good for the woman, then 'tis less for them to worry about. But I'm told that bed-play can be pleasant and not merely something a woman has to endure. How a man kisses can tell you a lot about how he goes about other things.'

'So what does it tell you when he uses his tongue?' Now that Elswyth had had the entire day to ponder that kiss and she was currently resolved to nothing but brutal honesty, she could admit to herself that it had been pleasant. Was that a sign that other things in bed with him would be pleasant? She wanted to ask, but it was too embarrassing.

Ellan gave her that sly, mischievous smile. 'It's very good, Elswyth. The boys at home were too sheltered to know to use it, but the men here know. It tells you that he's concerned for your pleasure.'

'Isn't it…wicked?'

'That depends on who you ask and who you kiss, I suppose. If it's only kissing and only for the purposes of finding a suitable husband, I think it's forgivable.'

'It seems…don't you think they kiss that way because they're barbarians?'

To her utter dismay, Ellan threw her head back and laughed and laughed. When she finally could stop herself from laughing enough to talk, tears were streaming from her eyes. 'Do you think a barbarian would care about your pleasure?'

Put that way… 'Nay, I suppose not.' It seemed silly that she had even been upset about it. Shame quickly overcame any lingering feelings of anger. He'd been attempting to please her and she had been cruel. Her words must have hurt his pride. The worst of it was that he was right. The true source of her anger had been because she was upset that she enjoyed it while being well aware that he was a Dane.

'Did you not enjoy it?' Ellan asked, her eyes solemn once more.

'I did, but I said some hurtful things.' Things that she would need to apologise for.

Ellan nodded, but seemed uncertain about Elswyth's mood. 'Did he…did he mention marriage or was he taking advantage of the fact that he had you alone? We can speak to Lady Gwendolyn and I'm certain—'

'It's not that. He does want marriage. Lady Gwendolyn mentioned that a marriage between us could be good for Alvey, but I refused.'

Understanding dawned across her sister's features. 'Because you won't have a Dane.'

Elswyth nodded. 'Ellan, you know as well as anyone the mark Mother left on our family when she left. The villagers all look at you and me as if they expect us to have the same weakness. Since she left I've done nothing but try to show them how proper and loyal I am. But this…the way he made me feel doesn't feel loyal at all—' She broke off to swallow past the lump that had formed in her throat. 'I feel as if I'm betraying

Father and Galan. Am I wrong?' she asked, genuinely confused. Days ago her position was so clear, but now everything was muddled.

Ellan rubbed her shoulder in sympathy. 'Mother's betrayal is not your burden to bear.'

'But it is,' Elswyth insisted. She had never understood how Ellan could brush off their mother's abandonment so easily, but it had never seemed to affect her as it had everyone else. Elswyth had always admired how easily Ellan could brush off the disapproving looks some of the elders had given them, the daughters of Godric's faithless wife.

Her sister shook her head. 'Mother's situation was different. She left her husband and children for a man we never even knew. You were always meant to marry and leave. It's only that the man is a Dane and not Saxon. It's not such a betrayal.'

'But you know how they feel about Danes. They'll see it as such.'

Ellan gave a shrug and said, 'You know my feelings on the matter. I think to fight the Danes is pointless. They're here. They're powerful. To survive, we must learn to live with them. The important thing is how do you feel about the Danes?'

'They do not belong here,' Elswyth couldn't stop herself from insisting.

'And yet they *are* here. Do you want peace or do you want to fight?'

The words were simple, but true. Sometimes Ellan had a way of making things seem not as complicated at Elswyth would make them. She did want peace. She wanted to go to bed every night knowing that the people she loved were safe. As that clarity came over her, she realised that she had amends to make with Rolfe.

'I need to go apologise for the harsh things I said.' Rolfe had been nothing but kind and had not deserved any of them.

Chapter Eleven

Wyborn pushed up on to his front paws and cocked his head to the side a moment before a knock sounded at the chamber door. Rolfe sighed and tossed down the writing implement he'd been using. His head was beginning to ache from trying to translate the Latin scrolls in an attempt to teach himself the written language. He much preferred the simple lines of runes to the unnecessarily complicated curves and swirls of the letters of that language. A simple letter could appear in numerous variations of strokes depending on the handwriting of the author, making it nearly impossible to keep track of which symbol it was supposed to be.

The tight muscles at the back of his neck begged to be loosened, so he rubbed a hand over them as he rose and crossed the few steps to the door. A talk with one of his men would be a welcomed break. Elswyth was the last person he expected to see, but there she stood, looking up at him with a timid smile hovering around her lips when he opened the door. He hadn't seen her after their return until the evening meal, where she'd avoided looking at him and had disappeared soon after serving Vidar and Lady Gwendolyn. He'd half-expected to receive a dressing down from Lady Gwendolyn for kissing Elswyth that morning, but one hadn't been forthcoming. Since she hadn't behaved any differently towards him at all, he'd assumed that Elswyth hadn't told her what had transpired.

'Good evening,' he said when it was clear she wasn't going to offer a greeting.

Her eyes had gone wide as her gaze had taken in his bare torso. He probably should have pulled on his under-tunic—he wore only his trousers—but he'd expected the late visitor to be one of his men. Not a woman and certainly not Elswyth. In fact, he'd been entertaining the thought of abandoning their morning sparring sessions. There would be no point if she felt so disgusted and uncomfortable with him.

A faint pink tinged her cheeks when she finally brought her gaze back to his. Satisfaction rose in his chest that she apparently liked what she saw when she looked at him. 'I'm sorry to bother you so late, but could I have a moment to talk?' Wyborn pushed past him, nosing her hand for a petting, which she eagerly gave him behind his ears, before he went back to plop down on his spot next to the bed.

A moment to talk. That probably meant she intended to lay out all the reasons he should not have kissed her, even though she'd given him very clear signs that she had wanted the kiss. Closing her eyes, leaning into him, parting her lips so sweetly when he had asked her, making those soft sounds of pleasure in the back of her throat. She'd given every indication of having enjoyed it, except for the dressing down that had come afterwards. He wanted to tell her nay and close the door in her face, but the reasonable part of him recognised that as his own wounded pride. Best to let her have her say and be done with her. Stepping to the side, he allowed her to enter, though he took perverse pleasure in closing the door a touch too hard behind her, making it clear that she was very much in his domain now.

She didn't so much as flinch at the sound, so he crossed his arms in disappointment and took in the straight line of her back as she let her gaze sweep around his chamber. Her hair had been left to fall loose down to her waist and it shone from a recent brushing. The candlelight caught notes of chestnut and amber in its richness. Did she have any idea how inappropriate her presence was in his chamber?

Her gaze finally came to rest on the table with the tablet and scroll laid out. 'What is this?' Her voice was tinged with awe and wonder as she took the few steps necessary to reach the table. Her fingertips moved almost reverently over the wood frame of the tablet.

'It's a writing tablet. Have you never seen one?'

Despite his wish to harden himself to her, the look on her face was rather endearing when she shook her head and asked, 'Do you cipher?'

'I write runes,' he explained, walking over and pointing out the marks he had written in the hardened black wax on the tablet. 'Almost everyone can write or at least read them.' He meant Danes, of course. He'd learned that many of the Saxons he'd come across in smaller areas did not write. 'Have you seen the runes on the men's belongings?' They frequently carved their names into the items to mark the owner.

'Aye, I have seen them.' She didn't lift her gaze from the tablet. She stared at it as if it was remarkable.

'It's a simple wooden frame.' He turned it over so that she could see all sides. 'Hot wax is poured in and when it hardens it's the perfect surface for writing.' Picking up the writing implement, he offered it to her. It was a slight iron rod set into a slender goat antler, but she turned it over in her fingers as if it were something truly amazing. 'Try it.' She shook her head, but a smile tugged at the corners of her mouth. 'Go on,' he encouraged her, momentarily forgetting his bruised pride.

A soft laugh escaped her and she took the tablet and made a line in the wax at the bottom with the iron end of the stick. Smiling at her handiwork, she tried again, this time copying the runes he'd already written there. 'What did I write?' She gazed up at him with a look of such joy on her face that he was mesmerised. Luckily, he didn't have to look down to know the word he had written before she'd disturbed him.

'Home.'

'Home,' she repeated, running a fingertip across the runes. 'These look different. What does it say?'

He was forced to tear his gaze away from her to see what she meant. She was pointing to the Latin word he'd written at the top of the board. He'd been working on coming up with a way to match the runes with the Roman letters. The work was giving him a horrible headache. The reminder made him squeeze the muscles at the back of his neck again to relieve the tension. Turning, he walked to his bed where he'd tossed his undershirt in frustration earlier and pulled it over his head.

She tried not to stare, but he could see her peeking out from beneath her lashes to watch him. The satisfaction he'd experienced earlier came back to burn within him. 'It's the same word in Latin. From the scroll.' He walked back to her and gestured to the partially unrolled parchment. 'I'm attempting to learn to read that language, but it's difficult.' He'd memorised the Latin passage written on the scroll and had thought to write the runes as a sort of translation.

Briefly, he considered donning his tunic, but rejected the thought. The under-tunic was the most he could offer her in the way of preserving her modesty. She'd seen more than this when she'd come to help him with his bath. He nearly smiled at the reminder, but didn't dare to dwell on that memory with her here. It was certain to awaken a part of him better left to sleep in her presence.

'How so?' she asked, a line forming between her eyebrows as she dragged her gaze from the portion of his chest and shoulders still exposed.

'For one thing, the letters are more complex. See this one?' He pointed and she nodded. 'It's a "G", but here it is again and it's written differently. There are too many curves in the language. It makes it difficult to follow when every writer makes the curves differently. Runes are simple with straight lines.'

He glanced at her only to see that she was staring at him in much the same way he must have been staring at her earlier. A little bit of awe and sadness tinged her expression. 'If only all the world were simple and straight,' she said with a miserable little smile.

The poignancy in her tone tugged at him. It nearly drew him right into touching her, sweeping the wealth of her hair back from her cheek and soothing her. He wouldn't do it, though. She had more than made it clear that any touching in that way from him wouldn't be welcome. Instead of comforting her, he stiffened his shoulders to block the impulse and took a step back. 'What do you need?' he asked, crossing his arms over his chest again.

As if she knew the moment of tenderness was over, she gave a slight nod of her head and set the tablet and utensil down on the table. Drawing in a deep breath, she turned to face him fully. Her expression took on an almost pained look and he knew that what she was about to say wasn't easy for her. He braced himself.

'I came to apologise for the way I behaved this morning.' His face must have revealed his surprise, because she elaborated, 'When you kissed me.'

'I'm aware of what you mean.' His voice came out gruffer than he intended so he cleared his throat and tried again. 'What part of that are you apologising for?'

'The way I behaved after. I called you a heathen and a barbarian—'

'You never said barbarian,' he pointed out drily.

She shrugged. 'In my head I'm afraid I did. The point is that I shouldn't have scolded you and, if I hurt you, I am deeply sorry. Ellan explained that by using your tongue you were only trying to make it better for

me. I've never been kissed, you see? I thought it was…
well, something other than what we did. Something that
only involved lips and not— Oh, why are you laughing at me?'

The more she had talked, the pinker her cheeks had
become, but her anger changed it completely. She was
so red that it looked like she'd blistered from standing
too long in the sun. Unfortunately, it only made him
laugh harder.

With a huff of anger, she made to move past him towards the door, but he managed to pull himself together
and cross the line he'd sworn never to cross again with
her. He took her by the shoulders. She snatched away,
so he held up his hands palms out and said, 'I apologise
for laughing. It was terrible of me.' He even managed
to stop the smile that threatened, though his lips still
trembled from the urge.

'You don't look sorry.' She glared at him through
narrowed eyes. The green slits glittered at him dangerously.

'I am. I wasn't laughing at your apology, only at the
image of you getting your sister to explain kissing to
you.' He could tell from the way she drew herself up
taller that his explanation was hardly any better. 'Let's
start over,' he said into the uncomfortable silence. 'I
accept your apology. Do you want an apology for even
daring to kiss you?' He didn't intend to offer one, but
he wondered if that was what had prompted her own
apology.

Much to his surprise her shoulders slumped and she
looked down at the floor between them. 'Nay, that's not

what I want. I gave you every indication that I wanted you to kiss me. I did want the kiss.'

He frowned. Certain that she was after something from him, he asked, 'Then an apology for using my tongue?'

She was shaking her head before he finished. 'Nay, I understand now why you did it. In fact, I should offer you another apology. I wouldn't have become so upset if you were Saxon. I was surprised and I used the fact that you are a Dane against you. It wasn't fair or right and I'm so confused.' With a groan of exasperation she turned away from him and sat down on the bench at the table.

For the first time he began to believe that her apology was sincere. Taking hold of the three-legged stool he sometimes used to prop his feet on, he drew it up to her and sat down. She had put her face in her hands, but she looked up at him when he was settled. He was surprised to see her eyes bright and miserable.

'I've been horrible to you. Both this morning and yesterday morning,' she said. A slight husk softened her voice and he was a little unsettled at the way it raked at something inside him, sending a flicker of awareness down low in his gut. 'How can you still look at me like that?'

'Like what?'

'As if you like what you see.'

He grinned. 'Because I do like what I see.' It was the undeniable truth. He was attracted to her. The comely length of her hair swung down around her hips, shining and glossy in the candlelight. He wanted to run his hands through it to see if would feel like spun silk. Her eyes always held a glimmer of mischievous daring, but somehow that seemed to be present in them more tonight. Or maybe it was that he was more focused on her now that she was in his chamber. Alone. Dangerously alone. He realised that he'd been leaning in and forced himself to sit back.

She took in a deep, wavering breath that made her lips tremble and she squared her shoulders. Obviously, she'd come to some unknown resolution and he was curious to find out what it was. 'I've decided that I have no choice but to be very honest with you.' Her fingers toyed with the horn end of the writing utensil on the table as if she was nervous.

He gave her a nod of encouragement.

'The absolute truth is that I admire everything about you. I have since you arrived. I look at you and I know that I should be afraid because you lead more warriors than I've ever seen assembled in one place in my life. I know that my father doesn't trust you and that I shouldn't trust you. That with one command from Lord Vidar, you could lead those warriors and completely decimate my village, my farm, my entire way of life, and it wouldn't even be that difficult of a task for you. I know all of that as plainly as I know my own name, but somehow it doesn't seem to matter. I'm not afraid. I look at you and I see the gentleness that you try to hide. I see how you care deeply for everyone under your command…everyone around you. I see you with Tova and I see a man who would care profoundly for his own children. I also suspect that same concern and tenderness would convey to a wife.' She swallowed, but rushed forward as if she were trying to get the words out before she lost her nerve. 'I cannot fear you. I cannot hate you as my father would have me hate you. I can only admire you, though it tears me apart.'

A tear had gathered at the corner of her eye as she spoke and it fell, landing on her soft cheek and sliding down to the corner of her mouth. He followed its path like a thirsting man, wanting to lap it up and taste the salt on his tongue. 'Elswyth—'

She held up her hand to stop him from speaking. 'I hope that isn't unfair to you, because I genuinely don't know where that leaves us. You see, you were right this morning. When you said that I was only angry about the kiss because I had enjoyed it and I had known you were a Dane the whole time…you were right. From the moment your lips touched mine, there was no pretending that you were anyone other than Rolfe. You are the only man I've ever wanted to kiss.'

Silence descended as he tried to take in all that she had revealed to him. He'd never expected this level of honesty from her. Even Hilde had never been so bold, preferring to hide her feelings and make him suss them out. Had he been wrong about his Saxon all this time? He had a difficult time believing that she could make herself so vulnerable to him while at the same time hiding the fact that she was a spy.

'Rolfe?' She said his name a moment before her warm hand touched his shoulder. The heat from her palm seeped through the soft linen and his skin prickled, reaching for more of her touch.

'It seems we are a matched pair.' His voice came out low. That line between her brows appeared as she tilted her head to the side in question. 'The first night you came here and tended to me, I had no idea who you were, but I liked you. You were tender and fierce, kind and spirited. I liked that about you. You challenged me in a way no woman has for a long time. Then I found out you were Godric's daughter. I, too, had my prejudices. I thought that Godric's bloodline was too bitter to hold any goodness, yet here you are.'

You are everything that I ever wanted in a wife.

The thought sent a shock like lightning through him. It pushed him to his feet where he paced unseeing to the door and back again. This couldn't be happening, not again. How did he always end up with the women who could hurt him the most? He had known that eventually duty would call him to marry. His wife was supposed to be passably pretty, dutiful and certainly kind, but she wasn't meant to inspire this mad longing inside him. She would give him strong children and in return he would keep her safe and in comfort. He was not meant to lose his heart to her.

In a moment of madness he imagined rushing down to tell Vidar that he would marry someone else, anyone else, but Elswyth. Only that would leave her free to take a Saxon as her husband, or worse—Aevir. He grimaced as soon as the thought crossed his mind. He'd rather die than see her with anyone else.

'Rolfe?' Her hand on his arm made him turn to see her standing before him. 'I would like to explain to you why my father is so bitter about the Danes.' Unable to do anything more, he gave her a nod. She dropped her hand and clasped them both together in front of her and explained to him what had happened with her mother, and how her father had handled the betrayal very badly. She ended with, 'It doesn't excuse his hatred, but I wanted you to understand. It's why I've fought my feelings for you so hard. I… I don't want to become her.'

He sucked in a breath, hardly able to speak past the tightness squeezing his chest. 'Your feelings for me?'

She nodded, looking shy, and a wave of tenderness came over him and he nearly swept her into his arms, but he managed to hold himself back. 'I feel affection for you, Dane. Except I…can't turn my back on my family.' Her eyes were pleading as she stared up at him.

'What if you're not turning your back on them? What if by our joining we can stop more bloodshed for all of the Saxons and Danes alike?' Why was he encouraging her, when to push her further away would end this madness inside him? 'What if our marriage could help foster peace?' His heart pounded hard against his ribs, almost as if it was trying to jump out of his chest. He didn't know why he was trying so hard to convince her to do something that terrified him. Marrying her would be one small step away from loving her. He saw it as clearly as he could see a storm approaching on the open sea from the bow of his longship and he was just as helpless to stop it.

The tender flesh of her throat worked as she swallowed. Her pulse was a soft beat at the hollow where it met her shoulder. He wanted to nuzzle that depression and lap at it with his tongue.

'Do you truly feel that's possible?' From her tone he could tell that she was moments away from telling him aye.

'I do.'

'Then I—I think that I could see myself as your wife and it wouldn't be so bad. Except...'

'Except what?'

'I'm afraid to feel more for you than what I already do. When my mother left...it hurt me deeply. I hesitate to open myself up to that pain again and I wonder why you would want me when there are so many other women who would have you.'

'That's only because you don't see yourself as I do.' A fierce need to possess her came over him. Her lips parted on a nearly inaudible gasp as he stepped closer, slowly walking towards her. With each step she moved back until she came up against the wall. 'You're a desirable woman, Saxon. Beautiful, kind, fierce when you need to be.' She blushed and glanced away. 'And you must know that if we were wed, I would never abandon you.'

Her gaze darted back to him, wide with an odd fear. 'I suppose I don't know that.'

He cupped her cheek in his palm. 'If you were mine, I would never let you go.'

'If...?'

He let out a soft laugh. 'I admit that I cannot let go of the doubt that you carry Godric's hatred for us within you.'

'I... I do not. I wanted to, but I can't.' She shook her head, and a tear fell. It landed on his wrist and they both looked down to see it shimmering there on his skin. Without even thinking, he brought it to his lips, letting the salt tingle on his tongue.

'Of course you can't. Hate is not in you, Elswyth, no matter how hard you try.' He wanted to leave it at that, but he had to know for certain. 'Have you given your father information about us?'

She didn't even hesitate in her reply. 'He sent me to spy, but I have not seen him since. When he comes I'll tell him the only logical conclusion from what I've seen: We must join with the Danes. To do anything else would be disastrous.'

None of that was a surprise, but relief lightened the weight on his chest none the less. 'Have you met with the Scots?' He sent up a silent prayer to all the gods he knew that she would tell him nay. As long as she had not betrayed them then he could have her. He still didn't know how he'd have her while keeping his heart away from her, but he'd manage it. He had no other choice.

'Nay...' She hesitated and looked away.

He touched her cheek again. 'But your family has?'

She gave him a slow nod.

'It's not a betrayal to tell me that.' He soothed her. 'We've long suspected their meetings.'

She swallowed hard and before he could say anything else, she pushed his hand from her cheek only to throw herself into him. Her arms wrapped around his waist and he pulled her against him, closing his arms around her. He buried his face in her hair and breathed in her sweet scent. She felt perfect against him, her softness filling in all the hard planes of his body.

'Why can't things be simple?' Her voice was muffled against his shoulder.

'They can be, Saxon.' They would be, he decided. She was no spy, not really, and one day she would find out about Banford and what he'd done there. One day soon, probably, but by then she would be his. He didn't fool himself that the knowledge would be inconsequential; only that in the end she would be happy things had turned out the way they had.

'How?' She looked up at him with shimmering eyes. Emeralds. They were like the deepest, darkest emeralds he'd ever seen. He determined then and there that if they wed he'd find her an emerald some day that matched her eyes.

'One choice at a time. Would you have me as your husband if your father bid it?'

She held his gaze without wavering as she said, 'Aye.'

'Then you have to decide if you'd have me if he tells you nay.'

She dropped her gaze to his chest and he could sense the panicked tension within her. 'I struggle with being disloyal to my family. After my mother left, well, I suppose I've spent my life trying to prove that I'm not like her. That I won't betray them. This feels like betrayal.'

Holding her closer, he lowered his voice. 'It's not betrayal to want peace.'

She took in a shuddering breath and closed her eyes.

'You don't have to decide now,' he whispered, running his palm down her back. 'Think about it, but know that if you have me I will protect you always and you will want for nothing.'

'And what of my family?'

He swallowed thickly, knowing that what he wanted was within his grasp and unwilling to say the wrong thing to have it taken away. But neither could he lie to her. 'Betrayers will not be tolerated, but I vow to you that I will treat them fairly.'

She gave him a wry grin. 'You would treat them fairly even if I did not become your wife.'

In that moment, he realised something profound about her. She would not take him to simply better her own life. She needed something more, something for her family to push her over the edge. It endeared her to him even more—however, he could not turn his back on traitors, even if they were her blood. 'What would you have from me?'

'Meet with my father and talk to him. Give him a chance to take your side.'

It was so simple. No jewels or gold required. She asked him for things that were so easy to provide her. Yet, a vain and undeniable part of him wanted her to want him without conditions, so he said, 'I vow to do that even if you tell me nay.'

She smiled and it was so blindingly beautiful that he could only stare at her, taking in her loveliness. 'Thank you, Dane.'

He couldn't help but smile at the word that had somehow become an endearment between them. 'Don't answer me now. I want you to think well before you tell me what you've decided, so we'll have no morning sessions for two days. On the third day, I'll come for your answer.' She nodded and, unable to resist, he bent his head to whisper into her ear, 'If you tell me aye, know that I will spend our nights together using my tongue on every part of your body,' he promised, alluding to the kiss that had brought her to his chamber tonight.

Her fingers clenched in his under-tunic and she let out a little breath of surprise, followed by a breathless laugh. The sound awakened the beast sleeping within him. He wanted to toss her on to his bed and show her what he meant. To spread her open beneath him and plunder the sweetness between her thighs.

'Kiss me again before I go,' she whispered.

Unable to deny that request, his lips brushed across her cheek on the way to her mouth. She turned to meet him, her soft lips pressing to his. He took them hard beneath his, the fierceness of his mood driving him to show her exactly what would be waiting for her if she told him aye. He'd try to be tender with her, but she stirred a longing in him that was too intense to be dampened. To his surprise, she didn't pull away. Instead, she parted her lips to accommodate him and made a sensual sound when he touched his tongue to hers. All it took was one tentative stroke of her tongue against his to bring him to full arousal. His hands tightened on her hips to pull her closer, practically grinding himself against her. It wasn't nearly enough and he was on the verge of taking her to his bed when he forced himself to pull away.

Panting as if she were as affected as he was, she smiled at him. It was the daring and mischievous smile he'd come to associate as being a part of the very fibre of who she was. She stretched up on her toes and gave him one last kiss to his cheek before hurrying from the room, leaving him there gasping for air and wanting her with a madness he'd never felt before.

Not even with Hilde. Gods help him.

Chapter Twelve

By the end of the first day Elswyth had made her decision. By the end of the second day she had admitted that decision to herself. It hadn't come as a certainty, but as a creeping and crawling suspicion that choosing not to marry Rolfe was unthinkable. Both he and Ellan seemed to think things were simple, so she had resolved to follow the advice he'd given her. Make one decision at a time.

Her first decision would be to marry him. Her second one would be how to tell her father about it. He would disapprove. Nay, he would despise her choice. She knew it as well as she knew that Rolfe would do everything in his power to make her a happy wife. She hadn't been lying when she'd told him that she'd watched how he interacted with those he cared about. He might be a Dane, but he had a kind soul and he would make her a good husband.

If only her father would see it that way. She'd need help to tell him, which is what had brought her to Lady Gwendolyn's chamber. An afternoon snow had driven many people inside, and Lady Gwendolyn had disappeared to her chamber a little while ago with Tova. Elswyth could hear the baby squealing in delight from behind the door as she knocked.

'Come in,' Lady Gwendolyn's voice called out.

Elswyth stepped inside to see the lady seated at the table in the chamber, smoothing out a gown she was attempting to embroider for her daughter. Everyone knew that Lady Gwendolyn was the best archer in Alvey, but her skills with the needle were lacking. Elswyth found it admirable that it was a deficiency she was trying to rectify.

Lord Vidar had been lying on the large bed across the room, tossing his daughter into the air which was the source of her squeals of delight. He stopped when he noticed Elswyth and sat up with Tova in his arms. He held the infant with a tenderness that brought an ache to her heart.

She thought with a start that if she followed through with her plan to marry Rolfe, she might have her own child by this time next year. Happiness warmed a spot in her chest and she knew that she was making the right decision in her choice of husband.

'Apologies for disturbing you, my lady, my lord, but I wondered if I might talk to you? Alone.' The last she directed at Lady Gwendolyn.

'You're not disturbing us.' Lady Gwendolyn smiled and seemed very happy to toss her embroidery to the side.

'Not at all,' Lord Vidar added as he rose. 'I suspect my wife is happy to be distracted from her needlework.'

Lady Gwendolyn laughed and said with mock tenacity, 'I'll conquer that needle if it's the last thing I do.'

Lord Vidar gave her an indulgent smile and held Tova against his chest as he bent over to press a kiss to his wife's forehead. 'Leave it. You don't have to learn embroidery if you don't want to.'

'But I do want to. It just won't co-operate.'

He laughed and shook his head as he left with the baby, closing the door behind him.

'Might I see, my lady?' Elswyth asked as she came to stand beside the table.

Lady Gwendolyn nodded and handed her the gown with the partially embroidered hem.

'It's much improved. I can see you've started taking note of the pacing we discussed.' The lines were straight, but the stitching itself was of irregular lengths, but it was better.

'Aye, it's coming along. I think the trouble is that I'm not accustomed to sitting still for this long. It takes patience that I'm afraid I don't have.'

'Nonsense, my lady. You have plenty of patience. Look how you taught me to shoot an arrow.'

Lady Gwendolyn inclined her head. 'I'm afraid that's an entirely different kind of patience. Besides, it's action. Working with thread is simply too tedious for me to enjoy, but I will conquer it before I set it aside. Now...' she took the gown back and set it along with the thread back into the basket she kept on the table 'sit down and tell me what you need.'

Elswyth took the bench on the opposite side of the small table. 'I've come to a decision.'

'Oh?'

'I'm going to marry Rolfe.'

The woman brought a hand to her mouth, but a smile lurked behind it. 'Truly?'

Elswyth nodded and gave her an abbreviated version of the events leading up to her decision. 'The truth is that I can imagine no one else that I would want to be my husband. I think of returning home when my father comes and there is no one there that makes me feel the way Rolfe makes me feel. Perhaps it's unfair of me, but I don't want to be a simple farmer's wife.' Rolfe had seen so many things, been so many places, she wanted to spend the years of her life talking and learning about those places. But more than that, she wanted more of how he made her feel.

'I don't think it's unfair of you at all. You've found someone who is special to you. That is rare and I'm glad you've decided to try to hold on to him. I'm even happier that it will mean you will stay here. I've become quite fond of you while you've been here.'

Elswyth felt her cheeks turn pink. 'Thank you, my lady. I've come to like it here as well. However, I am concerned with how to proceed. I'm certain you're aware of the potential issue with my father. I can't imagine that he'll agree to this match.' Would he perhaps even turn his back on her? The very idea made her heart stutter. It wasn't out of the question, however, because her own mother had done just that. She didn't know if she could stand losing both of her parents, so she focused on the fact that she was doing this to further peace and save lives.

Lady Gwendolyn nodded in agreement. 'Aye, I expect him to put up quite a fuss. However, I know this is the right choice for you, and for Banford, though he'll be too stubborn to see it at first.'

'At first? Do you think he'll eventually come around? I don't want to lose him.'

'I do. It will take time and it won't happen overnight, but it will happen. Your father cares for you, Elswyth. I don't think you'll lose him.'

Elswyth smiled, the weight of her choice starting to slip from her shoulders for the first time. 'How do you think we should proceed? Tell him when he arrives and talk him into agreeing to the marriage?'

Lady Gwendolyn shook her head and for the first time her smile slipped. 'Nay, I'm afraid that won't work. I've given it some thought—oh, don't look at me that way,' she teased. 'You know how I hoped you'd say aye. I've been thinking of how to approach this ever since. I think the only way forward is for you to marry as soon as possible. That way, you won't have to go against your father's wishes to marry. He won't like it, but at least we avoid the situation where he tells you nay and you have to defy him.'

'I can see the wisdom of that, but what happens when he arrives and I am wed?'

'Lord Vidar and I will talk to him.' Reaching across the table, she patted Elswyth's hand. 'We can plan for that a little later, don't worry. Right now we must plan for your wedding. Have you spoken to Rolfe?'

Elswyth shook her head. 'He's given me a couple

of days to think about it. The last time I saw him was two days ago.'

'Ah, that's why he hasn't been at the table the past two evenings. I thought you both had quarrelled.'

Elswyth could feel her face burning again as she thought of their last moments together. That kiss had been anything but a quarrel. She could hardly fathom what he had meant by using his tongue on her body, but she couldn't stop thinking about what he'd said.

'So we should have the wedding soon then?' Excitement leaped in her belly at the very thought.

'Aye, as soon as possible. Ordinarily, we'd plan something, but I'm afraid, with your father due soon, we can't wait. There's every chance that he could come early with the snow falling.'

The butterflies in her stomach took flight. Rolfe could be hers sooner than she'd dreamed possible. 'As soon as possible then.'

Lady Gwendolyn smiled broadly and clapped. 'How exciting!'

Elswyth left Lady Gwendolyn's chamber a short while later. It was nearly time for the evening meal and she wanted to talk to Rolfe before then. Since her decision had been made, there was no point in waiting until the morning to tell him. Besides, from the open door in the hall she could see that the snow was beginning to stick. They might not even be able to have their practice as planned. She wanted to tell him now and, if she was honest, she wanted to see his face before Lady Gwendolyn or Lord Vidar mentioned it to him first.

He hadn't been in his chamber, so she walked through the great hall. Some of the men had started to congregate around the fire, drinking their ale, but he wasn't among them. Holding her cloak closed, she hurried out into the cold to find him. The wind was strong, promising more cold would be heaped upon them earlier than usual this winter. It had been snowing off and on for days.

Shivering, she hurried to look for him, finally finding his broad form as he spoke with the blacksmith. She was struck by how jovial their conversation was. Rolfe laughed at something the man had said and laid a hand on the man's thick shoulder. The blacksmith was a Saxon with bristles of white hair on his head and jaw who was nearing the age when he'd hang up his hammer. He could have hated the Danes like her father did, but here he was laughing with one of them in an easy manner. The sight reaffirmed that she was making the right choice. Saxons and Danes could co-exist peacefully in Alvey and she would do her part to make it so.

Pulling the folds of her cloak more firmly around her, she came to a stop at the edge of the wooden overhang shielding the forge. The blacksmith saw her first and his attention drew Rolfe's gaze. He straightened when he saw her, the smile dropping from his mouth as he searched her face for her answer. The blacksmith murmured a greeting, but Elswyth couldn't be bothered to pay attention to him. She was too drawn to her future husband. The fur he wore across his shoulders made him appear even more powerful than he was. He quite stole her breath away.

Rolfe's gaze narrowed in question, so she smiled. 'Aye,' she said with a nod.

A large smile curved his mouth and he left the blacksmith to come and stand before her. 'Aye?' he asked again, the flicker of uncertainty in his eyes only endearing him to her.

'Aye, I will be your wife.'

His smiled broadened, eventually becoming a laugh that was laced with nerves. 'You're certain? Even if your father—'

She cut him off, wanting to enjoy this moment of happiness without bringing dark thoughts between them. 'As soon as possible. I've talked to Lady Gwendolyn. She believes that it's best for us to marry before my father arrives. She and Lord Vidar will explain things to him.'

'As soon as possible. Tonight?' he teased.

She couldn't help but to give in to her nervous laughter. 'Nay, but as soon as things can be planned.'

'Tomorrow, then.' This he said with more certainty and her heart gave a little jump.

She could be married to him by this time tomorrow night. Her future was set on a course and for once, she didn't want to alter it. Her heart pounded and her stomach churned in a way that was far more fierce than the butterflies from earlier, but somehow it was a good feeling all the same. 'How do you feel?' she asked.

'Happy.' He gave her a tender smile and pulled her in close, though he stopped short of taking her in his arms as people rushed around them going about their evening. 'There is no one else I want as my wife.'

Though the words were tender, there was a hesitance in his eyes that she couldn't help but notice. If she was honest, there was some hesitance in her own heart as well, but it didn't stop the happiness she felt.

The wedding was two days later. Lady Gwendolyn had insisted on preparing a small feast while Elswyth and Ellan had hurried to make her bridal tunic, all of which took time. Although Lady Gwendolyn had offered to lend her something to wear, Elswyth thought that it was important to go to the wedding wearing only her own clothing. It wouldn't be right to pretend to be grander than she was—Rolfe needed to understand what he was getting: sadly only her and nothing else. So she and her sister had spent the past two days adding embroidery in fine blue and yellow thread to the bodice and hem of her best tunic, which was a pale green that she thought matched her eyes nicely.

They finished just in time for Lady Gwendolyn to help her to a steamy soak in the bathhouse. It was a new building in Alvey, built since Lord Vidar had been in residence, and was an entirely new experience for Elswyth. The only baths she'd had up until that point were hastily taken before the fire at home. This was luxurious. The entire chamber was filled with steam that left her feeling cleansed inside and out. That feeling was only enhanced by the way Lady Gwendolyn and Ellan scraped and polished every part of her body with a sea sponge. It left her skin pink and she felt as though she was glowing. Afterwards they rubbed a sweet-smelling oil into her skin that left her feeling soft and relaxed.

She tried not to think of why they were paying this much attention to her physical appearance, but it was impossible to keep her thoughts from the night ahead. As the warm water slid over her skin, she kept remembering Rolfe's kisses and his promise to use his tongue on her body. There was no telling what that meant and there was no way she could discuss it with Lady Gwendolyn or even Ellan, but every time she remembered his words and the husk in his voice as he'd said them, her stomach gave a little leap of anticipation. It hardly seemed real. He would be hers tonight. The old guilt that she was turning into her mother was still there, but now she was able to push it to the back of her mind, secure in the fact that she was helping her family. Rolfe had helped her see that and she was forever grateful to him for it.

'We have to hurry.' Lady Gwendolyn's eyes were bright in the shadowed light of the bathhouse. 'Rolfe will come soon to his own bath.'

Her face went hot at the thought of him preparing for the night ahead—for her—and both Lady Gwendolyn and Ellan laughed. They wrapped a soft woollen blanket around her and Lady Gwendolyn asked in a gentle voice, 'Do you know what to expect tonight, Elswyth?'

'I think I know enough. I *was* raised on a farm.' She tried to laugh as if she weren't nervous. However, the closer the time came the more worried she became. It couldn't possibly be exactly like she'd seen with the sheep, could it?

As if she sensed her unease, Lady Gwendolyn took her hand and brushed her wet hair back from her face.

'There can and should be pleasure for you in the act. Remember that. I believe that Rolfe will ensure that for you, but if he doesn't, then talk to him or, if you feel you can't, then come talk to me. Promise?'

Elswyth nodded and then hurried into her under-dress and pulled her cloak tightly around her. There was no snow today, but the wind was biting as they hurried to the great hall and upstairs to the chamber Lady Gwendolyn shared with Lord Vidar. The rest of the time before the wedding was spent with Lady Gwendolyn telling them stories that kept them laughing from when she'd first met Lord Vidar while they combed Elswyth's hair dry and dressed.

Rolfe paced before the fire in the hall, anxious to see Elswyth and make her his wife. He hadn't wanted a feast and he couldn't have cared less what she wore to wed him, but Lady Gwendolyn had seemed to think both of those were important. He'd relented, because he'd had no choice, but as each day had passed it had only made him long for Elswyth more. He told himself that it was only the night ahead that he was anticipating and he almost believed it.

Night was beginning to fall when she finally made her way down the steps to the great hall with Lady Gwendolyn and Ellan trailing behind her. She looked lovely in a pale green tunic that only made her eyes appear deeper. The apples of her cheeks held a bit of colour as she stared at him, barely able to look away as she made her way to him. She was clearly nervous, her palms running anxiously down the side of the overdress. She and her sister had taken great pains with the stitching, but he could hardly notice it. His eyes were only for her face.

Aevir, who had returned from the north to attend the ceremony, said something about the night ahead from his place beside him. Rolfe was too intent on his wife to comprehend the words, but he knew they were crude by the way the other men snickered. Elswyth hesitated and Rolfe growled out, 'Shut up', which only made the men laugh harder.

'Enough!' Lady Gwendolyn scolded them in a harsh whisper when they were close enough. They quieted, but there were a few snorts among them.

Even though Elswyth's blush had deepened with obvious embarrassment, she didn't let that stop her from reaching out to take his hands. Pride swelled in his chest as she took in his form. He wore a well-fitted tunic of midnight blue, embroidered with gold-silk trim at the shoulders and hem. The material stretched tight across his chest in a way that he knew emphasised his broad shoulders. He knew that she liked what she saw by the way her eyes widened a fraction and she couldn't quite bring herself to meet his gaze.

'You're beautiful,' he whispered. And she was. Her deep chestnut hair had been pulled back from her forehead in an intricate weave of plaits, but the heavy length had been left to fall around her waist. He couldn't wait to wind the silk of it around his wrists as he took her beneath him later. He was half-hard from watching her come across the room to him, knowing that she was his, knowing that nothing could stand in the way of his finally having her tonight. When he'd first seen her a primitive part of him had wanted to take her in his arms right then to let everyone know that she belonged to him.

'Thank you,' she whispered, drawing him away from the dark fantasy. She wore a wreath made of wheat and straw with rowan berries set around the crown of her head and she let one of his hands go to touch it as if she were ashamed of it. 'This is your last chance to make a run for freedom.'

'Why would I want to do that?'

'I…' She trailed off, but then seemed to resolve herself and she finally met his gaze. 'I'm sorry I can't come to you with more. I've heard some of the stories told around the hall at night. I know that you deserve a woman who can come to you with a crown made of gold.'

She meant the stories about great men and their prize brides. He grinned and gave her a slow shake of his head as he recaptured her hand. 'Nay, I don't want that. I wouldn't miss all the Saxon vengeance you have in store for me.'

The bright smile she gave him settled inside him, warming some deep place he hadn't even known had needed her sunshine. In the back of his mind lurked the very real danger that their happiness might be short-lived, or that their happiness might blind him.

But right now she looked at him as if she could love him and he felt himself sliding towards that abyss and losing himself in her. He wanted to bathe in it, to drink it all in until he was drunk on that feeling.

Tomorrow would be soon enough to face the future. Tonight was only about him and his Saxon bride.

For the next few moments, the world kept moving around them, but he only saw Elswyth. Alvey's priest spoke, but she never broke Rolfe's stare, seeming to be as fascinated with him as he was with her. When it was time he spoke his vows in a clear and deep voice that he hoped conveyed to her how much he meant them. When her turn came, she made him proud by doing no less than he had, speaking in a strong, clear voice.

Finally, he broke the spell to look at Vidar who stood next to him. The man pressed a ring into his palm, the light from the candles glittering off the gold. Rolfe turned back to her and took her small, graceful fingers in his as he spoke the ceremonial words, 'With this ring, I take you as my wife. I give you my protection and my loyalty, and I pledge to you that I will give my life before allowing any harm to come to yours. We are one… from now until eternity.'

Her lips trembled as she took in a deep breath and her eyes reddened with unshed tears. Yet happiness shone out from her as she smiled at him and something around the vicinity of his heart threatened to break open. It didn't matter that the words were ceremonial. He meant them and her voice was steadfast when she said, 'I accept you as my husband.'

Gently, he nudged the band of gold down her finger until it settled into place, claiming her as his. He gave her hand a gentle squeeze before letting it go to turn to Aevir at his other side. Aevir held up the new sword wrapped carefully in linen. He unwrapped it carefully before handing it off to Rolfe. If they were back home, it would have been his family's sword, passed down from generation to generation. But they weren't home, so he'd had the blacksmith working for days—since before Elswyth had told him aye—to make a new one. The hilt was ornate with a scroll pattern on the guard.

Rolfe presented it to her on the flat of his palms. 'I am entrusting this into your care to be given to our first-born son. May we have many children.'

A nearly overwhelming feeling of pride swept through him as she took it from him and said, 'I accept.' Then with reverence—for the sword was symbolic of Rolfe entrusting her to further his bloodline and bear his children—she handed it to Lady Gwendolyn and took Rolfe's hands in hers. 'I will be proud to bear your sons and daughters.'

He squeezed her hands and pulled her close, brushing his lips against hers. A cheer went up through the great hall. As his arms slipped around her, he whispered against her ear, 'You are mine now, Saxon.'

They were officially man and wife.

Chapter Thirteen

The rest of the evening passed in a blur of activity. It was full of food, good wishes for their future, Elswyth pretending not to hear the many jests regarding their wedding night and drinking the special honeyed mead that had been prepared for them. Finally, although many people were still feasting around them, Rolfe put his arm around her and pulled her to his side to whisper, 'I can't wait any longer, Saxon. Are you ready for bed?'

She knew what he was really asking. The truth was plain in the way his eyes burned into her. At some point during the evening her nerves had given way to anticipation. Oh, the nervousness was still present, but excitement burned hotter. Admiring the comely bow of his lips, she said, 'Aye, I'm ready.'

Rolfe rose and pulled her to her feet, causing another exasperating cheer to go up through the hall, nearly shaking the rafters. She was confused when six men, including Lord Vidar and Aevir, followed them to the stairs. There had been no visible signal so she could only assume that the six had been predetermined, but no one had told her to expect this part. Squeezing Rolfe's fingers tighter, she wrapped her other hand around his upper arm. He gave her a smile that she was sure was meant to reassure her, but it was too wolfish to help.

The men followed them right up to Rolfe's chamber, where he paused only to swing her up into his arms and carry her over the threshold. Thank goodness he kicked the door behind them, blocking everyone else out, even Wyborn.

As she slid down his body, Rolfe reached back to secure the door, ensuring their privacy. 'Do you need time to prepare yourself, Wife?' The way his arm kept tight around her waist coupled with the look on his face told her that he might give her time, but it wouldn't be much. The blue of his eyes had deepened to almost the same midnight hue of his tunic.

'Nay.' Her whisper was so low she couldn't be certain that he'd heard her, so she gave a quick shake of her head to make sure.

'You're so beautiful. All night I've only been able to think how lucky I am.' He touched her cheek, her hair, his palm eventually moving down the long sleeve of her linen underdress. The heat from his touch nearly scorched her through the material.

'Will they stay at the door until…until…?' She couldn't bring herself to say it.

He nodded. 'The ceremony is useful, but we're not truly married until we drink the honeyed mead and I spend my seed inside you. Should the validity of the marriage ever be questioned, and there's a good chance it might, we need witnesses to stand up for us.'

God knew she didn't want to tempt fate and have them actually wait inside the chamber while the deed was done, but curiosity wouldn't allow the question to go unasked. 'But how will they know the deed is done?'

He grinned a grin that was full of sin and need. 'The walls are thin and there are sounds that...' Swallowing visibly, he said, 'I think things will become apparent as they happen.'

She nodded, satisfied with that for now. Having her curiosity sated only allowed her earlier misgivings to return. 'I'm sorry I have nothing for you.' Nerves coupled with the shame of coming to him in such a humble wedding ceremony made her start to babble. 'Lady Gwendolyn told me about the usual custom of gifting you with a sword. I don't even have a proper dowry.'

'I don't care about those things.' His voice was gentle and deep as his fingers came to rest on her jaw, slowly lifting her face so that she met his gaze. 'Jarl Vidar gave me the choice of any woman. I chose you because I want *you*, not because I want the things you can give me.'

'Are you saying that I should be grateful to have been chosen by you?' Seizing on his words, she attempted to bring levity to the moment and gave a curtsy. 'Thank you, oh, Lord Dane, for choosing such a humble wife.'

He chuckled and tickled her waist to make her straighten. It worked and she laughed as he hauled her back into his arms. 'Why do I think I might long for the missed opportunity to have chosen a biddable wife?'

'You won't. You'd get bored with biddable.'

'I would,' he agreed, his eyes already losing the humour that sparkled within them. 'Kiss me,' he said.

His mouth was only a breath from hers so it was no trouble to lean forward and close the gap. He quickly took control of the kiss, covering her mouth with his and gently scraping her bottom lip with the edge of his teeth. She gasped at the sensation and he took advantage, thrusting the tip of his tongue against hers. The sensual stroke made her body come alive as his earlier kisses had, only this time her reaction was more intense because she knew there would be no stopping. Heat raced through her core, throbbing deep down inside her.

His hand moved from her waist, up her ribcage, to mould itself against her breast. Her flesh filled his palm briefly before he cupped the weight, allowing his thumb to stroke over the tip. Her nipple pebbled in response, her entire breast seeming to swell as it ached for more of his attention. But he kept his touch slow and leisurely, continuing his tender assault of her mouth while his thumb moved in a teasing circle around the tip of her breast. When she arched against him, silently pleading for more of his touch, he moved his attention to her other breast, teasing that nipple until it, too, ached for more of his touch.

'More, Rolfe.' Without meaning to, her hips pushed against him and she grasped at the back of his tunic, wanting to get beneath it and feel the heat from his skin against her own.

He drew back to look at her and the admiration shining down at her was enough to take her breath away. He moved slowly and deliberately, as if he was afraid he would frighten her, to work the brooches at her shoulders, unfastening one and then the other until her overdress dropped to the floor with a swishing sound. She stepped out of the slippers she wore and kicked the dress away, watching as his long and graceful fingers went to remove his own tunic. He tossed it towards the trunk at the end of his bed and moved to sit down on the edge of the bed, working at the fastenings of his boots. His fingers shook a little.

'I'll help you.' She moved to kneel before him and together they worked to rid him of his boots. When they'd both been set aside, her hands went to the hem of his under-tunic and she lifted it over his head. She tossed it over her shoulder, but had no idea where it landed. All she knew was that he was perfect and she allowed herself a moment to appreciate his singular male beauty.

His chest was lightly furred with dark blond hair and his skin had a golden sheen that she assumed he'd acquired from going without an under-tunic and tunic over the summer. She'd itched to touch it ever since she'd attended him in his bath. The two candles that were lit caressed him in equal parts shadow and light, revealing the strong lines and sculpted curves of his muscled torso.

'You can touch me.' He was grinning at her, drawing her into the space between his knees.

She moved reverently, almost afraid to claim that which was now hers. His skin was warm and supple beneath her palm when she finally made contact. Slowly, she allowed her hand to move down over his solid chest, his hard nipples and down farther to the ridged planes of his stomach. She would have gone even lower, but when her fingertips touched the waist of his trousers he stopped her by grabbing her wrists. She looked at him in question and he shook his head. 'Not yet. By the gods, if you touch me there I won't trust myself.' He kept his smile, but the fierce need in his eyes made her gulp. It wasn't fear as much as anticipation that coursed through her heated blood.

'Take off your dress.' He stared down at her body as if willing himself to be able to see through the material.

Setting back on her knees, she wrestled with the hem of the billowy dress and slowly pulled it up. There was a brief moment when fear kept her still, but she wanted to go further and she even wanted him to look upon her as she had looked upon him. Hoping it would increase his pleasure, she pulled it over her head and tossed it behind her, leaving her in only her winter leggings.

'So beautiful,' he whispered, bringing his hand up between them to touch her as he had earlier when she'd been clothed. Only this time there was nothing between his fingers and her breast, so the pleasure was more intense. His fingertips and palms were hardened from years of sword work and battle, but the coarse touch only seemed to please her. His fingers rasped against her tender skin, making her ache as he plucked at her nipples.

A soft groan escaped her, prompting him to say, 'Come.' His hand went to the small of her back, lifting her up on to her knees and pulling her towards him as he dipped his head down. Before she fully realised his intent, he took her nipple deep into his mouth, the rough and silky stroke of his tongue laving her. So this is what he meant when he'd said he'd use his tongue in other places. A dart of pleasure shot straight to her core, making that place between her legs throb. She wanted something there, but she didn't know how to say it or even what to ask him for. Instead she tangled her fingers into the dark blond hair at the back of his head and held him close, unwilling to relinquish the pleasure he was giving her for the unknown.

As he continued to suckle her, his hand moved down past the small of her back to fill itself with the generous curve of her bottom. She moaned a little in the back of her throat as the rhythmic squeezing of his palm combined with his mouth at her breast made the ache inside her seem nearly unbearable. She shifted, rubbing her thighs together to alleviate the throbbing between them, but nothing seemed to help.

His mouth finally released her and his hands moved to the fastenings of her leggings, pushing them down over her hips before helping her to stand so that she could step out of them. In but a moment she was nude and standing before him.

His admiring gaze stole over her, finally making its way up to her face where it settled on her eyes. 'You've done me a great honour in becoming my wife,' he said.

She wanted to tell him that she was the one who was honoured, but she couldn't speak past a throat that was swollen nearly closed with emotion.

'Lie down for me?' His voice was textured with emotion and longing.

She nodded and moved on to the thick furs piled on the mattress. His bed was a hundred times more comfortable than the one she shared with Ellan, she thought as she settled on to her back on a fur, sinking into its warmth. He made to turn and join her, but she didn't want to be deprived of the sight of him. 'Can I see you first?' When he raised a brow in question, she nodded towards his trousers, biting her lip in mild embarrassment at how forward she was being, but it was her wedding night and he made her feel like she could say anything to him.

He grinned at her and rose to stand beside the bed. Powerful and beautiful, he looked down at her as he unfastened his trousers and pushed them down his muscled thighs. Once free from the confines of the fabric, his manhood sprang upward, nearly reaching his navel. Her lips parted on a silent gasp as she stared at him. Somehow she'd never thought that part of him would be quite so large or quite so domineering. It stood there as proud as a conquering…well, as proud as a conquering Dane. She nearly laughed at her own jest, until she realised that *that* part of him would have to somehow work its way inside her to spend. To say that it was as thick as her wrist might be a slight exaggeration, but not by much.

He released the ties that held the bed curtains back and they closed around him, sending their world into shadowed darkness as he joined her on the bed. She pushed up on to her elbows at the same time he lowered to his knees above her. 'Rolfe, I don't—' His mouth took hers in a deep and searching kiss, leaving her breathless when he pulled back to trail hot, open-mouthed kisses across her jaw and down her neck. Her skin prickled in absolute adulation to be the recipient of his attention, but she couldn't put the sight of *him* from her mind.

'I don't think…' Her voice trailed off. How did one properly address this? No one had told her he'd be so large. Maybe everyone had known but her.

'Hush…' he whispered, coming back up to take her mouth. 'Don't think about it yet. Lie here and let me love you. I'll tell you when it's time to think about that.'

'Do you vow it?'

His easy smile against her lips somehow reassured her. 'Aye, you have my word.' With a gentle hand on her shoulder, he pushed her lightly until she relented and laid back. Then his hand trailed from her shoulder to her breast and down farther to ease over her belly. His mouth followed, trailing hot kisses over her skin. When he stopped to lavish each of her nipples with attention, she closed her eyes and sank her fingers into the silk of his hair. With his mouth working over her, it was easy to forget the coming invasion and even the men waiting outside their door to listen as the deed was done. In the dark cocoon of their bed, there was only the pleasure he was giving her.

Much to her surprise, his mouth moved even lower, past her breasts, scaling over her stomach as his arm skilfully moved under her thigh, sending it farther across the bed so that he could slip between her legs. She stiffened, but he didn't take his mouth from her, moving down to her hip and then her thigh, shifting lower so that he could kiss the inside of her knee. Rotating her slightly, he let his tongue dip into the sensitive crevice behind her knee. She relaxed immediately as the slick pleasure of the caress. It wasn't until he was pushing her thighs farther apart that she realised he'd worked his way upwards, settling his shoulders between her thighs.

He placed a kiss on the dark curls guarding the mound of her womanhood. 'Rolfe!' He did it again, this time letting his tongue dip out to touch her. 'That's wicked.' Remembering his comment about the thin walls, she was sure to keep her voice very low.

'It's not. I'm your husband. Nothing we do together in this bed is wicked.'

She couldn't think of an immediate response and he'd spoken so loudly she was certain the men had heard. She'd never be able to face anyone tomorrow if they guessed what he was doing to her now.

'How does that feel?' he asked. When he repeated the action, he pressed deeper, his tongue penetrating the folds to the tender and throbbing flesh beneath. How did one answer that? There were no words to convey how the slick and rough slide of his tongue against an area so intimate she didn't even have a name for it felt. Instead of answering with words, she settled for an incomprehensible sound that she hoped he took for aye. He couldn't possibly mistake how her thighs fell open to welcome him.

With a soft laugh, he renewed his attack on her body. His fingers held her open, so that his tongue could swipe out in slow and lazy glides against her aching flesh. She didn't mean to, but she bucked beneath him in response, somehow needing more of that delicious stroke. Her thighs fell open even wider and her fingers curled in his hair to hold him against her. His attack became less lazy and more focused. His tongue swirled around the aching nub, giving her just the right amount of pressure, but somehow not enough all at the same time. She needed more...*of something.*

Then his finger stroked her as he continued to lick her, the coarse pad moving through her wetness and pressing inside. She moaned when he filled her with it and retreated, only to press inside again. The rhythm was mesmerising and she moved with it, seeking even more. Much to her delight, another finger quickly joined the first, stretching her, leaving her feeling deliciously full of him.

He growled against her flesh as he pleasured her. 'Come apart for me, Saxon. I want to taste your pleasure.' That harsh and raspy command was her undoing. Combined with the steady rhythm of his fingers and tongue against that swollen nub, she felt a tidal wave of pleasure cresting over her. It took her over completely, making her body tighten and pulse, trembling around his fingers where they pressed so deeply inside her.

Delicious tremors were still pounding through her as he moved smoothly up her body to hold himself just over her with his weight on his right arm. His hips settled into the cradle of hers and she felt the broad tip of his manhood pressing against her.

'Now,' he whispered against her lips and she tasted pleasure on him. 'Now I must come inside you.'

She nodded, but she wasn't as afraid as she might have been without the pleasure still coursing through her and weighting her limbs. Her arms went around his shoulders to hold him close and fit herself against him. Distantly, she heard his gasp as he pushed inside her a little. The fit was tight and it burned a bit as he stretched her, but at the same time she wanted more of him, wanted to be as close to him as she could get. She could feel her channel grasping at him and he must have, too, because he groaned in the back of his throat and pressed forward. Pulling back a little, he thrust forward again. In the little bit of light that seeped in around the curtain she could tell his face looked pained.

'Only a little further,' he whispered.

She wasn't certain what he meant until he retreated, only to thrust until he was fully seated within her. She couldn't help the little cry she gave and he immediately tried to soothe her, his lips brushing across her temple and whispering tender words. A hand came to her breast, his thumb strumming over the nipple.

She felt completely full of him, but after a moment of his careful attention, a tug of longing began where they were joined, an echo of the pleasure he'd given her. She shifted, testing the tight fit.

'I can't wait any more.' His voice sounded pained.

She realised that he was asking for permission to continue. 'Aye,' she whispered, wanting to give him the same pleasure he had given her. The pain had receded to discomfort, aided by the tremors that still occasionally shook her.

He moved his hips and she was surprised at the pleasant sensation. It wasn't nearly as intense as that he'd given her before, but it made her want more. She lifted her hips to meet his motion and he made a harsh sound, his hand moving to her hip to stay her.

'Don't move or I'll spend now. I want to make it

good for you again,' he whispered as he rocked his hips against hers.

Spending now didn't seem like a bad thing to her. The entire point of this was to get him to spend, but his strong hand on her hip kept her in place. So instead of moving her hips, she clenched her inner muscles, tightening around his thick manhood where it was buried deep inside her, testing her ability to give him pleasure.

'Ah, Saxon!' He made a low, groaning sound deep in his chest and said something harsh in his language that she didn't understand. As if he had no control, his hips bucked against her and he took her with an intensity that stole her breath away. Aching to get even closer to him, she tightened her arms around him and wrapped her legs around his thighs. With his face buried in her hair, he gave a deep guttural cry as he found his release, pumping his hips in a few last desperate thrusts as he spilled his seed. His voice was so loud and deep, so unmistakably filled with male satisfaction, that she knew that's what the men outside had been waiting for.

She kept holding him when he fell over her, in awe of the power she had over him and the wonderful thing that had happened between them. She'd never dreamed that such pleasure was possible. It seemed like sorcery. As his body shook with leftover tremors, much like her own had, she buried her face against his chest and stroked the hair at the back of his neck. Fate had given her a gift in the form of Rolfe and she never wanted to let him go.

Chapter Fourteen

Sounds of feasting filtered into the chamber from below, but here in their warm, dark bed, there were only the sounds of Elswyth breathing and the echoes of her cries of pleasure ringing in Rolfe's ears. For as long as he lived he would never forget the sweet sound of his wife—his Saxon—coming apart in his arms. The soft and desperate cry had urged him to lead her to an end whose existence she probably hadn't even been aware of, yet she'd trusted him to take her there anyway. Brushing a palm along the length of her lithe body, he squeezed her hip and placed a kiss to her temple as his heart swelled with tenderness for her. He was dangerously close to losing himself to her. He could feel it, but he had no way of stopping it from happening, save walking away from her and that was something he couldn't do.

Easing from the bed so as not to wake her, he pushed back one of the curtains to allow in some candlelight. It swept across her breasts, giving him a view of the lush mounds of flesh with their pink tips. By the gods, she was beautiful. His manhood tightened and swelled, so he forced himself to look away. She'd be too sore for any more bed sport tonight.

Some thoughtful servant had left a pot of water along with a pitcher of mead on the table before they had retired for the evening. It had grown lukewarm, but he still used it to clean himself and then picked up a square of linen and wet it for Elswyth. She roused when he sat on the bed, smiling up at him with a flush on her cheeks. He eased her knee upwards and with gentle strokes washed away the evidence of their joining before tossing the square away. To his surprise she hadn't resisted, only lain there watching him with joy and contentment shining in her eyes.

'How do you feel? Was I too rough with you?' He couldn't resist dragging a fingertip down the sweet, intimate flesh that was still open to him. She smiled and he ran his hand down her soft inner thigh, unable to stop touching her.

She shook her head. 'I'm a little sore, but that's to be expected. You were actually quite gentle for a barbarian, Dane.'

Chuckling, he grabbed her hips to hold her in place as he moved quickly to lie on top of her. She giggled and swatted at his shoulders, but he grabbed her wrists and held her arms to the furs at her back. 'Is this more of what you had in mind, Saxon?'

'Aye, I knew the tenderness wouldn't last.'

She didn't sound as if she minded, turning her head and offering more of her neck to him as he kissed her. He was awed and surprised when she curled her legs around his waist to hold him in place. After the way she'd reacted to their first kiss, he hadn't known what to expect from her in their bed. His fear had been that she wouldn't allow herself to enjoy the things he could show her, but she seemed to have put her initial reservations behind her.

Unfortunately, this position wasn't conducive to his resolution to allow her sufficient time to recover before he took her again. He'd already swelled to his full length against her and was aching to be inside her again. Instead, he let her go and pushed away to sit back on his knees. 'The rough bed sport starts tomorrow. Every bride deserves one tender night.'

She pushed up on an elbow, shocking him even further when she looked directly at his engorged shaft with curiosity. 'You're…' She paused as if searching for a way to describe him. 'Hard again?'

'Aye, it's possible to spend more than once a night.' It was also possible that he'd pass the rest of his life in this particular state with her as his wife.

She glanced up at him as if she'd never considered that possibility, before staring back down at his length. 'May I touch you?'

He nearly groaned, knowing it would only make him desperate for her, but wanting her to be comfortable with him, so he nodded, not trusting his voice to speak. Her initial touch was tentative and soft, but she soon grew bolder and took him in hand. He could tell that she grew aroused by touching him; her breathing came faster and her eyes darkened. Finally, she whispered, 'I won't mind if you want to…put yourself inside me again.'

A deep groan of frustration escaped him before he could stop it and he moved away from her touch. 'I would love nothing more, wife, but you must heal.' If he was honest with himself, there was a healthy dose of self-preservation in his refusal as well. Bedding her had broken down the meagre barrier he'd been able to erect against her. He needed some time to put the pieces back together before taking her again.

Picking up a fur, he wrapped it around his waist to hide his desire from her. Not that hiding it did anything to make it go away. Deep pulsations of need continued to pound through him, so he moved to the table in his chamber and poured himself some mead before taking a long swallow.

'Is something the matter?'

He turned to see her sitting up in bed, holding a fur to her breasts, but her soft shoulders and the curve of one hip was still exposed. Emotion squeezed his lungs so tight that he couldn't breathe as he took her in. How could she tell? How was it possible this slip of a girl could break him down so easily? He gave a shake of his head in answer.

'You don't still suspect me of treason?' Her mouth smiled in jest, but her eyes were wide and serious.

The question was nearly his undoing. 'I know how difficult of a choice it was to marry me.' As he spoke, he set his cup on the table and crossed to her. 'You chose peace and I believe that peace is in your heart.'

Her face brightened and she took his hand and

brought it to her chest. The steady rhythm of her heart beat beneath his palm. 'Once I thought of losing you, it wasn't that difficult a choice.'

Fighting the urge to crush her against him and never let her go, he closed his eyes. Every fibre in his body told him that this was dangerous. It was too soon. He hadn't even known this woman a month ago, yet she called to something deeper within him. It reached for her, needed her, longed to drink up her every touch.

'Then it must be something else,' she whispered.

'What do you mean?'

Taking his face in her hand, she said, 'Ever since I told you aye there's been something…you've been holding yourself back from me. There's been a distance.'

He let out a breath on a laugh because he knew she was right. 'There wasn't any distance between us earlier tonight.'

She blushed, but she didn't back down. By the gods, she was fierce and he was doomed. 'Not that.' Her lips curved in another smile and she continued gently, as if afraid to scare him off. 'Perhaps wariness is a better description. If it's not me and my family, then why are you wary of me? Did… Is it something that's happened to you?'

Her eyes were so open and honest when she stared up at him that he couldn't stop himself from putting his arms around her and holding her against him. This woman had more courage than he. The notion struck him with a certainty that he couldn't deny and he felt shamed and proud at the same time.

When he couldn't speak of his fears, she had come to

him with hers and spoken of them openly. She'd sought his comfort as she'd told him of her mother's betrayal and her family's hatred. It had quite literally cost her the life that she had known to come to him as his wife and he'd had to give up nothing in return. The least he could do was be honest with her and let her know that there were certain boundaries he couldn't cross. Perhaps he'd been selfish not to tell her before they had wed, but it wasn't something he'd rectify even if given the chance.

She was his.

Pulling back enough to look down at her without letting her go, he said, 'The truth is that there was once another woman. I thought that I loved her, but I realise now that I was merely infatuated.' He'd never felt this bone-deep pull with Hilde. There had been excitement and affection, but not whatever was happening with Elswyth. He held her close as he told her everything, even how it had driven him to become a warrior. She watched him with a mixture of sadness and understanding.

When he finished, she said, 'Hilde was a fool, but I can't say that I'm sorry for it. Had she not been, I wouldn't have you now.' Taking his face between her hands, she rose to her knees to meet him at eye level and the tip of her nose touched his as she spoke. 'And you have me. I won't betray you, Rolfe. I give you my word.'

'I know that you won't.' It was all he could manage against the swell of tenderness he felt for her. The barrier had crumbled with her words and he was tumbling headlong into the abyss with only her to catch him. It didn't matter if he trusted her to catch him or not. He was already lost.

She kissed him with all the passion smouldering between them. A groan tore from his lips when her hand came between them, tightening around his semi-hard length and bringing him to full arousal again. 'Saxon,' he murmured, though he didn't know if it was a warning or a welcome.

'Is it possible to pleasure you without you being inside me?' she whispered.

He nodded, somewhat amazed that in her innocence she was able to conceive of such a thing. 'Aye.'

'Show me.' Her hand tightened slightly, pulling the breath from his lungs.

So he showed her how to use her hands to bring him pleasure, then he spent the rest of the night making good on his vow to use his tongue on every part of her body.

Rolfe left her the next morning to go meet with his men, but when Elswyth had moved to rise with him he'd pressed her to stay in bed. Exhausted from their activities the night before, she'd slept a fair amount of the morning only waking up when someone knocked on the door. She had barely donned her underdress when the knock came again.

'Elswyth?' Ellan called, her voice insistent.

Rolling her eyes at her impatience, Elswyth opened the door, barely getting out of the way before her sister barrelled in holding a tray of breakfast. 'You are awake,' she said as she set the food on the table.

'I am now. Thank you for bringing breakfast.'

Ellan shrugged off the thanks and walked over, looking her up and down as if she expected her to be different somehow. Elswyth laughed at the expectant look on her face. The truth was that she did feel different, but she was certain she still looked the same from the outside.

'How was it?' Ellan asked. Subtlety had never been her strong suit.

'What do you mean?' Elswyth smiled, intentionally baiting her sister, as she walked over to take a seat at the table.

'Elswyth,' Ellan groaned and sat down on the bench beside her. 'Was he…gentle? Did you enjoy it?'

Taking pity on her, Elswyth nodded. 'Aye to both. It was perfect and I went to sleep knowing that I am a lucky woman to have him as my husband. This morning I can still scarcely believe it.' If not for the fact that she had awakened in Rolfe's chamber and her body bore a slight tenderness from the night before, she might think she had dreamed it. Never had she expected marriage to be like this.

'If I had to guess, I would say he feels the same.'

'Did you see him?'

Ellan's smile widened. 'I did at the morning meal. He seemed happier than I've ever seen him. The men were teasing him, but he didn't get angry once and smiled the entire time.'

Elswyth felt her cheeks burn hot. 'I suppose everyone knew what we did.'

Ellan laughed and rubbed her shoulder with affection. 'Well, it was your wedding night.'

She was embarrassed, but she couldn't find it within her to regret the night or their lack of privacy. There was no room for regret in her happiness. Turning her attention to the bowl of pottage, they spoke for a while about the wedding. When Ellan turned the conversation back to the wedding night, obviously desperate for specifics, Elswyth shook her head, laughing. 'You'll find out soon enough for yourself. How goes your hunt for a husband? Any prospects?'

Ellan shook her head and looked away. The change in her mood from borderline rude curiosity to meekness immediately made Elswyth suspicious. 'You've met someone.'

'Nay.' Ellan shook her head again, but the look on her face had turned serious. 'We've not met. Not really.'

'But there is someone who's caught your eye?'

Nodding, Ellan rose to her feet as if the strength of her thoughts couldn't be contained to merely sitting. 'It's too soon to think of marriage. He's unmarried, but I don't know if he's promised to someone. I don't think he is.' She wrung her hands and paced, a faraway expression in her eyes. 'He's tall, handsome and quiet. He doesn't say very much, but when he does the men listen and his eyes… Elswyth, his eyes say so much. He watches me sometimes and I swear to you that the feeling is more powerful than the flattery of any man.' A pretty blush tinged her sister's cheeks and she smiled like a woman in love.

'Such emotion for a man you've never met.'

Ellan grinned and nodded her agreement. 'I know you won't believe this, but I can't seem to find my voice when he's near.'

'Who is it?' When Ellan shook her head, Elswyth rose and took her hands. 'You must tell me.'

'It's Aevir.'

An image of the powerful warrior came to mind. There was a quiet intensity about him that might have drawn her interest as well if she hadn't been so consumed with Rolfe. He was handsome, but where Rolfe was gentle, there was a hint of something dark in Aevir. Not cruelty, exactly, but something complicated. 'Does he return your interest?'

Ellan ducked her head. 'Aye, I believe he does. I see him watching me and once...'

'Once what?'

'Before he left for Banford we found ourselves alone one night and I think if we hadn't been interrupted he might have...well, it hardly matters. We were interrupted.'

'You kissed him?' Elswyth's voice rose in surprise.

'It was an accident really, but, aye.'

'Do you want me to talk to Rolfe? Find out more about him?'

Ellan shook her head. 'Nay, please don't mention anything. I'd rather wait for Aevir to return and see if there is even anything to consider first.'

Elswyth assured her that she wouldn't ask about Aevir, but she couldn't help but worry at her sister's choice. Aevir was respected among the warriors and he treated them well, but there was something about his quiet intensity that unnerved her. His eyes sometimes seemed almost haunted, making her unsure if he would be a good match for her often playful sister.

* * *

On the first morning after their wedding, Rolfe knew that he was enamoured of his wife. He had wrongly assumed that he could go about his duties and his life would stay much the same as it had been before. The only difference would be that his wife's lush and lithe body would be waiting for his pleasure in bed every night. But she'd invaded his thoughts as well as his bed.

She was always there. While on the sparring field, he'd try to catch glimpses of her with her bow and arrow and secretly long to be with her instead of his men. While in the bathhouse, he tried to think of ways he could get the place to himself so that he could bring her there and take her while their bodies were slick with sweat and steam. In the evenings while listening to the stories told by the skald, he would seek her out to hold her against him, savouring how well she fit with him. At night, long after their bodies were sated, he enjoyed talking with her about his childhood home and learning how she had spent her days before him. It was this that frightened him more than his physical attraction to her; it was this intimacy that was far more potent than anything he'd known with Hilde.

By the time several days had passed, he knew that enamoured wasn't a strong enough word to describe his feelings for her. Obsessed would more closely name the feeling. Or, if he were a bitter sort, he could claim that she had bewitched him. Only he knew that women held no such power and that she herself was as lost in him as he was in her. Any fool could see how her eyes lit up when she saw him. When they spoke, even at the table eating their evening meal with everyone around them, the world fell away and it was just the two of them.

But even their obsession with each other couldn't keep the world at bay for long. Her father would arrive soon, which meant that news of what had happened in Banford would finally reach her. As each day had passed, the lump of dread in his stomach had become more noticeable. He knew that it would be best if she heard the news from him, rather than some other source, yet he couldn't bring himself to disturb the bliss they'd found.

Each morning when he awoke, he told himself that he had to tell her today. Except she'd awaken next to him, warm and soft and eager, and he'd lose himself in her for a time. Afterwards, as the day wore on, he'd find himself beguiled by her happiness and he couldn't bring himself to say anything that would change that for her. Then he would make a deal with himself to let them have today and he would tell her in the morning, only to have the whole cycle start again.

Finally he ran out of time. Men had come in late that morning to alert them that Scots had been seen on Alvey land to the north, just outside Banford. Rolfe would have to ride out immediately to see to the problem. Hurrying inside, he found his wife seated near the fire with Lady Gwendolyn and Ellan, helping the former with her embroidery skills. Tova sat next to them on a pallet on the floor near Elswyth's skirts, playing with a woollen doll. Wyborn lay near the group, far enough away to discourage the baby's curiosity, but close enough to keep a watchful eye on Elswyth. He'd become her protector, as if he knew that she belonged to him and Rolfe now.

The group laughed at a particularly crooked line Lady Gwendolyn had sewn and Rolfe felt a tug near his heart as he stared at Elswyth's happy face. He didn't want to rob her of her happiness, but he had no choice. She would probably hate him for what he'd done in Banford before they had wed and what he was about to do would guarantee it. There was little doubt that the Scots had been seen because they had met or had planned to meet with Godric.

'Elswyth.' She glanced up and the ready smile fell from her face as she took in his grave expression. His heart twisted as she stood, the blood leaving her face as she approached him.

'What's happened?' she asked, taking his arm.

He drew her to the side of the room for a bit of privacy. 'The Scots have been sighted on Alvey land.'

'Where?' But it was as if she already knew. Her brow creased and a pain came into her eyes.

He nodded. 'Near Banford. We have no proof, but we suspect they are here to meet with your father.'

Shaking her head, she said, 'But they've never come this far south before.'

'I know. It's a bad sign that they've grown bolder.' He rubbed her shoulders in a steady motion to soothe her. 'I have to go.'

'Let me come with you. I can talk to my father.'

The idea was so abhorrent he immediately shook his head. 'Nay. I won't have you in danger.' He was certain there would be a fight. If they caught the Scots crossing the Alvey border, there would be a battle.

'As far as Banford, then.'

'We can't be assured the Scots won't attack Banford. I won't take the chance. You must stay here behind Alvey's walls.'

She opened her mouth to argue, but he tightened his hold slightly on her shoulders. 'I have to go, Saxon. We can't argue about this.'

Throwing her arms around him, she squeezed him as if she never wanted to let him go, but the hall was abuzz with action now as the word had spread and they had no choice but to part. 'I'll help you pack your things,' she whispered, a husk in her voice as she blinked back tears.

He let out a groan and pressed a kiss to her forehead. 'I will come back.'

She nodded, but her fists tightened in his tunic. 'Soon.'

Chapter Fifteen

It took Rolfe and his men two days to hunt the Scots down. The longships took them north, but the Scots knew enough to stay away from the waterways, forcing the warriors to travel on foot across the frozen earth for much of the journey. Cnut brought men from Banford to join him, bringing their count to nearly eighty strong. Finally, when the sky was still dark and the moon covered with low-hanging clouds, Rolfe and his men approached their encampment.

They crept silently, but the scream as the first battle axe found its mark quickly alerted the men to their presence. A surge of vigour drove Rolfe forward—suddenly the battle wasn't about taking land or maintaining territory, it was about protecting his home. An image of Elswyth as she slept flashed before his mind's eye. More than anything else this battle was about protecting her and ensuring that she could continue to sleep and live in peace. A guttural battle cry fell from his lips and his warriors followed suit as they attacked.

The Scots rose, but many of them met their deaths before fully coming to their feet. The ones towards the

middle of camp stood the best chance. They stood in
a circle three rows deep, facing their attackers on all
sides, but Rolfe's men were too fast, too ready and prepared to be held off for long. Rolfe's sword took men
down faster than he could see their expressions and
soon there was a gap in their defence as a group ran off
towards the wood instead of fighting. The grey light of
morning spread over the camp, illuminating their path.

'After them!' he yelled to the man on his right. 'Keep
as many of them alive for questioning as you can.' The
warrior took the group of men under his command,
running after them, and Cnut quickly took his place so
that Rolfe would not be left undefended.

The clang of steel on steel sounded close, drawing
Rolfe's attention away from the fleeing men to the action before him. As if his face had been culled from the
depths of Rolfe's deepest nightmare, Osric loomed before him and time itself seemed to grind to a halt. The
pale skin of the Saxon's cheeks was burnished with exertion as he hacked at an attacker. The Dane warrior
deflected, surging to his left to meet yet another Scot,
leaving Osric free to skewer his unguarded ribs if he
so chose. But something caught Osric's attention and
he turned towards Rolfe, meeting his gaze.

Fury transformed his features, his teeth shining
white as he bared them and trudged forward. Rolfe
stared, hardly able to breathe as he heard Elswyth's
voice near his ear as she laughed about the time Osric,
then a boy, had helped her convince her father that one
of the sheep could talk. She had told Rolfe that story
one night as they'd lain abed. Her throaty laughter had

filled the cocoon of their curtained bed as she remembered how her father's bewildered disbelief had turned to grudging acceptance when he'd been unable to find the source of the voice and then anger when he'd found out he'd been duped.

This boy—now a man—was important to her.

Rolfe's muscles froze, unable to carry out his natural instinct to protect himself as Osric came closer. His grip tightened on his sword, but his arm stayed up, caught in that moment of slackness before attacking. 'Osric! Don't!' His words fell on deaf ears as the Saxon lunged, swinging his blade.

Cnut yelled, plunging before Rolfe to intercept his would-be attacker. Before Rolfe could even call out, Osric fell to the ground, blood pouring from a deep wound across his torso. It was a death blow. The light had faded from Osric's eyes before his shoulders landed with a dull thud.

The horrible moment was over as quickly as it had begun. Rolfe was forced to step over him and continue the battle until it was finally over. Whether Osric had been there as a messenger or had joined the Scots, Rolfe didn't know. Despite the order to take prisoners, no men had been left alive. They had defended themselves too fiercely, clearly determined to die fighting.

With Osric's death, the glimmer of hope Rolfe had carried that he and Elswyth might be able to find their way to happiness had died. She would never be able to forgive him for the killing her friend. But even if she could, Osric's presence only furthered the theory that Banford was ripe with treachery. Godric had to be behind it and Rolfe had no choice but to try to prove that theory.

Elswyth would hate him. It was a certainty, but if only that had stood between them, he might have found some reason to hope. As it was, his standoff with Osric had proven that which Rolfe most feared. Elswyth had made him lose his focus. Because of his growing infatuation with her, he'd allowed himself to shirk his duty, to feint when he should not have hesitated in meeting Osric with his sword. He might be dead now if not for Cnut. Or worse. Had Osric posed an immediate threat to one of Rolfe's men, could Rolfe have saved him? Would he still have hesitated? That hesitation was an unforgivable crime as far as Rolfe was concerned.

Darkness settled over him as he made his way through the next hours. Men were sent with Cnut to Banford with the news of Osric's treachery. Aevir was to be called in and Godric was to be brought to Alvey for questioning. Rolfe went home to his wife with a heavy heart.

They arrived near midnight and Rolfe stayed downstairs long enough to relay what had happened to Vidar and to wash the stench of battle from himself in the bathhouse. Only then was he able to take himself to his wife. Silently pushing open the door to their chamber, he lit a single candle and pulled the bed curtain back to watch her sleep. He was exhausted, but his body still stirred at the sight of her. In fact, he'd left Wyborn downstairs by the fire, because he wanted one more night with her before seeing the hatred on her face.

Before he had to put necessary distance between them. Tomorrow he would have to somehow figure out a way to remove her from his heart.

Stripping off his clothes, he crawled into bed with her and pulled her soft, warm body against him. She sighed, instinctively curving herself into him.

'Saxon,' he whispered against her neck as her familiar scent washed over him.

'Dane,' she answered back, but her voice was still thick with sleep and dreams. The woman could sleep through an invading army.

His palms moved over her body through her nightdress, remembering the planes and curves, filling themselves with her softness. His mouth found hers, drinking her sweetness, as one of his hands found its way beneath the linen to her bottom. It was the touch of his bare skin on hers that finally broke her sleep.

'Rolfe,' she whispered against his lips, then repeated his name with more urgency as she pulled away, turning in his arms, to see him. 'You're home!' Her arms went around him and she kissed every part of his face as if checking for damage. 'Are you injured?'

'There was a fight, but I'm not injured.' He hoped she didn't ask him for details, because he couldn't talk about it now. He only asked for one more night with her. Tomorrow would be soon enough to push her away.

'Thank God.' She said it like she meant it, repeating it as if she'd spent the hours of his absence praying for his return. Perhaps she had. Perhaps she had missed him as much as he'd missed her. Her hands travelled over his naked chest and farther down as if she couldn't quite believe he was unharmed.

Rolling her on to her back, he rose above her, taking in her precious face as she stared up at him.

'What's wrong?' Her brow furrowed and she touched his cheek even as she widened her thighs so that he could settle between them. 'Something's happened.'

He shook his head, too overcome with her to talk. Instead of asking again, she only smiled and pulled him down to kiss him. He closed his eyes and put all of his regret and, aye, even love into that kiss. Her hands worked between them, pulling her clothing out of the way to make way for him. Finally, her fingers wrapped around his length and she guided him to her. He gasped as his rigid length slipped into her moist heat. She arched beneath him, beckoning him for more and sighing against his lips when he gave it to her.

He took her slowly, knowing that tonight might have to last him a lifetime.

When Elswyth awoke the next morning, Rolfe had gone. Downstairs the men had already sequestered themselves at a table in the corner, discussing the battle, she assumed. Lady Gwendolyn hadn't been very forthcoming with information, only saying that aye, the men had battled the Scots and that her family had not been involved, before keeping her busy all day in her chamber with mending and embroidery. It had been enough for a time, but as the day had become night and she'd only been able to share quick glances with Rolfe, Elswyth was losing her patience. It was as if everyone had made a concerted effort to keep her from her husband.

Aevir had arrived during the evening meal, and when she thought that meant the men might break for the night, it only sent them into another round of discussion. Elswyth had finally taken up a stool by the fire where she played a dice game with Ellan, determined to wait them out and approach her husband as soon as he rose.

Something was wrong. She didn't know what it was, but something had happened in the time Rolfe was gone and it had changed him. It was in his face. She had seen it last night and cursed herself a fool for letting him distract her before finding out the truth. Whatever it was, it scared her and she wouldn't rest tonight until she got to the bottom of it. There was a distance between them that frightened her.

The door came open and a man rushed in. She recognised him as one of the men who stood guard on the wall. His eyes were wide and determined as he walked to Lord Vidar. The dice slipped from her hands and she rose to her feet, knowing instinctively that something had happened.

'Godric is here,' he said a bit too loudly.

'What are you doing?' Ellan asked, coming to her feet when Elswyth turned to go get her cloak.

'I'm going to see Father. Something has happened and, if Rolfe won't tell me, I'll ask him.' There was also the small issue of delivering the news of her wedding to him, but somehow that seemed secondary now.

She hurried upstairs and came back down just in time to see Rolfe heading out the door. Determined to find out what was going on, she hurried through the hall before anyone could stop her. Lady Gwendolyn called to her, but she pretended not to hear and kept moving forward. When she stepped outside, it was easy to see where to go. A group of men had gathered beneath the light of the torches inside the wall.

'I asked for my daughters.' She heard her father's deep voice through the crowd as she pushed her way through.

'And we have come instead.' The iron in Lord Vidar's voice was unmistakable.

'You would deny me my own daughters?' Godric's voice rose a fraction.

'Nay, but I would know what you're about first. My man tells me you left Banford days ago,' Lord Vidar answered.

She neared the front to see Father grin, revealing well-kept teeth, though a few were missing. 'Went hunting. No harm done. I've come to take my daughters home and I'd like to leave in the morning.'

'Won't you stay and take a meal with us tomorrow?' Lord Vidar asked.

He shook his head and at his side Galan crossed his arms over his chest. 'No time for feasting.'

'Elswyth won't be returning with you,' Rolfe answered, drawing the man's astute gaze. 'She's my wife.'

Elswyth winced at the words. She had a speech prepared, one in which she would have gently let her father know what had happened. Instead of the anger she had expected, her father only looked pensive. Galan was the one who grew angry. His arms dropped to his sides and his fists clenched as he took a step towards Rolfe. 'Did you force her?'

'Nay, I didn't force her. She was very happy to become my wife.'

'What did you do to her, you bastard? She would never marry a Dane willingly.' Galan's voice rose a notch on that last part.

Elswyth winced when confronted with the bald hatred she had known to expect from them. They would think she had betrayed them when they learned the truth of Rolfe's words. Part of her wanted to go back inside before one of them saw her.

Rolfe's voice interrupted that thought. 'She did marry me and she did so willingly. The marriage is valid with witnesses and the endorsement of your lord.' She couldn't see his face, but his voice was hard, nothing like the man who had come to her last night 'We regret that it had to be done in haste and without your agreement, but I'm prepared to reimburse you for the omission and to give you a fair bride price. I'd like to offer you twenty-five pounds of silver.' It was more than double the typical amount.

Father scoffed. 'Do you think silver is all it will take to buy my acceptance of this farce?'

'It's no farce.' Rolfe's voice had gentled, but only slightly. 'The deed has been consummated and she is content as my wife. I have vowed to give her my protection and keep her safe.'

A flicker of uncertainty appeared on Father's face and for the first time something very close to pain displaced the hatred. She longed to reach out to him and tell him that she was happy. It was time to reveal herself.

Father's next words brought her up short.

'Safe,' the older man said. 'Does that include her home? Her family? Did you tell her about your actions in Banford before or after the wedding? Have you told her about Osric?'

She had expected Rolfe to scoff, to deny any knowledge of the wrongdoing her father's tone implied, but that didn't happen. A damning silence fell over the men. A sick feeling formed in the pit of her stomach and she knew that this was why Rolfe had appeared so hollow. Something had indeed happened.

'Rolfe?'

He turned, eyes wide with guilt as if he were stricken to see her. The crowd made room for her and she stepped into the clearing in the middle of the circle they created. When Rolfe didn't speak, she turned to her father. 'Father, what happened in Banford?'

'Go back inside.' Rolfe's voice was hard, leaving no room for argument as he pressed his hand to her waist. It wasn't the sort of touch she associated with him. It was cold, almost impersonal, as if she were an object and not the woman he'd held with such tenderness in the past. A shiver worked its way down her spine.

Elswyth stared up at her husband, having been aware that this side of him existed—the forbidding commander of warriors—but she'd almost forgotten it. Nor had she expected to see it directed at her. It only reinforced the distance she had felt growing between them since his return. Telling herself that she was mistaken, she pressed a hand to the one at her waist and gave him an uncertain smile. 'I want to stay. What is he talking about?'

'We'll talk about this later. Inside,' came his immediate and unyielding reply. There was something in his face lurking behind the command, something that she dimly recognised as fear, and it frightened her. She'd never seen Rolfe afraid. It told her that whatever they were talking about was important and it concerned her. She wasn't going anywhere.

Turning to her father and Galan, she stepped away from Rolfe's hand on her waist and asked, 'What happened in Banford and what is this about Osric?'

Her father opened his mouth to speak, but before a sound came out Lord Vidar said, 'Do not, Godric.' His voice was deep and strong with authority.

She stared at his hard face, taken aback that the men she thought she had come to know so well were behaving in this way. A threatening wave of premonition came over her, and she looked to Rolfe. He appeared angry, but the fear was still there, twisting his handsome features with pain. 'Elswyth.' His voice had gentled a bit. 'Come, let me tell you in our chamber.' There was a subtle question in his voice as he held out his hand to her.

Her gaze fixated on that hand, wavering. She so wanted to disappear with him, hiding away in their chamber from whatever horrible thing was about to happen. She wanted it more than she'd ever wanted anything. She might have actually taken his hand. Her palm tingled, already anticipating his familiar warmth and comfort, but Galan spoke. 'He killed Osric.'

'Lie!' Rolfe yelled, staring at her brother as if he could strike him down with one look.

Elswyth reeled from those words. She thought of Osric's boyish smile and the way his hair always had the one curl that would flop over his forehead. The way he would tease her about getting too attached to the baby lambs who lost their mothers, but he would stay up late right beside her the entire time helping her care for them. His heart had been just as soft as hers when it came to them. And now that kindness was gone, stripped from the world as if it had never existed.

'He can't be gone,' she whispered to herself, but Rolfe was there behind her and he heard her, confirming her worst fears.

'I'm sorry, Elswyth.' His voice was soft, but it was cold and distant. The man she knew would have called her Saxon and his voice would have ached with the admission as he touched her. This man was not the husband who had left her.

She whirled to face her husband. 'You killed him?' She couldn't even conceive of a scenario where that event was likely.

'Nay.' His voice hardened and he glanced at her brother in annoyance, before looking back to her. 'Come inside with me. I vow I'll tell you everything that happened.'

'You'll lie to her, you mean,' Galan said before she could answer. 'Your men killed him because he was talking to the Scots. Because you're so arrogant a man must be cut down for even talking to someone you dislike.'

'Damn you! Shut up and let me speak to my wife!' Rolfe shouted.

'You've had plenty of time to talk to her,' her father cut in. 'You came back last night, didn't you? That's plenty of time.'

'Last night?' She stared up at her husband and she knew he was remembering just as she was how they had passed the night in bed. He'd known this horrible thing and he hadn't come to her once today to tell her. The guilt was shining from his eyes, proving that her father spoke the truth.

'You've had even longer than that to confess the destruction you wrought in Banford.' Father's voice cut between them.

'What did you do in Banford?' she asked, feeling very much as if the man before her were a stranger.

Rolfe swallowed and proceeded in a precise voice as if he were explaining something complicated to someone slow, or trying to distance a deranged person away from the knife in their hand. She wasn't certain which scenario applied to her at the moment. It seemed that everyone knew everything except for her and she very much felt as if she could strike out at someone if she wasn't let in on the secret soon. 'Osric was with the Scots we found,' he said. 'He fought alongside them when we attacked. Our plan was to take prisoners, but it was clear from the beginning that they only wanted victory or death.'

A lump welled in her throat and her lip trembled with the force it took to ask, 'He's gone?'

Rolfe gave a curt nod and her vision blurred with tears.

'Even before that they burned Osric's home and Durwin's, too,' Father said. 'Claimed they found Durwin across the border in Alba where they killed him.'

Her hands were shaking when she brought them to her face, needing a moment to take in what had happened without everyone staring at her. But it didn't help. She could feel their eyes on her. A spasm of pain tore through her body as she imagined Osric cut down by Rolfe's order. The sight of his dear face wouldn't leave her. She'd never see his smile again, or his kind brown eyes as he brought her a pudding from his mother. And poor Durwin. He'd been married with a child on the way. Why had he been with the Scots?

Then a thought came to her. If she had married Osric, none of this would have happened. He'd still be alive and smiling at her. Father had wanted her to marry him. He'd not made a secret of it, not really. She'd pretended surprise when Ellan brought it up, but only because it wasn't something she had wanted to entertain. Osric had been like her brother, or maybe she'd been too stupid to understand how to pick a proper husband. He would have been kind to her and she had no doubt that she could have talked him out of joining her father's cause. Had she married him, he would have been home and not out with the Scots. He would be safe and alive. Guilt nearly made her drop to her knees.

As she'd had her crisis the conversation and shouting had continued around her, but the words, 'grounds for divorce', spoken by her father brought her back to what was happening.

'There will be no divorce,' Rolfe was saying.

They spoke as if she wasn't there. As if deciding her future wasn't a conversation worth including her in. But then that should come as no surprise, because no one had bothered to tell her any of this before the issue had been forced. She barely managed to stifle a sob as she pushed her way through the crowd, needing to isolate herself from the madness around her.

Chapter Sixteen

No one approached Elswyth as she ran back to the chamber she shared with Rolfe. Behind her the men's voices rose in anger, but she couldn't be bothered with them any more. She had too much to sort out. The only problem was that once she was alone with the door latched behind her, there was no feeling of sanctuary, no clarity. Only more confusion.

Osric was dead and her husband had caused it. Rolfe might not have held the weapon, but he had ordered it when he had ordered the attack. She couldn't wrap her thoughts around that and she didn't know how to accept it. Where did this leave her? Them? Father would never come to see the logic in her marriage to a Dane now. Even if her earlier argument would have convinced him, Osric's death would weigh too heavy on his heart. He'd loved Osric like a son.

In the silence of the chamber, there was only one conclusion that became clear in the madness. If she did not turn her back on Rolfe tonight, she would lose her family. Father and Galan would shun her, casting her from their lives as her own mother had been cast out. If she chose to be with her family, then Rolfe would be lost to her.

That thought brought her to her knees. They fell out from under her and she crumpled into a heap next to the bed. If today and tonight had been any indication— a terrible shudder tore through her as she remembered his cold touch, his hollow voice—then he might already be lost to her. Guilt or something more powerful was driving him to keep his distance from her.

The knock on the door drew her from her thoughts. There was no one she wanted to talk to, so she asked, 'Who is it?' without rising.

'It's me,' Ellan answered. 'Please open the door.' Her voice was as distinct as if she stood inside the chamber. Elswyth found herself thinking no wonder the men had had no need for further confirmation of the wedding-night consummation. They had heard it all.

Torn with the need to be alone and to find comfort from the only person she knew who still accepted her as she was, Elswyth ultimately rose to her feet and un-latched the door. Ellan came into the room and took her into her arms. Much to Elswyth's shame, she started to sob. Ellan crooned softly, 'I'm so sorry', and led her to the bed where she sat beside her on the furs, gently rub-bing her back. Once the tears came, it was a long time until they stopped and, once they had, she felt drained. But she knew what she had to do.

'What are you doing?' Ellan asked as she jerked away to get to her feet.

Elswyth was already at the door before her sister's

voice stopped her. 'I have to talk to Father. I want him to know why I married Rolfe.' She needed to hear his reaction, to know for certain if he would truly reject her.

Ellan nodded and stood. 'I'll come with you as far as the gates. I can't chance him making me return.'

Not for the first time, Elswyth wondered how choices could be so simple for Ellan. She always seemed to know how to get what she wanted. Elswyth always struggled, because what she wanted seemed to be at odds with something else she wanted.

The pair were able to move through the great hall undetected as excitement was still high and the house was in general chaos as the men drank. It wasn't until they were outside that Elswyth saw Rolfe's broad shoulders as he stood talking to Lord Vidar and Aevir. She hoped to make it past their group unnoticed, but Aevir saw her and spoke to Rolfe, who turned to regard her. She sucked in a deep breath as he walked over.

'Where are you going?' he asked, his eyes sharp as she pulled the fur cloak tighter around her as if that could shield her from his coolness.

'I'm going to spend the night with my family. I wasn't able to speak to my father alone.'

Rolfe immediately shook his head, but she couldn't tell what he was thinking. His eyes were closed to her. 'Nay. It's late. You can speak to him in the morning if you must.'

'If I must? Rolfe, he is my father. I wed knowing that he would not approve. I must speak with him.'

His mouth pressed into a grim line as he stared at her. Part of her wanted to throw herself into his arms and seek the comfort that she knew he was capable of giving her, but he seemed so far away from her.

'He's camped outside the gate. You can stay tonight, but you'll come back in the morning.' He spoke as if she were no one important to him and her heart broke a little bit more, if that was possible. It wouldn't be possible to break her heart if she didn't love him so much. The realisation of how quickly she had fallen under his spell was enough to make her nod. Words failed her.

Turning quickly, she hurried to the gates. Once there, she glanced back to see that Rolfe had moved back to the men. Ellan took her in a quick hug. 'Please remember that you are not our mother,' her sister whispered against her ear. 'No matter what Father or Galan say, you married Rolfe because you chose peace.'

A lump of gratitude towards Ellan formed in her throat and she nodded, afraid that to speak would bring more tears and she needed to be strong now. Giving Ellan a squeeze, she turned and walked through the gates.

Her father had made his camp near the village of tents set up by the Dane warriors outside the walls. He was squarely outside of Dane territory, though not so far as the forest.

'Elswyth!' Galan called to her as soon as he saw her and ran to take her in his arms. 'He let you go?'

Father stood by the fire, holding his hand out to her. She nearly sobbed as she moved from Galan's arms to take her father's hand. 'How is Baldric? Were you able to get him back?' In her pain and confusion, she'd forgotten to ask about her younger brother earlier. That guilt was heaped on to the other that was weighing her down.

Her father's brow furrowed and he shot a glance at Galan. Galan cleared his throat and said, 'Aye, Sister. We were able to get him back. He's at home.'

Relief swept through her. At least taking the bloodstone hadn't been for naught. She'd helped to save her brother. Father put his thick arms around her and her shoulders started to shake. Sobs threatened again, but she managed to hold them back.

'Did he hurt you, girl?'

'Nay.' She shook her head. 'He'd never hurt me. I married him because I thought it would bring peace to Banford. Osric wasn't supposed to die. Why was he there, Father? Why was he with the Scots?' Her fists clenched in his tunic, but his expression was impassive as he stared down at her.

''Tis true then? He didn't force the marriage?'

A lump lodged in her throat. 'I wanted to.' She wanted to claim that it had only been for peace, but she wouldn't deny that she loved Rolfe. 'I cared for him deeply.'

Pain lashed across his face and it was quickly followed by white-hot fury. 'How could you care for one of them?'

Taken aback at the abrupt change in him, she let her hands drop and stood rigid. He looked at her the same way he'd looked upon their mother that night Elswyth had heard them arguing. It was exactly what she had feared would happen, yet she had somehow made herself believe that she could make him see things differently. 'He's not a monster. Rolfe is a good man.'

'A good man who killed Osric.'

She winced at the accusation, because it was true enough and she couldn't deny it. 'That's not all he is. He wants to help us. He believes that if we work together then we can make Banford even more prosperous. The Scots only seek to enslave us, but the Danes could—' Father's hand came up as if to strike her. She broke off and cringed, waiting for the blow, but Galan stepped forward.

'Father!'

The harshly spoken word was enough to stay his heavy hand. He lowered it with a look of pure disdain. 'Will you stay with him or leave with us?'

The ultimatum wasn't unexpected. It was her worst fear realised, and yet still she asked, 'Wh-what do you mean?'

'You've disappointed me deeply, girl. If it were Ellan, I could understand. She always was most like your mother. Faithless and silly. But you... I expected more from you than to lay yourself down for the first Dane who showed interest.'

Blood whooshed in her ears as every cruel word hit her with the force of a blow. 'That's not what happened. He loves me.' Loved her. As soon as the words left her mouth, she realised that he didn't any more. Perhaps he'd realised how impossible their love was in the face of battle.

'Your mother said the same thing, even when she came to me with the Dane's bastard in her belly.'

Elswyth gasped. Mother had been with child. 'Is that the night you argued?'

His brow furrowed, surprised that she'd heard them, but then he nodded. 'She sobbed and claimed to be torn. She loved the Dane, but loved you children, too, so I did her a kindness and took her choice away.'

'You made her leave.' The accusation shot out of her like an arrow aimed true to its target.

'I wouldn't have a wife who had sullied herself with one of *them*.'

'And what of a daughter?' She held her breath, very much afraid to hear the answer. Despite his faults, he was her father and she cared deeply for him.

He stared her down and she sensed Galan at her side, holding his breath as he awaited their father's judgement. 'You can choose. You either stay here or you come with us.'

Lose her family or lose Rolfe for good. 'Back to Banford?'

He shook his head. 'The time has come to act. Killing Osric was a step too far.' He lowered his voice as if realising that the enemy might overhear him. 'We'll get revenge now.' His words implied that the Scots would help in that.

'Father, nay, you cannot mean that you will join them?'

He nodded and she felt the press of Galan's fingers on her back. 'We will.' Galan's smooth voice confirmed her worst fear. 'I believe Father is too hasty in forcing you to choose,' Galan said, drawing her gaze to him. He stood tall and as proud and defiant as the leader of a rebellion should look. Her heart ached, because she couldn't help but to imagine that he could be dead soon.

'I am not,' said Father with a bite in his voice.

Galan narrowed his eyes at the older man before looking at her again. 'With you as Rolfe's wife, you'll have more insight into their battle plans. You can tell us everything we need to know.' The world started swimming around her and her heart sank. Her father's face blurred only to be replaced by Galan's smiling features. 'I'd be proud of you if you had planned this,' he teased. 'You'll be the perfect spy.'

Her knees went weak and she would've fallen had Galan not grabbed her. Her brother expected her to spy on her husband and her father was forcing her to make an awful choice. Her entire world seemed to be caving in on her.

'Nay, Galan. There will be none of that. It's too late. Either she leaves with us in the morning or she stays here to lie in the bed she made.' Father levelled her with a glare and said, 'If you stay, you will no longer be my daughter.'

She brought a hand to her mouth to stifle the sob that wanted to escape. Father didn't know it, but Rolfe had already withdrawn his love. There was no reason for her to stay here. But neither could she meekly go with him. She wasn't that dutiful daughter any more, hoping that if she didn't make a misstep that she would earn his love with her loyalty. She had to get away from all of them. She'd go to Banford. Perhaps she'd find some clarity there, away from this madness. If not, at least she could go to Baldric and keep him safe.

Chapter Seventeen

'Where is my wife?'

The sun had not yet crested the horizon, but Rolfe hadn't been able to wait any longer to take Elswyth back. He'd spent a fitful night in their bed, barely able to find any sleep because every time he drifted off he'd reach for her and become aware of her absence all over again.

It was only a slight exaggeration to say that he felt as if he'd been waiting for her all his life. In the short time he'd been with her he knew what would make her laugh and what would make her only smile, and somehow he knew just what to say to make her eyes go very fierce before her temper flared. He could hardly credit the thought, and he'd never give voice to it, but it was as if the gods had meant for her to be his. She *was* his and he would do everything in his power to keep her with him, even if he was forced to keep his distance from her.

If only he knew where she was. As he stared down at the empty place near the embers of the fire where she should have been, Godric and Galan roused in their blankets.

'She won't be your wife for long,' Galan muttered as he sat up.

The anger that coursed through Rolfe's body was so spontaneous and fierce that he was on top of Galan before he could think better of it. 'What have you done with her?'

'Nothing.' He didn't miss the way Galan looked towards the place where she should have been.

'She's gone, you fool.' Rolfe stared into the distance, hoping she'd merely walked away for a bit of privacy, but genuine panic was started to rise within him. The warrior tents were back towards Alvey's wall, but there was no sign of her wandering among them. He briefly wondered if one of them had taken her inside for his pleasure, but none of them would be so stupid. She was his and everyone knew that. He twisted towards the forest, but her form wasn't visible through the dim light of the waning moon. He told himself that she'd merely gone into the forest to relieve herself, or to walk and think things over, but he knew—*he knew*—that she was gone. There was a great void inside him that said she was already far away from him.

'She's gone.' Godric's voice, still harsh with sleep, broke the silence. 'She chose her family over you and she left to go home.'

Pain as sharp as a knife's blade slashed through his chest. The man couldn't have found better words with which to wound him. 'You lie.'

Galan sneered, standing next to his father, 'We have

no need of lies when you've made certain she hates you. She found out who you really are and she left.'

Anger surged through Rolfe, so hot and furious that it propelled him across the glowing embers of the nearly dead fire. He swung his fist and knocked Galan to the ground. 'What sort of brother are you to tell her about her friend in that way?' he shouted. She should have been told in soft, gentle words that would take into account her deep grief.

Wiping the blood from his mouth, Galan smirked from where he'd fallen to the ground. 'What sort of husband are you to have killed him?'

The words were meant to wound and they did. They hurt deeply, nearly bringing Rolfe to his knees with the agony. Stifling a groan of anguish, he ran back to the safety of Alvey's walls hoping that he would find her there, but one quick search of the stables proved that Gyllir was not among the other horses.

Elswyth was gone.

He couldn't move for a moment as that horrible reality pulsed through him. She must have really left for Banford. There was nowhere else she could go. She had chosen her family over him. The devastating pain of that was enough to make him stumble, his hand grasping for the wall.

'Grim!' Rolfe shouted for the boy who guarded the horses at night.

He poked his head over the railing of the loft, straw in his hair as he rubbed his eyes. 'Aye, Rolfe?'

'Have you seen my wife? Gyllir is missing.'

The boy's eyes grew round and when he shook his

head, Rolfe's heart sank. He didn't bother to berate the boy for not watching as well as he should have. There was no time. He had to get to Elswyth. Whether she had chosen her family or not, he needed to talk to her, to hear her tell him herself. By the gods, he might just bring her back anyway.

The blow of the horn sent another shard of terror through him. A blow this early meant something was gravely wrong. 'Ready my horse,' he ordered Grim and ran to the gates to figure out what was happening.

The Saxon Aldred stood heaving for breath, his horse beside him lathered in sweat. The men on watch had gathered around them, listening.

'What's happened?' Rolfe asked, and they relayed the story to him. There were Scots in the north. Aldred had come upon them during his routine ride through his assigned territory. The area Aldred described wasn't directly on the path that Elswyth would take, but it was close enough to make Rolfe fear they might find her. Turning to the men of the night guard, he asked, 'Did any of you see my wife leave on Gyllir?'

'Aye,' one of them said. 'Around midnight she came and took the mare out.'

He stared at them, incredulous. 'Not one of you stopped her?'

They looked at each other in discomfort before one said, 'Should we have stopped her? Is she a prisoner?'

'Nay, but she was alone at night. Did you not suspect anything? You could have sent for me.'

They shuffled in discomfort again. 'She said that she

was staying with her family tonight. We didn't know that you had forbidden her to leave.'

He hadn't forbidden her to leave, but neither should she have gone. He wanted to yell at the helplessness he felt. 'Send for Jarl Vidar and Aevir. Tell them we leave within the hour.'

That hour seemed endless. If Rolfe could have gone, he would have, but he couldn't simply ride out with the threat of the Scots lingering. They needed to assemble the warriors and prepare for battle. Finally, Rolfe had gathered his men and took Aevir, leaving before the allotted hour. He'd leave Vidar to take the other warriors in boats up the river. They'd make faster time and come from the west.

Rolfe set a brutal pace, the horses of more than forty warriors tearing up the ground in his fervour to find Elswyth. The Scots would have to come second to that. He'd never felt such an obsession in his life as he did now, needing to know that she was safe more than he needed his next breath. His only goal was to find her and take her in his arms. She could hate him for ever, but he was never letting her out of his sight again.

They had ridden hard for over an hour—the sides of his horse were already lathered in foam and he heaved in deep breaths—when they broke through the edge of the trees to see a single horse on the path ahead. The gathering sunlight glinted off its golden coat as it grazed on the grasses of the valley floor. Even from this distance, Rolfe could tell that it was Gyllir. His heart gave a leap in his chest as he urged Sleipnir even faster.

As soon as he approached, he vaulted down before his horse had even stopped, landing hard on his feet. He ran past Gyllir, expecting to see Elswyth resting in the tall grasses, but she wasn't there. A quick survey of the small valley found that it was empty.

'Elswyth!' He yelled her name over and over, but there was no response.

'Rolfe!' Aevir's hand on his shoulder finally got his attention, but Rolfe could tell from his expression that it wasn't the first time Aevir had called his name.

'She has to be here,' Rolfe said.

Aevir shook his head, then said very carefully, 'She's not here, Brother.' He led Rolfe back to Gyllir where it was obvious she was wounded as she favoured a foreleg. Dried mud caked one side of her as if she had fallen. She must have thrown Elswyth as she fell. An image of his wife, hurt and broken on the ground, came to mind.

With more than a day's travel to Banford ahead of them, there was no chance she'd reached the village and sent the horse back on its own. Something had happened to her. Either the horse had spooked and thrown her or she had come across the Scots.

Fighting nausea and a bone-deep fear he'd never felt before, Rolfe gave the order to keep riding.

They had been forced to a slower pace, so it was a few hours later when they reached the area where she'd been taken.

It was obvious a skirmish had occurred. Horse hooves had made deep prints in the mud left from the snow earlier in the week. There were at least a score of horses, maybe more, it was difficult to tell. One horse had taken a tumble, probably hers given the mud on Gyllir's side and her injury. The disturbance in the mud where the horse had lost its footing and slid on to its side was unmistakable. It appeared that Elswyth had been ambushed or had run right into the unaware Scots. Either way, they had her. He couldn't think too deeply about what that might mean. He only knew that he had to find her.

Elswyth had been lucky. Her arm had been scraped when Gyllir had fallen, tearing the sleeve of her under-dress, but she'd managed to jump free to avoid the horse landing on her leg. It had been small consolation, because she'd had no chance to gain her footing before the Scots had captured her. It had happened so fast that she'd not even had a chance to pull her axe. One moment she'd been racing through the trees and in the next she'd come upon them. Her impression had been that they had been just as surprised as she had, but it hadn't changed the fact that they had taken her.

They had stuffed a cloth into her mouth to keep her silent. She hadn't made it easy, fighting until one of them had boxed her ear, sending her into a world of pain and stars. When she'd regained her senses, her arms had been tied to a horse and a Scot rode behind her. Struggling only sapped her strength and bruised her body, so she'd resolved to wait until they stopped.

Turned out that struggling with the Scot behind her had hurt her worse than falling from the horse.

She had counted a group of seventeen. All men. All warriors. She didn't know what they were doing this far south. Were they scouting? Had they become lost? Surely they hadn't come for battle with so few men? After they had taken her they'd travelled fast, as if they were afraid of pursuit, but after a few hours it had become apparent that they'd succeeded in their crime so they'd relaxed. A few of them had even given eerie calls of victory that had made her blood run cold.

If she had to guess, she would say this was no sanctioned jaunt to the south. They had probably escaped their leaders, hoping to return home with a Dane prize. They reminded her of adolescent mongrels testing their boundaries with the way they jested and spoke to one another, and they all seemed fairly young. The oldest and apparent leader was probably only a few years older than her. He was clean and well dressed, making her think he was someone of power. It was only later in the day when someone had spoken his name that she realised he was Domnall, the King's son. Though the most frightening thing about him was that he wore the bloodstone she had stolen from Rolfe on his cloak. She recognised its size and the gold filigree, though it was missing its chain.

She had debated if it would be better to tell them her identity or to keep quiet. Not that there was much time for talking. It appeared they were trying to make it back to their own territory with all possible haste. They had stopped only briefly a couple of times to water the horses and eat a little bread. Night had long since fallen and they'd shown no signs of stopping to camp, which was a relief. She feared what would happen to her if they made camp. But she was also starting to fear what would happen if they didn't. Snow had begun to fall the farther north they travelled and as day had become night a layer of it had accumulated on the ground. Somewhere during the struggle she'd lost her fur so her limbs were numb from the cold and the Scot at her back showed no signs of taking pity on her.

Light of a new dawn was just beginning to crest on the horizon when a shout from behind them drew the attention of Domnall. He pulled up short and all the other men stopped to watch as he doubled back. A figure rode out of the darkness and she recognised him as one of the group who had dropped off some time back. Apparently he'd been left behind to watch for Danes. She'd been so tired that she'd drifted in and out of sleep on the horse, so she wasn't entirely certain where they were. She'd guess they were north of Banford, perhaps already in the Scots territory.

Domnall shouted back to his men and she cursed herself for not being able to understand his words. There was no mistaking the change in momentum that ran through the group, a potent mix of anticipation and bloodlust, but all of it was tinged with fear. The fear was in how the men darted glances from one to the other as if attempting to draw strength from their own arrogance. A battle was coming. Her heart pounded and she knew the man had brought news of the Danes coming. It was Rolfe.

Domnall rode back, dismounted and walked straight towards her. She tried to keep her fear in check, but she couldn't control the shaking of her limbs as he cut the bonds attaching her to the horse from her arms and dragged her off. He set her on her feet, but they were numb from the cold and the hard ride, so she sank down before she could find her strength. He left her there and walked back to his horse. Her heart leapt as she thought that maybe he'd decided to leave her. Perhaps he thought she wasn't worth the risk and if he left her here the Danes would halt their pursuit. Her hopes fell when he walked back to her holding another set of rope and she realised he meant to tie her up again.

By this time she was able to get to her feet and she tore the cloth from her mouth. 'Let me go and I'll make sure you are not followed.'

He grinned and spoke in her language. 'How will you ensure that?'

'I am Elswyth. My father is Godric from Banford and I am the wife of Rolfe from the Danes of Alvey.'

He paused in his approach, but his smile only widened. 'Godric's daughter.' Then he tapped the bloodstone affixed to his cloak. 'I've you to thank for this. Those Danes killed my brother and took this from his dead body. Your brother, Galan, says that you retrieved it from them. He did not say that you had married one of them.'

She hesitated, uncertain how much glory she wanted to accept for an act that she despised. 'Aye, I took it,' she finally said. 'But only because you had Baldric. I did it to save him, not to help your cause.' The last thing she wanted now was to help the Scots. All she wanted was peace.

He watched her curiously, his head tilting to the side. 'Baldric? The boy?'

She nodded and a feeling of unease came over her as she remembered her father and the peculiar look on his face the previous night when she'd asked about Baldric.

'We never had Baldric,' the man said easily. 'Godric secured the bloodstone as a gesture of his loyalty.'

Her knees nearly went out from under her again as the pain of her family's betrayal tore through her. Baldric had never been in danger. They had told her that to make her steal from Rolfe. She'd betrayed Rolfe's trust for nothing. For a foolish test of loyalty to a king she had no love for.

'Your father lied to you,' he concluded, taking a menacing step closer to her.

Despite the fact that she knew she would get no help from his men, she looked for it anyway, only to see that they were all busy scurrying in every direction. They were planning to hide and lie in wait for whoever was coming.

'Tell me, Elswyth, to whom do you give your allegiance? Your father or your husband? You cannot serve both of them.'

She flinched from the question. Dear God, was it meant to follow her always? But what else had she expected? She was a Saxon who had married a Dane. Tangled loyalty and distrust would haunt her for ever.

Her family needed her and Rolfe...even thinking his name brought physical pain. He'd spent hours worshipping her body, but that alone wasn't enough to earn her devotion. Nay, he'd earned that with his noble strength, his sense of honour and gentle teasing. He'd earned that with the way he had always made her feel safe and protected. The memory of the way he had looked at her as he'd spoken the words that would make him her husband came back to her, as if she were the only woman he wanted, as if he had truly meant every one of them.

It was all those tiny moments added up to create a bond that she had known would only grow stronger in the days to come. Until it had all come crashing down around her.

'What does it matter to you?' she asked him coldly.

'It doesn't, but we're about to find out whether it matters to your husband.'

His eyes gleamed cruelly as he came for her. She screamed, hoping that the sound would warn Rolfe and the others, but it was cut off short by his open palm against the side of her head. It hadn't been terribly hard, but the strength hadn't yet returned to her legs so the blow knocked her to the ground. Her knees landed with a heavy thud on the hard ground, followed by the nearly dead weight of her exhausted body. The cold wet snow seeped through the fabric of her tunic and leggings. He tore the cloth from her hand, intending to tie her mouth again, but she refused to make it easy.

Drawing on the last of her reserved strength, she lashed out, catching him in the groin. He groaned in pain and fell to his knees, but he was only momentarily slowed, enough to allow her to rise, but not escape him. He grabbed her arm and with his greater strength was able to pull her beneath him so that he could tie the cloth behind her mouth and then wrench her arms in front of her to tie them. She fought him mercilessly so that by the time he'd finished, galloping horses could be heard coming up the slight hillside.

Her heart gave a leap of joy the moment she saw Rolfe's beloved face in the pale sliver of the coming dawn. His hair had come loose from the usual way he wore it pulled back from his face to swing in a wild mass around his shoulders. His eyes widened with visible relief when he saw her. In that moment everything became clear to her. She hated what he'd done and she despised the coldness with which he'd treated her, but she should have stayed and talked with him. Anything to keep him from danger. The rest of the Scots were out there hiding. One of them might even now be waiting to jump him.

Chapter Eighteen

Rolfe drew his mount up short the moment he saw Elswyth with Domnall, heir to the Scots King. Her eyes were round with terror. The sleeve of her dress was torn and much of her hair had fallen from her usually tidy braid, but otherwise she looked whole and unharmed. Domnall stood behind her with a dagger at her throat. It was only one of the many reasons Rolfe wanted to see him dead.

'You've taken my wife, Domnall. You will die for the crime.'

Domnall's laugh sent a chill through Rolfe's body. It was said the man was touched in the head and, looking at him now, Rolfe could believe it. His eyes were those of a man unconcerned with his current situation, which was an unbelievable show of arrogance in one so young and undermanned. Rolfe knew that he had at most twenty men. Aevir had split off a while back and had managed to pick off a few, but the rest were probably spread out in the shadowed dawn, watching them. Rolfe had ten men at his back, the rest silently closing in from the other sides. Domnall had to know Rolfe would come with more than ten men.

'If I die, then so does she.' Domnall pressed the tip of the blade closer to her tender neck, drawing a bead of blood. However, Elswyth didn't flinch, she stared at Rolfe as if attempting to warn him with her eyes.

Rolfe wanted nothing more than to attack and pull her away from Domnall. He'd take her in his arms and thank the gods she was safe while vowing to never let her out of his protection again. But he couldn't think of that now. First, he had to get her away from the madman.

'Why were you on Alvey lands? It's an act of war,' Rolfe said, attempting to distract the man while showing no sign of the rage that pounded through him at the sight of his wife's blood.

'We're already at war, Dane. You know that. The truth is that I didn't come with the intention of taking such a prize, but I'm glad to have found her.' He ran his hand over her torso, from her breast to her hip. Elswyth's wrists were tied in front of her but she still managed to send a sharp elbow into Domnall's side.

Domnall grunted and tightened his arm around her in what looked to be a merciless grip.

'I doubt you could handle her.' Rolfe forced an unconcerned grin.

'It seems that you couldn't handle her either. What was your wife doing wandering the forest on her own in the night? Did she get away from you or was she going on a spy's mission to report to her family?'

'She's no spy and it's none of your concern what she

was doing unaccompanied. Hand her over and I *might* let you live.'

Domnall laughed again. 'Your words are very compelling, but I'll keep her. I quite like her. Had I known Godric's spy was such a beauty, I'd have demanded he give her to me as a sign of his loyalty rather than the bloodstone.'

The words were so odd, that Rolfe had to ask. 'What bloodstone?' From across the distance he met Elswyth's gaze and the guilt shining out at him nearly stole his breath. He didn't want to believe it was his bloodstone, but there was no denying the pained way she looked at him, as if her heart was breaking this very moment.

Domnall shifted her slightly to the side, revealing the stone fastened to his cloak. A surge of blinding anger tore through Rolfe. It was the same stone he'd brought home, set in the same gold-filigree design. It was supposed to be in the chest beneath his bed.

The guilt stamped into her features told him that Elswyth had taken it. When? Had she delivered it tonight? Was that the true reason for her mad dash in the middle of the night?

If he'd had any doubt about her guilt, he only had to look back to his wife to see the way her face scrunched with pain—or perhaps it was anger that her game had been found out—and the way she would not meet his gaze. It was clear that she had used him and chosen her family in the end. He had allowed his feelings for her to blind him to her true character. First Hilde and now his wife. He let out a bitter laugh.

He didn't want it to make sense, but it all came together perfectly. Her family had wanted her to wed him, probably in an attempt to eventually control him, or at the very least to gain insight to his plans. It was the perfect plan, because she was so unlike any seductress he'd ever come across. Instead of using pretty words and her body, she had used her innocence to seduce him.

The breath wheezed out of him in a hiss. The lies she'd fed him hurt far worse than the theft. Hilde had left him broken, but Elswyth's betrayal cut far deeper. Down to his core where it mangled him.

'Do you recognise it?' Domnall's voice had turned bitter. 'You took it from my bastard brother after you ran him through with your sword.'

The anger was followed by a very real and a very hated surge of fear that the man would kill her before Rolfe could save her. Rolfe shouldn't care any more. He didn't want to care, but he couldn't stop himself. Not yet. Perhaps soon he would be able to wrest control of the flicker of tenderness that still lingered for her and extinguish it like the hated spark that it was, but for now it was there and he could no more put it out than he could allow it to live.

Despite her crimes, she didn't deserve to die for them. He could devise a far better punishment than death. Besides, like it or not she was his wife and he'd vowed to protect her, to give his life for hers if need be. He'd honour that commitment.

'Aye, I recognise it.' He did not, however, recognise his own voice. It had gone soft and menacing with a raw thread he'd never heard in it before.

'Shall I cut off her cloth?' Domnall ran his dagger

up her neck and over her jaw, coming to a stop on the cloth that had been put between her lips and pulled cruelly around to the back of her head and tied so tight that it bit into the tender flesh of her cheeks. 'She can tell us how she came to have it and how she delivered it. Perhaps she could also tell you how we came to know where your sentries were so that we could avoid them.'

She finally deigned to meet his gaze again and Rolfe held it, refusing to allow her to hide from him. He'd get answers from her, but it wouldn't be with Domnall watching. It would be when they were alone and he would get the truth from her whether she wanted to tell him or not.

Elswyth could hardly bear the stone-hard hatred she saw in Rolfe's face. This was the commander she knew lingered beneath the surface of the man she had come to love. This was the enemy warrior capable of violence. It was not the man who had smiled at her so tenderly, nor the man who had whispered deliciously wicked things in her ear as he'd come inside her. This man was as cold and beautiful as the moors in winter, with hard plains and jagged edges that were as beautiful as they were inhospitable.

As the coldness of his gaze crawled inside her, making her shiver even harder, she had to wonder if he would even try to get her back from Domnall. He looked as if he could turn and leave without even giving her a second thought. And why wouldn't he? They were very possibly in Alba. Domnall had won. Any attempt to get her back now would be an act of aggression that would likely bring retaliation to Alvey. He knew she had stolen from him and she couldn't use her voice to tell him that Domnall lied about her supplying the Scots with information. Why would he want her? If she wasn't so exhausted and heartsore, she might have cried again.

'Nay,' Rolfe finally said, answering the question she had nearly forgotten hung in the air. 'I do not care to hear from her. Tell me what you want to give her back to me.'

She would have tumbled to the ground with relief had Domnall's grip on her waist not have been so tight she could barely breathe. It was a short-lived relief, however. She barely wanted to face Rolfe any more than she wanted to go with Domnall at the moment.

'You still want her, knowing she's a traitor?'

Despite herself, Elswyth stiffened, bracing herself for the answer.

'I want her because she's my wife. You will pay for taking her, Scot.'

It shouldn't have hurt, but it did. Rolfe wanted her back because the slight of taking a wife could not go unseen. It had nothing to do with her. He probably hated her. If the coldness in his eyes was an indication, he did hate her. She wanted to go back to the day before her father had come, when everything had been good between them and she'd been falling in love with her husband. She was afraid that now they could never go back. Nothing could change what either of them had done. She had lost both her family and her husband.

'Have you harmed her?' Rolfe asked.

'You mean have I taken her?' Domnall replied. 'Not yet.'

From somewhere in the deep shadows of the nearby trees a piercing cry broke through the silence that had fallen. Rolfe didn't react, but Domnall stiffened behind her. She didn't know how he knew, but it appeared they all assumed it was a Scot calling out as he lost his life. It was followed by another one on the opposite side. Rolfe's men had them surrounded. Domnall began to subtly tremble behind her while Rolfe looked on.

'Let her go and I'll give you a head start,' Rolfe said.

The sharp tip of the dagger pressed harder into her neck. A warm trickle of blood oozed out of the tiny puncture to slide down her neck. Before she knew what was happening, Domnall was pulling her backwards. Her feet stumbled over the uneven ground and she slipped a bit, but tried to hold her neck away from the blade's point. Rolfe and his men didn't move. They stayed vigilant.

Finally Domnall made it to where his horse was waiting. He mounted, half-pulling her up with him, so that she draped over the side of the horse facing Rolfe. 'Dismount!' the Scot yelled.

Rolfe and his men slowly moved to comply, but as soon as they did Domnall pushed her away and took off. His horse went flying off into the grey morning. Elswyth landed with a painful crash, her head throbbing and her limbs shaking as she rested on her hands and knees.

Strong hands grabbed her shoulders and pulled her to her feet. She knew without looking that it was Rolfe, she would know his touch anywhere. Though his face and eyes were still hard, he did keep his touch gentle as he cut the binding around her head. Hooves thundered past them on either side as his men set off after Domnall, but Rolfe stayed calm as he looked her over. 'Did he hurt you?'

She shook her head. 'Nothing that won't heal quickly.' Her tongue felt swollen and slow from having the cloth shoved in her mouth.

Rolfe turned back to Sleipnir and pulled a skein of water off his back, pressing it to her lips. She drank greedily, some of the water trickling down her chin to moisten the front of her dress. When she'd had her fill, he took it away to replace the stopper and she brought her bound hands up to wipe the water away.

'How did you know they had me?'

'We got word of the Scots being sighted as I was planning to ride out after I discovered you missing. We followed your path towards Banford and came across Gyllir.'

'Is she hurt?' Elswyth had been so worried for the gentle horse, not having seen what had happened to her after being taken.

'She has a slight limp, but it looked to be minor. We found where you had come across the Scots and it was a simple matter to follow them here.' He spoke without emotion. She could have been anyone he had saved in keeping with his duty.

'Thank you, Rolfe. I… I wasn't certain that you'd want to have me back.'

He paused briefly in tying the skein to his saddle,

but then he finished the task and looked back at her. She could not tell what he was thinking or feeling. Perhaps saving her hadn't meant he'd wanted to have her back at all.

'Would you untie me?' She held up her wrists to remind him, but he merely looked at them. His face was impassive and her stomach sank. 'Am…am I a prisoner?'

'Did you steal the bloodstone from me?'

She swallowed, hating the answer that she had to give. She hated that she had taken it. If she had to do it all over again… She closed her eyes and put that useless thought away. Nothing could change the past. 'Rolfe, I—'

His hard voice cut off her words. 'Tell me "aye" or "nay".' His tone brooked no argument, drawing her gaze to his impassive face.

'Aye,' she said, her voice a little more than a whisper.

'Then you're a prisoner.' His words were flat as he turned to pull a fur that had been wrapped up behind his saddle. He shook it out and wrapped it around her shoulders, his movements as impersonal as if she were a stranger. Though his hands moved up and down her arms to help warm her faster and get her blood flowing, there was nothing to hint at the tenderness or the passion they had shared.

'What will you do with me?' she managed to ask as he boosted her on to his horse.

He didn't say a word as he mounted behind her and turned Sleipnir around, heading south towards Alvey's border. His left arm hooked around her waist to keep her stable. Her body felt so tired and she trembled from the cold that had seeped deep into the marrow of her bones that she wasn't certain she'd be able to stay up without his assistance.

'Rolfe, you must know that I only took it because—'

'Enough! I can't talk to you now.' The bitterness in his voice was the only outward sign of the deep anger burning inside him.

Rolfe despised how good she felt in his arms. After a day and nearly two sleepless nights without her, he'd longed only to have her in his arms again, to hold her against him and know that she was safe and his. It didn't seem to matter that he had learned she had used him ruthlessly for her own purposes. He knew that and his anger burned so hot that he could scarcely contain it, but his heart and his body hadn't yet caught up to his mind. They craved her with the intensity of an animal too long separated from its mate. So he allowed himself this time to hold her. They should reach Banford by afternoon and then that would be the end. He'd turn her over to Vidar and she would have to answer for her crimes just like anyone else.

At first she'd tried to hold herself stiffly against him, but soon the motion of the horse became too much for her exhaustion and she slumped forward. That was to be expected. More concerning was the fact that she had yet to stop trembling. The sound of her teeth chattering along with the occasional sounds of Sleipnir's huffs of breath was the only thing that broke through the stillness of the morning.

'Elswyth?' He hoped to rouse her, thinking that even though they were in a hurry, he should make her walk a bit to get her blood flowing again. She didn't stir, so he repeated her name a bit louder and with more authority. When she still didn't rouse, a flicker of fear moved through him.

A few years ago he'd been to the Great North with a group hunting the great white bears that lived there. They'd been besieged by a snow storm and had sought shelter, but it hadn't stopped a few of them from being overtaken with the cold. They'd shivered uncontrollably even after they'd found the warmth of the fire. Two of them had fallen asleep and never revived. It had been much colder then, but those men had been stout and large-boned. Elswyth was smaller framed and more delicate and she'd been without a fur for at least a day and a night with steady snow. A twinge of guilt tightened his chest uncomfortably. Her clothing was the same as that she had come to him with, barely adequate for winter, much less the extended exposure she'd endured. They hadn't had time to commission new clothing for her in heavier fabrics. Or perhaps there had been time, he simply hadn't seen clothing her as a priority when he'd wanted her without her clothes as much as possible.

Allowing Sleipnir his head, he pulled the knife from his boot and cut the bindings at her wrists. Then he turned her in his arms to see her pale face and the faint blue shadows around her lips and beneath her eyes. 'Saxon,' he called.

She shifted and the relief he felt nearly sent him falling to the ground.

'Saxon, talk to me,' he said, unable to stop himself from cupping her cheek. It was nearly as cold as the snow.

'Dane.' It was the softest whisper, but it brought a smile to his face none the less. He found the pulse in her neck and breathed another sigh of relief when it was strong and steady beneath his fingers. 'So tired and cold,' she mumbled, seeking the heat of his body and turning into him. 'Please can I sleep?'

'Aye, Saxon. I'll keep you safe.' He held her against his chest and pulled away her fur, tucking her against him so that only their clothes were between them. She needed as much heat from his body as she could get. Then he wrapped his fur around them both and tucked hers around her so that she was doubly protected. The new position hindered their speed, but they were still able to make slow and steady progress. He checked her often to make certain she wasn't slipping into a deeper sleep. Each time the strong beat of her pulse reassured him.

Chapter Nineteen

Rolfe had not seen Elswyth in three days. She'd been sleeping—very nearly unconscious—when they had finally made Banford around nightfall. He'd meant to take her to one of the huts Cnut had built for his warriors, a small, thatched-roof structure that was little more than a place to sleep overnight. Instead, he'd taken one look at the inviting trail of smoke coming from the opening in the roof of her family's farmhouse and had taken her home.

An elderly woman—he'd later come to learn she was their housemaid—had been tending the fire when he'd kicked the door open with his booted foot. She jumped up and grabbed a cooking knife, but settled when she recognised him. Her wide eyes had gone to the fur-wrapped bundle in his arms as he'd ordered her to bring a straw mattress to set beside the hearth. That's where he'd laid Elswyth. The old woman had immediately began to cluck over her like a concerned hen. Rolfe had stayed until he was certain his wife would recover and then he'd left, commanding a Dane warrior to guard the front door. None of the Saxons in Banford could be trusted until he had questioned them all.

Aevir had returned at the end of the first day with Rolfe's warriors. Only a few of the Scots who had taken Elswyth had managed to escape, but Domnall was regrettably one of them. It was a fight Rolfe was more than prepared to fight another day. With Aevir's help, they were able to speak with every person in the village over the course of the next two days. All of them claimed innocence when it came to joining with the Scots and to his surprise he was inclined to believe them.

Godric, both of Elswyth's brothers, ten single men and four men along with their wives hadn't been seen for days. The popular opinion was that they had gone north to join with the Scots once it had become apparent that taking Banford would come to naught. In fact, many of the villagers seemed to breathe a collective sigh of relief when he spoke to them. Most of those left behind were families and the elderly who seemed more than willing to trade their anger for peace with the Danes.

Something told him that his wife not one of them. She had demanded his presence to every Dane he had stationed at her door, arguing when they wouldn't allow her to leave the home, and was once driven to physical violence so that he'd had to order every blade in the house confiscated. He told Aevir and even himself that he was content to await Vidar's arrival—after all, it was up to the Jarl to mete out justice for a crime done within his own walls. But even Rolfe couldn't hide from the truth late at night when he sought the meagre comforts of his bed.

The truth was that he was afraid of what he might do when he saw her again. Anger at her treason and lies had nearly burned him alive from the inside, but he couldn't deny the swell of tenderness he felt when he thought of her. As much as he tried to turn it to hate, he couldn't. She had betrayed him just as Hilde had—in some ways even worse—but some part of him would not let him forget how she had relaxed into him every night after giving him her body. How her elegant fingers would curl his hair around them absently as she stroked his shoulders and chest, whispering that she had never been happier. Most of all he couldn't forget how he'd thought they'd have the rest of their lives together and how happy that had made him.

Her mind was keen and eager to learn so he'd planned to keep teaching her the sword and even how to read and write the runes in which she'd shown interest. They were supposed to have had many long winter nights ahead when he'd tell her about his travels and his family. Perhaps he'd even take her back home to meet them one summer. And their children… His throat inevitably closed when he thought of those imagined, yet already beloved creatures with their loving mother. He'd already had their entire life in his head, but it was gone now.

Their future was gone and he couldn't decide between anger and heartache, so they both ate at him with vicious teeth until he was snarling at everyone and everything that crossed his path. He didn't *think* he would harm her when he saw her—he had sworn to protect her and he would abide by that until she was no longer his—but he couldn't chance what he might do. So he stayed away from her and he avoided his straw mattress—a sorry excuse for a bed if he'd ever seen one—for as long as he could until he could fall into it each night and have exhaustion overtake him. Unfortunately, he was a man of action and, while they waited for Vidar to reach them and for some sign of the missing Banford citizens, he only had to wait.

The evening of the third night found him sitting at the hearth in Cnut's longhouse with Aevir at his side. He had long ago finished his mead, but he held the tankard in his hands as he stared at the fire.

'Go to your wife, Brother,' Aevir said, giving him an infuriating smile before he threw back the remainder of his own mead.

'Don't call her that,' Rolfe said, his voice husky from disuse.

'It's what she is, isn't she?'

Rolfe shook his head. 'Not for long.' He'd already decided that divorce was the best option. Vidar would grant it given the circumstances.

'You'll have to talk to her for the divorce.' Aevir's easy voice was grating on his nerves.

'Then I'll talk to her at that time.'

Aevir sighed and then said the words that could have been his last had Rolfe not known him so well. 'I've never known you to be a coward.'

Rolfe threw his tankard to the floor where it landed with a loud thwack and dented the wooden plank. He was on Aevir before the man could defend himself, knocking the bench he sat on backwards, taking Aevir and the two men who sat next to him to the floor with it. 'Words of a dying man,' Rolfe growled, drawing back his fist to blight out the infuriating smirk Aevir still wore.

Aevir managed to dodge the blow and struggled upwards, reversing their positions so that he had the upper hand. Grabbing Rolfe's tunic, he said, 'I know the look of an infatuated man when I see it. Go talk to her and put us all out of our misery.'

Rolfe managed to knock him in the stomach, taking the air out of him and startling him enough so that Rolfe could flip their positions yet again. This time when he had Aevir beneath him he swung and managed to clip his chin with the edge of his knuckles before Aevir dodged away completely. 'You know nothing about what I'm feeling.'

Aevir twisted and managed to get a foot under Rolfe's knee, knocking him off balance. Aevir used the momentum of his fall to get behind him, locking his arms around Rolfe's torso to confine him while his heavy thighs worked to contain Rolfe's struggles. The men were evenly matched in strength so it was anyone's guess who would come out on top, though Rolfe could hear several men calling out wagers.

'I know what it is to love, you fool, and I know what it is to lose that love,' Aevir growled in his ear as they struggled. 'I would give anything to have her back for even one day, to say all the things I didn't have time for. *You* have time now, don't waste any more of it than you already have.'

'It's not the same,' Rolfe hissed, knowing that no one else would hear him over the cacophony of noise the men were making as they cheered them on. 'She lied to me. She stole from me. I cannot forgive that.' Everyone knew how Rolfe's own wife had betrayed him.

'Then go and tell her you're divorcing her now. Go talk to her before you get yourself killed.'

Rolfe hated Aevir's interference, but deep down he knew that his friend was right. He needed this resolved so that he could stop being consumed by Elswyth—if such a thing were even possible. He'd lost his focus and it would go badly for him and his men were they needed for battle while he was like this. Resentment fuelling his struggles, he twisted free enough to drive a powerful elbow into Aevir's side which made his friend huff out a breath of air and loosened his grip so that Rolfe could escape. Coming to his feet, he shoved Aevir away and strode for the door, but not before Aevir's mocking voice called out, 'I hope you know that by "talk" I meant—' The slamming door muffled the vulgarity and the roar of laughter from the men inside that followed it.

Blinded by his rage, Rolfe kept walking across the moonlit field, not caring that the cold turned his breath to frosty puffs, or that he'd forgotten his cloak inside. The cold couldn't touch him. Nothing could touch him and that was the problem. Only one name pounded inside him, driving him forward until he approached the farmhouse door. He hadn't even been aware of his destination until the warrior who was her sentry came to his feet, then stepped aside quickly when Rolfe showed no intention of stopping.

The door opened easily and Rolfe stepped over the threshold, slamming it behind him and setting the latch with a perverse satisfaction. She had come to her feet the moment she'd seen him and there was no mistaking the momentary flare of joy that had crossed her features. It made her cheeks flush with health and her emerald eyes brighten. He'd not seen her since he'd left her here and the rush of relief he felt at seeing her whole and thriving staggered him. It had the effect of cold water thrown on hot metal and cracked through the anger hardening around his heart.

'You look well,' he said rather lamely.

'I am well…thanks to you.' Her voice was like a balm to his ravaged heart and the way she looked at him…

That balm came with a warmth that threatened to further assuage his anger. Desperate to keep stoking the flames so that he wouldn't have to face her without them, he said, 'Why are *you* mending clothing?' The pile had dropped to the floor when she'd stood, but she still held the needle with the thread attached, binding it to the clothing at her feet. 'Where is your servant?' The woman could have been standing right next to her and Rolfe wouldn't have seen her. His entire awareness was consumed with Elswyth.

A flicker of unease marred her joyful features. 'She spends her evenings elsewhere.'

'What? Why?' He'd thought Elswyth would have someone with her at night. He hadn't meant for her to be confined alone.

'We…argued.' She dropped her gaze and he finally took in the state of the small house. Several stools had been overturned and their legs broken, a pitcher—nay, several pitchers—had been shattered, their pieces swept neatly into a pile in a corner. It seemed that only a few basic items had been spared her wrath.

'You did this?' he asked.

Her eyes met his and her chin raised a notch higher than was necessary. 'I wanted to leave and your warriors wouldn't let me. I tried to overpower them and she said I was deranged and she wouldn't stay here at night alone with me.' Drawing in a deep breath as he stared at her in shock, she asked, 'Is there something you want?'

'You asked for me.'

'Days ago.' Accusation burned in her eyes.

'I'm here now.' He shrugged and her eyes burned bright with fresh anger. Good. He wanted her anger.

'I want to leave.'

'You're a prisoner.'

The words hurt her and though that hurt brought him a small measure of satisfaction, it brought him far more pain. And this was why he had avoided her, he realised. To hurt her was to hurt himself.

'Then at least let me see Baldric, my brother.'

'He's not here. We suspect he's already with the Scots to the north and awaiting your father.'

She took a moment to digest that and he would have sworn her surprise was genuine. Drawing herself together, she said, 'The reason I left Alvey was so that I could come here. I wished to see Baldric and visit Osric's mother. I'd like to see his grave, if that's possible.'

He clenched his molars so hard he was surprised they didn't crack under the strain. 'You're a prisoner,' he repeated.

'Then I would like the chance to answer for my crimes. Surely I deserve that?'

'Aye, and you will have that. Jarl Vidar will hear your pleas and decide on a punishment.' Silence descended between them, so Rolfe gave her a brief nod and turned towards the door, quietly cursing Aevir. Nothing had come of this talk with her. He'd been foolish to allow Aevir to goad him into it.

'Rolfe, wait!' Leaving her mending behind, she hurried across the distance, stopping just short of reaching him. 'My crimes were against you, not Lord Vidar. Let me explain to you.'

He was already shaking his head before she'd finished. 'You were a spy, so your crimes were against Alvey. Vidar will hear you, I don't care to hear more of your lies.'

She drew back as if he had struck her and the pain reflected on her face hit him twofold, so that it was momentarily difficult to breathe. 'Damn you and your stubbornness, Dane. I never spied.' As she started to explain, he stepped towards her, but she only stepped back out of his reach. 'Aye, my father sent me to spy, but I never gave them information. I told you all of that already. The only contact I had with anyone in my family aside from Ellan was the night after you returned and Galan came to me.'

'Nay, I don't want to hear more!' He raised his voice

to drown hers out and leaped for her, but she easily sidestepped him.

'Why don't you want to hear?' she yelled back as she moved to the other side of the open hearth to avoid him. 'Are you afraid that the truth will make you realise how cruel you've been keeping me locked up here?'

'Because I cannot believe anything you say.' He stepped around the hearth which was in the centre of the house, leaving her with half as much space to run from him.

'Can't you identify the truth when you hear it?' She steadily backed away from him as she spoke.

'Not when one is as skilled at lying as you.' It seemed he was blind when it came to women.

Her mouth dropped open. 'I stole the bloodstone because Galan told me the Scots had Baldric and were demanding it back in exchange for his life. I barely knew you then. It wasn't personal when I took it from you.' She had come to the back wall of the house when she finished. She made to dart around him, but he grabbed her around the waist and pulled her back against him. Her familiar scent washed over him, stealing his breath, so that they stayed a moment like that until he could speak.

'Even if what you say is true, you made it personal when you married me without confessing. You took me as your husband, you drank the mead and took me into your body, all while knowing what you had done. Perhaps I could forgive your reasons had I known them earlier, but I cannot forgive your lying to me.' Or her betrayal. He'd didn't know if the pain of that would ever go away.

Her breath hitched, but when he thought she'd lost her fight, she stomped on his booted foot and pulled away. She slipped from his grasp, and he prepared to chase her, except she didn't run. She stood with her back pressed to the wall and glared at him. 'You know all about lying by omission, don't you? You didn't tell me of Osric, or the destruction you wrought in Banford. You never gave me the chance to choose to forgive you and yet you expect me to do what you couldn't.' Her voice might have been bitter, but the tears on her lashes ruined the effect.

'Damn you, Saxon.' Her tears were his undoing, just like the night she'd come to him in his chamber. The fight left him, leaving only pain, aching and bleeding, in its wake. He brought his hand to her cheek and his voice was raw when he spoke. 'I knew you would hate me for what I had done, so I wanted to wait to tell you until after you loved me.' It was perhaps the most honest thing he'd ever said in his entire life.

A sob stuck in her throat. With a groan he slid his hand around her nape and pulled her close. His mouth covered hers and she opened to him, eagerly, greedy even. The tip of her tongue touched his and he growled at the fierce need for her sweeping through him. It was like adding kindling to low burning fire. He went up in flames.

Chapter Twenty

The need to take her...own her...*possess* her tore through him with a savageness that left room for nothing else. He needed her once more. She was his mate and he'd not touched her for days and days. The want was primitive and tinged with a deep-seated urge to make her come apart in his arms. He wanted to feel her trembling beneath him with want and hunger, knowing that he was the only one who could assuage her desire.

The soft heat of her mouth pulled at him as he kissed her. She opened beneath him and invited him inside. He wanted her hard and fast and panting with desire. Pulling away from the touch of her eager tongue, he caught a glimpse of her heavy-lidded gaze as he tore at her nightdress. The linen came apart with a loud rending sound that seemed to echo in the small house. She gasped and that sound only spurred him onwards.

Turning her so that her breasts pressed to the wall, he tore the back to match the front until the linen fell from her shoulders. The smooth skin of her back called to him and he couldn't resist touching it in a slow caress as he pushed the dress to a puddle at her feet. She arched into his touch and he couldn't bring himself to stop until he reached her bottom and filled both of his palms with her. She moaned deep in her throat when he squeezed and kneaded, shifting and pushing back against him in a silent plea for more.

Possession was what he wanted. Simple and crude. He wanted to bury himself deep between her thighs and own her as she writhed, begging him. The image of that made him swell to aching.

Elswyth turned abruptly against the wall to face him. She was nude, her beautiful body flushed with pleasure and desire as she pulled him against her, her mouth seeking his as she fitted herself against him. Her leg came up to hook around his thigh and he couldn't resist taking her mouth savagely and pressing her back to the wall. His arm went under her knee, opening her to him so that he could grind his hardness against her willing body. She gasped into his mouth and writhed. His fingers found her slick with arousal and he was surprised to find her as ready as he was.

Abruptly he pushed away from her, letting her settle against the wall as he backed away. 'Get on the bed,' he growled out in response to the question on her face, his hands going to his trousers.

Her gaze fastened on that movement as she hurried around him to comply, rushing to the straw-filled mattress near the fire. Almost immediately, his hands were on her waist, shifting her around so that her hips pressed back against him. The absolute need to dominate and reclaim her coursed through him. They belonged to each other no matter what might happen and always would. She complied so sweetly, as if she needed the reaffirmation, eager and ready to be his again.

His. The mere thought made blood surge into his groin, pounding through him as it urged him to take her.

He nudged her thigh and she opened to him, spreading herself so that he could settle on his knees between them. His trousers around his knees, he guided his manhood to her. There was something wild and primitive about having her nude before him, ready to receive him while he was clothed. It made him mad with excitement. As he pushed the swollen head of his manhood into her, she made a low sound of pleasure in the back of her throat and pressed back, seeking more of him. A rush of triumph burst through his chest.

Aye, beg me.

Gritting his teeth, he was determined to fight the surge of need that bid him to simply take her. So he played with her to draw out her pleasure, withdrawing, moving in a maddening rhythm along her crease, only giving her a taste of what she wanted. He paused at the drenched entrance to her body again, teasing her with his plump head, when she suddenly lurched back in an attempt to fill herself with him. A hoarse groan escaped him and he was helpless to do anything except jolt forward, joining their bodies in a hard thrust that rooted him deep within her. Spots of white light played behind his eyelids as he fell over her, keeping the bulk of his weight off of her on a straight arm while his other wrapped around her hips, holding her tight against him.

'Please, Rolfe.' Her voice was barely coherent, but the desperate rhythm of her hips was unmistakable as she moved beneath him, begging for more.

There was only her beloved softness beneath him, squeezing him in her tight grip as he moved. She sighed in a sound of unmistakable appreciation as he pulled out nearly all the way and slid hard back into her. She angled her body so that he could sink even deeper and he was lost. His hips began a hard tempo, pumping in and out of her in a desperate rhythm of possession. No longer able to keep himself away, he buried his face in the back of her neck so that her scent filled him. His name fell like a mantra from her lips as she clawed at him, her hand coming around to hold his thigh as if she was afraid he might leave her.

Soon she cried out in a hoarse sound as her sweet body clenched at him, convulsing around his shaft in delicious shock waves that drained him of his release. But even then he couldn't stop. He kept pumping until every last bit of his seed had been wrung from him and his tremors had subsided. He fell against her heavily, his heart threatening to pound out of his chest as he struggled to catch his breath.

He couldn't believe how consumed he'd been by her. For those few brief moments nothing else in the world had existed. Only her. Tenderness for her welled in his chest and his hands clenched at her, already wanting her again and afraid that something might take her from him. For a man who considered himself to be strong, she made him weak. He could never trust his judgement of her.

With a soft cry that he couldn't contain, he pulled himself from her body and struggled back into his trousers. A contented smile curved her lips as she turned over on to her back to look at him, but alarm quickly set in when she saw that he was getting to his feet.

'Don't go.'

He shook his head and she made to rise, but he held out his hand to ward her off and said, 'Nay!'

His voice was harsh to his own ears and it startled her, but it only made her pause briefly before getting to her knees to beseech him again. 'Rolfe, let us talk. I don't want you to go—'

The door closed behind him as he made his way out into the frigid night air. The woman consumed him without even trying. He had to get away from her before he did something foolish like forget his anger or even the reason he was angry. One entire night with her and he was certain he'd forget all about her treachery.

Damn it all—he loved her.

Elswyth passed a fitful night and finally gave up attempting to sleep when the grey light of dawn shone through the edges of the door. For the very first time she allowed herself the absolute despair that her marriage with Rolfe might be over. For a few moments last night she had made herself believe that a future was possible.

The truth was that he despised her. She'd throw another pot if she had any anger left within her, but there was nothing left. He'd wrung it all out of her last night. Instead of behaving like a child, she'd dressed in her winter clothes and doled out a bowl of pottage for herself with the first morning light. There was nothing to do but wait until Lord Vidar arrived and then she could finally tell her story. She didn't know what would happen after that and she couldn't bring herself to care.

Then something extraordinary happened. After she had finished her meagre meal, a man opened the door. He was the Dane who had been sent to guard her on a previous day. The man she had attacked with her blade when he'd refused to summon Rolfe, to be exact. He stood inside the door and gave her a wary stare.

'What do you want?' she asked with very little patience.

He bristled, looked out the open door as if he didn't like what he'd been tasked with doing, and then glanced back at her. 'I'm to take you to visit a grave,' he mumbled.

The hope bursting through her heart brought her to her feet. Rolfe had sent him. He'd remembered her request from the night and sent this man to take her to see Osric. After everything else that had happened, she had assumed he'd forgotten the request. What did it mean? Did he still care? Was he merely attempting to assuage his conscience? Whatever it meant, he was thinking about her. Last night hadn't been some final goodbye. He might have meant for it to be, but he was still thinking of her this morning.

Biting back her smile, she hurried to find her cloak and in moments had joined the Dane at the door. He held up a rope made of hemp and she glared at him. 'I'll not be restrained. If you must, then you can go find your master and tell him that I won't be bound. Let him come do it himself if he insists.'

Shifting from one foot to the other, he sighed, clearly wishing to have any other duty than to deal with her. She crossed her arms over her chest, feeling very much within her rights to insist that she be treated better than a common criminal.

Evidently deciding that he'd rather have the deed over with quickly than to return to Rolfe and explain his failure, he glared at her and stepped outside, indicating that she should come with him. He wound the rope back up into a coil and affixed it to his belt as he led her around the house and to the path that would take them to the village.

Despite the morbid reason for the outing, she was happy to be outside again. The day was clear, if not blue, and there was no new snow so the path was easy to navigate. She'd nearly worn holes in the plank floor of the house, pacing with unexpended energy over the past several days. In the distance a man—though if he were Saxon or Dane she couldn't tell—put out hay for the sheep, their anxious *baas* making her feel more at home than she had since she'd arrived. How easy it would be to slip back into her old life, as if what had happened in Alvey had been a dream. But it hadn't been a dream and she still had the telltale body aches from last night to prove it. Rolfe had been real and he'd been hers.

Her eyes moved of their own accord to find him. There were men sparring in the clearing outside Cnut's longhouse, but he didn't seem to be one of them. Aevir seemed to be the one running them through their paces. As they approached the village, men, women and children were moving about their daily chores. Not one of them seemed concerned with the additional Danes in their midst. She shouldn't have been surprised. Without her father and the other agitators, there was nothing to keep life from happening as it should.

Lady Gwendolyn had been right. Everyone served someone and most people didn't care who it was as long as they could live their lives in peace. As long as there was enough food and work and time to enjoy life, what did it matter? The Danes were here, but they were not a hindrance and they were not malicious invaders. If only her father could have seen this, perhaps life could have been different.

What would have happened had her mother never met that Dane and run off? Would her father have been more willing to work with Lord Vidar? In the days since talking to Father, she'd not been able to stop thinking of Mother. Somehow knowing that she carried the Dane's child made the woman's decision more poignant. She hadn't simply left her family because she'd found a man more exciting than her husband. She'd been forced to choose and she'd followed her heart. She hadn't left them so much as she'd chosen a future for her unborn child.

The knowledge gave clarity to Elswyth's own dilemma. If she was allowed to follow her heart, it would lead her to Rolfe. She only hoped it wasn't too late to choose him.

'Good morning, Elswyth!' They had walked close enough to the outskirts of the village that a few of the women paused to set their heavy baskets of laundry down to call to her.

She called back and smiled, happy to see familiar

faces. She would have stopped and talked, but the Dane looked back at her. 'Let's go,' he grumbled.

Biting back a retort, she followed him and gave a regretful wave to the small group. Soon he led her to a grave, a fresh mound of dirt covering it. A wave of sorrow came over her. Though she'd had days to come to terms with his fate and she had, it still didn't seem possible that the boy she had known was gone. She wanted to laugh with him one last time, but she couldn't and that wasn't Rolfe's fault. She could accept that now.

Rolfe was no more to blame for Osric's death than he was to blame for the Dane presence in their lands. Osric had made his own choice and he'd been fully aware of the consequences. Even so, she found that she had to be angry with someone, because Osric wasn't here to bear the brunt of it. In the days she'd spent in that farmhouse, she had come to realise that if anyone should share the blame with Osric that it was her father. Father and his bitter sense of betrayal towards Mother had led them all to this. Osric had not been a warrior. He would've been content living his life in peace. Father must have encouraged him to meet the Scots.

The sharp whinny of a horse caught her attention. Sleipnir raced across the ridge separating the field from the village. Rolfe was on his back, leaning forward as the stallion ran beneath him. Her heart clenched with longing as she watched him and it was quickly followed by a surge of possessiveness. He was hers. They had taken vows and nothing could change that. His people might believe in divorce, but hers didn't and nothing he or Lord Vidar could say or do would change that.

Rolfe would always be hers.

She hadn't realised she'd started running towards him until the Dane guarding her called out. She'd caught him unaware as he'd left her to pay her respects in peace and watched some of the women in the village. His heavy footfalls came up behind her, but they only spurred her faster. Rolfe had reached Aevir and had vaulted from his horse to talk to him about something that seemed rather important.

'Wait!' The Dane grabbed her arm, tugging her to a stop. Jerking away from him, she nearly succeeded in running again, but he was too determined. 'You can't go there. I have to take you back to the house.'

'Nay, I need to see Rolfe.' She swatted at his hands in a way that might have been comical had she not been so desperate. She opened her mouth to tell him in no uncertain terms that she wouldn't be returning without speaking to her husband when a great roar sounded from the forest north of the longhouse. Men on horse-back flooded the valley, spilling in from the forest as if they had no end.

Scots! That's why Rolfe had been moving with such urgency. He must have seen them from the rise and come to warn everyone.

'Go to them!' she yelled when the Dane seemed intent on dragging her away from the sight in the opposite direction.

'I can't leave you!' His voice was stern, but he wasn't looking at her. He stared at the coming violence as if he itched to join in.

'Rolfe needs you more. I need to lead the women in

the village to safety.' One look showed her that the villagers were aware of what was happening. They ran for the forest to the south, prepared years ago by her father for the eventuality of invasion with peace with the Scots and Danes being so uncertain. Something must have happened with her father's truce with the Scots to make them invade. Or perhaps they only came for the Danes and planned to leave the village in peace. Either way, someone needed to make sure they all hid in safety.

'Nay, they'll be fine. Jarl Vidar arrived with his men late last night. We've more than enough warriors.'

Relief overcame her. At least there was that. 'But what if they need you?'

The Dane wavered, but his youth eventually won out. It was clear that he'd much rather fight with the men than hide with the women, so he shoved the grip of his dagger into her hand. 'Run!' he ordered. 'Do you know where to hide?'

'Aye, the rise in the forest.' She indicated the direction in which the villagers were fleeing. Father and the warriors had made certain everyone knew to hide behind the rise. It was difficult to see for anyone who didn't know the landscape and it would give the villagers a safe point from which to view the battle. It would also give them ample time to see any attackers who might approach.

He gave a curt nod. 'Go then!' But as he ran towards the battle, he didn't even look back to make sure she followed his orders. Why would he? She was a woman and she was meant to obey.

Only she wouldn't.

She ran as fast as her legs could carry her into the village. By the time she reached it most everyone had gone. A few of the men stayed back with weapons to guard their houses should the Scots get past the Danes. Sliding the dagger into her belt, she picked up a short-handled axe that had been left carelessly by the wood-shed. Taking it in hand, she hurried towards the battle. Already the sounds of steel on steel could be heard ringing out as warriors clashed.

The echo only made her legs pump harder. Her only thought was to get to Rolfe, to make certain that he was safe. She could make out his head and shoulders at the edge of the sparring field. She couldn't see clearly from the distance, but he moved fast, striking with his sword as it seemed one Scot after another came at him. She lost sight of him for a moment as she was forced to run around the forge, the tall stone wall blocking her view.

When next she saw him, he had two men coming after him at once. Blood dripped from his sword as he stepped over the bodies of the slain enemies at his feet. Aevir was across the way, fending off his own attackers. A man sneaked around the longhouse, walking silently but briskly into the open to approach Rolfe from behind. She called out, but her voice seemed to be lost in the noise of battle.

Bracing her feet against the dirt, she pulled back the arm with the axe. Excitement and fear ran through her entire body, but she forced a calmness she was far from feeling and breathed in. On the exhale she let the axe fly. It whooshed through the air and somehow that sound was louder than her own cry had been. The weapon was a blur as it sailed, coming to a rest with flawless accuracy in the back of the man who would have attacked Rolfe.

The attacker let out a startling cry as he fell to his knees. Having dispatched the two men he'd been battling, Rolfe turned, his eyes finding her before landing on the man at his feet. 'Get down!' he yelled.

It was only at that moment that she realised she was standing in the middle of a field, the battle swarming around her, with only a dagger in her belt for a weapon. Her heart too frozen in fear to pound, she looked for a place to hide as Rolfe finished the man off. The longhouse was farther away than the forge, so she turned back to it, hiding herself behind the solid stone wall and drawing her dagger.

She could hear Rolfe's voice calling to Aevir, but she couldn't tell what he said. By this time her heart had resumed its pounding and seemed to have taken up residence in her ears. All she could hear was the blood rushing through her veins. It might have been only moments or maybe it was hours that she stayed there, but Rolfe came around the stone wall. His eyes found hers and he rushed over.

She rose to her feet just before he caught her in his arms and pulled her against him.

'Elswyth,' he whispered against her ear, his hand going to the back of her head to hold her tight. 'You're safe.'

'Is it over?' she asked against his neck. He smelled of sweat and horse, but it was the most glorious scent ever. He was safe and whole.

'Aye.' His voice was little more than a hoarse croak as he tightened his arms. 'Why didn't you run to the forest?'

'Because you needed me.' She pulled back just enough to glare up at him.

He grinned, his arms still so tight that she could barely draw breath. 'Aye, I did. You saved me.'

She'd been prepared to battle it out with him, not thinking that he'd relent and admit that her axe had taken the man down before Rolfe could handle him. So she stood stunned, not certain what to say. Rolfe seemed to know what to do because he kissed her deeply, his tongue plundering her mouth with determination. When he pulled back to take a breath, he said, 'Thank you.'

She shook her head, wondering how he could ever think she could do anything less. 'I would give my life for you.'

He looked stricken, as if her words pained him. Dropping his forehead to rest against hers, he said, 'Nay, never do that. I love you too much. I couldn't live without you.' He took a deep, wavering breath. 'I'm sorry, Saxon. For ever thinking that I could live without you. For doubting you. For believing that you were anything less than you are.'

She laughed, though it sounded rather like a sob. 'I forgive you as long as you spend the rest of your life making it up to me.'

His deep laughter moved through her as he swung her up into his arms. 'You can count on that. I love you.'

Chapter Twenty-One

It was evening before Elswyth was brought before Jarl Vidar to explain her crimes. The Scots had been soundly defeated, thanks in part to the arrival of the Jarl and his fleet of warriors. As before, this attack seemed to be a test. It wasn't the whole of the Scots horde, but enough to check their weaknesses. It had been a foolish ploy, because far more Scots had been cut down than had escaped—though Domnall hadn't been among either group, much to Rolfe's displeasure. They had even taken a few for questioning. The whole of the afternoon had been taken up with dealing with the battle's aftermath.

Now Elswyth sat at the long table in the hall with Rolfe at her side as she recounted what her family had called upon her to do. Her chestnut hair was pulled back, but left to flow down to her waist, the fire picking up streaks of red and gold. She was beautiful as she fearlessly answered the Jarl's questions. Rolfe was proud to see that she didn't shirk her own responsibility—she *had* after all agreed to spy—but neither did she deny how she had been misled by Galan and, ultimately, her own father. She would never have stolen the jewel without the threat of Baldric's safety spurring her on.

He believed that now. A strong thread of honour ran through his wife, guiding her actions and judgement. It had been there all along, which is why he'd been called to her from the beginning. Perhaps she would have opened up to him earlier had he shown her that he loved her, instead of allowing Hilde to cast her shadow on their union. He stroked a hand down Elswyth's back as she finished her story and sat silently awaiting Vidar's judgement. She seemed to take strength from his touch, notching her chin a bit higher as she met Vidar's harsh gaze head on.

'Do I understand you to claim that you never actually gave your family any beneficial information?' Vidar asked, his brow furrowed as he looked down at her.

'Nay, my lord. After seeing Alvey with my own eyes, I came to the conclusion that peace would be best. Your forces were too strong to fight, but more than that, I saw how peaceful it was there. With Lady Gwendolyn's help, I came to believe that we could find that peace here in Banford if given the chance.'

Vidar took in a deep breath as he stared at her, his expression still fierce and hard. 'Then it appears your only crime is that of theft.'

He raised a brow and she nodded. 'Aye, my lord. Again, I am very sorry for that. I only took it because—'

He held up his hand, palm out, to stop her. 'I understand what prompted the theft, Elswyth. I cannot fault you for your intentions, but neither can I ignore the outcome.'

Rolfe clenched his jaw and gently pressed his palm into her back, reassuring her. He didn't believe that Vidar would treat her harshly, but he had no idea what his friend intended. If he set out to make an example of her... He couldn't even allow the thought to finish in his mind. Knowing how her family had used her and forsaken her was punishment enough.

'Aye, my lord. I understand.' She stiffened under Rolfe's touch, steeling herself for the punishment.

'You stole from Rolfe, so I will remand you to your husband for him to mete out a suitable punishment. However, I would urge you in the future to come to us should you or your family need assistance.'

She nodded, but relief was postponed at the mention of her family. 'What will become of my family?'

No one had seen her family since Rolfe had confronted them outside Alvey's walls. In the rush to find Elswyth and deal with the impending Scot threat, they had slipped away. Yet with several of the villagers missing along with her family, it could only be assumed that they had wilfully left. Perhaps to join with the Scot cause, perhaps not. The next few days would tell. Rolfe burned to get hold of her father and tell the man what he thought of him and his treatment of his daughters.

'It's good that your father and brothers were not with the Scots who attacked. I won't leave Banford until this problem is dealt with once and for all and that includes finding your father and brothers. I'll give them the same chance I gave you to answer for their crimes.'

She nodded and Rolfe took her hand in his, giving it a squeeze. She hadn't given up hope that her family would turn up soon. 'What of Ellan? She never entertained our father's hatred.'

Vidar nodded. 'I've already sent for her to join us here. I'll question her, of course, but if that's true then she'll be free to do as she'd like. She can return to Alvey or stay in Banford.'

Unable to wait another moment to be alone with his wife again, Rolfe rose to his feet and pulled her up with him. Murmuring his thanks to Vidar, he put an arm around her waist and ushered her from the building. She smiled up at him when he tucked his fur cloak around her shoulders and let the door close behind them.

'Where are we going?' she laughed. 'We should at least check on Aevir.'

Aevir had been wounded in the battle, but had been tended to hours ago. Rolfe shook his head. 'You already made him a poultice and he's resting. It's time to discuss your punishment, Wife.'

She pulled a face, but he could tell it only hid a smile. 'I knew you wouldn't let that go.'

'Of course not. Jarl Vidar specifically said that I was to punish you. I can't defy an order.' He swung her up into his arms and ran with her through the cold to the farmhouse, her laughter floating behind them. The housemaid had left the fire burning in the hearth with a pot of stew bubbling over the flame before she'd left for the night. His stomach growled at the aroma, but it would have to wait. He had another hunger to assuage first and it was for something far more important than food.

After he set Elswyth on her feet, she hurried to the hearth to warm her hands as he secured the door closed behind them. After hanging up his cloak, he walked up behind her, putting his arms around her and drawing her back against his chest.

'You forgot your gloves in Alvey.'

She shook her head. Her voice was soft when she said, 'Nay, I left them on purpose. At the time I couldn't keep them. They were your first gift to me and it hurt too much to look at them.'

He breathed in her sweet scent and ran his lips along her temple. 'At the time…but not now?'

'I'm sorry I left the way I did. It was wrong.' She turned in his arms as she spoke and looked up at him, her hands cupping his face. 'I want us to always talk going forward. I know that there will be things you have to do that I won't like, but we can't allow that to come between us. We can't forget that we are better together than we are apart.'

Lacing his fingers with hers, he kissed down the tender inside of one slender wrist, smiling when she sucked in a breath. 'I'm sorry for what happened with Osric. And more, I am sorry for not telling you and being honest with you from the beginning.'

She nodded. 'I love you, Dane. I love you far more than I could ever hate you, no matter what happens. Please believe that. Always.'

His answer was to press his lips to hers and hold her close. With the bitter winter wind raging outside, treachery and heartache was forgotten as they explored the love that burned between them.

* * * * *

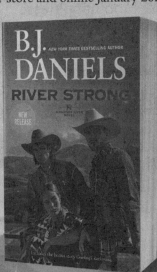

Subscribe and fall in love with a Mills & Boon series today!

You'll be among the first to read stories delivered to your door monthly and enjoy great savings.

WE
SIMPLY
LOVE
ROMANCE

MILLS & BOON

JOIN US

Sign up to our newsletter to stay up to date with...

- Exclusive member discount codes
- Competitions
- New release book information
- All the latest news on your favourite authors

> ## Plus...
> get $10 off your first order.
> *What's not to love?*

Sign up at **millsandboon.com.au/newsletter**